Book 1

JASON THE JUGGERNAUT

The Unstoppable Light

by

TIMOTHY CARAWAY

SUTTON, ALASKA

This book is a work of fiction. Names, characters, businesses, places, events and incidents contained within are either products of the author's imagination or used in a fictitious manner. If any long-standing institutions, agencies, public offices or events are mentioned, the characters involved are wholly imaginary. Any resemblance to actual persons, living or dead, or actual events is merely coincidental.

Relevant Publishers LLC
P.O. Box 505
Sutton, AK 99674

www.relevantpublishers.com

Publisher's Cataloging-In-Publication Data

Names: Caraway, Timothy, author.
Title: The Unstoppable Light / written by Timothy Caraway

Identifiers: LCCN: 2018955037 | ISBN 978-1953263254 (paperback) | ISBN 978-1953263261 (ebook)

Printed in the United States of America

A Christian Inspirational Classic

For more books in this series, please visit:

www.relevantpublishers.com

ACKNOWLEDGMENTS

I greatly appreciate the help of friends and family who provided critiques, suggestions and inspiration in developing this book. I especially appreciate Scott Crockett has been a good enough friend to tell me when something stinks and all of his efforts to set me straight. I also appreciate the patience of my wife Kelly and the numerous times she has helped to edit this work and Hannah Cross, my niece, who helped with the illustrations in my first edition.

Through all of this, my part was the least and the most fun since I merely wrote as inspiration struck. And to the one divine being for which nothing is impossible, my deepest thanks.

Plains
Vorkana
Village
North Fort
Plains
Sulter
hill
East
Fort
10 Miles
Harville
Chanderlon
Plains
Werton's
Fort
Hundar
South Fort
Plains

PROLOGUE

Tracking a wounded boar is a dangerous job as the boar could charge from the underbrush at any moment. His initial shot was good, but long, and the arrow must not have penetrated deep enough. The blood trail was thin and spotty. Armed with a light hunting bow and a short spear, his stride showed confidence he could handle any charge, given enough time to face it.

However, this hunt was leading him into unfamiliar territory. The boar had run toward a mountain valley where Barex had never been. In his own territory, he knew the places to avoid— places of magic or haunted by a spirit or even the area around the cracks in the ground where certain monsters dwelt. But here, a misstep or moment of inattentiveness could spell instant doom.

Because of the extreme danger, he was tempted to let the pig go, but this was a spring hunt after a sparse winter, and game was scarce. His family and tribe needed meat, and this pig was a prize to be pursued. The nights were still cold, and snow lingered in the high country; he hoped to get his kill, then head home before dark. If he could make it back to his normal hunting grounds, he could even travel throughout the night.

The spore led him atop a ridge, and he knew he was getting close, for he could hear an occasional labored grunt. The pig was tiring and would soon drop. He paused at the top of the ridge, taking in the late afternoon view of the valley and mentally mapping the mountains before him. He looked for anything unusual that might indicate habitations or lairs of more intelligent creatures, such as smoke or cleared areas that should not be there.

Seeing none, he started down the slope. Weaving around the boulder-strewn trees, clumps of brush, and occasional patch of snow, he followed the course of the pig. The cool smell of moisture indicated a stream nearby.

He paused for a moment to study the pig's path through some snow. Suddenly, with a wild squeal, the pig charged out of some brush from the side, its eyes full of avarice and hate. It was a medium-sized boar, but still its three-inch tusks were enough to do him damage.

He stumbled as he swung his spear around, falling to one knee; it was not necessarily a bad move since this allowed him to jam the butt end of the spear into the ground to meet the force of the charge. His spear was not a boar spear, which are designed with prongs to keep a large pig or bear from running the spear through its body as it pushed to get at its sole objective of tearing apart the hunter. It was simply a straight spear, light and streamlined enough to be easily thrown.

The pig, however, tired from loss of blood, fell over before the spear penetrated deeply into its chest. He thanked the gods he was not hurt, but checking the sky, realized it was later than he would have liked. It was evident now that he would have to spend the approaching night in the woods. Again, he entreated the gods for protection from the unknown. Not that the gods ever listened much, but Barex tried to keep on their good side just in case.

He gutted the carcass but did not butcher it further. Being a strong man, he lifted what remained of the animal around both shoulders, heedless of the blood that smeared him, and walked back up the hill.

He rested at the top and surveyed his surroundings again. The waning sun made dark shadows in the valleys, and he felt reluctant to spend the night down in those dark areas where he may not be able to see anything stalking him. Instead, he made a fireless camp at the base of a tree and sat back against the trunk, chewing some jerky he carried. He laid the pig beside him for additional warmth and gathered his sparse fur jacket around him to ward off the chill of the evening.

Dozing off and on throughout the night, alert for unusual sounds, he was suddenly awakened by a distant crack of thunder. At least, it sounded like thunder coming from the direction of the mountainous valley to the east. He rose to look, and his eyes were met by a brilliant glow. Although a great distance away, it looked like the sun setting on the ground, except the light had a strange silver color.

The thunder continued to rumble, accentuated by explosive cracks as he watched the light increase in brilliance, then slowly wane. After the light and noise disappeared, he could still make out a reddish glow that lingered for some time. Wisps of white smoke or steam rose from the area.

He had seen magical lights before, and certain creatures could produce a dim glowing light, but what he just witnessed was a scale of power he had never seen before. What did it mean? Was it a sign from a god? It was an omen for sure, but was it for good or ill? Was this something he was meant to see?

These thoughts troubled him so much he knew it was no use trying to sleep, so he gathered his weapons and carcass and started into the night toward home. The village elders would surely know what this meant. If not, then the witch doctor Krundor would know, though all the tribes avoided him if they could, for he was evil despite his great knowledge and would demand a large payment.

A chill of fear crept up his spine, and he had a premonition... A premonition of change.

CHAPTER 1
Climbing Jacob's Ladder

"Let me see your license and registration, please," the New Mexico police officer said to the large aging man in the driver's seat of a rickety old pickup truck. The man obliged and waited patiently as the officer went through the registration. "The reason I stopped you, Mr. Bristol, is because your license plate is about to fall off...Bristol, Jason Bristol. Jason the Juggernaut Bristol?"

"Yes, Officer, that's me," Jason replied. He did not consider "the juggernaut" the greatest of honors because in mythology, it was a sinister, nearly unstoppable monster, but that did not matter to those who had crudely dubbed him the nickname.

The patrolman suddenly became animated, his breath misting in the cool fall air. "I have seen every one of your fight videos that went viral on the Internet. You were great!"

Jason shrugged. He and his family had participated in a year- long house-swapping deal, exchanging their home in Wasilla, Alaska, for a small place in a suburb of Los Angeles. As an independent martial arts instructor, he had opened a dojo in a community where several martial art schools already existed. The challenge to his unwelcome presence was almost instantaneous. He was ambushed several times outside his dojo by several small groups of so-called martial art experts. He managed to resist them without breaking bones or sending anyone to the hospital. Someone caught some of the challenges on video, and suddenly, he became an Internet sensation.

The officer returned his license and registration and said, "Could you autograph your picture for me?"

"Sure," Jason agreed with a good-natured grin. Jason opened the door and stepped out as the patrolman returned to his car. He turned up the collar on his heavy blue jean jacket lined with sheep's wool to combat the brisk fall air. It would be even colder in the high country, but this light jacket was more than warm enough for what he considered mild southern climates.

The officer returned with the magazine Real Martial Artists, which had printed an interview with him about his Alaskan style of fighting. The story included a picture of him standing in front of his LA dojo. Adjusting his glasses, he searched for his photo in the magazine.

"I like how you didn't waste moves and didn't even go into a fighting stance. You used moves I would expect from the military. These guys jumping you were experts, yet it was obvious you weren't even trying," the officer enthused, momentarily forgetting his professional demeanor.

"Thanks." Jason scribbled below the photo. "Most martial arts nowadays are not really designed for that kind of fighting, so I had an advantage."

The patrolman shook his head. "That can't be all of it, because some of those guys were well-known street fighters and mixed martial artists."

"They have missed the point of martial arts. They won't have a powerful system until they design it so a child could use it to defend themselves against an adult effectively."

The officer paused. "Is that even possible? I mean, a kid just can't stand toe to toe with an adult fighter and even hope to win," said the officer skeptically.

"It has been done many times, even by children with little or no training. However, there is another element, and that is in spite of our plans and strategies, in a desperate situation, I believe it is God who gives the victory."

The officer stared at him blankly, then mumbled, "I never went much for that religious stuff. I think God helps those who help themselves."

Jason shrugged. People always needed proof, proof that God cared for them enough to intervene in their lives, so he replied, "No matter how good we are, we can never be prepared for everything, but that does not prevent God from showing us that he cares—"

The officer cut him off. "I'd love to stay and chat, but I am on duty and must be off. It was nice to meet you, Mr. Bristol."

Jason returned the signed magazine and pulled out his folding pliers as he walked to the back of his truck. He had hoped to be known for his faithfulness rather than his toughness. During his interview for Real Martial Artists, he had mentioned his beliefs, but they were edited out of the magazine's final edition.

Even then, he felt a little chagrined that his religious testimony was not as effective as he thought it should be. Although he had been a Christian nearly all his life, he had times of doubt even as a child. Sometimes, he wondered if he was foolish to believe in the unseen. Then he would remind himself that he would rather believe there is eternal hope than just an empty non-existence, even if there was no evidence of God's existence.

Fixing his license plate and relieved to have gotten out of a ticket, he waved to the police officer as he pulled the pickup back onto the highway. The blue bomber belched smoke, probably violating five EPA codes as he brought it up to speed, heading for the New Mexico high country.

That year in California had launched his martial arts career in ways he had never dreamed of. Martial art schools began opening all over the country, copying his style, and he spent much of his time traveling from dojo to dojo. This also gave him opportunity to speak as a guest at churches and martial art schools and seminars as he and his family traveled about. His wife, Molly, and homeschooled kids, Trevor and Cassandra, loved the opportunity to travel. Sometimes, though, he wished he was back home hunting moose or exploring the Alaskan fjords in his kayak.

In spite of the lack of pleasure time, he was in for a special treat this day. Brad, a student in the newly established dojo in Albuquerque, also worked as a lab assistant for the Navarone Corporation. A leader in the field of longevity, the company was promoting a tour for government officials and wealthy investors with hopes of generating financial support.

As an amateur explorer and martial artist, Jason was keenly interested in all of the natural sciences and when he discovered the type of work his student was engaged in, Jason eagerly pumped him for information. From Brad's perspective, it was rare that anyone took an interest in what he did, much less have the ability to talk about it intelligently. Brad could not help but boast of their most recent breakthroughs, even though it was not to be released to the public yet. He did not relate the details, but invited Jason to go along with the tour group and witness firsthand the ground-breaking discovery of significant age reversal. How the lab assistant was able to get him on such a VIP list, Jason didn't know.

A "jack of all trades" in his fifty years of life, Jason had worked on small farms, fished commercially, built and rehabbed houses, invested in stocks and commodities, was an artist and martial artist. Despite not being wealthy, he also volunteered his time in his local community and to ministry. Hunting, fishing, sailing, skiing, kayaking, and snowmobiling filled out his repertoire. As a result, he was familiar with the open seas as well as surviving in the wilderness, orienteering with stars, maps, compasses and a few traditional Alaskan native tricks to find his way around.

Using his small-time investing resources, he had checked out the Navarone Corporation and found it to be a struggling US company in the biotechnology sector. At only fifteen cents a share, it seemed in danger of bankruptcy. Oddly, it did have some big financial backing from some place not mentioned in any of his research.

Meanwhile, the rest of his family had rented an RV and driven down to

Carlsbad to visit his sister's family and explore the many caves and caverns that riddled the area. They were not interested in this super scientific stuff, and they welcomed the break too.

As he drove the old truck to Santa Fe, he pulled out the handwritten instructions and followed them to a small dirt road winding into the hills. He could see several game and ATV trails crisscrossing the dirt road. He felt himself relax as he left the crowded byways and was glad to be driving a vehicle which matched his surroundings.

Although it was late fall, you would not have known it from the trees. The scrubby pine and cedar evergreens were the same color year round. He was beginning to suspect he had taken a wrong turn somewhere when the road he was looking for appeared.

He stopped before a chain-link fence hung across the road with a metal No Trespassing sign wired to it. He climbed out of the truck and inspected the gate. A chain wove through the links but was not locked. He unhooked the chain and drove his truck through the gate. As he secured the gate back in place in the manner he had found it, he noticed the hidden camera among the rocks at the side of the gulley, verifying he had found the right place and was not just trespassing on some old-timer's homestead.

His truck groaned on the steep road winding to the top of the mesa. About halfway up, he spied a small, dark hole beside an outcropping of rock. He would not have noticed it except his kids had been looking for any possible cave at every rest stop while they explored the state. Perhaps he could bring them back here to explore. He stopped the truck even though he knew he was late, thanks to the diligence of New Mexico's highway patrol.

A quick jog up to the rock revealed that it did indeed hide a small opening to a cave. He was a little disappointed to discover that almost every cave in New Mexico was explored, mapped, and required a permit with a small fee to enter it. He would have to check to see if this was on the list of known caves.

As he walked back to the truck, he reflected on his family's interest in caves. He tended to feel claustrophobic in one but still felt a thrill, like entering another world. Some caves with their weird limestone formations gave the effect of being an alien environment.

His kids made believe they were transported into another world. Although he shared their wonder, he knew that as an adult, he no longer experienced such things as they did. Sometimes, he wished he were a kid again to re-experience such journeys of imagination.

Releasing the truck's hand brake, he continued in low gear the rest of the way to the top. A brisk wind and blowing dust met the truck just as it breached the rim. A security gate beside a guard hut blocked the road, which continued toward some large buildings about a half mile away. The rest of the mesa had been cleared, making it appear very bleak.

A large white sign attached to the fence read Navarone Corporation in fresh red paint. Navarone, Jason mused, was a fictitious island somewhere near Italy in a novel written in the 1950s depicting a World War II gun battle. Why this organization had chosen the name Navarone, he could only guess.

A security guard, dressed for the cold, walked to the driver's side carrying a clipboard.

"Identification, please," intoned the guard.

Jason handed him his driver's license. The guard briefly checked the list on his clipboard and handed his card back.

"Thank you, Dr. Bristol. Everyone is waiting for you at Building A." The guard reentered the hut and lifted the gate.

"Dr. Bristol?" Jason wondered to himself. Is that how Brad got him on the list? Perhaps the guard was so used to scientists visiting, he just assumed everyone who came had a doctorate degree.

He parked his rickety junk heap next to a shiny new car covered in military stickers. Other high dollar cars and even a few limos lined the parking lot. A small knot of drivers gathered out of the wind at the corner of the building, smoking and chatting. He nodded in their direction as he walked by and entered the door designated by a big red A over it.

Stepping into the warm, moist room, his glasses immediately fogged, so he slipped them off. Inside, a receptionist and several young men in lab coats stood behind a counter. A dozen or so other men, dressed in business suits or military uniforms with an air of importance, stood around as if impatient to be somewhere else. An attendant offered to take his jacket. Although he wore his nicest clothes, he still felt a little out of place.

A tall, wiry man in a lab coat stood in front of the group with a laser pointer and a large free-standing map of the facilities set on the counter, Winding up his orientation speech, the man sounded dry and self-important. Jason was relieved his lateness spared him this monologue of the history and physical layout of the place. Everyone was then directed to line up at a security station while an elderly guard painstakingly ran a wand over each of them after having them empty their pockets into small plastic trays to be pushed across the table and picked up at the other side.

As his spot in line approached the guard, he groaned inwardly. He had forgotten to clean out his pockets. Although most of his really incriminating stuff was in his jacket now hanging on the coat stand, such as a box of .22 long rifle bullets and his pliers, he also had in his pants pocket a medium-sized folding knife. Not knowing what else to do, he put it on the plastic tray along with his cell phone and glasses.

The guard picked up the knife and, after turning it over in his hands a few times, opened it and suspiciously eyed the wicked serrations along its edge. Being familiar with knives and how to fight with them, these theatrics amused Jason. Although it looked mean, it was only a pocket knife, not a fighting knife. Fighting knives were built much sturdier and often had such high quality steel that they could only be sharpened by a professional.

The elderly guard looked at him as if to gauge his mental stability. He smiled disarmingly and shrugged. The elderly guard laughed, put it back on the tray, and proceeded to wand him. To Jason's surprise, he was allowed to pick up his knife along with his cell phone and glasses. Security must not be as tight here as in an airport or government building, he thought to himself. Later, when he saw the knives, scalpels, drills, and various saws just lying around in the labs, his knife seemed trite. Slipping on his now clear glasses, he walked over to the group of men who had already passed security and introduced himself. He stuck his hand out to a white-haired military man nearby with five stars pinned to his collar and a pin with the name of "General McHannon" printed on it. "Hi, I'm Jason Bristol," he offered.

The general scowled and pretended not to hear as he continued to stare down the hall toward an open area lined with glass covered counters, similar to a cafeteria. This was the first time he had ever gotten a cold shoulder from a military man and thought it odd, considering in numerous encounters throughout his life he had always found a camaraderie with soldiers.

He inwardly shrugged it off and turned to focus his attention in the same direction. Two armed guards, a stocky man and a tough-looking woman, came down the hallway past several office doors and stood beside the group, privately conversing among themselves.

When everyone had completed the security check, a man sporting a lab coat and clipboard appeared out of an office and introduced himself, "Good afternoon, gentlemen, I am Dr. Kuenning, head of the Navarone Longevity Project. I know that you have heard rumors and are impatient to see this operation for yourselves. So after a brief tour of our facilities, we will bring you to the main lab where you will get to witness our latest experiments. I think you will become as excited as we are with what you see. Would you please follow me?"

Dr. Kuenning was not an imposing man, small and frail, bald with a heavy set of black glasses set upon his nose. To Jason he looked to be more at home in front of a microscope than leading a tour of soldiers and scientists. Jason liked him because he seemed to be much more interested in his work than impressing the present, high brass from Washington. With little fanfare, the head scientist led them all to the first room. This room, which at first seemed to be a cafeteria, was actually a laboratory with a variety of plants and animals and many technicians currently involved with various phases of research.

An animated young technician in a green lab coat with wavy brown hair appeared at Jason's elbow. "Hi, sensei... I mean, Dr. Bristol."

"Hi, Brad. Dr. Bristol, huh?" Brad grinned sheepishly. Jason continued, "Thanks for inviting me. Is this the lab where they discovered the fountain of youth?"

"Oh, you haven't seen anything yet," Brad asserted, waving his hands around. "This tour will change what you think about life and death, perhaps even the way we understand reality itself."

"Why the military guys?"

"We're hoping the government will help fund this project. We have a few ideas how this will change the way we treat injuries on the battlefield, perhaps heal a person almost instantly, although we have yet to prove this in animal tissue."

"So you have done this with plants?" asked Jason.

"That is correct, Dr. Bristol," answered the young mad scientist smugly.

Jason thought to himself how there is a huge difference between plant and animal tissue and that selling the military on this would be tough. Besides, instantaneous healing sounded like a supernatural miracle, and Jason could feel his own skepticism rise.

At that moment, a loud harrumph at one of Dr. Kuenning's statements distracted Jason.

"And who is the grumpy one?" he asked, nodding toward an angry looking elder with a powerful build in a pinstriped business suit.

"Oh, that is Horace Mansfield, a very wealthy contributor to this project," Brad replied. "I think Mr. Mansfield is here to make sure the new equipment upgrades are safe, and with good reason, because his son died here. His son, Trent, was a technician working on a cooling conduit when a nearby radiation containment shield ruptured, spraying hot radioactive plasma all over him. He died before we could get him to a hospital. It shut us down for a while. That's when I had some free time and started taking martial arts—"

"You have a nuclear reactor here?" interrupted Jason, surprised.

"Yes," said Brad. "Some of our experiments are based on a Jacob's Ladder, which requires a tremendous amount of energy to make a big one."

Jason reflected on this. He had seen Jacob's Ladders in high school science demonstrations where a wave of current would travel down two parallel bars. Other than looking interesting, he could think of no useful purpose for it. "Why a Jacob's Ladder?" he asked.

Brad leaned over conspiratorially and whispered, "If given enough power, it creates a field that seems to alter time."

Alter time, thought Jason to himself. Suddenly, he had all sorts of questions, but Dr. Kuenning hurried them outside, heedless of the brisk cold wind, to stand before Building B. There, he gave a small lecture on the history of previous experiments and attempts at rejuvenation and how they were underfunded and underpowered. Horace Mansfield had provided them the funds to build this nuclear reactor, which had just recently been made fully operational. He then herded the group inside the general viewing area.

The nuclear reactor was huge, encased in a cement structure inside the building. As they walked into the small control room, a low rumble could be heard and felt. Technicians were alertly monitoring the gauges and computer consoles.

"Are you doing an experiment now?" Jason asked Brad.

"We're warming up the machine for a demonstration for you guys. In fact, this will be the first time that full power will be available to us."

"Will it always take this much power to use the machine?"

"Oh no, this is just the beginning. Once we accomplish our goal, then it would be a simple process to fine-tune it, reduce the power demands, and perhaps even make a portable unit."

"Was Dr. Kuenning the one to come up with this process?"

"No, we were stuck in our experiments until Dr. Phil Nexlar, a quantum physicist, suggested we use a lens of unusual crystalline materials for the base of the Jacob's Ladder to focus its energies and transform the field into a particle wave. With some adjustment, we were able to make it work."

"Doing what?" asked Jason.

"We're not sure what it's doing, but we've been able to reverse the age of living things."

"By how much?" Jason asked, surprised. An age reversal machine? The financial implications of such a technology staggered the imagination.

"You'll see." Brad beamed like a kid who could barely contain himself.

"Isn't this kind of interrupting the natural order of things? I mean, it's almost like you're trying to play God."

"If Dr. Kuenning can pull this off, then we will become gods. Think of it! Sickness and disease eradicated, old age is a thing of the past, even near fatal injuries undone almost instantly."

After examining some of the power dials, Dr. Kuenning jotted in his notepad and led the group out of the room. The third and final building they toured had one large room with an incredibly large machine in the center. Numerous counters with computer stations and monitoring screens lined the walls. The main attraction was a giant, horseshoe-like projection coming off the machine with a crystal globe affixed to two rods at its base, suspended three feet above a mirrored table.

The project head was describing the machine when Jason overheard Horace Mansfield ask an assistant, "Is that the new radiation containment shield?" and point at a smooth rounded box concealing the plasma conduits that attached the machine to its power source through the walls. It was painted yellow with radioactive warning symbols all over it. The assistant nodded and turned away. The elder looked down mournfully.

Dr. Kuenning placed a large potted flower on the table and moved behind a screen. Donning thick black rubber gloves, he pulled down the high-voltage lever. Immediately, a three-foot arc of electricity shot across the gap and slowly made its way down the forks toward the crystal. More arcs followed, creating a classical Jacob's Ladder. It was as though the dancing energy bolts were being absorbed by the crystal, and it glowed with an increasing intensity.

The power level slowly built, generating brighter and more furiously gyrating arcs. After about thirty seconds, a silver ray of light shot over the flower from the crystal. The flower seemed to phase out and disappear. Five seconds later, it reappeared. Only this time, it was no longer a flower but a small, slender shoot of green with only a single leaf.

Jason was stunned, for this was not merely age reversal, but it was as if the machine reached back in time and snatched a younger version of the plant and then brought it back! Among the gasps in the audience, one of the visiting scientists shook his head and declared, "That is impossible!"

Nonplussed, Dr. Kuenning continued his narration, struggling in his excitement to keep his voice modulated and professional, "What you see is still the same plant but a much younger version of it," he intoned. "The mirror works to attract and stabilize the ray."

Brad pulled Jason away from the others and excitedly whispered, "When we did this before, the plant came back with a butterfly on it from a species we have not been able to identify."

"Then the plant traveled someplace else? What made it young again?" asked Jason.

"I don't know," said the technician, "but Dr. Kuenning thinks it is some sort of time travel!"

The project head continued, "So far, no living animals placed in this ray have ever returned. Inanimate objects and dead organic matter are not changed by this procedure. Gentlemen, I believe this discrepancy will soon be solved, but my theory is that we have actually altered the space-time continuum. Once we have stabilized the energy fields to enable a living being to regress through time, well, the possibilities are limitless."

After producing a cage with a white albino rat, like a magician, Dr. Kuenning continued, "One of my colleagues, Dr. Nexlar, believes he has found a setting to allow living animals to return, so you will get to actually witness our latest effort in this endeavor."

Setting the cage on the mirrored table, the scientist went back to adjusting dials and increasing the power to the Jacob's ladder. A computer monitor Jason could see showed the power setting on a bar graph go from twenty-two percent to sixty-five percent. The machine groaned and whined as the Jacob's ladder snapped and buzzed with the additional energy. It seemed that translating a live animal took a great deal more energy than needed for the plant.

The white rat sat back and looked up at the monstrous device above it. It squeaked fearfully as suddenly the silver ray pulsed over the hapless creature and slowly the rat, cage and all, faded from sight. Almost immediately, Dr. Kuenning began the reverse procedure. A shadow image of light showing the cage and a blob of light within it momentarily appeared and faded again.

"We need more power," one of the techies yelled as someone ran to a panel where the power conduits came from the wall. Another woman in a lab coat vigorously punched the keyboard while monitoring a console flashing warnings.

Again, Dr. Kuenning slowly pulled another lever and even more power surged through the silvery ray that came from the orb. A quick glance at the monitor Jason saw earlier, showed the power increasing to over ninety percent.

Brad had to whisper loudly in Jason's ear to be heard above the ever-increasing noise from the machines. "We have never used this much power before. I hope it doesn't burn anything out."

At that moment, Jason's cell phone, set on silent mode, vibrated with an incoming call. He moved further from the group to see who was calling, but the noise of the machine made it impossible to answer. Rounding a counter, he flipped open the phone, but a sudden commotion on the main floor prevented him from seeing his caller's name.

A glowing mass of something not there before, like a reverse photo image, made a huge indistinct shape, just barely able to fit on the table underneath the light-emitting orb. It faded again but came back as Dr. Kuenning pulled another lever, and the machine trembled as another crescendo of humming began.

When the lighted image came back this time, Jason got the fleeting impression of a strange, bear-like creature holding a mangled cage. It stood, bumping its head into the orb above it. He wasn't sure if it was this action or if the overloaded machine just simply blew on its own, but smoke and sparks began spewing from various places in the machine and the creature, or whatever it was, vanished as the light destabilized.

Crackling bolts of lightning arced from the pulsating crystal striking walls, pipes—anything in its path. The light, once a single focused beam, now became a myriad of little beams shooting throughout the room and wherever those little beams touched, things vaporized, even metal.

Dr. Kuenning desperately struggled to switch off the main power levers, but they seemed to be welded open. The visitors stood momentarily stunned as chaos erupted around them and technicians frantically worked switches and punched keyboards. One man cried in despair, "Doctor, the cooling valves have failed, we're going into meltdown!"

"Shut it down, shut it down quickly! Call the power plant, have them shut it down from there!" commanded the doctor, trying another lever.

An angry jolt blasted out the overhead lights so the only illumination in the room, apart from the sizzling electric whips, was the disorienting flicker of a thousand different warning lights on the damaged control panels.

Suddenly, sensor warning alarms blared, and a calm woman's voice over the loudspeaker instructed everyone to exit the building in an orderly fashion. However, technicians at the panels were less composed and cried out for everyone to run because the machine was going to blow any second! Momentarily shocked by the pronouncement, Jason surmised that with that much built-up power, if the machine did blow, he would never see it coming before the blast ripped him apart.

From that moment on things seemed to move in slow motion. The noise of the machine coming apart mingled with the panicked cry of people trying to leave. Jason gave a silent prayer for safety as Brad ran past him. Seeing the powerful energies unleashing behind him, Jason moved to push his young friend to the floor, but the man had already moved on past.

Despite Jason's training, panic overtook him and it was as if his limbs refused to move, so he dropped behind a heavy counter to protect himself, the unanswered cell phone still in his hand. He could feel himself falling, but he never hit the floor. The explosion happened simultaneously with his move and drove the counter into him. He was vaguely aware of a larger beam of light that seemed to be part of the explosion create an implosion, sucking him back through the desk and spinning him like a boat caught in a whirlpool.

He felt himself pulled through the desk, scraping himself on splinters of wood and metal that seemed to be going the other direction. The whine of bending and tearing metal was so loud, Jason thought his ears would burst, and he seemed to become a different substance, on a different plane of reality, being pulled on a wave of light.

As if in slow motion, he could see the machine exploding, the fire, the smoke, and even pieces of human bodies going past him, even through him, as he was sucked in the opposite direction...Then, everything went gray and silent, then black, as he lost consciousness.

CHAPTER 2
Born Again

Cold...Cold...Darkness...Hunger.

Jason could feel the warmth of the activated cell phone still clutched in his hand.

Call...call for help, he thought. His body hurt from the cold, and he felt stiff throughout his joints. Something was in his mouth—metal and broken teeth? He pushed them out with his tongue, tasting blood and the acrid taste of ozone. As awareness slowly returned to him, he realized he lay on his belly. Painfully he forced his head up and opened his eyes. Through cracked eyelids, he could see the bright glow of his cell phone screen. It flashed Call Disconnected and No Service Available. Darkness suddenly overwhelmed him again as he slipped back into unconsciousness.

The sensation of a chill night wind woke him sometime later. The roof must be gone. God help me, he thought to himself. He realized another strange sensation. His cell phone was held by someone else's hand, a child's hand. Then darkness overwhelmed him again.

Cold again and sound—was that a magpie he heard calling? He opened his eyes, and it was now daylight...morning, to be exact. He immediately pushed himself up. Soil, moss, and a pile of metal fillings mixed with gold crowns lay below his face. He left his glasses where they fell. He felt around with his tongue, and although he seemed to have fewer teeth, they were in perfect rows as they should be. A mane of blond hair veiled his face. His cell phone screen was dark. Slowly, he rose to his knees to take in his surroundings.

He was in terrain very unlike the plateau he had been previously. Steep mountains rose on either side of a small, forested valley. He was kneeling in crusty wet snow in a clearing of grass and low brush, surrounded by young birch and alder trees. The patchy snow seemed to indicate it was now early spring rather than late fall.

The sound of a stream could be heard in the distance. There were other things around him as well—pieces of busted computer equipment and twisted wreckages of metal. He spied the unmoving hand of another person behind a hummock of brown vegetation. He got up to run but immediately fell, tripped by clothes several sizes too big for his body. Looking down at himself, he was shocked to see the proportions of a much smaller self. The hands he saw—his hands—were those of a kid!

His entire body had shrunk. A gust of wind blew the thick hair across his face. As he brushed it back, he had a horrible thought he had turned into a girl! He quickly dug into the oversized pants to check.

Whew, he thought with relief, everything still there. As that comforting realization passed, he was astounded to realize he no longer needed glasses to see clearly.

He felt like he had awakened from a deep sleep and didn't know who or where he was, except that this time the confusion remained. He wanted to take some time to get his bearings, but there might be others in desperate need of help.

Although he didn't feel any pain, he wasn't sure he was not hurt, for there were burns and tears in his clothing, along with blood stains. Doing a quick check with his hands over his clothing, he felt curiously free of wounds. Disoriented he could not remember why he was here or what caused the wreckage around him. He knew something terrible had happened, but what was it? Rubbing his temples he tried to think, but a dull burning sensation in his head made him feel nauseous, so he just looked around for now.

Feeling lost, he trudged to the unmoving hand, hiking up the too-long pants. The hand was attached to the mangled body of a middle-aged man in a military uniform. His chest had a piece of what looked like a metal chair embedded in it. There were several holes the size of a quarter going clear through the body, with clean edges as if made by a laser and burn marks on his clothing as well.

He scanned the area again for some movement or sign of other survivors. Not immediately seeing anyone else, dead or otherwise, he noticed a hunk of the Jacob's Ladder machine in the center of the clearing. The metal appeared to have wormholes all through it. The large crystal lay beside it, now unattached from its support rods but otherwise seemingly undamaged. Upon seeing the Jacob's Ladder, memories started to come back in a jumble of disassociated facts, but they still did not make sense.

Walking around, he found several more bodies. All apparently died in a similar fashion to the first soldier he had found. Two wore laboratory smocks and another was in a military dress uniform similar to the first. They all had body parts missing or holes in them. He also found the remains of young girl, around seven years old, dressed in an oversized security guard uniform. She seemed undamaged except, oddly, her nearly severed arm was that of an adult woman. Her arm was burnt and full of holes and a pool of blood blended with the frozen moss and crusted snow underneath her.

These people looked vaguely familiar as he sat down on a nearby moss covered stump that was free of snow and slowly pieced together what had happened. Starting with the present, he worked backwards, the aftermath, unconsciousness, an explosion, an experiment out of control, a chance phone call, Dr. Kuenning, Brad, a VIP tour. Suddenly it all came back in a rush that made him dizzy. His identity, his wife, his kids and the rest of his life slammed into his brain like a ship hitting an iceberg.

Reeling from the impact of it all, he slumped down and grabbed his head in pain. When the wave of pain passed, he slowly shook his head and marveled at what he remembered.

Even his jumbled memories did not explain why or how he survived the explosion and was apparently reduced in age. The earlier, successful experiment had succeeded in reducing the age of a flower to that of a sprout. Did it do the same to him? If so, then that might explain why he was so free of injuries, but what about the young girl, who must have been one of the security guards?

He remembered Dr. Kuenning had said non-living items were not changed by the ray from the machine. Evidently, the guard had nearly lost her arm from the exploding machine before the wild rays struck her and reduced her in age, while her nearly dead arm remained unchanged. She then must have died from blood loss while he was unconscious.

Then he remembered the sight just before the explosion, a large creature. What was that? Was that what the lab animal was changed into, or was it a predator that chanced upon an easy meal of the caged rat, but was accidentally caught up in the ray? And if so, was that creature or more like it still around?

Jason shook his head. That was an important consideration, but there were things here he needed to attend to first. Turning his attention back to the immediate area, he surveyed the blast site.

Among the scattered parts, he found the guard's pistol, fully loaded and unfired. This he took with him. He walked over to where he had dropped his cell phone, hoping to reach someone, anyone, for help. He definitely needed to contact the authorities, and he needed to talk to his wife, Molly, to let her know he was okay.

Okay? That is, if you could call being reverted to a child as being okay, a voice in his mind said. Perhaps this was only a dream, for it did not seem real.

Flipping open the phone, he eagerly waited for the screen to power up, but to his disappointment, it showed no bars for reception. He dialed 911 anyway and an "Unable to Connect" message appeared. He checked the last call and verified it was from Molly. Trying to answer it had probably saved his life by moving him farther away from the initial blast, but not far enough away to avoid being drawn in by the strange rays. To his relief, it appeared his student Brad had escaped. At least his body was not among the victims he had found so far.

He had to find his way back home but had no idea where he was. Was he teleported to a new location? He certainly was not in the same desert he had driven through a few hours ago, if it was only a few hours ago. Was he transported through time? If so, his diminutive size suggested he had regressed several years—many years, actually. Or was he in another dimension completely? Maybe he was suffering some sort of mental trauma, and he only imagined he had aged backward several decades.

Maybe he was injured worse than he thought. Maybe he was in a coma, and his mind was creating this alternate reality around him. He denied this because the gun and cell phone felt too solid in his hands, and details of wind, sun, and sensations on his skin were often overlooked in dreams.

Could he be in heaven? If so, then where was Jesus, who should have been here when his eyes opened? Where were the welcoming angels or saints who had gone before? Was he in an intermediate place? Well, wherever he was, it was obvious he had needs to take care of. He was in a survival situation.

Full of questions and having no other options, he resolved to climb one of the higher snow-covered ridges and try to pick up a signal on his cell phone, but first, he needed to modify his clothes to improve his mobility and take care of immediate needs.

Although it should not be his priority, he had to do something about his gnawing hunger. He did not know why this was so important. Perhaps it was being in a child's body. He remembered once when he got lost in the woods as a kid and had missed several meals, yet even then he did not notice how hungry he was until afterward.

Moving around had warmed him up some, and the climbing sun gave its warmth, but he surmised the nights would be well below freezing. If he didn't find help right away, he would need to make a shelter of some sort.

The female security guard's shoes and clothing were the easiest to adapt to his size. He figured his newly acquired biological age to be close to ten years old. He took the general's jacket for warmth, using a belt to tighten it around his waist.

Very thankful for his pocket knife, he trimmed the shirt and his pants and put another notch in the belt. He adjusted the security guard's belt and holster to fit so he could more easily carry the gun. It was a nine millimeter semi-automatic, not much good for hunting, but better than throwing rocks.

It held a clip of ammo holding ten shots, not much, but probably more than enough for him to get back to civilization.

Digging around the security guard's vest pockets, he found a can of mace and a pair of handcuffs. He couldn't see himself needing these but started a pile under a tree of potentially useful items. He then checked the mutilated bodies of the other four men but found little of use. Their billfolds contained identification and credit cards but very little cash. These he placed back on the bodies to help identify them if discovered.

He wanted to try his cell phone again. Though not ready to climb the mountain ridge, he saw a small hill nearby and cautiously headed toward it. With the handgun in the holster over the outside of his coat, he felt fairly ready for any predators that might be about.

While climbing to the top, he was surprised he had to rest three times. It was as though he had no reserves of endurance. With the pale sun overhead in the gray sky, he figured it was about noon when he reached the summit. Because of his exhaustion, he knew that climbing the higher ridges that day was out of the question.

At the top of the hill, he tried to look out across the valley for some sign of civilization, but the trees and brush, although still leafless, interfered with his view. After climbing a thick birch with spreading limbs for a better view, he could see the rest of the valley with a stream running through it. The lower end of the valley opened to a hilly area with a plain in the distance and more mountains beyond that. The upper end of the valley continued into the mountains. No signs of smoke, roads, planes, or jet contrails were anywhere to be seen.

From the top of the tree, he again tried for a cell phone signal. Still nothing. After climbing down, he contemplated where he might be. Even though this high mountain valley was similar to his home in Alaska, the lower areas reminded him more of the Northeastern United States, except the surrounding mountains were greater. Perhaps the Midwest? Colorado, maybe? Montana?

He rested as he contemplated his next move. "What will I do now, Lord?" he prayed quietly to himself. After a moment's wait and receiving no direct answer, he tried to focus his thoughts. Since no one else survived and there was no medical emergency, he did not have to rush and risk his own welfare in order to find help.

In fact, all the advice in standard survival manuals is to stay put until help comes to you. But with his unusual method of arrival, in the midst of an explosion, he had a sinking feeling no one was looking for him or the others beyond the immediate wreckage of the ruined science lab atop the plateau in New Mexico. Even a thorough search for someone as important as the general would probably not lead them here.

Wherever he was, he felt more comfortable staying in the area as he learned about his surroundings rather than moving to the lower, warmer area he could see from this hill. There would be fewer predators up here, and he could spend more time trying to get his bearings. As far as he knew, he could be in another country hostile to him, being an American.

Having worked most of his life in the Alaskan bush, he was no stranger to cold weather survival methods. Water was provided by the stream. Now he needed to salvage what he could, make a shelter, procure food, and eventually, tend to the dead. He would also make preparation for a signal fire in case a plane flew over. Having not seen or heard a plane since he awoke made him feel perplexed. He could not imagine some place in the United States that was habitable but with no plane traffic.

He momentarily thought of his wife and kids and was surprised to find tears rolling down his face. He didn't feel particularly sad, but as a kid again, he seemed to be more vulnerable to his emotions. A breakdown was not a luxury he could afford right now, however.

He wondered what his wife would think if she could see him now. What would it be like to be married to a ten-year-old kid? His youngest son was twelve. They could be best pals, but what about filling the role of a father? Would his fourteen-year-old daughter even listen to him?

He knew he was a man inside, and that made all the difference to him, but would it make a difference to anyone else? Would he have to grow up again to regain the respect he once had? Speaking of growing up—cavities, colds, wisdom teeth, puberty, and the awkward pimply teenage years would have to be relived. That was a perturbing thought.

Then again, he had stumbled on the fountain of youth. He was ten again. He had great memories of that age. It was an exciting time of exploring and carefree fun. He found himself laughing—young again. The excitement of renewed vigor coursed through his veins. In his youthful exuberance, he tore down the hill, jumping snow patches and logs, dodging trees in reckless abandon, and letting out loud whoops of delight.

He hit the bottom, exhausted but happy. As he rested, he reflected that his exuberance came just as naturally as did his tears. He could have been hurt running down the hill the way he did, and he wasted precious energy needed for survival. Unless he kept strict discipline, his emotions could betray him. Just as he came to that conclusion, he also felt the urge to brush it aside. However, the older, wiser part of him won out though he could definitely feel the rash, invincible adolescent within him struggling to express itself.

He smiled ruefully. He simultaneously felt like a father admonishing his kid and a kid rebelling against his father. He suddenly thought of the song "I'm My Own Grandpa" and walked back to the clearing humming it to himself.

Able to move more easily with his oversized clothes well secured, he could now scrounge around better. He found pieces of a computer desk with several drawers intact. In one drawer, he found computer storage discs, some paper and pen, a small hole punch, and some scissors. The scissors were the kind of snips that surgeons use, with a blunt protrusion on the lower blade to make it easier to cut skin without damaging the flesh below. He also found a metal attaché case full of important-looking documents.

He dumped the documents, so he could use the case for carrying useful items. He also found a large black garbage bag partially filled with office trash. He dumped the trash and neatly folded the bag, adding it to his growing survival kit. The garbage of mostly paper items he saved as fire starter.

The middle desk drawer was stuck, but after a little effort, the drawer opened to reveal a half-eaten box of doughnuts and two granola bars. These he devoured instantly and gratefully.

Thirsty now but feeling re-energized, he carefully made his way to the stream as he considered his next step. He made his way around a patch of snow noting broad, deep indentations of something that had crossed it sometime ago. It was too melted to make out clearly, but from the size of them, they might be bear tracks. He couldn't see marks from the front paws to verify this, but sometimes a bear walks in such a way that its hind tracks partially cover the front tracks. He remembered again the bearlike creature that was at least partially returned to the lab during the experiment. Were these tracks from a similar creature, perhaps even the same one? His eyes scanned along the perimeter of the clearing again, hoping not to see anything large and furry. Seeing everything normal, his thirst urged him back toward the running water.

The stream had completely melted the winter ice and was slightly swollen with spring melt. Going down the bank, he stood on some slippery rocks, then crouched to scoop some water to drink. Not trusting to anything, he tested the water first with his tongue. It tasted cool and refreshing, so he took a drink but limited himself to a small amount.

Standing and turning to go, not being used to his new body and the clumsy oversized shoes from the security guard, he slipped on the rocks and landed on them hard, feet and hands in the icy cold stream. Pain shot through his left knee as it hit a sharp edge of the large rock on which he had been standing.

He painfully regained his footing and stood erect, angry with himself.

Any injury, no matter how small, could threaten his chances for survival. Checking the wound, he saw this was more than a mere skinned knee; there was a deep, three-inch gash bleeding profusely. Even worse, he was crying again. The pain seemed to paralyze his body, and he was stuck in the middle of a stream blubbering like a baby.

When he was a boy, he was considered tough. There must have been something he did when he got hurt, afraid, or was frustrated. Then, it came to him. He'd always growl to bolster himself. It was his imitation of a tiger. This seemed so silly, but he'd do anything to help himself get moving again.

At first, it came out as a little "grr." He could do better than that! He let loose with a half growl-half roar. To his amazement, it worked. He could start moving again.

Limping up the bank, he checked his pockets for anything to make a bandage. He could feel the warm blood running down his leg. He sat on an exposed patch of moss, pulled up his pant leg, and wiped the blood, leaving a red smear along his calf and hand. He pulled out a handful of cool green moss and pushed it down hard over the wound to try to stop the bleeding.

Not having a way to bind the moss to his knee, he just sat there awhile, monitoring the bleeding. Using his other hand, he cleaned the blood off his leg with more moss. To his relief, it stopped bleeding after about ten minutes, so he stood and limped his way back to the entry site very carefully, so as not to reopen the wound. His leg was already beginning to feel better.

All was as he'd left it and he returned to salvaging, this time a little more thoroughly, systematically placing materials in stacks. He found some plastic conduit straight enough to fashion into a blowgun. He saved this in his survival pile and kept an eye out for stiff wire or shards of metal with which to make darts.

By late afternoon, Jason began his shelter. He wanted his camp far enough from the bodies to avoid predators and scavengers. He located a large rock about half the size of a house a quarter mile away with only one steep access to it. A rock was not the best place for a warm shelter, but he worried about bears, and this would give him some security. He built a low lean-to on top out of dead branches.

The shelter was just long enough for him to lie down inside. He was going to cover the branches with moss and dead leaves, but instead, he found a fallen birch that provided a ready supply of bark that came off in foot wide strips. This he held down with sod to help insulate from the cold surface of the rock, which would undoubtedly leach away his warmth if he tried to lay directly on it.

If he still had the full strength and size of an adult, he probably would have risked putting his shelter in a hollow part way up a hill, above the cold that would settle lower in the valley and better insulated with moss and grass. But that would also make him more vulnerable to predators and despite the gun, he wanted as much time as possible to see something coming.

Adding more birch bark to the roof bestowed a modicum of water proofing should it rain. He had been in the high desert where rain would seldom be a concern, but his current surroundings were more temperate. He also spread pine bows as bedding over the rock and covered that with birch bark as well.

Recovering coats from the other men was a gruesome task, but he needed some to serve as bedding and blankets. One thin blood-stained lab coat served as a makeshift door to cover the entrance. He would try to wash the blood off and dry the coats later. His shelter looked like a trash heap, but it should keep him warm and dry. Survival shelters never look pretty anyway.

The overcast sky was dark by the time he finished, and he was hungry again. Tomorrow, he would try to set a snare or catch a fish, depending on what seemed most available. He had forgotten his knee in his focused preparations, and he checked it now.

Pulling up his pant leg, he expected to see a swelling, oozing mass of scabs and blood, but to his astonishment, there was no wound at all. His knee was blood-stained everywhere except the spot of the wound, and in its place was fresh new skin. There was not even a scar. Was there some curative property in the moss? He marveled, wondering what part God's hand played in all this. Everything seemed so familiar and yet so strange at the same time.

Wandering through the clearing before turning in for the night, he stumbled upon the crystal globe, lying unbroken in the brush among the wreckage. It had no value in his survival preparations, but it had brought him here, wherever here was, and could be his only hope for returning to his own home and his normal, middle-aged self.

The confrontation with the unknown and a feeling of loneliness in the dark evoked in him the sudden urge to pray. As the only survivor in this valley, God must have had some hand in bringing him here safely, perhaps even for some specific purpose. Anyway, he knelt and thanked God that he had survived this incident at all, let alone without even a scratch.

He felt unworthy of this miracle and even a little guilty that he alone should survive out of all the others. He prayed for his family and thanked God for the renewal of his body.

Heavenly entreaties completed, he picked up the crystal and examined it. At his touch, a small spark of light began dancing in its depth, then faded away. The crystal seemed to emanate warmth, so he wrapped it in some cloth and took it with him into the shelter. For some reason, he felt it important he not lose this mysterious link to home and slept that night with it tucked at his feet.

CHAPTER 3
Living Legends

The next day, Jason awoke from dreamless sleep, wondering where he was, lying in dirty rags with a canopy of sticks and bark above him. He could feel lumpy branches under him and cool air about him. He wasn't cold, but he wasn't warm either. The quietness reminded him of many solo hunting trips. Was he on a hunt?

He rolled over and looked at the stained, dirty-white fabric over the door. He moved his hand to lift the tarp-like door and stopped, staring at a small pale child's hand. He pulled it back and huddled for warmth. All the events of the prior day came rushing back as a bizarre nightmare.

He felt his face and his long-tangled hair. He was definitely a kid. Perhaps he was only a kid who dreamed that at one time he was a man. But if that were true, then why was he lying in a survival shelter? Where were his parents? They would never allow him to grow his hair so long.

The memory of his wife, Molly, and kids, Cassandra and Trevor, evoked too great a sense of responsibility for them to have been a dream. The memories of a lifetime flooded him; too much to have only been a dream.

Where am I? he thought to himself urgently. He lay there, reminiscing the events of the prior day, looking for some kind of clue as to his whereabouts. He had a sudden thought. Perhaps he was somewhere in the Southern Hemisphere. That would explain the spring-like conditions, even though it was previously fall when he'd entered the lab. That would mean a five-thousand- mile jump. That stretched believability, but what was believable about any of this?

Finally lifting the fabric of his makeshift door, he saw that during the night fresh snow had fallen, blanketing the valley about an inch deep. Getting up and moving was his best defense against the cold. Reluctantly and awkwardly, he exited his comparatively warm dwelling like a grizzly bear leaving its den after a winter's hibernation. He felt as hungry as one, too.

Squinting against the white glare of the fresh snow, he explored his surroundings anew from the perch of his rock, noting fresh animal tracks. He could see tracks of some small creature close to the thickets by the stream, probably rabbit. He walked down to verify, and indeed, they were rabbit tracks. He could try to hunt them by making a blow gun, but using snares was far more energy efficient.

Selecting electrical wire from his survival pile, he set some snares, looped together along the rabbit run at the edge of a patch of alders close to the stream. He remembered learning how to set rabbit snares from an old native man when he was a kid. He chuckled to himself...when he was a kid.

The snares were a simple noose propped with small twigs and placed where the rabbit was likely to jump over an obstacle such as a log or rock. This increased the likelihood for the rabbit to become ensnared when it either starts its jump from one direction or on its landing from the other direction. The speed of the jump helps tighten the noose around the unsuspecting varmint. The old native who taught him this used about five snares and always had at least one rabbit a day to supplement his diet.

After setting his snares, Jason visited the stream to quench his thirst and look for other sources of sustenance. He knew man cannot live on rabbit alone since they do not have enough fat to fulfill a human's need for energy. Sweeping the snow off a log he hunkered down to watch for fish.

After a while, his eyes wandered to the bank. Dark-brown remains of ferns hung limp over the rocks along the water's edge. He remembered as a kid his family would harvest and cook fiddle- neck ferns that sometimes grew under the earth and snow in the spring. These were immature ferns, which grew like sprouts. He quickly dug into the base of a nearby plant, pulling up five green fern heads. Peeling off the outer brown husks and stuffing them into his mouth, it felt satisfying to eat something. Despite the rich earthy smell, the immature ferns had a very mild taste. The next few he dug, he took care to not take the whole plant so as not to decimate this area as a future food source.

It seemed strange to remember things of his childhood with crystal clarity while recent events, which led to this misadventure, were more of a blur. Even some important things such as his family and parts of his martial arts seemed to be missing in chunks. Perhaps the accident that contributed to his change had wiped some of his memories.

Taking up his log perch again, he spent more time studying the water. Finally, a small fish swam into view. So there were fish here. He could easily make a conventional hook and line but decided to make a fish trap of some sort instead. A trap over a period of time would provide more with less effort.

As a commercial fisherman, he was more familiar with nets and had heard about the ancient Kenaisti Indians in Alaska who made nets twisted from spruce tree roots. There were similar trees here, but harvesting roots out of the still frozen ground would make this option very difficult.

He had several choices for fish traps. Basket traps made from interwoven slender branches were intended for deeper and wider rivers. The second choice came from the old days before commercial salmon fishermen in Cook Inlet were restricted to nets only. They used weir traps made of posts driven into the mud flats at low tide.

These posts were interlinked with heavy netting, making a corral with a wide V leading fish into the narrow opening. Fish swimming along the shore toward their spawning river would get corralled. The fishermen would scoop them out with a netted pole or spear them with a pitchfork.

This second design could be easily scaled down. He wanted the corral to be fairly small, so he could more easily corner the fish. Also, the overall trap would not be so labor intensive. In fact, he could have two openings, one for catching fish going upstream and the other for catching fish going downstream.

Using his pocket knife, he cut down some slender willows as well as heavier ones to be sharpened into stakes. It took him the rest of the morning, about four hours, just to get everything cut.

By noon, the snow had melted, and he took off his shoes and socks and waded into the stream's cold water to start hammering his stakes with a fist sized rock. The stakes did not go in easily. The rocky mountain stream bed split his stakes or pushed them out of line, so he had to cut still more stakes to finish the job.

Next, he wove willow saplings between the stakes, forming a wicker wall. He took special care, making sure there weren't any holes where fish could slip through. By the time he was done, his feet and hands were so numb from the cold, he could not feel them. He made the wall of the fish trap to extend several inches above the water to prevent fish from jumping over.

During this time, he observed a few very small song birds, which he could have easily shot with a blow gun, if he had one. But knowing they're mostly feathers, it would take ten or twenty of them to make a meal. Hunting for a larger grouse sized bird, or whatever sort of creatures inhabited the area, would make that effort worthwhile. Getting close enough to such a bird for a blowgun shot would take patience and a whole lot of luck.

Perhaps this or a larger creature would justify him spending one or two of his precious bullets.

Leaving the stream late afternoon, he spent the better part of an hour gathering firewood for the signal fire and made a little pile of bark and grass for a quick start. Strangely, he never found matches or a lighter among the bodies or debris. Score one for the anti-smoking lobby. He did find a flint striker for lighting Bunsen burners. Although it wasn't very good for lighting cooking fires, it was better than rubbing two sticks together, so he would make do.

The lighter consisted of a piece of flint held in a springy metal wire construction that when squeezed and released would throw sparks hot enough to light a gas burner. The lighter could potentially light tender made from the shredded paper from birch bark if one was quick enough to blow it into a flame.

From his experience, this usually took great effort. Once, he had even experimented with lighting a fire with a bow drill. Although he could eventually do it, he learned to appreciate the Indian method of carrying a live ember from a previous fire in a fold of moss and bark to save time and energy. If he were to be prepared to light a signal fire in time for any plane, he must keep a small fire going nearby at all times.

After gathering and stacking a sufficient amount of wood, he surveyed the disaster site for a convenient way to protect the bodies. He could pull the bodies into a depression and cover them with logs, brush, and rocks that could keep scavengers at bay until they could be recovered. This would take a lot of work, which he planned to do the next day.

Upon checking his snares and fish traps that evening, he was rewarded with a couple of fish. With much splashing around, he caught them one at a time in a corner and grabbed them with his hands. It took a while to light a fire, then he cooked the small fish whole on a flat rock. He knew better than trying to cook fish speared on a stick since its flesh was too soft and would fall into the fire as it cooked.

After a quick prayer of thanks, he devoured them hungrily, leaving only bones. He supplemented the meager protein with more fiddlehead ferns, which left him without hunger pains but still unsatisfied.

That evening, he made his supplications sitting on the rock outside the shelter. It occurred to him that he should put some brush and rocks on the steep path to his shelter as an early warning system should any creature venture near.

He went back down, grabbed some wood off the wood pile, and carried it back to the top. He made several more trips to the creek to gather stones, which he placed carefully along the slope and in cracks in the rock up to his frail dwelling.

He considered keeping his cooking fire going all night but was already getting the sinking feeling that no one was going to come looking for him.

How could they? They would only look in the vicinity of the accident. Who would guess where the strange rays of light had sent them?

Perhaps they would think the explosion great enough to have vaporized their bodies. Maybe there was a fire afterward, perhaps a spilling of radioactive plasma...maybe even the nuclear reactor itself was compromised. No, no one will come. He was on his own. Of course, God was with him, and he did have a gun. What more did he need? He would walk all the way home if necessary.

As he went to sleep that night, he could hear a pack of wolves howling in the distance in the direction of the lower valley. He placed the nine millimeter handgun close to his side with a bullet in the chamber. He wished he had his old .44 revolver instead. It could handle almost anything up to the size of a grizzly bear and even take out a grizzly if you hit it in the right spot.

Despite this, he knew from experience that all he could do was make careful preparations; it was all in God's hands. It was hard to think there was some good reason for him being here. Sure, Christians believe everything works out for the good of those who love God. He should be able to sleep with security, knowing nothing bad was going to happen to him. These thoughts helped to comfort him.

That night, he dreamed for the first time since coming to this place. He dreamed he was back home and the fire had gone out in the wood heater. He was trying to get it going before his wife and kids froze. He felt cold and every time he got the fire going it would go out. He felt as if he worked on the fire all night long.

Of course, he woke the next morning, freezing. He hated to leave his shelter to venture into the brisk morning air, but hunger drove him into action. As he crunched through the frozen snow toward the stream, to his amazement, he noticed the sapling one of his snares was tied to shaking. It had caught a white rabbit; its winter coat had started changing, giving it a mottled appearance.

He quickly dispatched it with his pocket knife and cleaned it for breakfast. He was a little pleased with himself, since this was a decent-sized hare and would go a long way toward calming his gnawing gut. It had been a while since he had cleaned a rabbit but made short work of it with his pocket knife—messy but adequate. He noticed toward the end of the job that the knife was in need of sharpening, a sure testimony to the cheap metal in the blade.

He tried to stoke up the fire from the night before, but it had gone fully cold, so he had to start again from scratch. It went more smoothly this time now that he had some practice. Not having any seasonings, he cooked the cottontail with some green bark added to the fire to smoke it a little.

As the bunny breakfast cooked, he attempted to sharpen the knife on a smooth stone, making slow circles with the blade. With some effort, it became razor sharp again. After about an hour, the rabbit was cooked and tasted excellent, considering the circumstances, and now, his full stomach enabled him to better concentrate.

After washing his hands in the stream, he took a long drink. The chance of picking up a parasite was small, he hoped. So far, he had not seen any animals or plants that would be out of place in North America. In fact, he could be back in Alaska for all he could tell. But even if he were in a place hostile to Americans, he doubted most people would take it out on a little boy. They may be suspicious of spy activity, but he didn't think they would suspect him directly of being a spy. Perhaps being a kid had some advantages.

He decided he had nothing to lose in drawing attention to himself. He checked his pile of wood for the signal fire. It seemed adequate to create a fire large enough to attract the attention of a search party. Still, he gathered some leafy branches and set them nearby to help create a goodly amount of smoke, just in case.

Having eaten and with nothing left to do to ensure his survival, he turned to the task of first cutting his annoyingly long matted hair and then burying the dead. Cutting his hair was a simple task of shearing off handfuls with the surgeon's scissors. He was sure he looked a mess when finished, but was seldom concerned with his looks even when he was around people.

When done, looking at the pile of hair, he contemplated of what use it might be to him in this survival situation. Thinking of none, he placed it in the notch of a tree.

As far as the dead were concerned, though his own survival did come first, the truth is he had been delaying this task as long as possible. Using the small saw blade on his utility knife, he cut a pair of poles from two young trees. He then created a simple sling between them out of electrical wire to form a travois. It was the best way he could figure to move the bodies.

Realizing string was a valuable commodity, he removed all shoelaces. Moving the dead was a grim task. Thankfully, the weather had been relatively cool so decomposition had been slow to set in, and he detected none of the noxious odor he had feared. Still, after several days, the deceased's skin had taken on the sickening pall of decay that turned their flesh translucent and gray. They were stiff and unwieldy. Moving them would have been difficult for a fully grown man, let alone a child. They were all more than twice his weight.

Thankfully, he did not have to move them far, perhaps only fifty feet.

As he covered the bodies with logs from the dead fall, he prayed for them. Some of the dead had name tags along with their driver's licenses and the general had badges and military decorations. He checked their names and tried to memorize them in case he got back to civilization. Pushing logs and debris over their faces filled him with remorse, despite knowing they were well beyond pain.

It was late when he walked back to his shelter after the last victim was finally laid to rest. Checking his traps and snares, he found he had caught another fish. After dinner, it felt dark and gloomy, depressingly lonely. He stayed up late, staring into his small fire and occupying his evening with prayers. The night sky was clear in the rarefied mountain air. He could not recognize any of the constellations, giving credence to his Southern Hemisphere theory.

Some distance up the snowy mountainside came an eerie, inhuman call. It sounded like an eagle's screech, but deeper and more throaty. Jason looked intently into the night, scanning the moonlit valley walls before him. Something larger than an eagle was flying silhouetted against the mountain. Its wings were definitely flapping, so it was no airplane. He had the impression of a winged dinosaur like a pterodactyl but longer in body and neck. A dragon? His mind rejected such a notion but tried to be realistic to the possible dangers.

His eyes strained to follow the apparition in the darkness as he watched it disappear over the mountaintops. The crypto- zoologist in him wanted to chase after it, but the small boy he now was felt very exposed on top of his rock. He considered he might be seeing things. The morbid day's work and his long isolation were compounding his fatigue and causing hallucinations. Still, the image seemed real enough that he slept uneasily that night.

The following day, he snared another rabbit. He could hardly believe his luck but was feeling more confident in his hunter- gathering abilities. His old Indian mentor would be proud of him. A rabbit every other day would sustain him, but he was certain the local bunny population would not hold up for long, and he would need to move farther afield to find meat.

After eating, he searched the trees for some grouse but did not find any. Most of the game would probably be down in the lower regions where it was warmer, and the foliage, thicker. He would have to go down there soon not only to hunt but to try to follow the stream to civilization. This being the third day and still no sign of any sort of aircraft, he resigned himself fully to the idea of self-rescue. He needed to make preparations for travel. His wife and family must be very distraught over his absence and might even think him dead.

To travel quickly, he needed to build up a food reserve, so he wouldn't have to hunt and fish much on the way. He was tempted to make a quick foray to the lower areas but decided to check the upper valley first. There must be animals in sufficient numbers for the huge flying creature he saw the evening before to hunt up there.

After spending another uncomfortable night, he hiked up the valley around the bend. The trees were becoming smaller and more sparse along the valley bottom, with thick brush filling the lower half of the mountains.

Walking another mile, Jason spied a discoloration in a snow patch. Upon investigation, he discovered animal droppings and round deep tracks, perhaps from a variety of goats or sheep. To be ready for an opportune shot, he carried his pistol in his hand.

Moving quietly he peered ahead, alert for any movement that would betray his prey. He would have to stalk it to get close enough to use his short-ranged gun. A hoarse, cawing sound could now be heard ahead. Hiking toward it, he could tell there were several birds fighting over something.

Among the rocks of a slope, he came upon ravens fighting over scraps from a kill. Coarse white and brown hair were scattered everywhere. Before him were the remains of a sheep whose bones and viscera were shattered and scattered over a twenty-foot area. Only the skull identified the remains as being that of a sheep. The horns were more tightly curled than any Dall or Bighorn sheep he had ever seen. He did not think there were wild sheep like this in North America, but he was not sure. How the animal died, he could not tell.

The shadows were becoming long on the mountainside, so he scanned the valley and ridges one more time, disappointed he had not found any game, and made his way through the rocks, trees, and brush toward camp. As he approached the grave site, something made him stop and freeze in place.

There was something different about the brush-covered ditch. He warily examined every nook and cranny in sight before slowly turning his head to check the rest of his surroundings. Seeing nothing else out of the ordinary, he approached the mass grave with gun drawn.

Some of the brush and logs were moved. A bare foot had been exposed, but as far as Jason could see, it had not been molested. Checking around again, Jason laid the gun down and pushed the debris back into place. As he finished, he heard a strange whistling noise, like what a marmot would make, but instead of a single note, it was more musical with several tones. It seemed to come from the direction of his camp.

He felt foolish for having laid his gun down when he knew there was something big around and quickly picked it up again. He should have at least put it in his holster. He was tempted to not go to his camp at all and just sit here on the rocks, but then, whatever it was could come back, and in the dark, he would never see it until it was on top of him.

It would be wiser, he thought, to investigate and assess the danger of this creature before it got any darker. So again, he made his way cautiously toward camp. He considered it strange that he did not think the whistling noise was made by a man. After all, man is one of the few creatures that whistle.

As Jason approached the camp, his hair stood on end. It was not from anything he could see, for he could see nothing extraordinary. Everything looked to be in place. It was more like he could sense a presence, as though something were watching him, yet as quiet as he was, how could it even know he was there?

Climbing his rock, he sat and looked for any signs of an intruder. By now, it was getting very dark, and he was hungry. He felt foolish because he had yet to see anything at all that indicated an intruder was actually still present.

Climbing back down, he lit a fire before checking his traps. If there were nothing in his traps, he just wasted his effort, but the fire gave him comfort and perhaps would scare whatever it was away. Checking his rabbit traps first, he discovered one of them indeed had caught something, due to the scrapping signs, but it was gone. The wire snare was broken halfway down its length.

Spooked, he checked to make sure the safety was off his gun and drew his pocket knife to carry in the other hand. He decided to leave the fish trap for morning. He would rather go hungry this night than risk an encounter in the dark.

As he approached the fire, he avoided looking directly at it to preserve his night vision. His plan was to go back up his rock, set his alarms and wait for morning. Still seeing nothing he cautiously climbed backwards up the rock, alert for anything that might come from around the rock or from the clearing near his fire.

Just as he made it to the top of the rock, something made him freeze in his backward ascent. It was a smell—a musky, salty smell that was suddenly overpowering. A small sound, a slight rustle of something behind him on top of the very rock he was on. Was it the flying creature?

Deciding immediate action necessary, Jason flung himself forward and down off the rock without looking behind. He planned to hit the bottom running and leap to the right to get offline of any predatory creature pouncing after him.

Hitting the bottom hard after a twelve-foot drop, he leaped clumsily to the side. A good thing he did, for a large creature landed right where he had been with a loud, thunderous roar. Through peripheral vision, he got the impression of a large, dark- brown, furry creature the size of a grizzly bear. But the way it landed was odd for a bear, back feet first.

He didn't take time to get a better look, scooting around the rock as fast as his feet could take him. Only then did he notice he somehow managed to retain his hold on his gun and the open pocket knife. Supposing the creature would be following closely behind, he continued around the next corner of the rock. Trying to gauge how close he was being followed, he glanced back as he rounded the corner.

Not watching where he was going, he felt his foot hit a rock, causing him to stumble and he fell, landing hard trying to protect his gun and keep from cutting himself on the knife. He felt the jarring pain of impact as his shoulder crushed on the rocks and a broken stick, wedged in the crack of another rock, simultaneously jammed into his ribs.

He lay there for a moment stunned by the pain. Knowing that danger may soon be following, he forced himself to move as soon as he could. He rolled off the rocks and forced himself to one knee, pistol pointing to the corner of the large boulder and waited.

As he waited, he checked his body for any wound. The pain in his side made it so he could hardly breathe, indicating some broken ribs. His shoulder hurt and blood ran from a cut in it, but it would be okay. Grateful to be alive, he gave a short prayer of thanks.

After a few minutes, he heard a branch crack some distance away. He slowly stood and listened. Further away, he heard a strange, deep-throated cry, then nothing.

Trembling uncontrollably and breathing painful, shallow breaths, he cautiously returned to the fire and threw on some more sticks. He felt certain that creature was not a bear. He searched for tracks and found deep imprints of what looked like a bear's hind feet coming off the boulder, but it lacked the claws. Could it have been the legendary Yeti or Big Foot? Or perhaps it was some other creature native to this country?

This and the large flying creature he saw didn't necessarily indicate he was on a different world, but he wondered. Because of his exhaustion, he slept deeply despite his near brush with death.

The next day, he arose late and in pain but already feeling better. The cut in his shoulder was already healed, but the rib bones still needed time to mend. This proved it was not the moss that had helped him heal earlier. It was either a miracle of God, or he had somehow been gifted with the ability to heal quickly, along with his youthful rejuvenation.

Checking his weir, he was rewarded by a catch of three fish and made repairs to his snare. Just before noon, he began a hike up to the snow on top of the high ridge to see if he could make his phone work. He did not reach the saddle until mid-afternoon. The climb was strenuous and would have been difficult under normal circumstances, but the lack of energy-rich food made him weak, and the climb all the more taxing. After trying several minutes, he failed to get a signal on his cell phone and turned it completely off. Phone service did not seem to exist in this area.

While he had the advantage of elevation, he tried to catch a view of any form of civilization or evidence of man—a road, a power pole, anything. He saw nothing and suddenly felt very small. The cold wind whipped through his baggy, oversized clothes, and he turned back to what he was beginning to call home.

CHAPTER 4

The First Human Encounter

Back at camp and preparing his evening meal, Jason considered trying to walk out the very next day. He had a gun and moving lightly and quickly, he could possibly find civilization in what, three or four days? And what if he didn't? What shape would he be in after an exhaustive hike with little or no food after four days? To be depleted that low in a survival situation could mean death.

And what if he ran into more creatures of the evening before or the large flying beast he saw? His mad dash to find help would make sense if there was a reasonable chance that help would be available in that time, but so far, he had seen no sign of man.

The encounter with the yeti—or whatever it was—highlighted the importance of a backup weapon, one that could handle a beast of that size and wouldn't run out of bullets. Having only ten bullets made them more precious than gold; he should weigh their value carefully in using them to hunt. If he missed the opportunity to get a sheep, goat, or deer, that meant he only missed a few meals; but if something big was trying to kill him and he didn't have the firepower, he would die right then and there.

Thus, Jason vowed to only use the gun in self-defense. He would continue to use primitive methods of survival as long as he could. He mentally ran through what he knew of primitive weaponry. Although he was an expert at sword, having studied the live blade seriously in his martial arts, the amount of effort to produce a workable blade from the scraps of metal lying around would take way too much time.

He considered it reasonable to take an extra two days to prepare, but to make a sword could take a week or more to grind the metal housing of the machine into proper shape. Plus, a sword does not fair as well against larger beasts, such as a boar pig or a bear. A spear is much better for that, simple and relatively easy to make. So for protection, making a spear would be his top priority, but a spear is very poor for hunting. He already had the tube from the conduit for making a blow gun, so it was just a matter of making the relatively simple darts to procure small game at short range.

The bow and arrow was the ideal hunting tool, for it could take larger animals at a greater distance and also offer some degree of protection, but for now, he would survive with smaller game. He would work on a bow along the way.

The spear was fairly easy to make, taking only about an hour and a half. Using a sharp stone, he hacked down a slender tree with some help from the serrated blade on his folding knife, then tied a piece of metal shrapnel from the machine to the end with electrical wire. It was sharp as it was, but he would sharpen it more as he traveled.

There was nothing in his traps that night, and he was glad he would be moving on soon. He was tired of eating fiddlehead ferns. He also remembered that ferns contain a high amount of silica which was not very healthy for continued eating.

He decided to depart tomorrow, even if he was not totally ready. Suddenly, he saw a pigeon-sized bird fly by. He scooped up a rock and flung it, but it seemed the bird flew faster than his rock could fly, and he missed by a wide margin.

The need for more power caused him to remember a simple weapon he had made as a kid. It was tremendously powerful for all its simplicity—a sling, similar to what David in the Bible used to kill the giant Goliath.

Procuring materials from his stash, he quickly made one in about ten minutes from the cut-out tongue of a scavenged shoe and two shoe strings. He ran to the stream and picked out four smaller than hand-sized rocks.

Going back to his huge rock with the lean to on top, he tried hurling a stone at it. The stone hummed with great speed and hit way off from his intended spot, but the boulder was so large, he still hit the edge of it with great force. The small stone shattered to pieces.

This brought to memory how inaccurate he was with the sling as a child, sometimes releasing the stone so it actually went behind him. It was a wonder he didn't destroy anything or hurt anyone. Sometimes, it went straight up, and he had to run for cover. But now he thought surely he was a better shot after thirty years of martial arts training.

He tried firing the remaining three stones at a stump. One hit out of pure luck, but the other two were so far off that if it were an elephant, he would have missed.

I am a better shot than I was as a kid, he thought to himself cheerfully, but not good enough. So he wound the strings around the folded leather and decided to keep it just as a fun diversion, stuffing it deep into his coat pocket. In some ways, he was beginning to think like a kid again.

Taking a technician's lab coat and folding it back on itself, he used ringlets of electrical wire to pierce the fabric to hold it together. Then he affixed the ends of the sleeves to loop back to the jacket for shoulder straps. This made a medium-sized backpack to carry assorted items, such as the mysterious crystal globe and the attaché case.

He started packing his attaché case and improvised backpack. Preparations were completed ahead of his estimated time schedule, which would astound his wife, Molly, if she ever found out. She used to joke that if he said it would take one day to get something done, it usually took three.

Again, it seemed like his traps were telling him it was time to go, for there was nothing in them that evening. He was going to dig up some extra fiddlehead ferns but was so tired of eating them he just couldn't bring himself to do it. Perhaps on the morrow's travel, he would find a new source of food.

The next morning, he removed his fish weir trap from the stream, threw the stakes into the bushes, and collected his snares. Lastly, he rolled up the collection of coats he used as blankets and stuffed them into the top of his backpack.

Ready to go, he hefted his back pack and secured his weapons. Jason looked every bit like a kid raised in the wild. He stuffed the blowgun into the backpack and tied a cord to his spear so it could sling over a shoulder. He carried the gun under his jacket in case he came across people alarmed to see a little boy carrying a gun. His pocket knife had a clip on it, so this he attached to his belt.

He had no idea how long it would take him to hike to civilization, but if the absence of aircraft was any indication, it may take a long time. If he was on another world, which he surmised as a wild possibility, then civilization may look very different, assuming there were even people at all. He did not want to even think about that.

Right now, he just wanted to believe that in about four or five days of traveling, he would walk into a small country town, meander over to a fast-food restaurant, order a large pizza and four hamburgers with a gallon of root beer soda to wash it all down. He could call his wife and kids and be on the next plane to meet them someplace.

His plan was to follow the creek down to a river, then the river to a town. If there were no towns, he would follow the river to an ocean. From there, he would follow the coast. Forcing himself to think of all the possibilities, if worse came to worse, as an experienced seaman, he would build a sailboat and use that to continue his explorations. As a last resort, he would chance his fate to the crystal he carried and hope he could recreate the experiment that had sent him here. He would need a source of electricity, but the complexity of the endeavor was more than he could think about right now. It would all be iffy at best, and he did not really think he had a chance to make it work.

Beginning his journey at noon, he found a well-packed game trail along the creek on which he could travel at a good speed. Just before leaving, he paused where the trail overlooked the valley and asked for God's blessings on his journey. He was a small boy going into a big world, and he needed a big God beside him.

Leaving the patchy snow in the high country, the birch trees became larger and thicker, most just beginning to leaf. The deeper forests further from the stream were lodge pole pine with moss growing several feet up the trunks. The freshness of spring was everywhere—young birds in nests, tracks of a large deer with those of newborn fawns beside it, and squirrels carrying food.

He stumbled upon a young buck with its head down about fifty yards away. He froze in place just as it raised its head. It then put its head back down to eat, nibbling on fresh green shoots.

Jason again debated with himself over whether to use his gun for hunting or save it solely for self defense. This was a prime opportunity to get a quantity of meat to have on hand as he traveled. If he had to trap and fish along the way, that could extend the time frame of his journey considerably. His rumbly stomach made its winning argument as he remembered he hadn't eaten since yesterday morning.

Albeit he had never hunted deer before, only moose or caribou, and that not very successfully, he decided to allow himself two shots from the pistol, and they needed to be taken with care. He wished he could have practiced some since he had no real feel of what the trigger pull was like or how accurate the pistol. He would have to stalk it to get a closer shot.

He pulled out the pistol and froze in place again as the buck raised its head and took a few steps. It looked around, then started browsing again. He was sure it had seen him, but it probably relied more on sound and smell than sight. Not feeling any wind, Jason hoped he could get close enough for a sure shot before he spooked it.

He took three more steps, then crouched, waiting for the deer to raise and lower its head again. He repeated this three more times but must have made some noise or a random current of air wafted his scent that direction, for he could see the body tense.

The buck raised its head quickly this time, and Jason fired broadside at the lower chest area, just behind the front leg where the heart should be. The shot sounded like a cannon in the stillness of the woods. At this range, about thirty-five yards, Jason could tell the real size of the deer was much smaller than he anticipated, being not much bigger than a large dog. He froze into position after the shot. The deer bolted like a rocket, leaping over the brush. Jason feared he had missed but after waiting, listening, and watching, he knew the deer had not gone far.

Not hearing anything at all, he walked to the bush and found the deer struggling to get to its feet on the other side. He felt bad he had not made a clean shot and had to use another round to finish it off. He justified the use of another precious bullet by the fact that a semi-conscious deer could hurt him if he had tried to use his knife.

It looked pitifully small, but it would be enough to feed him for a week, and he was glad he wouldn't have to waste much meat. Being familiar with processing moose and caribou, taking care of the meat and hide of such a small deer was relatively easy. He built a fire and added green boughs to smoke the meat, putting strips on racks made of branches. He made a separate fire to cook deer steaks, eating to his fill with much pleasure. This food was much more satisfying than the rabbit and fish he had been eating. It took most of the day for the smoking and that evening he used the deer skin to secure his meat high in the tree branches, out of reach of predators.

Making his camp farther away from the meat, he built another fire for warmth. After saying his evening prayers, he retrieved the crystal, set it on a log, and watched the fire play off its surface. The reflected fire seemed to dance inside it, producing an illusion of magical life.

He thought of the man who had found the crystal—who was it Brad had said? Phil Nexlar he seemed to recall. How did he come to think this translucent lump of stone could do anything beyond what any other rock could do? Did he shape the stone into its ball shape or did he find it that way?

Jason did not believe accidents happen to Christians. Everything happens for a divine purpose. Perhaps God had gone through great trouble to make sure he was at this experiment at the exact time it met disaster, so he would be brought here.

He rejected the idea that God willed all those others to die, just so he could be brought here. The "accident" probably would have happened and killed the others anyway, but God made sure Jason was in the vicinity at the right place at the right time and survived.

But why? he thought to himself. He could see no reason to be in the middle of the woods with no one around. He heard a far off howl. The wolves would probably visit that night. He would keep the fire going and a good tree to climb at his back.

He dozed. In the middle of the night, something awakened him. He was still propped against the base of a tree and without moving his head opened his eyes just enough to look through the slits. At first, he saw nothing unusual, but across the embers of his nearly extinguished fire, he saw the reflected glow of eyes. He remembered his crystal orb, but the eyes were from the wrong direction. Calmly and almost imperceptibly, he moved his right hand to grasp his pistol.

With pistol in hand, he opened his eyes to see more clearly. It was a wolf. If there was one, likely there were more nearby. Now he turned his head and looked around. Suddenly, there was a snarling sound from the direction where he had first killed the deer and left the gut pile. The wolf turned its head to look, and Jason took the opportunity to stand. The wolf facing him slunk down low, as if ready to pounce or flee. Jason didn't want to waste any of the eight shots he had left on a minor predator like a wolf. As a full-grown man, he would have no problem scaring it off, but he was not a full-grown man anymore, and at his current size, even a single wolf was a force to be reckoned with.

The wolf didn't move, so Jason kicked some broken branches he had piled near the fire onto the glowing embers. As the flames flared up, the wolf slunk into the shadows and, after another moment, turned to join its brethren. He could hear the wolves now fighting over the gut pile and bones. After about a half hour, the wolves made no more noise, but he had no way of knowing if they had really left or not.

Putting his spear beside him and keeping the fire going, he dozed off and on throughout the night. Near morning, he awoke to discover he had slept, if fitfully, the last few hours, as his fire was completely out.

He cooked some more of the meat for breakfast and spent the rest of the morning smoking and cooking the remainder of his meat. He tied his roll of coats to the outside of his backpack to make room for the meat. He was tempted to put the smoky- smelling meat inside his plastic bag but knew that would make it rot, so he just layered it into the cloth backpack so it could continue to dry more.

Repacking the brief case and the crystal orb on top of the meat made a pack so heavy, he could hardly lift it. He sat it down again and went through the contents of his attache case, trying to eliminate the heaviest objects and stuff he could do without. He removed two small pulleys, the Mace, handcuffs, and about two pounds of wire, bolts, and metal shards. He repacked the spray can of Mace, thinking it might work against smaller predators like wolves, thus saving his ammunition.

When he was done, his pack was still heavy. It was tempting to leave the crystal orb, since it weighed around eight pounds. Perhaps if he could find a good place to stash it, he would do that since it was something he could not immediately use or, if he found his way home, never would use.

The next few days, he traveled slowly, following the stream. He would have preferred to stay at his mountain retreat, but the need to find out where he was and how to get home pressed him onward. Other streams ran into this one, forming a river—wild and loud with small waterfalls and rough haystacks. Earlier, he had wished for a canoe to help carry his load but was now glad he didn't have one, for he would undoubtedly get dumped, losing his precious survival items.

On the fourth day of traveling, toward evening, just before making camp, he caught a whiff of smoke and the faint smell of cooked fish. Someone was close by! He felt like leaping for joy and running to find these people, screaming like a maniac, except that his backpack was still heavy enough to keep him from doing more than a clumsy trot. He took it off, looking for a good place to stash it. A fallen cottonwood by the stream, hollowed at the base, seemed a likely spot.

He contemplated his survival weapons. Since most people would help a lost boy, he didn't want to give away the fact he was armed. He considered going completely unarmed but wasn't so confident in his martial arts ability that as a little boy he didn't need an equalizer. He decided to take only what he could conceal under his coat, the gun in a shoulder holster and the little can of Mace. He opened his pocket knife and reclipped it to his belt, blade pointed down and ready for use.

Even though his knife was not really very good for fighting, he knew how to use one well enough for most purposes, and it would work in an emergency. One of the keys of success for a martial artist is to have a number of backup plans.

Going down to the river, he washed his face. He felt strangely self-conscious and full of anticipation at the idea of human contact. He imagined a family of campers or a sports fisherman trying to beat the spring weekend crowds. He stashed his pack and weapons in the hollow tree and carefully made his way along the river. It was farther to the camp than he thought. Just when he started to think he had imagined the smell, he saw smoke from a campfire drift through the trees ahead.

Entering a small clearing, he was surprised to see, hovered over a fire, a stout-looking man with tan skin and shoulder- length black hair held in place with a headband. His upper body was bare, and his legs were covered with loose leather trousers that came to his knees. Purple scars crisscrossed his entire back, and when, by chance, he turned halfway toward Jason, he could also see scars on his chest, some in a pattern as though done in some ritual. He wore a necklace made of bones that suspiciously looked of human origin. Propped on a nearby stump was a bow with a quiver of arrows and a large sword. There was a large, heavy knife belted to his side.

The man was big by any standards. If he wasn't so filthy Jason would have suspected he had stumbled onto the set of a Conan movie. He made a quick survey of the surrounding woods. It appeared the man was alone.

Perhaps he was a hunter, but if so, he preferred to hunt primitive style.

Despite the fact that Jason had spent days alone in the wilderness, was tired of sleeping on the ground, and was powerfully concerned about his family, something did not feel right and his instincts warned him not to approach the stranger. But if anyone could tell him where he was and how to get back to civilization, it was this man.

Because his need was great, he had to risk contact but decided an escape plan would be a wise precaution. However, other than jumping into the river, which would have been foolish, he could think of nothing. His only option seemed to be to walk into the open and say nothing, just see what happened. Let the big man be uncertain of everything and reveal his nature by his questions.

Taking a deep breath, he stepped into the clearing. The big man immediately froze in place like a statue, his squinting eyes darting from side to side as if he expected an ambush. Jason couldn't tell if this man was a representative of the local culture or an escapee from an insane asylum.

When nothing happened after a long moment, the man relaxed a little and spoke in a soothing voice in a language he'd never heard before. To Jason, the words sounded a little like Korean with some German tossed in. The big man spread his arms in an obvious effort to appear nonthreatening as he spoke again while turning in a circle, peering into the growing shadows of the woods.

Jason could speak a little German but decided against trying it and waited. The big man tried another tactic, which was a mistake. He smiled. His top teeth were filed to fine points. Jason had read about this characteristic of many cannibalistic tribes and involuntarily stepped back at the sight of the stranger's fierce grin. Suddenly, the big man moved, surprisingly quick, leaping across the distance and grabbing Jason's arm so firmly it hurt. He was shocked to feel pain because as a grown man he would not have even noticed it.

His captor laughed in triumph, speaking to himself while smacking his lips. He produced a leather strip from somewhere and forced the boy to turn away from him as he began to wrap one end of the leather around the wrist behind the boy's back.

Recovering from the shock, Jason's martial arts training took over, and he kicked back into the man's shin. When his blow landed, he jerked his arm loose while simultaneously stepping back into the big man's chest and grabbing the man's other wrist. On reflex, he tried to do a hip throw but failed. He was a boy, not a man. After slipping an arm around the waist and pulling hard on the elbow, to his dismay, he only managed to trip the big man up a little.

The man, initially surprised at the speed and agility of Jason's retaliation, quickly recovered and responded with a backhand that sent the boy flying to the ground. Jason instinctively rolled, years of training teaching him how to fall, and was back on his feet in time to meet the big man's charge.

He made the mistake of trying to grab for the can of mace in his pocket. The man hit him hard with a body slam that sent the little can of pressurized irritants flying into the woods and Jason falling to his back. As the backwoods warrior stepped in to grab him again, Jason kicked hard to the inside of the knee, throwing the man down for a second time.

Both man and boy regained their feet at the same time and the man again charged. Had Jason been fighting as the large muscular man he was only a few days ago, he would have had no trouble throwing the charging barbarian, but he had to remind himself to fight as a kid would against someone over three times his weight. He sidestepped the charging man and kicked backward into the joint of the man's leg, driving him down to one knee. The man fell painfully, giving Jason some precious moments, so he ran. He had a head start, but the big man had instincts like an animal and was apparently no stranger to fighting or killing. Ducking into some thick brush, he hoped to dissuade his pursuer from continuing the chase, but the large man crashed through the brambles as though they were wisps of fog and grabbed him around the arms from behind. Jason flung his heel into the man's groin and was quickly released as the man groaned in pain. Seizing the opportunity, Jason did a kid's move. He jumped straight up, driving the top of his head under the man's jaw and laying the pointy-toothed cannibal out flat on his back.

He ran again, hoping that might be the end of the attack and not wanting to stick around to find out. He ran back toward the hollow tree where he had stashed his gear. He was breathing hard as he crossed a clearing when a hand grabbed him from behind a tree. The big man had recovered more quickly than he would ever have expected and made up the distance between the two of them remarkably fast. This time, the barbarian was playing for keeps, and capturing Jason was not on his mind as he raised the heavy knife to strike a deep blow in the lad's chest.

Instinct took over as Jason reacted to the latest attack. His hand on the handle of his own open pocket knife clipped to his belt, he bent and dove through the only opening he had between the big man's body and the edge of the descending blade.

As he spun, he popped out of the man's grip. The opening he escaped through was between the large man's legs, a move he never could have executed as an adult. He then rolled to standing again with blood dripping off the small pocket knife now held in his hand. He was not even aware he had done anything with it.

The barbarian looked down at the blood flowing from his thigh where Jason's tool had left its mark. He looked shocked for a moment, then screamed in bestial rage as he charged Jason with his own knife held high.

Jason felt surprisingly calm as he stood his ground. He would have pulled his gun if there was time, but in this moment, timing was everything. Waiting until the last split second before he kiai-ed (the karate yell used to focus effort), he leaped past the big man's good leg, purposely slashing it deeply to the inside. The enraged cannibal tried to spin with him but stumbled and fell at the end of the turn.

By now, Jason had the gun in his hands and had it trained on the sitting barbarian, who simply stared at it with no comprehension, not seeming to understand the danger it represented. Knowing he was defeated and now bleeding profusely, the man looked at Jason pleadingly as he dropped his knife and grabbed at his wounded legs. An artery had been cut, and blood flowed freely.

Jason squatted and considered doing what he could to save the man's life—after the man lost consciousness. When the weakened barbarian finally closed his eyes, Jason holstered the gun and used the man's knife to cut a strip off his pants to serve as a tourniquet. He bound the first wound as best he could to staunch the flow of blood, but before he could apply the second of the strips, the man was dead.

He had never killed anyone before. Strangely, he did not feel as bad as he thought he would. The guy did try to kill him, after all, and he only defended himself. He said a prayer for the big man's lost soul and left the body to replenish the forest from which he had made his living.

There was no way this man was of his own civilized world. The man's language and tribal markings contradicted the idea that he was a lone kook acting out some role playing game. He could no longer deny the evidence; he was not in his own world.

He felt a crushing weight as he pushed aside the thought that he may not be going home anytime soon.

"I am sorry, Molly," Jason whispered to himself, as he felt tears roll down his cheeks. He could not bear to think of his family living without him, nor he without them. He continued on to the hollow tree to recover the rest of his items.

Returning to the dead man's camp, he took stock of the tools left behind. The big man's bow and arrows were better than anything he could make, so he took them and the large knife that almost killed him, but the deceased left little else of value.

The large sword was too big for him to use and had nothing that bespoke of value anyway, a plain rust-stained blade with an ugly-wrapped leather grip. It was notched from many battles against other bladed weapons. The barbarian's world was better off not knowing that one of its better warriors had been defeated by a ten-year-old kid.

While searching, he was stunned to find the dead man's pack contained the cooked, gnawed and rancid remains of a human arm, hand still attached. Moreover, it appeared to be a woman's hand. He had an inkling the man's pointed teeth were indicative of cannibalism, but the proof made him sick to his stomach.

He dropped the pack in disgust. What kind of country had he fallen into? Was he really not on earth any longer? Or was he still on his own home planet but in a different time? Was there really a dragon he saw flying over the mountains some nights past? Or was he just in a particularly remote and wild part of the world, a part National Geographic had just not gotten around to yet?

He thought for a moment what his next move should be. Was it worth the risk of running into more cannibals, maybe next time a whole village of them and end up as Jason soup? Or should he just return to his original shelter in the hills and wait longer for a plane to fly overhead or some mountain climber to come along? It was hard to know. Nothing like hand-to-hand combat with a cannibal to inspire worry.

That night, Jason dreamed he saw his wife searching for him, calling his name. He would run toward her and answer in his little boy's voice, but his wife would turn away and call again. He woke up crying, and to make matters worse, it was raining.

CHAPTER 5
Deologue 1

The woman wore a black dress, an orb on a gold chain about her neck and sat, bored, on a sofa overlooking the sea. A gentle breeze blew, causing ripples on the ocean surface. With one hand, she would make a gesture, and all the water would change color. Currently, it was purple. With her other hand, she formed clouds of various shapes that danced about her. Her black hair acted as if it were alive, constantly weaving itself into a new hairdo.

Finally, in anger, she clapped her hands, and it all, including the ocean, disappeared into a puff of smoke. With a wave of her hand, she produced a forest setting and a throne upon which to sit. Much more satisfied, she sat on the throne and began producing forest creatures. Rabbits first appeared all around her, jumping and frolicking.

"Oh, you are all so cute, so peaceful," she crooned. Her hands poised for another spell, and with a fierce look, she said, "But what if suddenly you are beset by wolves?"

She started to wave her hands, but at that moment, a man ran from the trees toward her. She stopped to stare at the man as if he were some odd creature. The man indeed was odd, for he wore a wooden hat in the shape of a hawk's head, with the beak extending over his face. He wore furs and what looked like miniature human skulls, threaded by a leather cord to make a grotesque necklace, and carried a spear ornate with feathers.

He came before the woman and prostrated himself.

The woman chastised him. "Krundor, I have given you the power to walk on the winds, and this is how you repay me, by interrupting my spells? I should turn you into a carrot and let my pets eat you."

The man shivered and cried out, "I am sorry, Axialla, my queen, but I have returned as you bid me."

"Then get on with it and give me your report," she snapped.

"I questioned the hunter, Barex, as you asked, and indeed, there was a bright light flashing from the mountains. I sent Magootoh, the hairy mountain monster, to investigate. Magootoh told me there were only dead men at the place of the light."

"What?" exclaimed Axialla. "Then either the prophecy is wrong, or it is not yet time."

Krundor interrupted, "But there is one thing more, my goddess, something Magootoh almost neglected to tell me. A child made a rough camp and buried the men near there. I sent a warrior to retrieve or to kill him, but the man was killed before he made it to the valley. Should I send out a war party?"

"Let me see..." The witch goddess held the small orb on her necklace and stared into it. "Hmm... Did Magootoh give a description of the child?"

"Only that it was young and human. The monster could not tell if it was a boy or a girl."

"That description is too vague, but never mind. A child does not fit the prophecy even if it grew...I must advise Xan Rukkah to look elsewhere. You did well, Krundor. You may go," she said dismissively.

Krundor left, running as if fleeing the goddess's presence. As he reached the edge of the wood, he thrust his spear forward and penetrated the fabric of Axialla's dimensional dwelling, thereby propelling him to his own place.

Axialla reclined onto her throne and looked about with a contented smile. "Now where were we?"

Upon seeing the rabbits, she said, "Oh, yes, we were about to call in a wolf..."

CHAPTER 6
Speaking in Strange Tongues

Traveling along the river for the next few days in a rainy drizzle dampened Jason's alertness. His nerves were on edge for a long time after his encounter with the big man, but the steady drizzle, fatigue, and hunger wore him down, so his attention began to slip. He practically walked into the opening of a village—small, well-constructed houses of wood on both sides of a road. Smoke curled from chimneys, and light shown through windows. Wagons designed for horses or oxen stood in front of several buildings. On the bank of the river rested three flat-bottomed boats with poles or paddles propped inside.

No one noticed him. All the villagers appeared to be inside, not venturing the rain. The poncho he made from one of the large garbage bags kept the rain off him and his dwindling portion of meat. However, the humidity was causing the meat to spoil. He desperately wanted something besides dried venison to eat. His nose detected what smelled like fresh bread baking, but he was not yet ready to make contact.

First, he needed to stash his survival tools, not knowing how these people might react to him. It did not look like the sort of place cannibals would live, but he did not want to take a chance. The night before, he had spotted a cliff on a hill with a natural stone pinnacle atop and decided that would be the perfect landmark by which to hide his crystal and briefcase.

He trudged with soggy shoes back the few miles through the woods to the pinnacled hill. The southern side dropped off in a steep cliff nearly seventy-five feet down, with large rocks at the bottom. At the top of the hill, a slim column of stone rose another fifty feet straight up, jabbing into the sky like a bony finger.

The rain had stopped, and the sky began to clear as he climbed to stand beside the base of the column of stone where he had a view over the trees. Although he could not see the river, thin wisps of smoke marked the location of the village. Beyond that, the clouds obscured the view.

His mind still refused to accept he was on another world and tried to place the area. This was not South America or South Africa, judging from the complexion and facial features of the barbarian cannibal he had encountered and the style of construction in the village recently discovered. Those clues and the landscape before him reminded him more of medieval Europe. Maybe he was in New Zealand. Either that or he had not only crossed an ocean but also gone back in time several hundred years.

If that were the case, and he was, in fact, in Europe in the Northern Hemisphere, then he should see some familiar star constellations at night. The Big Dipper, Orion, and the Pleiades should be easily recognizable, even thousands of years forward or backward from his own time. The strangeness of the evening sky lent credence to his Southern Hemisphere theory. He could not make out the constellation known as the Southern Cross, but New Zealand was still the best answer at this point, albeit a New Zealand with a few pointy-toothed cannibals running amok.

He made camp at the base of the cliff that evening after digging a hole for his cache. The sky had cleared and verified that although there was a moon, there were no familiar stars or constellations—neither the Big Dipper nor the Southern Cross. He must be on another world, maybe in an alternate dimension in an alternate universe.

The strangeness of the sky caused him considerable unease, and he suddenly felt really and truly lost. For the most part, other than when almost smashed by a yeti or skewered and eaten by a shark-toothed wild man, his ordeal had felt more like an adventure than a disaster. Now, staring into the alien heavens, he wondered if he really would ever see his home and family again.

If God had brought him here for a reason, then perhaps God would send him home when that reason was fulfilled. Maybe when he reached his proper age again, he would somehow be transported home as if no time had passed at all. Perhaps, like a dream, he would wake up and everything would be as it was. As he lay on the ground, covered in a trash bag and pondering the strange arrangement of stars above him, he could not help but wonder where God was.

The next morning, he emptied the contents of his pack and tossed out what remained of his meat. Reluctantly, he placed the pistol into the attaché case beside his other tools. He appreciated the power and security it represented, but even among primitive people, it would only be a matter of time before it would be stolen from him. With only eight rounds, he could fend off two or three attackers, but his success would depend more on how well he could fit in. He considered keeping the barbarian's bow and arrows with him since they were of this world, but not knowing the customs, he decided not to risk it. Let his martial arts be his secret weapon.

Wrapping the plastic trash bag that had served as his poncho around the attaché case, he placed it in the hole he had dug at the base of the cliff. He also carefully laid his weapons and tools alongside, including the crystal, then covered the hole with three large stones, sealing them with earth. To distinguish as well as camouflage his cache, he transplanted a small sapling over it, so it was the only one growing in the clearing.

By noon, he headed to the village. He felt naked without any weapons, not even his pocket knife or the barbarian's blade, so he picked up a stout stick with a pleasing shape. He left the river and circled the village to enter from the opposite direction.

Upon his approach, he came across a road rutted from wagon wheels and pocked with hoof marks, but he could still easily walk on such road. The first house he came to was about a half mile outside the village. It looked shabbier than the village houses, its roof thatched with straw instead of the split wood shingled roofs of the village. It was at the edge of a field with a small shelter behind it occupied by chickens. A vegetable garden grew on one side, and a quaint stone well was located on the other side.

His plan was to scout out the area and learn as much as he could about the inhabitants while keeping a low profile. He would try to stay unobserved for as long as he could before revealing himself to the locals, so he ducked back into the woods and watched to see who would come by, either along the road or from the cottage.

After a while, an old hunchback woman with gray hair and a black dress emerged from the shabby dwelling with a bucket and threw grain to the flock of chickens in the fenced area in back. Then she spent a little time tending the vegetable garden. The old woman went back inside and reappeared after a few minutes with a hooded shawl over her head. She carried a basket overflowing with what appeared to be roots and sprigs and made her way toward town.

He watched the woman go until she was out of sight and then approached the house. He tried to look in the window, but it was covered with an oiled cloth that allowed no visibility to the dark interior, so he opened the door and took a peek inside. After his eyes adjusted to the dim light, he saw a single room with a bed, a table, and a cooking hearth upon which a large iron kettle hung over cold ashes. Various knives and ladles hung over the table and on it sat a loaf of bread.

The temptation to steal a slice or even the whole loaf was nearly overwhelming, but he did not touch it. He figured ten-year-old boys were irresistible to little old ladies, and he would earn his food. He found an ax and split the meager supply of firewood the elderly woman had stored in about fifteen minutes. He then took the ax and marched off into the woods. Being no stranger to getting firewood, he immediately set to cutting dead fall. In about an hour, he had enough cord wood for several trips to the house.

When he returned to the house with an armload of wood and the ax, he discovered the woman had returned. She approached him with a broom held in hand like a weapon, and her voice shook with anger as she scolded Jason severely with harsh sounding words and motioned him to leave. But since he couldn't understand a single word she said, he ignored her, set the ax back in place, and started a new wood pile.

After a bit, the old woman grew quiet and watched him wonderingly. He walked off to the trees to fetch more wood. It took him four more trips to retrieve everything he had cut. The old woman, meanwhile, although keeping an eye on him, went about her business. He noticed the garden fence in need of repair in order to keep the chickens out, so he set to mending it.

He worked on the fence the rest of the day and stopped when it got dark. Tired, he sat down beside the back door to the old woman's house. She was inside cooking something that did not smell too appetizing to his nose. Still, he waited and hoped she would give him something, anything, to eat.

After a long while, the woman made preparations for bed and could be heard talking to herself. Then it became quiet. Jason was about to give up hope when the door opened a crack, and a crusted hunk of bread flew out. He snatched it up and smiled to himself. The old woman was coming around. The bread was tough but delicious, and he devoured it quickly.

He then drew water from the squat, stone well to wash it down. As he wiped the water from his chin, he saw something move at the edge of the trees. It was fast like a deer, but upright like a man and very tall. It brought to mind his encounter with the yeti, though this figure was much leaner. He suddenly felt very vulnerable, wishing he had stashed his gun someplace closer. Not seeing the creature anymore and having no idea what danger it represented, he retrieved the ax and carried it with him. He would investigate and search for sign at first light.

He gathered some straw and slept in a nest beside the house. It was a cold night, so he slept little and fitfully, still feeling exhausted in the morning. Forcing himself into action at first light, he patrolled the perimeter of the field but saw nothing out of the ordinary, not even tracks.

Feeling a little warmer, he drew water, gathered chicken eggs, and set them in front of the door before the old woman got up. He was finishing his work on the fence when the old woman called him. She bade him come inside where she had made breakfast of eggs and bacon. From that point on, she took ownership of him, commanding him to do tasks and chores. Of course, he couldn't understand her words, but she naturally gestured and pointed with every word she spoke, so even though he seemed a little slow mentally, he was able to get the chores done.

Jason imagined himself as a young martial artist trying to learn from a lone master in a remote area. The crone probably never knew she was teaching him her language, but he would repeat everything she commanded over and over as he worked. The words she used sounded similar to the Germanic language the cannibal had spoken and if not the same language, at least was probably a dialect of it.

She also seemed to use a specific form of sign language as she spoke. Once he tried to copy it, and the old woman became enraged. After another severe scolding, he never did it again in her presence. Perhaps it was only proper for elders and not youngsters.

Days went by, and he forgot about the stranger he saw the first night. Ever alert for any clue that would help identify his whereabouts, he spent his free time observing the villagers and travelers for signs of more modern technology. After he learned enough of the local language to get by, he would travel again and try to find his way home. He hoped to be gone by fall.

Over time, he learned the old woman's name was Haglar. More properly, Haglar the Watcher. Haglar would sometimes take him with her into the woods carrying extra baskets, which she would fill with tubers and herbs. He watched closely to learn which ones were edible and which were medicines or poisons. The good ones Haglar would croon over while with the bad ones she would scold and swat his hand. The medicinal herbs she would sniff carefully and then put into separate pouches.

He never asked questions but considered himself fortunate to have a language tutor who always talked to herself. He was picking up the language very quickly and could even discern the curse words she was prone to use every other sentence. He found it indeed very similar to the German he studied in high school and found himself substituting German sentence structures as he started to string words together.

Finally, after a few weeks, Haglar took him to the village with her with the intent of selling her herbs and concoctions. Although he had observed the village from afar, this would be his first chance to visit.

The village was much more active now than the rainy afternoon of his first encounter. It had a primitive feel to it despite the nicer roofs. The townsfolk appeared Caucasian but much more uniform in size and facial features than one would see in a typical group of people in the US. All had the same dark black hair, and although his own blond hair stood in stark contrast to theirs, it did not draw undo attention.

They dressed in what appeared to be homespun wool and cotton. Some of the men wore sloppy leather hats that looked sort of like a bonnet without the frilly visor in front. The street itself was soft dirt, and the main occupants of it were chickens, ducks, and the occasional goose, scratching and looking for food or bits of rock for their gizzards.

On this day most of the villagers and all of the children were down at the riverbank near a newly arrived barge. A few fur trappers had piled their furs on the ground in heaps to show the sea-traveling merchant. These trappers, rough men, looked similar to the cannibal.

The better-dressed traveling merchant wore a colorful red cotton vest and sported an extravagant purple silk hat. He and his four guards brought his barge upstream once a week to sell goods and to buy furs and other oddities, such as what Haglar brought. A small crew who worked the poles on the barge either lounged on deck or relaxed on the bank.

The merchant set up his wares—a large collection of pots and kettles, as well as some frivolous items such as bright silk scarves or little stone carvings that appeared to be men in stately poses. The villagers and traders clamored about, talking too quickly for Jason to understand them, about the deals they wanted to make; however, as he and Haglar approached, the crowd quieted and quickly parted to give them access to the trader.

The trader had just finished a deal with a trapper, counting out a handful of copper coins for the huge bundle of fur loaded on the deck. The trader grinned big when he saw Haglar and gave a deep bow of respect as his eyes eagerly drank in the contents of her basket. She nodded in return and offered her wares for inspection. He took the basket of roots and herbs almost too quickly as he made faces of distaste while sorting the variety of vegetation. His hands nearly shook as he turned his attention to the pouches.

Jason was astounded as he watched the merchant pull some gold coins out of his pockets and meekly offer it to Haglar, as if that were all he had. To Jason this seemed an incredible amount compared to what the others were trading. Haglar cursed violently, jerked her basket away, and started to leave. The merchant immediately apologized and bid Haglar to wait. He went down into the barge and produced a small chest. This he opened and carefully counted out a handful of gold coins and offered it to Haglar. Satisfied, she exchanged her basket for the gold and turned to leave, muttering happily to herself. Jason suspected, and later trading rendezvous confirmed, this was a ritual they performed every time in order to get a satisfactory deal. It suddenly occurred to him he was learning a valuable skill from Haglar when they went on their foraging trips. To have that much gold would make Haglar very wealthy in this region, but what she did with it, he did not know. She certainly didn't live like she was wealthy. He considered it none of his business.

Again, the villagers gave a wide swath for the both of them. Parents whisked their children away as they approached. He got the impression Haglar the Watcher was someone feared and respected, and of course, this extended to him. He had the gnawing feeling she was some sort of witch but also considered that in his own world's past, eccentric and unusual individuals were accused of being witches, so he reserved judgment. So far, he had not seen any evidence of what he would call magic.

At night, he still slept outside but had built a small American Indian dwelling called a wikiup made of brush and straw. This helped keep him warmer at night and sheltered from the occasional rain. Haglar fed him breakfast and a meager dinner but gave him nothing else. He continued his habit of evening prayers. Even though he did this silently, whenever Haglar caught him, she would look at him curiously and keep silent, as though she could sense something spiritual going on, and quietly return to the house.

A few nights later, as Jason finished putting new straw thatch on the roof of the house, he saw the strange tall silhouette at the edge of the woods. It was crossing the small clearing toward the cottage. He hurried down and retrieved the ax just as it came around the corner.

It stopped when it saw Jason. The creature resembled a man, though eight feet tall. It may have even stood taller were it not hunched over and drooling. Its reddish, glowing eyes were deep set in a caricature of a human face. A long nose sat over rubbery lips, which split to reveal sharp, pointy teeth. Its warty skin had a greenish hue, and its head was covered with sparse, coarse black hair. Its fingers and toes ended in claws like those of a bear.

The sight was such a shock and so unexpected, Jason nearly dropped his ax. His first impulse was to run, and run like he had never run before. He tended to attribute such flighty responses to his having all of the emotions of a kid again. While he determined to stand his ground, he knew that even the man he used to be would consider running. In this situation, it would be a very viable option. Before him was a true monster, one whose presence emanated malice and hate.

He considered the angry bears he had faced in Alaska as well as the yeti he encountered so recently in the forest, but never before had he faced a corporeal being that gave such a feeling of pure evil.

"Lord, give me strength, wisdom, and speed—especially speed!" Jason prayed to himself.

"Trombul," Haglar barked as she brushed past Jason. Haglar seemed to have an uncanny awareness of everything going on about her, though up to now the creature had made no sound. Haglar immediately switched to a guttural language Jason could not follow. Trombul answered with retching sounds, then turned and moved as if on a mission. Jason watched what he could only describe as a troll as it disappeared into the night woods. Haglar brushed back by him as though he didn't exist.

Astounded at Haglar's casualness, he was reminded of the myths and fairy tales back home. Here, they were reality. He could still smell the stench of where the troll had stood, the coppery smell of blood and fish, most likely from its last meal.

The aura of evil lingered as well. That awesome monster did Haglar's bidding.

It seemed the villagers had good reason to fear Haglar. He wondered what he had gotten himself into and if he had a reasonable enough command of the language to leave right away.

Not yet, he thought. Although he understood a lot of words and had a basic idea of sentence structure, he still couldn't communicate above a rudimentary level.

Summer became hot, and after the day's chores, Jason would wander to the river to bathe and cool off. He spent time trying to follow the conversations of men talking as they fished with dip nets. Sometimes, he went through the village. All the children avoided him. Even the older boys, from whom Jason expected trouble, would avert their eyes and pass by. He sometimes saw the village women glare at him with hostility and shake their head disapprovingly. Still in none of this did he find clues to his whereabouts or how to get home.

Up to now, he made it a point to never talk directly to Haglar nor to ask her for anything. He never gave her the opportunity to deny him permission to do as he wished, and he figured she was probably relieved to not be bothered by him. He was always there when she needed him and always doing more than she required. She had never bothered to learn his name. She just called him "boy" whenever she needed him.

Considering moving on and trying to find a new tutor, he decided to try out his new language skills. His opportunity came the following week after Haglar brought him into town again to sell more herbs. Haglar had just finished her trade when she went to strike a deal for some cloth with a nearby woman.

In the meantime, Jason wandered back to the traveling merchant directing his crew in the repacking of his goods and newly acquired furs and farm produce.

Getting the man's attention, he asked, "Excuse me, sir, what is the next town like?"

The man looked at him incredulously as Jason stumbled over the words of his request, followed by an explosion of laughter from the merchant and the men around who overheard. The merchant turned and walked off laughing as one of the guards swatted Jason with a metal-gloved hand, sending him reeling to the ground. He never did figure out what he said that was so funny. Perhaps he was not as ready to leave as he had hoped.

He redoubled his efforts and hung around town more often. He ventured to talk to a group of children playing with corn husk dolls near a field, but they ran from him to their parents, working nearby, who then looked angrily back at him for disturbing them. Finally, he was able to strike up conversation with an old fisherman who held a pole, with line and hook, down at the river.

The elder, dressed in scraps of leather, had a long ragged white beard and a face scarred and twisted by the battles of time. His long, floppy hat covered a nearly bald head. Jason asked about the fishing, and that was enough for this storyteller. Laying down his fishing pole, the fisherman had to use his hands to show the size of fish that had got away minutes before and then went on describing his many fishing exploits.

Jason continued to ply the man with questions. He often had to repeat himself because of his poor speaking skills, or because the man was nearly deaf, Jason didn't know. He made a fishing pole himself and joined his new tutor in the following days as frequently as he could. Neither of them were really fishing, so they almost never caught anything, but that did not matter.

From the man whose name was Rofin, he learned that the village's name was Vorkana, and they were in a country called Harvella. Other kingdoms surrounded Harvella, most notably Chanderlon to the west, to which this river flowed. The closest town down river was Sulter Hill, where the wagon road also led. Although the name Sulter Hill seemed familiar to Jason, he could not quite place it. He seemed to recall a US Civil War battle at such a place, but even if this was true, was the name similarities an indication of travel between the worlds or coincidence?

From the wizened ancient, he also learned about some of the strange creatures that populated the nearby forests and advice on what to do if a child like him should see one, which was frequently, "Run for your life!" Jason was never sure if the creatures the man spoke of were ones he had actually encountered or if they were myth but, after seeing the troll, he was ready to believe almost anything.

He ventured to ask the man about religion and if he had heard of Jesus. At the mention of religion, the elder shuddered and told Jason to stay away from all of them if he could, for when the gods walk the earth, no man is safe. It was better to live a simple life of ignorance than to draw the attention of spiritual powers. He refused to listen about Jason's God.

To also help while away his free time, Jason made another set of bow and arrows which he kept hidden near the edge of the woods and spent many hours practice shooting. He was getting pretty good, if he thought so himself. He experimented with a concept he once used in training with a gun called point shooting. This is where you aim as if pointing your finger at something. His first few shots with the bow and arrow missed, but as he got used to the aim and compensated for his point, he became more accurate. The advantage was he could fire without taking much time to aim.

As fall came, he had a better command of the language but wondered about the wisdom of leaving just before winter. The risks of traveling in the cold of winter and the possibility of starvation were very real. He thought perhaps he should wait until spring, but one night, something happened to speed his departure.

CHAPTER 7
There Are No Accidents

On a sunny fall afternoon, the day after the first frost, Jason was harvesting garden tubers, similar to long potatoes, when a messenger boy, a poorly dressed urchin from the village, banged on Haglar's door. Jason could not hear the exchange, but as the messenger sped back to the village, Haglar called to him, "Boy, clean the place up and do it quickly if you value getting any dinner. We have visitors." Just as the presence of the messenger boy was rare enough, he had never seen Haglar entertain any visitors. So at Haglar's bidding, he entered the cottage and began sweeping inside the hearth.

Haglar made different preparations. She wrung a chicken's neck, drained its blood into a bowl, and splattered the warm red liquid around the door while chanting. This reminded Jason of the biblical event where the Israelites sprinkled blood in a similar manner to protect the house's inhabitants from the Death Angel, one of the ten plagues on the Egyptians who refused to release the Israelites to leave with Moses.

Later that evening, five men on horses, all heavily armed and armored, rode toward the cottage. These were the first horses he had seen here, and they were fine, well-muscled creatures. The men wore cone-shaped helmets and chainmail covered with a yellow cloth tunic with gold embroidered runes, which, of course, Jason could not read. Shields hung from their backs, and maces and flails hung from their saddles. He dumbly stood, broom in hand, continuing to play the role of a simple farm boy.

An older man with a graying mustache rode forward and introduced himself. "I am Brother Dorrian sent by Father Varigold of Chanderlon to see Haglar the Watcher."

Immediately, the cottage door burst open, and Haglar strode out dressed all in black except for a scarlet scarf tying up her hair. "Excuse the boy, my lord, he is a dolt. I am Haglar. Please come in."

Dorrian motioned for the other men to stay, and they seemed relieved. He dismounted, gave the reins to one of the men, and followed Haglar into the tiny hut. Jason entered too, closing the door behind him and made himself small in the background. Haglar did not seem to notice or to care. The fact that Jason could understand them this well attested to his many conversations with the old fisherman.

Dorrian said to Haglar, "Father Varigold had a prophetic dream. He hoped you might be able to see where the subject of that dream is located."

"Such answers are expensive, my lord," Haglar replied as she held out her hand.

Brother Dorrian reached into a pouch and pulled out a small bag of coins—very heavy for their size. This he lay in Haglar's hand. "For the benefit of the Brotherhood," said Brother Dorrian, as if it were a mantra.

"Be seated, my lord." Haglar motioned to the cottage's only chair. "Go fetch some water, boy," she commanded in a nicer than usual manner. He ran out with the wooden bucket and quickly drew water from the well.

He glanced over at the men still mounted on horses. Something did not seem right about how they reacted to Haglar as if afraid and he felt even more suspicious of Brother Dorrian, who did not react that way. Was he this way because of his position of leadership and did not allow his own fears to show or was there something more? Was he simply more enlightened and less superstitious or was he ruthlessly ambitious and more dangerous himself than any small time fortune teller? Perhaps time would tell.

He raced back, sloshing water on his way. When he got inside, Haglar stopped him. "The water is for later, boy. Put it by the wall."

He saw a black kettle filled with an oily, highly reflective substance. He put down the bucket. The old woman produced what appeared to be a ruby and set it on the table. She then lifted the large pestle she used for crushing herbs and smashed the ruby, crushing the red stone to powder.

After brushing the crimson powder into her palm, she began her incantation, muttering and waving her cupped hands in intense concentration. At the end of her chant, she blew the dust over the oily substance in the pot. The mirrored liquid came alive with a swirl of colors.

"Ask your question, Brother Dorrian," hissed the old woman.

"We seek the hero of Father Varigold's dream, summoned from another world, a man of great power called the Juggernaut," said Brother Dorrian forcefully while standing and looking into the pot.

Jason did not understand the word the man used in his language to describe juggernaut, but it tugged at his very soul, and he knew it was significant. He could not help but peer into the pot as well. The swirling colors settled, and as if looking into a reflection, he saw a powerful-looking man slightly balding with touches of white in his hair. It was him as a man. They were looking for him!

Why him? Why would a dream on this world set a search of this magnitude for him? How could he as a small boy be a hero and what did these people even need a hero for? Did God bring him here for this or did he carry the guise of a small boy to escape this fate? And another question, how could a pot of oily substance show them anything? Was this really magic or some psychic ability?

"This is not enough," said Haglar. "Show us where this man is right now."

The pot swirled again and started to slow and then swirled some more. "Show us. Where is the man called Juggernaut?" The pot stirred faster and faster until it began to boil. It stopped suddenly, and the strange material within became perfectly reflective, like a flawless mirror, showing the faces of all three persons in the room, but Jason's reflection seemed to dominate. Suddenly, he felt shy, not wanting them to know who he was, and he pulled back.

"Ach, the spell has ran out," exclaimed Haglar in disappointment.

"I paid good money!" shouted Brother Dorrian angrily.

Haglar put up her hands. "The spell has never failed before. But wait, I have other, more direct means to find out, and it will cost you nothing more. My reputation is at stake, and I will bear the burden myself. Boy, pour the water into the pot."

Jason grabbed the bucket of water and began to pour it into the pot relieved that, for the moment, his identity was not discovered. The mysterious fluid in there previously was gone, somehow evaporating into nothingness.

Haglar pulled out of her pocket many small crystal globes the size of marbles and lined them on the brim of the pot. How they stayed there without falling off, Jason could not tell. The mystic lady then brought out a small diamond and placed it on a stone slab. This too she crushed. No wonder these sessions were expensive.

She lifted the remnants of the stone and blew the dust into the fire below the pot. The flames flared briefly, sending a plume of smoke toward the ceiling. Haglar began chanting again with fierce concentration. She seemed larger and stronger than before, and her eyes were wells of black.

He intuitively knew that interrupting her focus now would spoil the spell and incur her great wrath. He was seeing for the first time the hints of great power within her, and he had no desire to test her capabilities. The water in the pot started boiling sooner than it should have and made a cloud of steam above the pot. The cloud swirled and rotated vertically, like a living whirlwind.

The old crone spoke, her voice coming stronger and more resonant than her aging throat should sound. Suddenly, she called, "Akari Demontri, we summon you. Come to us now." At the same time, Haglar struck the cloud with her fist, creating a dark hole in the center. The swirling hole grew larger until a small tumbling creature came howling through the hole and fell across the room, bouncing off the far wall. The creature made a great show of dusting itself off and regaining its dignity. It stood scarcely two feet tall. Hairless except for a little tuft at the end of its tail, the gray creature was the perfect caricature of a devil, horns and all!

Brother Dorrian stepped back, greatly alarmed.

"You have summoned me quite forcefully this time, Haglar. I trust you have the proper appeasements awaiting me?" the demon spoke in a small, squeaky voice.

Haglar nodded. "Yes, I have what you require in waiting, oh great Akari. We have a question on a matter that defies divination. Tell him what you seek, Brother Dorrian."

Dorrian stammered. "B-b-but this is a demon. I... I...We do not deal with demons."

Haglar harrumphed at Dorrian impatiently. "It has cost me a great deal to summon this other worldly creature. You will ask your question." Her statement was a command, not a request.

"I will not...I cannot," stammered Brother Dorrian.

"Then I will ask," Haglar said, then turned to the creature.

"Akari, we seek the location in this world of the off-world man called Juggernaut," she said.

The little demon rolled his eyes and spat contemptuously. "There is no man called Juggernaut on your world," it snarled.

Brother Dorrian leaped forward. "What? Is he dead? Will he be coming in the future?"

"You have paid for one answer. Do you wish to pay for another?" asked the miniature demon, pointing at Brother Dorrian.

"Most certainly not," the man asserted.

"Good, then I will be going," declared the demon. Its eyes drifted into Jason's direction. "But wait, who do we have here? A new slave, Haglar?" asked the demon as he eyed Jason curiously. Jason felt like crawling into a hole and hiding.

"He is mine," shouted Haglar, "and you can't have him!"

The strange little creature stared hard at Jason for a long moment, then a strange look came upon its face, as if recognition had dawned upon it. It broke into a howl of laughter and flew around the room. Smoke, sparks, and miniature fireworks trailed in its wake. Akari spiraled into the vortex and was gone. All that was left was the smell of sulfur and the echo of maniacal laughter.

"I have never seen the demon behave so oddly," mused Haglar as the room quieted.

Dorrian walked to the door, his hand on the handle. "If I had known you were going to summon a demon, I would never have agreed to this."

"I had hoped to not have to resort to Akari myself, but I have paid the cost, and you have your answer, so no more complaints from you," she spat.

Brother Dorrian left into the night where his companions awaited. As they rode off, Jason heard Haglar mutter, "A most unusual evening," along with many curses as though trying to make up for her good behavior the hour before.

Jason slipped out the door and ducked into his wikiup. If there was any doubt he was on another world, it was gone now. The prophecy and the little demon verified he was an "off-worlder," someone from another planet. He was not walking, sailing, or flying home. There was still the orb, of course, but there was no guarantee it would work in reverse. Even so, God had sent him here for a reason—even sent a prophecy ahead of him. He marveled at that. There was a prophecy about him on this world! What great deed was he to do here? He further supposed that only through fulfilling God's purpose could he ever begin to hope to go home

It was time to leave. If there was any doubt Haglar was a witch, that doubt was now vanished. He took mental inventory of anything he should take, but there was nothing. Other than meals and unconscious tutelage, Haglar had given him nothing, and he owed her nothing, so he left without even a good-bye. He knew his destination now. He needed to see a priest named Father Varigold and learn more about this prophecy.

If he had revealed himself, Brother Dorrian may have taken him directly to this Varigold person, but because of his earlier suspicions, he wondered if he might not make it there alive. Besides, he had no idea what Varigold would want with him anyway, and the cautious approach would be to find out before he revealed himself to anyone.

He considered retrieving the crystal from his cache, but being a little boy traveling alone, it was safer where it was. Hazards of the journey, thieves, robbers, cannibals, and trolls were all dangers that could rob him of his orb, and for him, it was far too precious to risk. Even the pistol with its eight shots left would not help him much in the long run and was not worth the lost time going back for it now. He wanted to put as much distance between him and Haglar as possible so she could not catch him and bring him back, if she indeed felt inclined. He thought of her statement to Akari that he belonged to her.

Jason took comfort knowing he was on God's mission now and nothing would happen to him outside of God's plan. Even Yeti and trolls could not stop him outside of God's will, though he wondered if that was presuming way too much. He walked down the road away from the village, trying to get a head start on any possible pursuit. It was dark without a moon.

Rounding the first bend in the road, he was surprised to hear the squeaky little voice of Akari. "She thinks she owns you; you know." It was in English.

Jason did not stop walking. "Yes, you are probably right," he replied, trying to keep the tone of his voice calm and casual.

"She will try to get you back," Akari claimed, now trotting down the road beside him.

"Thanks for the warning."

"I could have told them, you know."

"Why didn't you?"

"Besides them asking the wrong question, I like the game you're playing—a joke of colossal proportions." The demon laughed.

"It is no game," Jason replied. "I want to go home, not get mixed up in some inter-worldly hide-and-seek match."

"Oh, I can send you home," the demon said sincerely, "for a price."

"And what is that price, demon?" asked Jason warily, the melody from "The Devil Went Down to Georgia" playing in his head.

"Oh, it's nothing too hard, just a small service. Not evil— quite good, actually." It seemed to Jason the demon also tried to sound calm and casual. He remembered the verse in the Bible: Satan is the Father of Lies. He reminded himself not to accept anything Akari said at face value.

He stopped and looked at Akari. "You travel through dimensional gateways with ease, so I have no doubt you can send me home, but I'm already in service of my God, and he can send me home whenever he pleases," he stated, trying to sound confident.

The demon snickered, "In service of your god? You were involved in an extra-dimensional accident. You are on a world your god has forgotten. You are forgotten. I am your only way home. You are nothing but an accident," he finished, the last phrase spoken with blatant contempt.

Jason stopped walking and knelt to one knee, so he looked the small demon in the eye. "Poor Akari. You must not know of Christians, because for Christians, there are no such things as accidents."

"You are choosing not to go home to your wife and kids? What about them? Don't they need you?" reasoned Akari. "Don't you need them?"

Jason wondered how much Akari knew of his family. The fact it even knew he had a family led him to believe the creature was fairly powerful or at least associated with some entity who was powerful. He would need to proceed with caution. Bargaining with the devil is a sure path to damnation, but at the moment, he needed to know what his options were. If nothing else, he could string the tiny fiend along just to get more information from it.

"Sure, I need them, but God has set my course, and like the story of Jonah in the Bible, I can't run from it." Jason was not sure Akari knew about the Bible, let alone any stories in it, but he threw it out there and let it hang without further explanation.

"How do you know this?" Akari asked, seemingly taken aback by Jason's response.

"Because I'm here and I have faith that things are unfolding the way they should," he replied, trying to maintain his confidence. The truth was, he had no idea what was going on, but faith was all he had so he clung to it.

"How do you know it is not God's will that I should send you home after doing a small service for me?" Akari countered, challenging Jason's resolve.

Jason paused before answering. He bemused over the strangeness of sparring with a real live demon. He crafted his answer carefully. "Because unless God shows me otherwise, doing a service for a demon, no matter how good it may seem, would most certainly be in opposition to anything God has planned." It sounded good to Jason anyway.

The demon screwed up his face. "Are you prejudiced against me because I look like what your home world people would call a demon?"

"Not at all," replied Jason, which was a bit of a fib. If pressed, he would have to admit that the little demon—the demon-looking creature— was right. Haglar and her visitor had also seemed to identify Akari as a demon, but that could be due to his own poor grasp of the language. "You're obviously a powerful creature, and until you prove the intentions of your heart, it would be foolish for me to trust you." Jason felt that a pretty solid recovery.

"And how do I prove to you my intentions?" Akari asked.

"Have you made a decision to work for God?"

"No. I only work for myself...and the occasional service of a more powerful demon." Akari replied, adding the last bit reluctantly, it seemed.

Jason stood and resumed walking before responding. "That's the way of most beings who think they're practicing free will. In the end, they'll discover they've become slaves to creation, or whomever it is they are serving, rather than the true freedom found in serving the Creator."

"I can't imagine God even allowing me to serve him, but the idea is different—intriguing. I will think on this," replied the demon with a thoughtful look.

Jason added, "And you did, in fact, just admit to me you're a demon, so now, I have even less reason to trust you."

At that, the Akari made a face, stuck out his forked tongue, and disappeared in a puff of smoke, leaving Jason alone on the road.

Walking on through the night, Jason felt strangely refreshed, alert to animals or strange creatures moving in the forest around him. In the predawn light, he came across a broken-down wagon. Climbing aboard, he fell fast asleep, despite the nipping cold and frost forming on the ground around him.

CHAPTER 8
Arrow Practice

Jason awoke in the early morning to the sound of creaking wheels. A wagon was coming down the same road he had walked just a few hours before.

Have they found me already? he wondered to himself.

The wagon was pulled by six oxen, and in it rode four rough-looking men in brown leather hats. The driver was very short and stocky, with a full black beard. The wagon seemed to be filled with rocks the color of burnt orange along with shovels, picks, and other tools tucked along the edges. Still groggy from sleep, Jason sat unmoving. His gnawing gut told him he was extremely hungry.

The wagon pulled up next to his broken-down wagon, and the driver pulled to a stop. The dwarfish man looked over at Jason and grinned. "Fine day for a wagon ride," he said.

The other men snickered at the joke.

"Yes," Jason said and then continued, struggling a little with the syntax. "I'm taking this wagon to the next town. You want to race?" He smiled and pretended to pick up the reins of an imaginary team. Jason was a little worried his slow and halting manner of speaking would make them think he was not mentally right, but they seemed not to notice.

"Oh, no, not this team of oxen against that fine team of horses you have," the man continued the humorous exchange. "But we would be honored to have you accompany us. Strength in numbers, you know. I have heard there are bandits about."

"Well, I would be happy to protect you from bandits," Jason quipped, speaking a little faster as he relaxed, "and it would only cost you a biscuit." He then added, "You should have seen what happened to the last bandit who tried to rob me—a cannibal at that!"

The other men guffawed and laughed heartily at this supposed joke from a feisty young lad, but the driver didn't laugh. He looked solemnly at Jason. "Well, in that case, it is good to have you aboard. What is your name?"

"I am Jason."

"Jason, I am Glandon, and my companions are Elgin, Byrinnar, and Maxmell," he said, handing introductions all around.

Jason scampered aboard the wagon, being offered a hand up.

Along the edge of the open wagon's interior were various bags and weapons such as short swords, bows, and arrows as well as a crossbow. An ornate war hammer rested close to Glandon.

It appeared Glandon was indeed a dwarf and leader of the other men, all human miners. He appeared as stout and strong, if not stronger, than any of them.

Elgin dug out a biscuit for Jason from one of the bags, and Maxmell offered a skin filled with water. The water had a stale, leathery taste, but Jason didn't complain, happy to have gotten anything at all for his perpetually hungry stomach.

After a while, Byrinnar produced a set of pipes and played a simple tune. It didn't sound like much to Jason, but the men seemed to enjoy it.

The wagon made its creaky way through the forest. In the early afternoon, a flicker of motion caught Jason's eye, so he asked the driver, "Do you mind if I hunt us some fresh meat?"

"Please do, young one, if that is your skill. We will stop and wait."

"No need to wait." Jason snatched up a bow and arrow that lay in the wagon. He immediately fired at a rabbit, which had frozen in place to avoid detection. His shot was accurate. He jumped down to retrieve his prey and climbed back on without the wagon even slowing. In the next half hour, to the amazement of the men, he shot two more rabbits and a medium-sized fowl. They stopped at a brook and had lunch over a small fire.

"You are one of the best shots with a bow I have ever seen," said Glandon to Jason. "And I never saw any of the animals until you shot them."

"Are you elvish?" asked Elgin.

"No, but I have lived off the land for a while, and it sharpens your senses." Jason then asked, "What are all these orange rocks you're carrying?"

"Iron ore. However, it has much gold mixed in. We are looking for a good profit when we get it to a crusher."

"There is a crusher at the next town," added Maxmell.

With his stomach full, the lack of a full-night's sleep caught up to Jason, and he spent the afternoon ride in slumber.

That evening, they made a simple camp, picketing the oxen in a nearby grassy clearing. They prepared a stew with some dried vegetables and leftovers from the meat Jason shot. After more piping and storytelling, the four men laid out their bedrolls underneath the wagon. Jason was small enough to sleep on the wagon's seat, and one of the men kindly offered his cloak.

Glandon cocked the crossbow with its crank, notched a bolt in place, and gave it to the first watch. Byrinner was on the first watch, and since Jason was not sleepy yet, he took some time to say his prayers for his family, then joined Byrinner by the fire.

"You okay?" asked Byrinner.

Jason nodded. "Just saying my prayers."

Byrinner did not reply, just studied the woods. Jason noted that Byrinner knew better than to stare at the fire, which would limit his ability to see any immediate threat.

Deciding now a good time to increase his vocabulary, Jason asked the night watch about the strange word he had heard Brother Dorrian use to describe the man in the prophecy.

Byrinner replied, "'Juggernaut' is a term used to describe a huge construct that's magically empowered to move. It has no feelings nor brain and is nearly unstoppable. If a person is called that, then it refers to his battle prowess as being nearly unstoppable."

Jason had to laugh, for now, he understood the prophecy used his old title, instead of his name. Prophecies always tend to be vague, even when very specific. Now he had no doubt this prophecy was about him, and he needed to find the full meaning.

The grizzled miner looked at him curiously. "Where did you hear such a word?"

Jason could see no reason to hide the truth and told him, "A priest from Chanderlon was searching for someone with that name."

Byrinner shrugged. "Never heard of him."

He readjusted the crossbow in his lap and stared out into the night. Now tired, Jason made his bed on the wagon bench. He rolled himself into the cloak, careful to tuck in the edges. The cloak was not as warm as a blanket, and it would be another cool night. His oversized military jacket would help, but he figured if he got too cold he could move over to the fire.

The other men took their turn at watch throughout the night, each taking command of the crossbow in their turn. When the frosty morning arrived, Glandon uncocked the crossbow and, after a breakfast of biscuits and cheese, hitched the oxen to continue their way down the road again.

As they resumed their travel, the men played a game of calling out shots to Jason. They would call a particular stump or large toad stool along the side of the road, and Jason would shoot it. He would try to shoot the called-out target before the men could finish their sentences. Then as they went by, he would hop off and retrieve his arrows.

By late morning the frost had melted, and the road crossed the river.

Glandon stopped the wagon halfway through the crossing to let the oxen drink while he took out a pipe and smoked it. Jason sat beside him, noticing the dwarf casually studying the forest beyond the far shore. There was a clearing a short way from the shore to the trees. Thick brush grew at the base of their trunks. The road continued on through the trees past the clearing.

"Good spot for an ambush," muttered Glandon. "The stream's too rocky to turn around. Pass the word along to the boys to keep a sharp eye out." Jason nodded and returned to the back of the wagon, but the men were already covertly readying their weapons. Someone had cocked the crossbow.

Elgin whispered to him, "Take the bow and hide behind the ore in back."

"Don't be afraid to let loose an arrow at the first sign of trouble," added Byrinner.

Jason sat and surveyed the forest on the side of the river bank they had just left, looking for any sign of movement. He saw none, turned, and half-drew his bow out of sight, lying across the ore. He laid out the arrows in a row on the pile so he could snatch them up quickly.

He could feel anticipation welling inside him. The man inside him would have no problem performing in order to defend himself and his comrades. Even if afraid he would do what was necessary, but now, he had a choice. He could hide and hope his companions won the battle, he could run and abandon them, or he could stay and very possibly shoot to kill. The man inside chastised him for even thinking such cowardly thoughts.

Some think running away to avoid killing to be the nobler path, and perhaps if he was alone, it would be. But now, these men had little choice but to enter a possible trap. To run would be to abandon his new found friends, good men who chose to make an honest living, while others choosing to kill as a way of life should have already accepted that the sword cuts both ways.

They would die if their chosen victims were too strong. To be blunt, kill or be killed were the options enforced here. They could surrender, of course, but surrender does not guarantee survival.

He then remembered his promise to protect this group of men when he joined them, for the cost of a biscuit. They may have thought it a joke, but joke or not, he had given his word.

With greater resolve, he gripped the handle of the bow, notched an arrow and glared at the foliage as if daring evil to show itself. Glandon finished smoking his pipe and cleaned it out by knocking it on the wagon before putting it away. Then, seemingly without a care in the world, he urged the oxen forward. The wagon rocked and creaked as it rolled over the rough stream bottom.

There is always one who is impatient. Just as the oxen cleared the water, climbing upon the shore, a man dressed in neutral brown and green rose up on a tree branch, exposing himself above a bough of leaves, bow drawn.

Jason loosed his arrow first, snatching up another before the first arrow even hit. He saw his first arrow had found its mark, spoiling the bandit's shot and knocking him screaming out of the tree. He had his second arrow pulled to a full draw before he even saw his next target.

The wounded bandit's cry roused his comrades to rise and attack. Five more men with bows in the tree limbs raised up as six men charged from the underbrush below. Jason hit another archer before he too could get a shot off. His own party had just begun to swing into action and since Jason was the only one already in motion, the remaining archers all fired at him.

Diving flat against the ore, he just missed being skewered as two arrows sailed over him and two more hit the ore in front of him. He rose to fire again just in time to see Glandon's crossbow bolt go through neck of a charging bandit. The man gurgled and fell, clutching his throat.

Elgin, Byrinnar, and Maxmell leaped from the wagon, swords in hand to meet the remaining five bandits. Jason had an urge to help the outnumbered companions but knew he needed to take out the archers if they were to have a chance. He fired again at an archer who just happened to duck out of sight behind a bough of leaves as he let loose. His aim was rewarded with another cry of pain from the trees.

Glandon had grabbed his war hammer and jumped down to assist the other men. One of the remaining archers changed his sites from Jason to Glandon. Seeing the archer's intended victim, Jason frantically grabbed for another arrow and started to draw but knew it would be too late.

It seemed as if time stopped, and he couldn't move fast enough, so he did the only thing he did have time for. Without thinking of the impossibility of it, he shot his arrow at a trajectory to intercept the bandit's arrow. The bandit already had a look of triumph on his face when Jason's arrow spoiled the dead-on shot. The heads of both arrows shattered with a loud snapping noise as they collided and fell from midair, swirling harmlessly down among the men fighting.

Everyone on both sides of the mêlée knew instantly what had happened and the fighting paused in a moment of stunned silence. Everyone except Jason, that is, already fitting another arrow to his bow string. He didn't have to fire, for the bandits were backing away. They had a look of awe on their faces, and one of them said something about an "omen."

Jason breathed a prayer of thanks. The bandits backed to the brush, then broke into a run, abandoning their fallen.

Glandon pushed the two broken arrows with his toe and said, "Mighty good shooting, boy, mighty good. By the way, thanks." The other men in their party checked the fallen bandits. Only one was still alive, sitting on a branch in the tree where Jason had shot him. The arrow had hit an artery in his arm, and he had lost a lot of blood.

In an attempt to save his own life, the desperado had cut his bowstring to make a tourniquet tied around his upper arm. The men helped the wounded bandit out of the tree, where he promptly sank to the ground and wearily leaned his back against the tree. Of the fallen bandits, one had been shot by Glandon and the other three by Jason.

Maxmell returned and helped Jason out of the wagon, and Glandon asked, "Everyone all right?" Everyone nodded in the affirmative. Then Glandon said, "Boy, go salvage what you want from the dead. You have earned first rights. Anything you want from that lout under the tree is yours as well."

Jason tentatively rolled one corpse onto its back. The body was still warm and smelled of urine. An arrow, one he had fired, lodged in the diaphragm and one lung, but what had killed him was the fall. The man had a knife visible and a quiver of arrows. Of course, with thieves, probably nothing was truly theirs.

He found an exceptionally well-made short bow from one of the dead bandits and two full quivers of arrows. He also found a long, slim fighting knife with a scabbard. In his youthful hand, it was more like a short sword.

Glandon offered him the fighting man's short sword, but after trying a few swings, it felt poorly balanced, so he declined. The other men found some coin purses among the bodies and gave Jason an equal share, which amounted to fifteen pieces of silver with the image of some distinguished king on the front and a dragon on the back.

They left the living bandit to fend for himself. He would probably die unless his comrades came back for him. Fair justice for someone of such a murderous occupation. But still, Christians were supposed to love their enemies, which goes beyond justice. So Jason brought to the wounded bandit some leftover meat from his previous hunting and covertly stuffed five pieces of silver of his share of the money into the suffering man's belt. The bandit's eyes bore into Jason's, and then he nodded his head with thanks.

The miners had pulled the rest of the dead into the bushes. Years of martial arts training had conditioned Jason's mind to accept responsibility for his actions. He had killed to save others, and his mind accepted that just as readily as it accepted the death of the cannibal who had attacked him. These men fulfilled Jesus's prediction that men who lived by the sword would die by the sword. He took the warning to heart, to not make a living by violent means even in this cruel and barbaric world.

Back on the road again, the men joked about taking Jason to a fair and winning a lot of money betting in an archery tournament. He instead asked them to keep his skill a secret. He knew they would honor his wish. They were simple men, but with a fierce loyalty to any they considered one of their own, and Jason had earned their trust.

The travelers soon reached the next town, Sulter Hill, situated near the river. It was five or six times larger than Haglar's village, with a smelter and ore crusher that ran day and night, making loud banging noises. The smelter spewed sulfurous smoke and black soot covered the men who tended the fires and worked the ore.

Driving the wagon over to a large metal trough, Glandon called to the workers from a nearby stone building who hurried out with wooden buckets. They began to unload the wagon, carrying the ore to the trough for sorting. A man wearing clean clothes, but with face and hands still smudged heavily with soot, approached the miners with a tablet and parchment. He made note of the delivery and gave the men directions to where they could pick up their payment.

Jason's companions, overjoyed to be at the end of their journey, offered to keep him on with them. He considered it seriously, but declined. He had to do what he could to return home.

He asked the miners if they had ever heard of someone named Father Varigold. They had not, but when he described the outfits Brother Dorrian and the men with him had worn, they surmised that Father Varigold was probably from a wealthy religious sect found in the capital city of Chanderlon. How far away it was, they were not sure, but they figured it was at least a month's travel westward along the Chander River.

He shared a room with them that night, and they parted ways the next morning after breakfast. Jason truly hated to leave the cheerful men and wished he could head back into the mountains with them. They had a log dwelling close to their mine in which to winter, though they considered bringing one more load of iron ore out before the winter snows hit.

He made some purchases with his silver—a backpack, a blanket, and some food. Gathering his things, he walked the packed earthen streets in the brisk morning air and appreciated the beauty of the day, clear skies, and a feeling of contentment. He could almost forget he was from another world. Almost.

CHAPTER 9
Deologue 2

The huge muscular man, with neatly trimmed gray hair and beard, was swinging a large sledgehammer, smashing rocks. Axialla admired the man's physique as she approached, his robe dropped to the belt at his waist, exposing the glistening tanned skin and rippling muscles of his upper body.

They were standing in a quarry on a cliff side as the sun beat down on them. The giant ignored Axialla when she stopped beside him. He intensely focused on turning a rock into little pieces of gravel.

"Xan Rukkah, why do you labor as if a common man?" asked the goddess.

"I do not labor. I am finding enjoyment. I have discovered I love to smash things," the god said as he showed her his maul.

"But you can smash this whole mountainside with just a word. Why do you mimic the actions of humans just to do so?"

"Eh, it is much more satisfying to actually feel things crush in your hands. Here, try it." He thrust the huge mattock toward her. Axialla threw up her hands and countered, "No, I have more important things to discuss. I want to talk about the prophecy."

Xan Rukkah set the head of the maul on the ground, resting his hands on the handle. "My servant Dorrian has concluded the matter. The prophecy is just another wild dream men sometimes have."

"I disagree. If Dorrian hadn't fumbled the meeting with Haglar, he would have discovered something meaningful."

"That old witch? I think you're just in a snippet because a spell of yours fizzled."

"It did not fizzle. The spell jworked. It showed them the champion, but they did not recognize him because he was in their very midst!"

"What? There was no champion there, even the demon verified."

Axialla folded her arms and said smugly, "He was there. It is the child."

"Nay, the prophecy spoke not of a child, but of a large man called the Juggernaut stepping from the mountains. The Creator's visions may be subtle, but they tend to be literal to a fault."

"Hmm, well...Perhaps this child is more than he appears. Perhaps he is the same child found camping at the flash site, and I cannot find a good explanation for how he arrived there, fifty miles from the nearest village."

Xan Rukkah dropped the handle, put an arm around Axialla, and walked her away from the quarry. "Perhaps you have a point. If he did not come from a nearby village, then it could mean he was the only survivor of the dimensional transport. If so, then we need to investigate where he came from and what significance, if any, it may have on the prophecy. I will set some others to that task. In the meantime, kill the boy, just in case."

Axialla smiled and bowed to the giant. "As you wish, oh Great One. But if this is the one who is sent, it will not be that easy."

Xan Rukkah looked a little frustrated. "Well, if you fail to kill him, then do what you do best. Seduce him with your promises of magic."

Axialla smiled even bigger. "It would be my pleasure, my king."

The goddess twirled like a dancer and, in a shimmer of lights, vanished.

The titan watched her display twinkle out, then clapped his hands. It sounded like the clap of thunder. As the echo rang, he bellowed, "Rastuken. Jazeel. Attend me."

Almost immediately two men appeared, one flying with wings like an angel dressed in battle armor, and another running swiftly, looking like a woodlands American Indian in bizarre war paint. The winged one landed before the god while the other leaped before him, arms folded stoically, not even breathing hard.

The winged one spoke first, "Xan Rukkah, it is rare for you to demand our presence. What is the emergency?"

"I have a mission for you two. You are to track the extra-dimensional rift that happened recently to its source and learn the identity of a child, who may have been a survivor in that crash."

Jazeel the Indian spoke, "I am the god of insanity. Why have you chosen me for this mission?"

"I chose you for your tracking ability and that you can see clearly where the more logical minded are confused. Right now, this mission defies logic, and you two are the best choice. Rastuken, you are the god of travel, and you may have to follow the convoluted trail Jazeel finds, drawing you two to a place we have never before ventured. Report to me who and from where this child comes."

Both lessor gods bowed. The one with wings opened a black hole through which they both jumped, vanishing as the hole collapsed.

Xan Rukkah nodded and looked up, "If you are coming back, Creator, then hear me. Is this child the best you can do? This place is ours now, and we will not give it up without a fight."

CHAPTER 10
Hunted

On a low hill that connected forest, river, and plain nestled the village of Sulter Hill. The road Jason chose led across the plain. Actually, it was more of a wagon trail than a road, sometimes splitting off into two paths, then rejoining. It was a beautiful morning, sunny with high clouds and a strong breeze blowing the tall golden blades of grass like sea waves. He was better equipped this time, with a well-made bow, quiver of arrows, long dagger, and recent purchases of a bedroll, leather backpack, bread, and a water skin acquired with the vanquished bandit's money.

He wondered how much he had grown since arriving as a boy but had no way to gauge, so he measured himself with his bow unstrung and marked it with a scratch. The bow was slightly taller than him, but at least he had a record for this fall. Perhaps he would eventually become the man Father Varigold foresaw. He felt uneasy about the prospect of waiting so long. Would his wife assume he was killed in the accident at the laboratory and remarry? He shook his head at such thoughts. A long time or short, he would try his best to get home. He would face the realities of home when he got there.

He focused on the task at present. It should take him two or three days to cross this plain. In the open, he felt vulnerable. With no place to hide if he was attacked, he would have to rely on speed and stamina to escape, and as a ten-year-old boy, he had little of either. Fighting may be just as futile, so his best defense was to be alert and wary and avoid trouble.

Taking his own advice, he climbed the tallest hill he could find and sat just below the top to study his back trail. By sitting in the tall grass below the ridge line, he would not be silhouetted for all to see. He watched for about fifteen minutes until satisfied no predators followed him. He did the same at other corners of the hill. He determined to do this frequently as he traveled the plain. He moved in a slow trot, keeping an eye out for tracks or any other sign of nearby animals.

At noon, a herd of antelope crossed the road ahead of him, leisurely grazing as they went. He considered shooting one with his new bow, except he could not carry so much, nor did he want to spend the time preparing it. He had bread for now, and perhaps smaller game would be available later.

That evening, he climbed another hill as he watched his back trail and all around. The nearest forest was to the southwest, to the northwest spires of rock and sandstone stuck out of the plains like claws.

He would have loved to explore the formations, but the trail led to the southwest, toward the forest. The wind had died, and after a brief meal of bread and water, he said his prayers. He was at a loss as to what to pray. He wanted to do God's will, but he also wanted to go home. Feeling a little unhappy about his circumstance and anxious to go home, he felt it all a little unfair.

But then, he thought of the others who didn't survive at all and realized that by all rights he should be dead too. A feeling of gratitude replaced his earlier melancholy, so he finished his prayers on that note and laid out his bedroll to sleep under the stars. Being very tired, he trusted the Lord to keep watch for him as he settled into peaceful sleep.

He awoke to the dawning sun and climbed the hill to do his vigilance. A mist filled the low-lying areas. Ahead were several herds of animals. Behind one of the herds, like stragglers, were lighter-colored creatures. Wolves, he surmised. Fox was hunting small game close by, so perhaps he might get a prairie dog or two himself.

He considered his restful sleep from the night before a gift from God and an indication of his increase in faith. To know God actually had a purpose for him, and he had, at least to some degree, God's protection until it was fulfilled felt empowering. But then again, God has a purpose for every Christian. We just do not often have the luxury of knowing what it is.

Taking one more glance around before traveling again, he saw something new on his back trail. He sat and watched. The figure, made tiny by distance, would stand up like a man, then hunch and bend over with its head close to the ground like a dog following a scent. Its figure was familiar even at this distance, burned into his memory like a nightmare from his one and only encounter with it.

It was Trombul. It appeared old Haglar had sent the troll to kill or retrieve him, and it was barely over a mile away. The troll probably traveled at night, but being so close to his prey may have pushed himself on into the bright daylight.

Jason predicted he would fare poorly in a fight against the monster and doubted he could outrun him, but perhaps he could slow the creature or even cause him to lose the scent by mingling among the herds, so he took off at a trot toward the herds. He wanted to fly at full speed to get away from the troll but regulated himself to the ground-eating lope he had used the day before.

He didn't look back until he topped a ridge almost an hour later. Ahead of him was a large herd of bison, but glancing behind, the troll was a mere two hundred yards away! Having caught sight of Jason on the open plain, Trombul was now running at full speed to catch him.

Jason had never been around bison before and didn't know how they would react to him. He charged at them, screaming and yelling in hopes they might stampede and he could perhaps catch a ride on the back of one. The antics of a ten-year-old boy had little effect on the herd at large. A few nearby animals bolted, but a large bull raised its head and lowered it again as it trotted toward him.

He stopped his yelling as he ran among the shaggy beasts who made way before him, keeping their distance as the large bull began his charge. Several other bulls also began making their way toward him, and he could feel the ground shake from the weight and power of their steps. Even the calves could have stomped him to bits, and these beasts seemed more irritated at him than afraid. Perhaps their attitude toward him affected what happened next.

The troll broke over the ridge with a growling, hacking noise, moving at a full run. The bisons near the troll stampeded away and toward the center of the herd with Jason. Even the big bull about to stomp him into the dust was distracted by the fearsome visage of Trombul.

Jason tried to climb aboard a large cow to keep from getting squished or stomped, but the cow veered away and shrugged him off. He almost tripped and fell in that attempt, and with the wall of massive heads, humps, and hooves coming at him, it would have meant instant death.

Suddenly, his world exploded with the sound of thundering hooves and bellowing of bison, the roar of Trombul lost in the din. The first wave of buffalo had separated slightly to go around him, and Jason ran with them, trying to match their speed to avoid getting trampled. Flying grass clods struck his face. To make matters worse, he could feel the breath of a cow on his back, letting him know he was too slow. He was about to get trampled, and with the bodies starting to press in, he had nowhere to go.

To get out of the way, he jumped hard against the rump of a bison next to him, then bounced back into the cow as it went past him. Feeling a hard kick against his thigh from the bison ahead of him, he felt like he was going down, so he did the only thing left for him to do. He sunk his fingers into the thick shoulder hair of the cow going past him and hung on, letting the beast drag him. The cow probably thought she was being attacked by some sort of predator and bellowed loudly but was unable to do anything about it at the moment, pinned in by the stampeding bodies.

At times, he thought his ribs would break from a body bouncing into him from the side, but his bow and quiver of arrows riding across his shoulder helped to shy the animals away, so they did not press against him too hard. Soon, the cow began pushing for the edge of the herd where she could maneuver to do something about the pathetically small "predator" clinging to her.

Other bison made way for the distraught cow as it bucked its way toward the edge of the group. At the fringe of the herd, he let go, and stumbling but still keeping his feet, he then tried to duck behind another cow. That she-bison made a halfhearted charge at him, more of a bluff, which he clumsily dodged, then he limped away, trying to put some distance between him and the river of flesh, horns, and hooves.

When finally a safe distance away, he lay down in the grass and crawled to the top of a hill, careful to not silhouette himself against the skyline and looked back in the direction he had come. He did not see the troll anywhere and hoped Trombul had gotten himself trampled.

Resuming his journey, he kept a hopeful eye out for circling vultures that could indicate the troll had died. Even if the vultures did indicate something was dead, though, it didn't necessarily mean it was the troll. Trombul was big and mean enough he could have injured or even killed a bison.

He was moving better, and the bruise on his thigh started to disappear, but still, he doubted he could make it to the trees by nightfall. The trees represented safety, where he could escape above the reach of most predators, perhaps even beyond the old troll.

Late afternoon, he came to a river meandering from the northwest, cutting across his intended direction. Low bushes grew along the banks. Up on the hill, sloping away from the river on the other side, cut stones stood about four feet high, spaced a quarter of a mile apart. Even from his side of the river, he could see runes cut into them.

He vowed to learn to read and write in the common language as soon as he could. Obviously, the rune stones marked some sort of boundary, such as a kingdom or a country. He surmised that perhaps the river marked the border of Chanderlon.

He checked the banks of both shores very carefully. The water was crystal clear, the riverbed rock and sand, so he felt it fairly safe to drink and to cross. Not wanting to get his weapons wet, he held his bow and quiver of arrows above his head. Halfway across, he bent down to dunk his head and get a drink.

Water dripping off his face, he was puzzled to hear a whistling sound. A quick glance around showed nothing in the surrounding river banks, but disregarding his weapons, he dove to submerge and hide himself anyway.

This quick thinking probably saved his life because something slammed into his back, driving him to the bottom. A sharp strike to the back of his neck would have killed him if it were not for the resistance of the water and perhaps his backpack hiking up.

He then felt himself jerked bodily out of the water. Just before unconsciousness claimed him, he was aware of an intense crushing pressure on his right leg. Something with claws large enough to reach around his right shoulder had pierced the flesh on his left and he heard the thunderous sound of labored flapping.

CHAPTER 11
Bird Feed

Jason awoke to pain and the noise of wind. He opened his eyes to see that he was soaring at a dizzying height, far above the plain. He tried to remain limp in the mighty bird's talons, which was not all that difficult, to prevent the predator from giving a final lethal peck. Moving his head as little as possible, he glanced upward and saw the face of an enormous falcon, large enough to carry even an adult man! He scanned the direction they were headed and thought it ironic that his fleeting wish was coming true—he would get to visit the badlands after all. Right now, though, he needed to plan a strategy before he passed out again.

If he struggled now, the falcon could simply drop him and pick up his dead body from below or pluck his head off with a quick bite of that wickedly sharp beak. The bird was so huge, he could not see how he could fight it in its nest or on the ground. Besides, he felt he had lost a lot of blood from where the falcon's claw had pierced his shoulder. Likely, the only reason he wasn't bleeding so much now was the squeeze the creature had on his chest.

He would have found it difficult to breathe, except his arm was between the bird's foot and his chest, providing space for him to get enough air. But he was wounded, and once on the ground, he doubted he would even be able to stand. Nevertheless, he needed a survival strategy. He took inventory—that was easy— all he had was his long knife attached to his belt. He probably dropped his bow and arrows, and he did not know what became of his backpack and bed roll, but they were gone, probably torn off with the initial attack.

Could he even move his arms? His right arm was in the falcon's talons against his side, but he was able to move his right hand and forearm without undue pain. His left arm felt numb and cold. He found he could move it with great pain to his chest, but still, it moved. His legs seemed okay despite the crush on his right thigh and was not lacerated by the falcon's talons. He could feel a deep gash in his neck, and a sharp pain shot from his head down his back. Not in the greatest of shape, he thought, but possibly good for a minute of action before he passed out again.

So that was it. He might have one minute of pure concentrated effort. It would take all his martial discipline, so he considered his plan carefully. The only similar situation Jason could think of was once hearing of a weasel that killed two hundred chickens in a blood lust, even though chickens are five times larger than a weasel. If a weasel, with a similar size disadvantage could do it, then he could do it too, although he didn't want to think a weasel might not do so well against a bird of prey. A weasel would gash the throat or bite the back of the neck. Okay then he too would do something similar, using his dagger.

He remained limp and waited, resting as he could. Strangely, he thought he could hear the distant sound of a woman laughing in the wind. Glancing around carefully, he could see no explanation for the sound; then, it stopped.

The monster bird now descended to an enormous nest, about thirty feet in diameter, constructed of giant feathers and sticks. It was on a spire two hundred feet tall. He was relieved to see the nest empty of chicks or mate. Perhaps the bird brought him to the nest to eat at its leisure.

He was crushed into the nest as the bird landed with its weight on him. If the hawk struck at him now, he would have no chance. However, the bird released him and stepped aside.

Jumping up, he drew his knife in the same motion. His immediate action caught the giant bird by surprise, and he continued his leap as high as he could, cutting simultaneously in Iaido fashion with a precision that would have made his sword instructor proud. Cutting upward, the razor-sharp dagger easily slipped through feathers, albeit short of the goal of the bird's throat, drawing a spew of blood immediately.

The falcon reacted swiftly and pounced with its talons, one pinning him on his back to the floor of the nest with a claw across his chest. He thought he would meet the follow-up attack of the bird's beak by striking the knife into an eye, but this proved impossible since he had to deal immediately with a huge sharp beak about to crush his head.

Jerking his face to the side, he simultaneously kicked at the beak and thrust up with the knife, heedless of its target. The beak grazed the side of his head and continued on past to slam deep into the excretion-crusted floor of the nest.

The bird's head pulled back quicker than he could get in another strike, but he saw blood on the blade. He had no idea where it had struck. The giant avian shook its head vigorously, slinging blood everywhere.

It then glared at him, blood dripping from under its jaw, and struck again. He knew he could not stop it this time and was as good as dead.

The monstrous head came in sideways with its mouth open. It apparently intended to bite him and tear his body in half, so he grabbed his knife in both hands and thrust it up with his head between his arms, as if trying to dive into that horrible maw.

The bird's head was not actually large enough to swallow him whole as he had envisioned, but it was close. The foul breath was nauseating, and the rough, dry tongue pressed into his left shoulder as he drove the knife deep into the back of the throat, the only soft spot presented by the bird in the attack.

He could feel the beak close in around him, and then suddenly open as the bird jerked its head away again, the curved point of its beak lacerating his back. He fell back limp, unable to breathe because of the weight of the talon across his stomach and lower chest. His back hurt from the flesh exposed to air.

The titanic falcon screamed its rage at Jason, but as it did so a spray of foamy blood spewed forth, some of it splattering in his face. The bird made a strange gurgling noise as it raised its head to the heavens, blood streaming from the corner of its mouth from the feathers below its jaw as well as from its neck, lower down. It was apparently dying, but would it finish him off first?

Still pinned to the floor of the nest, he made a feeble cut at the bird's feet, but was blacking out and couldn't stop it. The constriction of the impossibly strong talons made it difficult to breathe, and his head throbbed with pain.

Just before darkness overtook him, he formulated what he thought would be his last prayer. Surprisingly, it was not for himself but for his wife, Molly, and kids... "Protect them Lord..." was all he could pray before silently blacking out.

He awoke, perhaps several hours later. It was dark, but he wasn't cold because the enormous falcon's wing stretched over him. He listened but couldn't hear other noise. The temptation to just go back to sleep to regain his strength and finish healing from his wounds was overwhelming. His accelerated healing was nothing short of miraculous, and although he felt pain, he also knew it was lessening, and he would be fine in the morning.

Exhausted, he fell asleep under the giant falcon's wing again. Several hours later, he awoke, hungry as usual, to daylight showing from under the wing and the noise of something moving in the nest.

Carefully, he turned to where he could just see the bottom of the nest from under the bird's wing. A large-taloned foot stepped into view, larger than that of the giant falcon which had carried him up here. He readied his knife and froze in place, hoping this new giant bird of prey wouldn't discover him.

After a few minutes, he could hear the thunderous flapping as the falcon took to air. Risking discovery, he crawled out to make sure it had left. Sure enough, it was leaving, but he had no idea how far it would go. Falcons have keen eyesight, and he would need to be careful to not show himself in the open even if he did get down from the spire. He decided then that he could only risk climbing down in the dark, so he would have to wait out the day, perhaps starting at dusk.

As soon as he was sure the second giant falcon had gone, he walked around the nest to survey his surroundings. He had a beautiful view of the badlands in the mid morning light. He spied a spring not too far away but tried not to think of that because there was no water to be had on top of the spire. His wounds were large, ugly scars, and even those already began to disappear. The first thing he did was give thanks. He did not expect to still be alive. Also, unless the troll Trombul had witnessed his abduction and followed, there was a good chance he had also lost that fiend for good.

When he finished his prayers, he looked around. It would be difficult to climb down, but not impossible. As a boy in his own world, he was afraid of heights. He always feared he would clumsily lose his balance or his strength would give out on a crucial hold. He still respected it, although as a man he had learned to face his fears. He also learned to trust himself and to regard fear as an ally rather than an enemy. This attitude had helped him overcome many challenges in life.

Something shiny buried in the sticks in the floor broke him from his thoughts. He dug it out and discovered a bronze helmet, slightly dented. It must have not been very old since it was not too badly tarnished. Digging around among the nest branches, he found more shining objects, mostly shields and pieces of armor.

He remembered that many birds like to decorate their nests with shiny things. He also dug up bones, most of them broken, some human and some antelope, even the remains of a wolf or two. It seemed nothing smaller than a buffalo had been safe from this bird.

He considered trying to push the body of the enormous dead bird out of the nest but changed his mind, knowing that if the other bird returned, he would need a place to hide. His hunger made him want to carve out a piece of the carcass to eat, but after finding human remains, the idea did not seem so appetizing. Also, a cooking fire could set the whole nest ablaze with him in it.

Spending some time digging around, he found quite a treasure trove. Several torn-up leather backpacks (the best of which he set aside to repair) and belts with swords or daggers still in their scabbards. He looked over the collection of swords, most of which were rusting, and found one with a pristine blade and a fine-jeweled hilt. It was probably very valuable but felt clumsy in his hands compared to the Japanese katana he was used to. It was also overly heavy compared to his small frame. He did not need the weight, so he left it, and for the same reason, he did not take any armor.

Digging further, he did find a slim, straight blade longer than his dagger. It was jet-black, including the pommel and hilt, reminding him of a ninja's sword. At first, he assumed it was painted, but upon closer inspection, he discovered the metal itself was black, its hilt just long enough to allow a double grip.

He tried a few swings, performed a sword kata, and was very pleased with the feel. It had a shoulder strap with its scabbard, which he put on. He then found a length of rope woven through the nest. It was nearly fifty feet long with a metal grapple at the end. Perhaps someone tried to rescue a friend from this nest or even raid its treasures.

Close to the bottom of the diggings, he found a leather bag containing a few gold coins. There were probably more, fallen down lower in the debris. The thickness of the nest construction meant it would be difficult to dig to the bottom, but he reasoned it might be worthwhile to dig another hour or so. He needed to be careful. If he became too weak from hunger, he may not have the strength to climb down.

He dug some more, and his hour's worth of digging yielded a variety of coins and gems. These he put into the leather purse, now fairly bulging when he tied it off. It was heavy, but he could manage the weight in his backpack. Taking the best backpack, he fixed the broken shoulder straps with bits of leather cut from the others.

Then he dozed again and awoke mid afternoon. A breeze stirred, which shook his confidence. He did not want to get blown around while climbing down. The grapple was made in such a way that it would not dig too deeply into the nest and could be dislodged easily after the pressure released from the rope. At only fifty feet, the rope needed to be used several times in order for him to reach the bottom. The hemp rope was beginning to deteriorate, becoming splintery, but his tests showed it still strong enough to hold his lighter weight.

The breeze became stronger as the day wore on but began diminishing as dusk descended. He only saw the giant falcon, or perhaps another, far off to the north. The only way he could really judge the size of the bird was when a flock of geese traveling south for the winter flew between him and the beast. It also seemed to flap its wings slower and more majestically than a normal falcon.

As the light faded, he began preparations for his descent. Diminishing winds and the precipitous drop made him feel dizzy. He found a stout branch end and hooked the grapple over it. If the branch moved the grapple would slip off, so he made sure it would hold fast by giving it several hard test tugs.

He had seen a picture of Polynesian native cliff climbers in search of eggs with a rope tied to their ankle but was not sure if that was merely to keep them from losing the rope or if it was the best place to tie in case of a fall. He knew that without a harness, tying the rope around his waist could severely injure him if he fell against it, hurting his back or crushing his ribs. A hurt ankle seemed less dangerous.

After a quick prayer for protection, his treasures secured to him, and with the rope end tied to his ankle, he took a deep breath and lowered himself over the edge.

At first, his feet fought with the sticks on the outside of the nest, the rope around his ankle snagging branches as he descended. One of the sticks dislodged, and he watched it fall, bouncing off the cliff on the long way down. It was a mistake to watch it fall. He closed his eyes. That was another mistake, because he could imagine in full Technicolor his body plummeting and smashing to bits below. He just discovered he was still afraid of heights.

He opened his eyes and focused only on the terrain beneath his feet, looking for a ledge or crack in which to wedge himself. About ten feet below the bottom of the nest, he found a large crack into which he could wedge his foot and arm and cling to the cliff without aid of the rope.

He performed a test swing, throwing his arm up. Even that little motion was overly difficult, nearly pulling him from his perch. Then he saw the rope slacken and the grapple dislodge! Terrified, he let go of the rope and tried to avoid being hit by the falling grapple. He put his arm over his head and hunched further into the crevice. The grapple just missed him as it plunged below, only to jerk hard on his foot as it reached the end of the rope, again nearly dislodging him from his precarious perch.

There must be an easier way, he thought to himself, but it was too late to climb back up. He was committed to this course of action. He concentrated on his breathing. When his breathing slowed somewhat, he tried to pull his leg up in order to grab the rope. His whole body trembled involuntarily.

This was not the time to lose courage, so again, he focused on his breathing. It was the only thing he could do that was safe. With each breath, he moved a little, doing what was necessary, his foot and clinging arm cramping.

Finally, he was able to draw his foot up far enough to grab the rope tied around his ankle. His fingertips slowly worked the rope, so he could set his foot down again. Using his teeth and one hand, he pulled up the grapple.

Now what was he going to do? His foot was standing in the best spot for the grapple, but how to get it in there without falling, he did not know. He dropped his pack and weapons, not caring if they got damaged—better them than him.

He slipped the grapple into the crack and let it slide down against his body until it touched his foot. He then jerked his foot out and let his body slide in a controlled fall down the crack to where the grapple was lodged, and he was able to catch it with his hands. Slowly, he started climbing down the rope again, moving to the rhythm of his breathing. The rest of the descent was easier as he found better ledges and deeper cracks, but he felt as though he "breathed" his way down. When he finally reached the bottom, he again breathed a prayer of thanks, the dark of night full upon him.

CHAPTER 12
The Black Blade

In the pitch-dark, Jason groped around and found his fallen items, fortunately undamaged. To reduce the weight he had to pack around, he cut the grapple from the rope and discarded it. He prayed that was an item he would not need again. Traveling in the dark in the badlands was not easy, but he headed in the general direction of the spring he had spotted earlier that day, going around other tall spires and craggy boulders and leaping deep crevasses.

At that moment, he was more thirsty than hungry, if that were possible, and soon, he found the spring running from pool to small pool. He located a little waterfall from which he drank deeply. Refreshed, he was now ready to hunt.

Though armed only with a long dagger and a small sword, he was trained both in combat knife and spike throwing, where the blade doesn't spin. It flies straight like a spear and is accurate to a range of thirty feet. Although he did not intend to use the black bladed sword, he carried it in his off hand, so he could use it in case his first shot was not a clean kill. He moved very quietly, to be as close as possible to his prey; a miss could mean a broken blade.

Movement is the cause of noise and part of the skill of silent movement is to know when to freeze in position. He must have been hunting quietly enough because a lynx stalked past without seeing him. He mused that many sportsmen from his home world would not have believed it possible to out stealth the king of stealth. But as a boy raised in the backwoods, he had learned from his father, who was part Indian, the ways of walking in the wilderness. He often stalked moose without them detecting his presence. Once, he had even surprised a wolverine. He had learned how to call animals, though he was now hesitant to try that, not sure what strange, unintended creature might come.

He came to a larger pool of water and waited for some thirsty critter to approach for a drink. The moon came out in the three-quarter phase, providing better visibility. Making himself comfortable, he became one with the gray, moonlit surroundings.

Eventually, three small pigs of a species he did not recognize approached the spring pool. They sniffed and looked straight at him. He didn't move a muscle but froze, still as a statue. The porcine visitors looked around a bit more and, sensing no danger, moved to the water. He either resembled nothing they had ever experienced before and thus had no reason to fear, or their piggy eyes were unable to distinguish his motionless form from the surrounding rocks.

He threw a knife at the closest pig. At that range, even if he missed one, he would have hit another. His aim was true, but the pig ran nonetheless. It squealed loudly as it took off, the other two running likewise. Giving chase, he easily followed the squealing even in the dark. He didn't want to lose his dagger and caught up with the wounded hog just as it keeled over, his knife sticking from its side.

After making sure the pig was dead by slitting its throat, he then gathered wood for a fire. He wanted a fire for visibility, as well as to keep at bay any predators which might be attracted to the kill. Since he no longer had his striker, he had to start a fire the old-fashioned way, by making and using a fire bow.

As a boy, he had practiced starting fires like this. It wasn't easy, but after about twenty minutes, he had an ember glowing, which he quickly tendered to a respectable cooking fire. He then dressed his kill and got a hunk of meat cooking. He ate as though he could not get enough and stopped more out of exhaustion than satiated hunger.

He intended to keep the fire going all night but awoke to cold ashes the following morning. With a wary eye to the sky as well as his surroundings, he spent the rest of the day smoking the remaining pork, eating liberally as he did so. He unbelted his jacket and cleaned the crusted blood from his own wounds as well as that of the falcon. It had several holes from the talons, but they were not so big to need immediate mending.

That evening, he felt fairly rested. The area he was in seemed safe, but he decided to move closer to the stream and eventually made camp upon a ledge which would be easily defended in the event of an attack from either man or beast. He wasn't sleepy, so when the moon rose, he walked to the stream and listened quietly to the night noises around him.

By becoming familiar with the normal sounds of the night, it is easier to recognize the sound of danger, or lack of sound when danger is near. The night sky was clear, and the stars shone brightly. It would be freezing cold by morning, and without his bedroll, he needed to have wood ready to keep warm. He would then continue his journey the next day.

He said his prayers, especially remembering his family. Still not tired, he found a flat area of sand and did the katas (fighting moves) he could remember. It did not matter that he lost a few, because he always felt he had too many to begin with. What is inside of you is what really counts. That was something he had thought to himself frequently since becoming physically a kid again. He remembered while teaching how he would wrap his black belt around one of his students and then ask the class if simply putting on a black belt made a person a black belt. The answer, of course, was no. He would then reiterate that what is inside is what really matters.

Jason thought with irony how that particular system had an age limit on who could become a black belt. You had to be at least sixteen years old to even be considered a candidate for testing. If he went back now at the biological age of ten, despite what was inside of him, he would not be considered eligible. Was that hypocrisy? They would argue that the belt should not be important to him. Whether they recognized it or not, at least he would know the truth. The sad thing is they would not accept that same truth for themselves. That system reflected a prejudice, closing their eyes to real possibilities.

Some in that system held that the standard for a black belt was the ability to defeat a male adult, and a child could not ever really defeat an earnestly attacking adult. He challenged that belief. He knew of many instances where a child had defeated an adult to rescue another child or themselves. It is a weak martial art which does not teach such strategies. Perhaps that is why he was here, or one reason—to perfect his martial arts so he could better teach children how to defend themselves.

After his exercises, he retired to his ledge for the night and rekindled a small fire from the embers of his previous fire. There was a large flat rock to reflect the heat, and he had more fuel for the fire toward morning when it grew colder.

The next day loomed gray and cold. Keeping an eye out for danger from above as well as the surrounding badlands, he traveled out onto the plains again. By mid afternoon, he had arrived at the forest he had seen several days before. He traveled along the edge of the trees where it was easier to hide if he needed to.

Just before evening, a patrol of heavily armed, mounted soldiers thundered across the plain toward him, their helmets plumed with yellow feathers and their red, yellow-trimmed capes streaming in the wind behind them. They carried lances and shields with swords strapped to their belts.

They rode toward his position with purpose. He lowered himself in the grass, believing they had spotted him and began planning an exit strategy. But instead of riding over to him, they funneled into the forest ahead of him and rode down what was obviously a road cut into the trees. He felt elated, for he had found the trail again.

After waiting a few minutes to make sure the men were gone, he angled through the trees to the forest road. It was the same rutted track that had come off the plain he had been following days before, albeit now well beaten with horse tracks. He followed it quietly and swiftly for a few minutes until it suddenly opened into a large clearing.

The clearing surrounded a low hill with stumps of felled timber still in place. At the top of the hill was a log fort. The gate was open with a sentry posted. The sound of a smithy beating metal rang in the air, and the smoke from chimneys could be seen. The sound of children laughing and squealing with glee over an exciting game gave the indication of a good-sized settlement. Already he could see himself eating a real meal at an inn.

Not sure if they would let him in without an inquisition, he figured he would play the "harmless kid" card to the hilt. He found an appropriate stick and straddled it. He then galloped to the gate, whooping as he went.

The guard, a serious-looking middle aged man, stepped out to meet him. "What are you doing out here, boy?"

Jason could see just through the gate that the patrol had dismounted and young men were taking charge of the horses and a group of children paused in their game to gawk at the soldiers and horses. He snapped the guard a salute. "Just returning from patrol, sire. Sorry I could not keep up with the others. As you can see, my horse is lame."

The guard broke into a smile. "Of course, anyone could see that your horse is lame, Captain. Please bring it on in so the pages can tend to it. And try to not get separated from your troops again. A troll has been sighted lurking about and would likely attack any stragglers. Good evening, sire." The sentinel snapped a tight mock salute and allowed Jason entrance into the fortification.

So, he thought to himself, Trombul has not given up after all.

The troll was not smart, but one had to admire his persistence.

Perhaps having already checked out this area, the troll had moved on. He was safe for now, assuming he was not found an imposter and imprisoned as a spy by the fort's inhabitants.

Inside the fort, which he learned was simply called the East Fort, housed a small town with livery, barracks, several shops, family dwellings, and an inn. The children he had seen earlier stood in a circle playing a game, and he stood nearby watching.

Three children stood in the center of the circle while the rest held hands and chanted, "Escape the fort, escape the fort." As if on signal, all three in the center charged separately and tried to break out of the circle. If they couldn't break the locked hands of the ring and escape, they were added to the circle.

One boy, larger than Jason, had just broken free and ran out close to him, laughing gleefully. Upon seeing him, the boy grunted. "New kid?"

Jason nodded affirmatively.

"New kids have to be a prisoner first."

He took off his pack, sword, and knife belt and joined the kids in their game. They played about half an hour. He made sure he never escaped and always joined the ring, not wanting to stand out in any way. While he laughed and played, he also observed activities going on with the adults in the fort. Most of the soldiers returned to the barracks while the stable hands pitched hay from a wagon for the steeds, now secure in their stables. Other craftsmen and women were at work around their dwellings.

The game was interrupted by the dinner bell at the barracks. Some children left to their homes, but most rushed to the barracks. Not wanting to miss anything, he put his pack and weapons in a dry barrel out of the way and joined the ruckus at the barracks.

A large hewn wooden table lined with crude wooden benches filled a large room. Along either side of the room were bunk beds with armor and weapons stashed in bins or hung along sections of the wall. A few foot lockers were stashed here and there. Dinner was laid on the table without plates or platters. Men sat at the table drinking from goblets while women moved about, filling empty flagons from wine skins. It reminded Jason of a church potluck only with weapons and free-flowing wine instead of plates and silverware.

Piles of bread, venison, chicken, and vegetables scattered across the table as well as pots of stew. The men ate using their hands and field knives. A few used long, two-pronged forks. Children ran in and out snatching whatever they wanted, unheeded by the adults. Several dogs lurked under the tables, snatching what fell to the floor.

He was taken aback by the unsanitary and chaotic conditions but spied a piece of bread beckoning to his ever-hungry stomach. Without waiting for an invitation, he was in the fray, snatching food with the rest of the kids. The bread was delicious. He also grabbed some raw carrots and an apple. He was tired of his nearly all meat diet. He ate his fill and then some. The honeyed rolls were especially good.

After the eating frenzy, the pace of activity slowed, and a while later, a grizzled old warrior gathered the children around and kept them spellbound with stories of battles and heroic endeavors. Tales of dragons, giants, and monsters never seen by man before rolled off the warrior's tongue for over an hour. As children drifted off, women carried them to their corners to sleep.

Jason was so tired, he could have joined the sleeping children, but instead, he grabbed what appeared to be a community blanket and stepped outside. Night guards walked the wooden ramps along the wall. The fort gate was closed. Music began in the barracks behind him as the adults continued their nightly party. It sounded like a similar party was commencing at the inn for the officers and more genteel guests.

He checked his pack of treasures and weapons in the barrel. They were as he had left them. If he appeared too wealthy, his hosts might assume he stole the loot and take it from him, so he chose to be careful and to only spend a little at a time in different places. Some may still assume he stole the small amounts even then, but he figured they might not care as much.

He sank to the ground beside the barrels and fell asleep saying his prayers. Anyone looking at him would see the picture of innocence. But the innocence of a child is from naivety, and he was anything but naive. His dreams were that of a husband and father. He dreamed he was fighting hand to hand with a troll to protect his family. He awoke just before dawn, feeling hollow, chilled, and wet. It was raining.

He could hear some activity within the buildings, so he wandered into the barracks and dried himself before a large fireplace still smoldering from the night before. After a breakfast of leftovers, he joined the children in their lessons in one corner of the barracks. Here was an opportunity to learn to read from a matronly woman who scratched out words on the earth floor and asked the children to provide the meaning. He learned the runes that every backwoods child should know, such as bear, wolf, deer, fox, horse, wagon and ax. It was not much, but he could see that the runes followed a distinct pattern, which he might be able to apply to future lessons.

About midday, the rain broke, and the patrol rode out again. Several visitors followed them out in their wagons. Children began playing games once more, the same sort of games children everywhere play. Some of the boys gathered to battle with wooden swords.

Not in the playing mood, Jason sought out the matronly woman again. There's nothing a natural teacher loves more than a willing student, but he found her in one of the houses teaching a group of older girls to sew. He was hoping to get some additional lessons but gave up the idea since he was planning on leaving soon, perhaps that day or the next morning.

After a few hours, the patrol returned with a dead wild boar tied to a pole and held between two horses. Jason joined the children gathered around to admire the beast and to watch the butchering process. Meanwhile, one of them produced a leather ball and started kicking it around. Soon all the children joined in a free-for-all soccer match. It was more a game of keep-away than soccer with all the children chasing the ball around the courtyard.

The ball accidentally rolled to him once, and he kicked it. He was surprised at the mushy response as the ball was not filled with air, but something more solid, perhaps saw dust or rags. His comparatively weak kick earned him some jibes, but all the children were off again as another, stronger boy kicked it away.

That afternoon, he decided there was no reason to delay his departure and determined to leave that evening. He reasoned he might be able to sneak away in the dark if the troll was watching the place.

Going to his supplies in the barrel, he took some of the silver coins from his pack and put them in his pocket. Then he went among the various craftsmen who supported the fort and purchased a small bow and some arrows. They seemed to not mind where he got the money.

When the dinner bell rang, he snatched extra food and filled his backpack. No one noticed the missing blanket from the night before, so he also tied it to his pack. Feeling a little guilty, he went back and left a small pile of silver where he had picked up the blanket.

Walking out to the gate, he realized it was already closed. There were two guards on the wall whom he could ask to open it, but really, were they going to just let a child walk out into the dark?

Resolving to wait until morning and sneak out with the patrol, he found his resting spot again. It never occurred to him he could not just leave whenever he wanted. Sometimes, it was hard to remember the limitations he had in a kid's body.

That night, he rested better, although it was still chilly. After breakfast the next morning, he gathered up his things to leave and walked behind a wagon following the patrol out of the fort. As he hoped, the guards seemed to assume he belonged with the occupants of the wagon.

The patrol never looked back and took the road toward the plain, with the wagon following at a much slower pace, while Jason took the other direction on the road continuing through the forest. The forest road was little more than a well beaten path through the trees, rutted from wagons and carts. Every now and then, it would break into a grassy clearing or cross a swampy stream, but he wondered if he was on the wrong road since he did not encounter any travelers that day.

Worried that Trombul would pick up his trail, he walked all day and half the night, then curled up among the roots of a tree. Covered with the dark gray blanket with which he virtually disappeared, he fell right to sleep.

CHAPTER 13
The Black Blade

Over the next several days, Jason was met and passed by travelers on horseback or in wagons. They showed little interest in a boy apparently out hunting from one of the isolated farms along the way. He did not actually need to do any hunting, though several times he heard large creatures moving through the woods.

One night, as he was curled in the trunk of a tree sleeping, he awoke to a soft running noise coming quickly toward him. There was no time to scamper up the tree, his intended escape plan, so he drew his black blade, knowing it would be nearly invisible in the dark.

He remained as he was, not moving under his blanket, with only his eyes peeking out. Suddenly, someone of short stature jumped over him and continued running, followed by another. At first, he thought they were possibly elves dressed in some sort of leather armor which, according to the tales of the grizzled warrior at the fort, these woods were full of. Both carried shields: the first one also carried a spear in his hand, while the second carried a sword in his belt.

As he wondered who they were, he became aware of several others passing by around him, all headed in the same direction. Another jumped over his hiding spot, after which it paused, turned and looked directly at him. A cruel scowl glowered from a face with large luminescent eyes above a large nose, perched above a set of snarled teeth. The creature's skin looked a dark gray in the night gloom, but he suspected it would appear green in the daylight.

The ugly visage reminded him a little of Trombul the troll, but if his knowledge of folklore from his home-world was halfway applicable here, he surmised he was face to face with a goblin. Elves were known as the "fair" folk because they seemed to look good to humans; this creature was anything but good looking.

For convenience sake, "goblin" is what he decided to call them until he learned otherwise. Whatever it was, it did not look friendly. It was carrying a short, well-notched blade in a manner indicating it was ready for an attack. It also wore leather armor which appeared to have been made for an adult human but was pieced together for its smaller size—about the same size as Jason.

The goblin turned as if it had not seen him and joined its companions running through the woods. All the goblins were carrying some sort of weapon ready in their hands. Jason waited about a minute after the last goblin passed before moving. He could not tell how many there were, but they were numerous.

He was not sure why, but he gathered his things and followed. He told himself he should just let them go about their business, but there was something in the furtive way they traveled that made him feel they were up to no good. Perhaps he also forgot that he was only a very small boy.

He trotted along as silently as he could, following after the pack of goblins. He could still see the trailing runners from time to time. He reasoned that if he were going to live in this world for a while, he should learn as much as he could about it. That was the best rationalization he could think of at the moment for doing an irrational act.

The image he had of goblins in his own world represented evil, but he did not automatically assume it would hold true here, assuming they were indeed goblins. Just because they were ugly didn't mean they were evil. However, he thought it ironic that up until this point, living things he discovered on this world were myths, legends, and scary stories told to children on his world.

Perhaps people tapped into this parallel world in their dreams or perhaps all that happened on this world had happened in his own world in the past. Or maybe some travelers actually crossed over between the worlds and told the tales of what they saw! That last thought gave Jason some comfort. He might return home too. Although this life was definitely exciting, he figured he wouldn't mind a little less excitement.

More than anything, he missed his family. He wondered what his wife was doing at that moment. He thought of his kids and the time that had passed without seeing them. He tried not think that he might never see them again, but it was getting harder and harder to withhold that finality as the number of days in the strange land increased.

It had already occurred to him that his family might consider him dead. They might count him as lost among the casualties of the laboratory disaster. The fact that his body was not found would surely not be reason to place doubt on his demise. He himself had buried several others in the soil of this alternate world—why would his family not suspect that his flesh had just disintegrated along with the others?

He pushed those concerns out of his mind and concentrated on the moment. Running through the woods at night was a risky activity under the most carefree of circumstances, so chasing after a band of nasty-looking critters armed to the teeth would need his full attention. Although he couldn't help but think, *What if my family could see me now, a little boy running after an army of small alien creatures?*

He slowed and hid behind a bush as the goblins stopped by a clearing. He circled behind them to get a better view. There must have been at least several hundred of the small creatures in the immediate area; it appeared they had circled the clearing several rows deep. In the middle of the clearing was a farmhouse with a barn behind it. Wheat sheaves stood stacked in a field in front and a hayfield spread out back.

This could have been the home of some oppressive tyrant, and the goblins were fighting for their freedom, but he very much doubted it. More likely, it was exactly as it appeared: a simple farm family was about to be slaughtered and plundered by a pack of vicious fiends and the odds against the farm were distasteful.

Just then, a large dog came charging from the barn, barking his warning. At that moment, all the goblins arose screaming and charged. With bow in hand, Jason drew back in anger and shot the nearest goblin. The short marauder screamed and fell, but his companions took no notice as they made quite a din with their own awful war cries. He continued to fire as quickly as he could, picking off goblins at the rear of the horde. The attackers in front were so intent on their target they took no notice of his assault from behind.

A man emerged from the house to meet the first charge with a sword and shield in hand. A husky woman appeared to protect his back, with a spear, from just inside the doorway. A group of goblins leaped at the window, covered in real glass. The first little thug broke through the panes to be met by a spear, but others pushed him through and forced their way inside the house heedless of their comrade's welfare.

Jason emptied his quiver of about twenty-five arrows, counting a kill for nearly each shot; then, drawing both sword and dagger, he ran to the compressed group of goblins about the door. The farmer was pressed to the door, wounded and flagging. Sounds of fierce fighting emanated from inside the home. The human battle cries from within were made by women. He thought them very brave.

He sliced his first goblin from behind on one side of the neck. The black blade bit deeper than he expected, nearly severing the goblins head, dark blood spurting everywhere. Now he struck quicker, slicing the necks of as many as he could from behind before the mass of attackers realized they were being attacked from the rear.

He killed five goblins before one turned to see what was taking down his comrades. His face held a look of surprise when Jason's long dagger entered his throat. There was no scream. Jason thought it must have been such a surprise to suddenly see him there that the goblin did not try to defend itself. But he later changed his mind as he discovered the goblins had a difficult time seeing him at all!

It wasn't the dark that prevented them from seeing him since their night raid indicated they had excellent night vision. Something else was happening. Was it a side effect of him being an off-worlder? Or did it have to do with the weapons or an item he carried? Whatever it was, it appeared the goblins could not see him until he struck. He recalled the third goblin that stopped in its run earlier that night and looked straight at him and then went on; it must not have been able to see him even then.

After about twenty goblins were killed in this manner, half the goblins stopped their main attack to search for him. They waved their spears and swords in front of them in an effort to find the mystery attacker. Now confident that he was invisible to the nasty little assailants, he started taking his time, picking his targets and maneuvering unseen to slash his victims from behind. He would appear momentarily on his attack and then disappear again.

He tried an experiment since it seemed the advantage was his. He knelt and momentarily laid down the black sword, hovering his hand a couple inches from the hilt. Almost immediately, the goblins were upon him. He snatched the blade up again and leaped into a diving roll. The spot where he had been was filled with goblin spears.

Unfortunately, a spear also nicked him. He felt foolish for testing his sword in the middle of combat when so much was at stake. He was not bleeding badly, not enough to give a blood trail for the goblins to find him, but it did hurt and seemed to drain some of his fighting zeal.

Invisible again, he resumed his grim task. By then, all the goblins were transfixed by the carnage being wrought among them by this invisible warrior. Unsure where to attack, several goblins threw spears into thin air hoping to score a lucky hit on him. After he slew ten more and beset the eleventh, a lead goblin amongst the attacking group called a retreat.

The goblins ran for the woods with Jason in pursuit, slicing as he went. Even the woods were not safe for them as six more died by his blade amongst the trees. Soon, they were fully routed, fleeing to wherever they called home.

After cleaning both his sword and dagger on the clothes of slain combatants, he sheathed his blades. He attended to his wound, but the bleeding had already stopped. It was not yet healed, but he could almost feel the flesh knit itself back together under the scab. He picked up his bow and empty quiver on his way back to the farm house. Bodies of goblins were being dragged from the house by several women when he arrived.

The heavyset woman quickly grabbed a spear when she saw him nearing the house. She eyed him suspiciously, and for good reason since he, as a boy, was about the same size as their recent oppressors. He continued forward, hoping the light from the lamps in the house would reveal him.

The woman commanded, "Stop right there, you."

He called out, "I'm Jason...Is there anything I can do to help?"

The woman leveled her spear and stalked toward him. After what they had been through, he did not blame her for her caution. The woman came closer and then peered about.

Lowering her spear, she questioned, "Are you alone?"

"Yes," replied Jason.

"From your empty quiver and the blood covering your clothes, I might think you are our deliverer, but... But you are only a boy. This...this could not be," stammered the woman in disbelief.

"It doesn't matter to me where credit is given. I only returned to see if I can help in your time of distress. I'm merely a traveler on my way to Chanderlon and will leave when things are cleaned up here."

The woman nodded, decided the boy was not a threat, and turned toward the house. The dog had been killed in the first charge. The farmer and one-time warrior had died from his wounds. The woman and her three daughters, who were nearly adults, fought as well as any man. Together, the women had killed a score of goblins inside the house.

The eldest daughter had a severe gash on her arm, which was now bandaged. The large farm wife had multiple nicks and cuts of her own but had killed many goblins at the front of her house with her man. A time of mourning would be soon, but for now, she had tasks to complete.

They had a simple, predawn breakfast and set to the arduous task of burying the dead. The farmer had a wagon and an old mule, which Jason borrowed to haul goblin remains into the deep woods to deposit for the forest to take care of. With the help of the youngest girl, who was about seventeen, he labored to load expired goblins into the wagon.

They collected what valuables they could, an occasional precious stone or a copper piece or two. Some of the swords, bows, and spears were salvageable and could be sold, but none of it could make up for their loss.

The mother and two older daughters dug a grave for their deceased. Jason collected some of his arrows from goblin bodies. As he did this, he noticed the women talking about him in whispered voices. He ignored them and continued with his work.

It took seven wagon loads to haul all the goblin corpses away, and it was late afternoon before they finished. The farm wife brought him some food and water.

"You have done the work of five men, Jason. You deserve more than what we can give you, but we have talked it over and would like you to stay. We need a man here, and you are definitely that—despite being a boy. You are alone, and we would welcome you into our family," entreated the older woman earnestly.

Touched by her sincerity, he replied, "I appreciate your offer, but I am on a quest to be reunited with my own family. You and your daughters can run your farm if you have the will. As soon as men discover the beauty of your daughters, I am sure you will find many young men willing to sign on. But I will stay with you tonight to make sure the goblins don't come back."

That evening, the girls sang songs of mourning. They had beautiful voices. Afterward, Jason told them the Creator's love story, how God the Father sent his son to mankind, knowing that mankind would kill his physical form and how with the Holy Ghost all three raised Jesus's body, promising the way for mankind to do the same thing. He felt a little awkward telling the story since he was not sure himself how God related to this world. He felt a responsibility to tell what he could, but he had not thought it all through yet.

Did Jesus die for these people too? He remembered a verse saying that all of creation was waiting for the revelation of the glory of Christ to be revealed in us. But were these people a part of that creation? He did not know. Perhaps he would be enlightened upon hearing the full prophecy, assuming the prophecy was from God.

The next morning, he left after a breakfast of cooked oats and toast. The four women saw him off with a hug from each and made him promise to return if he needed a place to live. The farm wife packed him a lunch of bread and cheese and wrapped it in a thin cloth.

"God bless you," he said as he turned to leave.

The farm wife wiped a tear as she watched him leave and smiled to herself as she whispered, "May God bless you too, Jason."

The traveling that day was mostly uneventful. He grew tired eventually and looked for a place to sleep. He spied a tall hill through the trees and cut through the woods toward it. Before reaching it, he found a gigantic tree with huge branches. This was as safe a sleeping spot as any, so climbing into the tree, he made his bed upon a huge bole and finished the lunch the farmer's wife provided. He drifted to sleep, his thoughts shifting between his wife and children, the farm family he had left that morning, and the many events that had transpired in the months since the lab accident.

He slept through the night and into the predawn light before climbing down, feeling rested. He was about to find his way back to the road when he felt the need to pray, so he decided to climb to the top of the nearby hill. It was not an easy climb, with thorny brambles blocking the way. One side of the hill had a rocky face that looked like a lion's. When he reached the summit, he had a wide view of the forest he had come through as well as a hilly area up ahead. There was also a river to the east.

He prayed, asking the Lord to show him his purpose in the strange and dangerous world he had been brought to. He prayed for protection for his family while he was gone. He prayed his wife would hold out hope for his return and not seek another man. He also prayed for the farm family and their protection from the marauding goblins. Finally, he prayed for discernment—wisdom to determine who was friend and who was foe in this messed up world.

After praying, he pulled out the black sword. Did it only make him invisible to goblins, he wondered? Or did it always make him invisible? Or must there be some threat present to invoke invisibility? Did it work in the daylight? Why did he become visible the moment he struck with the blade in his hand? He knew nothing about it, really, least of all from where its power was derived. Was it magic or some kind of technology so far advanced even he would call it magic? What was magic anyway?

He knew God condemned the use of magic for the ancient Israelites, but Christians were not under the same laws as the Israelites. Jesus's resurrection from the grave brought about a new covenant, but he did not see how that would change God's commandments against divination or sorcery. But why would God condemn magic in the first place?

Perhaps magic was a natural force that could be tapped into in order to perform apparently supernatural things. Or was it a spiritual power granted by beings not of this physical realm? Was there good magic and bad magic, or was it all bad in God's eyes?

He had no answers to any of those questions, nor did he know of any way to get answers. No one in this world seemed to have anything that looked like a Bible, and few had shown any outward signs of religion of any sort.

The black blade, whatever it was, represented power. Maybe he was meant to find it. This might even be the whole reason God had brought him here—to find the ebony blade. With such a mysterious weapon, a warrior would be invincible in battle. Or, he thought with a shudder, an assassin from whom no one would be safe. He could sell such a blade and make a fortune, but think of the havoc it could cause if it fell into the wrong hands. He would be naive to think he could possess its power all to himself.

Jason did not like the way his thoughts were going. He remembered the warning of his home country's forefathers— "absolute power corrupts absolutely." He clung to the dark sword. With this blade, he was safe from Trombul, if the troll was still alive and pursuing him. He could do good with it. It would help him complete his quest and get home quicker.

Of course, he did not even know what his quest was exactly. If finding this black blade was all it took to be a hero, then God could have arranged for someone from this world to find it.

If powerful weapons were needed, he could eventually manufacture something like a Gatling gun. For that matter, God could have arranged for an assault rifle to be found amongst the debris of the destroyed laboratory with a good rationale for it being there. A martial artist should prepare to use every strategy available, but in the long run, a martial artist knows there are times when fighting is not always the best way, and winning is not always the goal.

While the black sword had served its purpose at the farm, he wanted to please God above all else. He made his decision. He must bury it right there. If God wanted him to use it, he could always come back to find it.

From the largest rock at the top of the hill, he took seven strides to the east. He scooped a deep hole in the earth and buried the black blade. He felt foolish doing it. Perhaps he was. After all, why toss away your greatest advantage? But he felt a struggle of morality and conscience within him, and in the end, he felt right in setting the strange and powerful sword down.

As he journeyed the rest of that day, he felt naked without the dark sword. As night approached, just before bedding down, he asked God if he should go back for the blade but received no comforting thoughts. Silence was not especially indicative of God's plan, of course, but he still found the silence within his thoughts an indication that burying the sword was the right thing to do—for now.

He dreamed as he slept. In his dream, he went back for the blade in the dark and climbed the lion mountain. The dark blade seemed to be calling for him, drawing him with its power like a moth toward the flames. But even in his dream, he struggled with himself and felt dread, while at the same time, he was magnetized, full of desire for the power of magic.

He went to the indicator rock and took seven strides to the east and started digging with his bare hands. Feeling the sheath he cleaned off the dirt and reached for the hilt as soon as he saw it, but something was wrong. As he touched the sword, it turned into a clawed hand and grabbed him around his wrist. He tried to jerk away, but it wouldn't let go. He heaved with all his might, but instead of pulling up the sword, he pulled a troll out of the ground.

It was Trombul!

Fear filled him as he vainly tried to get away while the troll laughed raucously, drawing him toward the hideously powerful fangs, dirt and mud falling from its face. The troll's other clawed hand raked at him, but instead of ripping just his flesh, it ripped to his very soul, opening tears that felt like they would never heal.

Kicking and raking down the monster's shins with the edge of his shoe should have been painful, but Trombul didn't even notice. Instead, he was jerked bodily into the air as the troll howled in triumph. Jason drove his left hand into the hideous giant's throat as he was drawn towards its maw full of pointed and snaggled teeth. The creature was overpowering him and there was nothing he could do.

At that moment, he resisted, not just physically, but spiritually, turning every fiber of his being toward God, calling on his Creator. Immediately, he felt himself falling from the gargantuan's grip, while the vision fled, and he awoke from his nightmare, breathing heavily. The ragged rips in his soul still gaped wide, but his eyes were on the Creator again.

Then, although he could not actually see anything, it was as though he were suddenly bathed in a soft light. It was a healing light, and he felt the reassuring presence of both the Father and the Son within it. The holes in his soul were filled with tangible glowing that knitted his being back together and he felt healed.

The feeling of peace filled him and enabled him to sleep deeply again, without fear, for the rest of the night. He was not afraid of anything, not even of Trombul lurking somewhere in the dark, seeking him, for his God was his protector.

The next day, Jason felt no longing for the sword and now realized he had taken his eyes off God for the lure of the power the sword offered. He traveled merrily the rest of that day, feeling light of feet and spirit. During the next few days he came across several more farmhouses, all of whom gladly accepted help with chores in return for food.

CHAPTER 14
Deologue 3

"We have discovered the source of the dimensional corridor to be a planet very much like our playground, although it was very difficult to get any answers from the inhabitants," said the winged being named Rastuken.

The two minor gods stood before Xan Rukkah, seated on a throne, in the hollow where a nose would be of a giant crystal skull. The house-sized crystal was set in an enormous cavern full of brightly colored stalactites and stalagmites. Other gods, including Axialla, were present as well, curious to hear the report.

"We have allies in spiritual rebels everywhere. Surely such an event didn't go unnoticed by them," responded Xan Rukkah.

Jazeel, the one wearing bizarre war paint and feathers, spoke up, "The event took them by surprise because the gate formed was the result of an accident. We tried more direct means with the humans but were blocked by spiritual servants of the Creator. We went undercover and disguised ourselves, but even then, it was amazing how little the humans know of opening gates. All we were able to discover was there were no children present at the time of the accident."

Axialla stepped eagerly forward. "It is as I said, the child is more than what he appears."

Xan Rukkah stood. "Or he is merely a lost child who stumbled onto the entry point and tried to help the dying humans. I assume you have killed him by now, though."

"No my liege, the boy has survived the attack of my pet falcon, but it seems to have been without interference from the Creator. The boy prevailed over it and killed it."

"Without the help of the Creator?" bellowed the giant god, outraged. "No child could have killed your giant avian monster without help."

"If the Creator helped him, it was very subtle, using the boy's own strength."

"Yes, yes, but with that failed, did you not seduce him with magic?"

"He did take the bait. A very powerful item that would have nearly made him invulnerable—the Moon Blade. He discovered the magic when he used it to route an army of goblins... But then, he buried it."

"Buried it!" cried the titan in disbelief. The other gods present echoed the sentiment. "Then you are right, Axialla. This is not a lost child from our world, for no one would bury such power unless they were confident in another source."

Rastuken spoke up, "Then Jazeel and myself will raise up an army of monsters and crush this lad."

"No, no," said Xan Rukkah thoughtfully. "The Creator has not tipped his hand in an all-out war, nor shall we. There will be time for that, but right now, we must not appear weak and afraid. Axialla, do you have another subtle strategy for dealing with this?"

"Yes, my lord. It has already been implemented, though it may take some time. Haglar, the witch of Vorkana, has sent a troll to retrieve the boy, and it has found his trail again. This troll is magically quested to not give up."

"Ah, that is good. Trolls are harder to kill than birds. I give this matter of the boy to you for now, Axialla. Let me know how it goes."

"Yes, my lord." Axialla bowed, turned and walked out.

She exited the cave and walked out on a dock misted with clouds, but instead of overlooking a sea, it opened to the immensity of space. With stars all around, both above and below, she leaned on the rail and looked upon a small planet with intense interest.

"Those gods are all fools," she said to herself. "They are not watching as they should be, and I alone know how much the Creator meddles in the affairs of men."

She thought back to the previous year when a king in the north raised an army of animated corpses, using magic which she provided. They terrified the locals and would have swept the populous off the coast, except for one seer who called for help from the Creator. The seer was only a young woman, a teenage girl, actually, who boldly stood blocking the way of the army and with just a word, undid all the mighty magic.

Yes, the Creator had his followers, even among those whose parentage had been corrupted by magic, yet the gods did not see it. Perhaps they did, but chose to ignore it. This boy was another.

She remembered back to when she, like the other gods, served the Creator. Even then, no one knew his name. He had made them powerful beings, each with a realm of powers that were their own. Their natural forms were nothing like they were now. They had been a huge variety of creatures that would fill the mundane world with wonder and awe.

But then, the Creator made, as the pinnacle of his creation, mankind.

A lowly creature with an animal structure but in the Creator's own image. These he proudly declared his own children, destined to eventually rule the universe with him.

The Creator even had the audacity to have them, the mighty spirit creatures, watch over and even serve mankind. This caused an uproar in all dimensions. Some even led open rebellions, declaring themselves the enemy of God and of mankind. Some rebellions were more subtle, such as theirs.

Over time, their nature, even their appearance, changed to become more like their envied enemy. At first, some used it as an excuse to help deceive mankind. Others, such as Xan Rukkah, found themselves lusting after mankind and changed to make themselves more attractive.

She had personally changed too, not only to more easily deceive humans, but to fit in with the fetishes of the gods so she could manipulate them as well. It was her step in power. Although she was considered second in command to Xan Rukkah, she desired to rule it all. Some day, at the right time, she would make her move.

There were no illusions she could ever beat the Creator in an outright war, but the Creator had made a mistake. When he created free will, he also created laws to give a semblance of order to the chaos he knew would follow. It was with those very laws that she would tie his hands.

She had a plan.

CHAPTER 15
The Prophecy in Full

Eventually, the woods opened to rolling hills interspersed with meadows, and the number of farmhouses and cottages increased. Wagons filled with grain, fruit, and vegetables carried farmers' produce from harvest to market. The laborers and traveling merchants ignored Jason and everyone else as they passed each other, characteristic of people accustomed to crowds.

By mid afternoon, he reached the outskirts of a large town which surrounded a tall, ancient-looking castle. Smoke settled among the variety of squat buildings from cooking or heating fires as the fall sun offered less warmth. Coming from the clean air of the forests, the smell of smoke was noticeable, along with the occasional whiff of raw sewage.

A passerby confirmed the city was, indeed, Chanderlon. There were no walls to define where Chanderlon actually started, but he eventually found himself on a cobblestone street surrounded by wood and brick buildings. People busily came and went in a hurried manner characteristic of all cities. He could see down a side street to a large river which ran through the south side of the municipality, a park district of groomed trees along the banks. Many bridges crossed the river, allowing easy access to both sides.

Feeling overcome by the sudden surge of humanity and the chaos of sounds and smells, Jason traveled furtively along the side of the main street, trying to avoid getting stepped on or run over by the frequent carts. Although archaic, the atmosphere of the town dispelled all thoughts of trolls, goblins, and giant birds. It was just too incredible, too unbelievable to think about such things in this setting.

Entering a market square, he could not resist buying some pastries and candy. The merchants seemed surprised at a little boy who actually wanted to buy their products, rather than steal them. At first, they tried to shoo him off, but when he produced a coin, they instantly became all smiles.

Not knowing the value of the baubles, he'd retrieved from the bird's nest; he only offered the coppery looking coins with a greenish tinge. The merchants seemed very pleased but did not offer to return change. He made it a point to observe other transactions to see if he could learn anything, although he could not see much similarity between his tarnished coins and the shinier ones of the townsfolk.

The sweets, made mostly with honey, tasted too strong at first. Accustomed to such a bland diet for so long, it was overpowering. The shot of sugary substances made him feel energetic, and he bought some more. After wolfing that down, he decided to buy more for eating later; however, once he got it in hand, he found he could not stop from putting it in his mouth.

He took a swig of water to help wash it down, and that is when his stomach rebelled. Not being used to such substances, he felt sick and made his way to an alley. Just making it to the entrance, his body repulsed the foreign stuff against a wall. An old man sitting at the back of the alley, repairing a basket, saw him, and broke out in raucous laughter.

The laughter followed him as he left the alley. He felt a little better but vowed to be more careful in returning to some semblance of more "civilized" food. He went by the sweets stands and wasn't even tempted to look at them.

Inquiring of a merchant as to the whereabouts of Father Varigold, she pointed without hesitation to a large temple that could be seen at the end of a nearby street. It had tall stately pillars with flying buttresses along the sides and base reliefs of gods, goddesses, heroes, and monsters lining the frieze.

The main public access to the massive building was up wide stairs in front. At the top a large open porch held many altars, apparently to the same god. A large statue or idol representing said god stood over the main altar with his sword outstretched. It was reminiscent of images of statues Jason had seen on his home world of the Greek god, Zeus.

Not being able to read the local language yet, he had no idea to whom this temple was dedicated and did not particularly care. He had not come to worship. Other people had, though, and several worshipers were placing their offerings upon the altars, mostly fruits or vegetables, although some placed money. When the worshipers left, priests appeared out of nowhere and cleaned the altars, taking items through side doors. He felt relieved to see neither blood nor child sacrifices as was often mentioned in relation to pagan gods in the Bible.

He approached a priest carrying a basket of offerings just cleared from an altar and asked, "May I see Father Varigold?"

He felt awkward in using the title "Father," since Jesus instructed his disciples not to use such terms in a spiritual sense, but still he did not want to antagonize or alienate people he needed information from. Even the Apostle Paul was willing to bend in order to be all things to all people so that some might be saved.

"Father Varigold is not seeing anyone right now. Come back next week," the priest responded tersely and abruptly departed.

Taken aback, but relieved he had stumbled on the correct abode of Varigold, he wandered about the temple in search of another acolyte, not willing to accept "no" for an answer just yet.

Upon seeing a younger priest, he hurried to him. "I have an emergency and must speak to Father Varigold. Can you take me to him?"

"Father Varigold cannot see anyone right now," came another brusque reply.

"Why not?" countered Jason hurriedly before the man could disappear.

The youngish altar attendant looked a little distressed trying to come up with an adequate excuse. "Father Varigold is indisposed, if you know what I mean..." he said, trailing off.

"No, I don't know what you mean. Is he going to the bathroom? I can wait," countered Jason reasonably.

"No, it is...it is more than that," stammered the acolyte.

"You mean he's dead?" asked Jason.

"No, no, nothing like that!" exclaimed the acolyte.

"Then he must be sick," declared Jason.

The acolyte quickly put his hand over Jason's mouth and drew him close and through a side door. "You must not say that in the temple," admonished the young priest in a harsh whisper.

Jason queried, "What's wrong with admitting a cleric is sick?"

The acolyte looked exasperatedly at him. "You must be new here. Our priests are healers. The curing of disease is one of our specialties. It is proof that Xan Rukkah is the strongest of the gods."

Jason shrugged. "Then why can't you heal Father Varigold?"

The young priest wrung his hands. "Our top healers say they do not know, but at some point, everyone dies and cannot be healed. They say it is a sickness of the soul and not the body, so physical healing does no good."

"I must see Father Varigold before he dies. It has something to do with his dream. Can you bring me to him?" asked Jason.

The young acolyte looked at him with surprise. "You...you know about the dream?"

"Why, yes," replied Jason, trying to exude calm and confidence, as if it should be obvious to everyone that he would know.

"No one knows of this outside the temple. Only Brother Dorrian has made very discreet inquiries on the temple's behalf. In fact, I think that whatever the dream is about, it must be very dangerous, because our leaders have forbidden us to mention it again. Father Varigold fell sick after Brother

Dorrian's return, and they think further mention will make it worse."

Jason looked pleadingly at the acolyte, sensing he had found an "in" with the young man by way of his insight into the priest's vision. "Father Varigold's dream might involve me, and I must know the rest of the dream if I am to complete my quest."

The priest looked at him with astonishment, then uncertainty, then compassion, a whole range of conflicting thoughts obviously coursing through his head. Finally, he whispered in a conspiratorial tone, "Come with me, and if anyone asks you, say you are here to make restitution."

The priest took him by the hand, which felt odd since he did not view himself as a little boy, and led him down a stairwell to a wide, pillared corridor. They passed several priests along the way who only glanced at the two curiously.

After a long walk, they reached a curtained room. A priest entered the corridor carrying a large tray of what looked like wafers. It was the one called Brother Dorrian. The older priest glanced at the two of them, then back again at Jason more closely.

"What have we here?" Brother Dorrian demanded.

"This boy was caught stealing from the temple." The acolyte squeezed Jason's hand conspiratorially.

"I am here to make restitution," Jason said on cue, trying to look guilty.

Brother Dorrian nodded and was about to go, then turned again. "There is something familiar about you, boy."

"I have seen the error of my ways, Father," said Jason, purposely misusing the title. "If I have stolen anything from you, I will repay it tenfold."

"My, that is generous," said Dorrian after a moment's pause. "But I don't think you owe me anything. Go in peace, my son." Brother Dorrian turned and continued down the corridor. Jason's faked contrition was enough to curtail the high priest's interrogation.

When the man was gone, the acolyte said, "You did well. Look, here is the room. I will wait for you out here."

Jason expressed his thanks, pushed the heavy curtains aside, and entered the room. It was mostly empty save a single bed, and without any ornamentation to cover the stone walls. The room was dark except for the sunlight streaming through the lone, barred window. The rays shone on a large, lavish bed in which rested an old man with white hair and a long flowing beard. A cleric seated on a stool next to the bed attended to him. Except for the splendid bed and the room's size, it looked like a prison cell to Jason.

"What are you doing here?" demanded the attendant harshly.

"I wish to speak to Father Varigold."

The attendant arose and started toward Jason with the obvious intent of expelling him when Father Varigold spoke. "Mussan, my son, who is here?"

"It is a boy, Father Varigold," said Mussan.

"A boy...how unusually brash. Have him come here," said the ailing man in a weak voice.

Jason walked over on his own, not trusting the attendant. "I am here to see you. My name is Jason."

"What is it you want, child?" The old man sat up higher against his pillows in order to see Jason better. As he sat up the blanket, a multicolored quilt of various shapes cleverly pieced together to create the scene of a golden sun with blue and green surrounding it, fell back to reveal the yellow robes and a sun shaped pennant of the man's office hanging from a gold chain around his neck.

White eyebrows and a long, slim, white mustache matched the man's white hair and beard. The thin, aged face, lined with wrinkles, sallow with illness and sunken eyes, smiled with kindness upon the sight of the boy.

Jason said, "I have heard part of your dream from a priest named Dorrian, and I wish to hear the rest."

Mussan, a stocky man in plain tan robes, prematurely balding, appeared to be in shock as he gaped at Jason and moved as if to stop him, but instead rushed out of the room. He could be heard shouting in the corridor, summoning others.

"I fear my fellow priests do not like my dream. But from what I hear, my dream does not matter, for the hero did not come." said Father Varigold woefully.

"Please, tell me the rest of the dream."

"First, young man, you must tell me how you know of the dream, for it has been kept a secret," said the elder priest.

"I learned of it from Dorrian when he inquired of Haglar the Watcher. I am the one who attended them," explained Jason.

"You traveled all the way from the realms of Harvella to ask me about my dream? Why would you do such a thing?" asked the old man incredulously.

Suddenly, a group of clerics armed with clubs and staves stormed the room. Jason became conscious that he had forgotten to stash his weapons and backpack prior to coming here and probably looked very suspicious. A man tried to grab him.

"I will tell you only after you tell me your dream," said Jason quickly, hoping to pique the priest's curiosity. The man was pulling Jason away.

"Leave the boy be," commanded Father Varigold in a voice that sounded stronger than a moment ago.

"But, Father," the attendant Mussan started, "the boy is armed. He may have been sent to—"

"Kill me?" finished Father Varigold, the irony fairly dripping from his lip. He coughed a few times and started laughing. He motioned to Jason. "Come near, my boy, and I will tell you my dream." The cleric holding him let go.

Just then, Brother Dorrian walked into the room and demanded, "What is the meaning of this? Father Varigold needs his rest."

Mussan bowed before him. "Father Varigold is about to tell his dream to this young boy."

Brother Dorrian went immediately to the bedside. "Father," he said, "this dream has upset you more than it should, and you have made yourself sick over it. Let us not revisit this painful vision, which has brought you such despair. There is no hero who will bring light into this world, for we must make our own light. We only have to believe in our god and look to ourselves for our answers."

"You are wrong, my son Dorrian, for the dream has power yet. See who it has brought us." Father Varigold gestured toward Jason. "You!" exclaimed Brother Dorrian in recognition. "The slave of Haglar. What are you doing here? Did Haglar send you?"

Jason replied, "I am no slave, and Haglar did not send me. I have come this distance on my own and paid the price in many trials to come and hear the dream. Please do not hinder me when I am so close to my destination."

Brother Dorrian opened his mouth to speak, but Father Varigold interrupted. "See, you did not come back as empty- handed as you thought, Dorrian my son, and we may understand more when we have met this youth's demand."

"Wait," said Brother Dorrian. "If you must speak of the dream again, it is not wise for so many to hear. Allow me to clear the room." Brother Dorrian herded the clerics out and gave Jason a parting look of distaste as he left.

Jason was at last alone with the old man again and spoke, "You have had other dreams before?" The old man nodded, his eyes bright. Jason continued, "This dream was different from the others?"

Again Father Varigold nodded and added excitedly, "It was more a revelation than a dream, for I was transported elsewhere, away from this bed and this temple. I walked by the river, feeling the grass beneath my feet, breathing the cool air into my lungs.

It was far too vivid, far too real to be a mere dream. This is what I saw...

I left the river and floated above the world, carried not by wings or sail but held aloft by the very wind. I sensed a presence—an intelligence—there with me. A winged man clothed in shimmering white and radiant with a light that emanated from within his body came to me. He spoke, 'Man of earth, sand, and clay, behold what has happened and what will happen to your world.' I sensed myself passing through time and age upon age, and I saw the world with all the gods and goddesses seated above it in the clouds. There was Palansod, Veridith, Scoron, and many others.

In a throne above them all was Xan Rukkah, the god I worship. He stood and summoned the attention of the gods and goddesses, all busy with their own conversations and diversions. 'Hear me, my fellow titans and powers of the universe. We have been given this plane by the Creator to nourish, to raise, and to make of it something valuable in his eyes, but do you think he will let us keep it? No. When he returns, he will take it back for himself after all our hard work. He says we will be rewarded—but the rewards will not be what we crave. We desire—no, we deserve—glory and worship. That is something we can have now and keep if we make this realm contemptible to the Creator. If we darken it with such evil that the Creator wouldn't want it, then he will forget it and forget us, and we will be free of his rule. So let us corrupt this world with our powers and deform all of creation, so it is no longer recognizable to him.'

The entire pantheon was pleased with this plan, but there was one problem. Man at that time only worshiped the Creator and would not accept the demands of the gods and goddesses. The plan was frustrated because man was gifted with free will. Finally, one of the gods seduced a woman to accept the gift of magic. From her were monsters introduced and magic spread through the universe like a plague. Men voluntarily gave up their free will for power and unwittingly became pawns in the gods' game of chaos and destruction, warring against those who exhibited free will or worshiped the Creator. Soon, darkness engulfed the whole world, and men became so deformed they were not recognizable as men anymore. Despair, chaos, and death were the future of our people. The Creator was forgotten. I felt horror and dread within my heart at this bleak revelation.

But then, a bright light came out of nowhere and fell from the sky, striking the world with great force in the mountains. From the fire of the explosion walked a powerfully built man, his countenance mighty, and his hair shining white. I knew he was a hero sent from the Creator, and a voice rang inside my head, calling his name: Juggernaut. Wherever he trod, light followed his path.

The gods hated the hero, and one at a time, each in their turn, sought to kill the Juggernaut, wanting glory for themselves. Each sent their greatest fighters and fiercest magic to seduce or kill the Creator's hero, but the Juggernaut was unstoppable. Light emanated from the Juggernaut and spread on its own—pure light from the Creator himself. The light circled and returned from all sources and strengthened the hero.

Then the winged man turned to me and said, 'The light of the Juggernaut is given strength by the light of others. Although the hero himself cannot be defeated, it is up to mankind to change.'

"Then I awoke from the dream, shaking and vexed in body, mind, and spirit. The memory of it burns inside my head, and I relive it all now upon the retelling of it."

"Why were you shaking?" asked Jason.

"Out of fear for my world and fear for myself. If the dream is true, then Xan Rukkah is no true god, and I can no longer serve him," whispered Father Varigold.

Jason held Father Varigold's eyes with his own. It was as if the elder had relived the dream as he told it and his eyes betrayed the fear he had felt before. "I will tell you now why I have come. It is because the dream is true, and I am the one the dream spoke of."

Father Varigold's eyes showed puzzlement. "But what of the man I saw, the one who is the Juggernaut?"

"I am that man, but I…" Jason struggled for the words to help Father Varigold understand. "I am…enchanted," said Jason finally. "My true age is fifty years, or at least it was when I left my own world. I was known as Jason the Juggernaut Bristol, a warrior's instructor and servant of the Creator. Somehow, someway, only the Creator knows, I came here to your world in the form of a little boy. Perhaps when time in this world passes, I will grow to become again the man you saw in your dream."

The priest's face showed his struggle in trying to believe. "I see you as only a boy, with a story any clever street urchin could come up with to get a hand out. How can you prove your identity?"

Jason paused, taken a little aback. He had thought of many ways he could convince his wife, someone who knew him intimately, but how could he convince a complete stranger on a different world that he was not just a child? He had the experience, knowledge, and skills of a lifetime, which he could demonstrate over time, but how to coalesce all that into a single statement he could say right now?

He shook his head and said, "I could tell you of my life, of wonders, of my wife and children who are older than what I appear now, but still an inventive child could make this all up. No, I will show you the light, for it is more important than believing in me anyway. The light is not something you can see with your eyes. It is something you see with your heart and with your spirit.

It is the knowledge that God, the Creator, loved us so much that he sent to us his son to be born and raised as a man.

"This son of God lived a perfect, guiltless life, and then broke the bonds placed on us by the law by paying the ultimate penalty of the law—death. An innocent man, who was more than a man, for he was the son of God himself, allowed himself to be slain for the redemption of man. The law of death was broken, for after three days, he raised himself from the grave.

"Because of this, not only do we have the hope of living eternally, but a promise to be adopted into God's own family through baptism—to become brothers and sisters to the Son. The light is this and more. It tells us how we can accept the gift of adoption."

The old man trembled. "We can become God's children? This is more wonderful than the legends of yore. Then your presence here verifies the dream is true. If I renounce my god, will the Creator be able to protect me from the wrath of Xan Rukkah?"

Jason thought for a long time, reaching for the best way to answer the frail priest's heartfelt query. It was obvious to him the old man was shaken to the core. He figured that he would have been too if he had spent his entire life in service to a false god only to discover at the end of life that he had been serving a lie the whole time. He directed his thoughts to God in the form of a prayer, asking for words of truth to relate to a troubled soul in desperate need of assurance and pardon.

"If you are not willing to face the wrath of Xan Rukkah, how can you be worthy of the Creator? You have spent your life in service against the Creator. How would you atone? I think a willingness to face the wrath of Xan Rukkah is an excellent way to start living in the light. Remember, the gods could do nothing to man until they left the light. But you have lived long in darkness, so it will not be easy and you only have a little time."

The old man was trembling fiercely, so Jason grasped his hand. It was cold, but his own hands were warm. Father Varigold felt the warmth and power course through him, and his shaking eased. "What will happen to our whole world if we do not accept the light?" Father Varigold whispered.

"On my world, the son of God came across a tree, expecting fruit, but when he found none, he cursed the tree, and it died. Your gods are wrong and do not know the nature of the Creator. When the Creator comes back, he will expect fruit. When he doesn't find any, he will be angry. He does not forget. He does not change."

Father Varigold rose off the pillow and swung his feet from under the covers. He stood up out of bed, imbued with strength. "I understand your meaning. The gods are doomed and us along with them unless we can break the ties with these so-called gods. You have healed me, child, and restored my courage. I will think on what you have said and please come again, for I would love to hear more about the Creator."

Jason turned to leave. "I would be happy to return, but if you hear the Creator calling you, don't wait. Answer immediately." Jason walked through the curtain. Brother Dorrian and a small group of older priests waited outside. They said nothing to Jason and let him pass, after which, they immediately rushed into the room.

Not seeing the young priest who escorted him earlier, Jason continued down the corridor and exited the temple from the other side, which opened directly to the market. There were tables lining the temple wall manned by priests, selling excess food items from the sacrifices. There were many customers cuing up to take advantage of the discount prices.

When the priests at the tables saw him exit the temple, they all stopped in mid conversation to stare. Word must have spread quickly; here was one of the few individuals granted access to the innermost sanctum and permitted to speak with Father Varigold about his dream. They seemed poised to hear some grand announcement from the boy, as if he would invoke some great power or utter a great prophecy. But all he did was ask for an apple from the priest nearest to him, who nodded and handed one over. Then the boy walked away.

As he circled around the temple to find the main street, he heard Father Varigold's voice ring out from the other side of the barred window. Several other pedestrians stopped and stared. "I, Father Varigold," he began in a strong, clear voice, "do hereby denounce Xan Rukkah as a false god, along with all other gods and goddesses, and I accept the Creator as the one and only true God!"

Cries of shock and disapproval rose from the bystanders, as well as the other priests in the room. Then came a cry of pain from the elder Varigold and the sickening noise of weapons striking flesh. The unwitting eavesdroppers quickly turned their heads and left, not wanting to be recognized, but Jason ran to the window with his bow drawn, rage and disgust rising within him. At the window, he discovered he was too short to look in and probably too late to do anything. Varigold was probably already dead.

He wanted to storm the temple, but it occurred to him that they might seek to kill him next. He felt torn. He turned right and left, seeking something he could do, somewhere he could run. His body sought to take action, but his mind sought to reason, like a truck with the gas pedal to the floor, but the emergency brake pulled tight. As he fumed outside, looking helplessly up at the window where Varigold had made his atonement to the Creator, reason caught up with his body, and he gave up seeking revenge and instead mingled among the crowded street to disappear. Eventually, he wandered to the river park area where the trees were beautiful in their fall colors.

Now he knew the entire prophecy, and he knew what he was up against. However, he still was not sure what he should do. Should he begin preaching on the street corners? Who would listen to the silly talk of a ten-year-old boy? It was now obvious God had planned for his arrival here and had work for him to do before sending him home. He felt a little impatient, but after considering he should be dead several times over, he would not complain. Still, he would pray for God to speed his way home.

And what of Varigold? Was he this world's first convert? The man feared the wrath of Xan Rukkah, and the clerics of Xan Rukkah dispensed that wrath swiftly and effectively. This man chose to follow the Creator and within minutes was dead. Why did God allow this? With the old priest's prestige, he could have done much for furthering the Creator's cause on this world.

Knowing how God sometimes works, he suspected there were many prophecies and people whose hearts had been touched to prepare the way. Were they preparing the way for him? But who was he but a mere child to all who saw him? Even as a man in his previous life, he tended toward shyness, despite the fact he had to overcome it daily as a martial arts instructor and part-time preacher. Now he felt like a small, lost boy who just wanted to go home.

He was probably in danger too, though hopefully not imminent. The clerics might suppose that he would slip back into the obscurity from where he came, a little boy whom almost none would believe.

Pulling a piece of smoked meat from his pack, he ate his evening meal. A town crier announced the news of the death of Father Varigold, who apparently died of old age.

Old age really falls hard, he thought ruefully. Also, the crier announced that Brother Dorrian had now taken the position of Grand High Priest and the title Father Dorrian. Jason felt weary and hid himself in the roots of a tree and, after his prayers, fell asleep.

CHAPTER 16
The Garden Secret

The next morning, Jason shook off the frosty morning chill and made his way to the main market square and bought more pastries for breakfast. As he sat atop a low wall studying the market, he wondered how he, as a child, could fulfill his mission for God.

Maybe the prophecy, even though there seemed to be no doubt it was about him, was not as it seemed and perhaps was not even from God for, after all, the priest who received it was not even a follower of the Creator. Then, feeling a little ashamed, he remembered the old man died because of that prophecy when he repented and chose to follow God.

Perhaps that was the whole reason for it, so that one priest could become converted, and now, his mission was done, and he could go home. That was a cheerful thought, although what about the part "it was up to mankind to change"? That sounded like this mission was more than just to one priest. Was he expected to undo all the damage these false gods had done, or was he only to be the beginning?

He finished the last of his pastries, and with his hunger satisfied, considered his situation. He must plan as if he were not going home soon. Would his gems and coins hold out or would he have to work? He could invest his treasure, which would be the wise thing to do, but it would also be a distraction. After all, since he was on a mission for God, would not God take care of him? Indeed, had not God already done so?

Of course, to gain the treasure, he'd nearly become feed to a falcon. His feeble efforts, with God's help, enabled him to kill the bird. God would bless him, but he needed to make an effort.

He watched the bustle as the push of people began their daily rituals. Most of the crowd here in the town's square were small- time businessmen and artisans. He also noted that some of the customers here were minor nobles, cooks, and seamstresses from the castle.

He must visit the castle sometime, the seat of government here. He must also keep an eye open for someone who could teach him how to read and write in the common language. Jason sighed. Too bad the old priest was killed. He would have been a logical direction for what to do now, as well as a valuable resource both for him personally as well as the cause of Christ. He felt his emotions well up into tears.

Jason overheard snatches of conversations throughout the crowd about Father Varigold's death and reports that he was murdered, despite the official news. He also overheard an occasional word about the Creator. News sure travels fast, even secrets. He was amazed how they did it so well without radios, TVs, and computers.

For the next few hours, he explored the town, working his way down to the dock district. The docks had a variety of small sailing ships with men and wagons loading and unloading cargo and hauling it back and forth between some log warehouses.

He loved the quaint and crude designs of the shallow draft vessels. Most were rigged with square sails, although a few had the triangular fore and aft sails that helped the ship to sail closer to the wind. It amazed him that men would trust themselves to the chance of winds in such frail crafts. He had a small sailboat of his own back home and, at one time, had rigged one of his fishing boats to sail.

It was late afternoon as he made his way to the castle. The castle had high walls and a wide drawbridge over a swamp moat with rusty lift chains which appeared to have not been used in many years. Guards checked visitors. Apparently, not just anyone could enter.

Contemplating his next move, he saw a family of minor nobles returning from their foray into the city. They were laden with bolts of cloth—a man and his wife and two daughters, passing right by him.

"I'll carry your cloth for you, milady," Jason volunteered to the noble woman.

The woman shook her head. "Help the little one, Amanie, if you would be so kind."

Jason took the load from a little girl, red-faced and grunting from her burden. She looked about eight years old and had reddish blond hair and freckles over her nose.

Amanie breathed a sigh of relief. "Thank you, kind sir. I could not walk another step without your help. What is your name?" He answered, and from that point on, Amanie chattered constantly as they crossed the drawbridge, the checkpoint, across the courtyard and through the corridors to their apartment.

The lord flipped a silver crown to Jason. "Thank you, young man. You will not get lost on your way out?"

"Oh no, sir, and thank you." Jason bowed with a flourish, and Amanie giggled.

"It is so nice to see commoners with manners," said the older sister, who was probably twelve. The father gave her a stern look as they went through the doorway.

Instead of leaving the castle as suggested, he found a niche behind a tapestry to stash his backpack and weapons, and began his exploration of the castle, walking through the corridors to large rooms with various purposes. Servants and lords went about their business, giving no notice to him. Even the guards stationed throughout the castle paid no attention. Although there were disadvantages to being a kid of little account, there were also benefits, such as moving invisibly among adults. Of course, other children took immediate notice of him, and he played the role of being impressed by their antics.

Two slightly younger boys engaged him in a game of tag- and-seek, where they raced over the castle hiding from each other. Jason found it a good way to scout and familiarize himself with the whole castle very quickly as his two playmates provided unwitting tour guides. Besides, he found he enjoyed the game. When they all grew tired, Jason made his way to the main hall where the royal table was laid. It had silver platters full of food and silver goblets filled with wine.

He was immediately chased out by a servant since this was only for the royal family, some lords, and special guests. He discovered later that meals were brought to the rooms of other minor officials, while the rest of the staff ate at a table prepared in the kitchen. The knights were served in their own halls with their pages attending them. The rest of the soldiers ate in the barracks.

Knowing he did not belong anywhere in the castle at all, he considered where he should eat, not wanting to draw attention to himself. However, this would be pivotal as to how he would be perceived at the castle if he did stay. He would always act like he belonged, so people would assume he did, but where exactly he belonged was a decision he had to make right now.

He returned to the main hall, might as well start at the top. If he failed, he could try for a lower station. He watched the lords and ladies as they seated themselves. Even the children were given a seat on benches beside the chairs.

After cleaning himself up a little at a wash basin, he saw the family he had helped earlier that evening. He went over and sat at the end, beside Amanie, her sister on the other side.

When Amanie saw Jason, her eyes grew big, and she exclaimed, "Jason, what are you doing here?"

"Your mother asked me to help you and has not discharged me from that service yet," he said in low tones, hoping that gave sufficient explanation for his actions.

"Really?" she replied. "I never had a servant before." There was wonder in her voice.

"I am not a servant. I have been asked to help you but not do your chores for you. You could view me more as your champion," said Jason.

"Really, truly?" quizzed Amanie.

"Yes, but do not tell the other children, for they would probably be jealous and throw a fit," he replied, reaching over and helping fill Amanie's plate. Her parents were busy talking with other adults, and Amanie's sister conversed with another girl her age on her other side.

Jason asked, "Since I am to be in service to your family, what are their names?"

"My father and mother, Lord and Lady Killensdale, and my sister is Nelda. Oh, and a cat named Scat," replied Amanie.

"Do you have a teacher for reading and writing?" asked Jason.

"Yes," said Amanie. "We have a tutor, and her name is Krucinda."

"Perhaps I can also help you with your assignments. Maybe tomorrow?"

"I go to the garden in the middle of the morning to work on my penmanship. It would be great to have my champion there!" she exclaimed. She chattered on through the meal, especially about Scat. It seems sewing was one of her least favorite chores and hinted that help in that area would be greatly appreciated.

Lady Killensdale glanced at Jason several times during the meal. She seemed to not recognize him as the common boy who had helped them, or perhaps she did and assumed Amanie had invited him. After dinner, he gathered his things and made himself scarce again. Going outside into the dark, he wandered to the garden Amanie had mentioned. It was well-kept, with stone benches under trees, a wishing well, terraced flowers, and a small shrubbery maze to the back. The shrubbery was short, about four feet high. The maze was obviously intended for young children.

Jason considered sleeping in the garden here safer than in a park by the river and intended to look for better quarters tomorrow. With winter approaching, sleeping outdoors was getting too cold, even with his blanket doubled over. In the morning, there would be frost coating the ground, and the water buckets would have a thin coat of ice.

In the dark, he could have slept anywhere in the garden and not be seen, but as an added precaution, he chose a hiding spot in the heavy shrubbery of the maze, lying down and curling up with his blanket in one of the many dead ends.

After his customary prayer session, he was soon fast asleep. About an hour later, the hushed voices of two men strolling about the garden woke him. He readied his long dagger, just in case he needed to defend himself. He was never challenged for carrying these in the city, except that one time in the temple, but here in the castle, they may not approve.

A voice interrupted his thoughts.

"Are you sure the garden is safe?" spoke the first man.

"No one comes to the garden at night anymore. It is too cold to be enjoyed by lovers, Master Griffon," spoke the second man. To Jason's ears, this second man sounded older than the first, with a deeper voice, but their hushed tones made it difficult to determine much else.

"Just the same, do not use my name. Is everything in readiness?"

The second man spoke hesitantly, "No, not yet. The ruins at Smitty's Hollow are not yet fixed to hold our hostages."

The first man growled impatiently. "There are only two weeks before the council meeting, and we must make sure we win the votes."

The second man complained, "But sire, it is hard to find workers we can trust."

"Then hire more, and if you must, kill them to seal their mouths."

Upon hearing this, Jason's guts knotted with disgust. From a cannibal in the wilds, to bandits on the road, murder of an old priest and now this! Although it changed forms, the evil in this world was consistent.

"As you wish, my lord." the elder man replied.

"Oh, and by the way, make sure there are beds. It would not do if our hostages are ill-treated."

The men walked away, continuing to talk, yet too far away to be understood. Jason could not get a look at them without revealing himself. Soon, the men were gone, leaving him alone with his thoughts. Who was Master Griffon? Where was Smitty's Hollow? And to whom should he tell who was not a part of the conspiracy—or should he tell?

Castle intrigue and influence of policies by force all sounded bad, but what if their cause was good? He doubted anyone who would kill workers to silence them was working for a good cause. He decided he must do something but needed to get to know someone familiar with all the governing leaders, yet neutral. He had less than two weeks to find someone in position of leadership whom he could trust.

He also found it amazing, almost too amazing, that during his first night in the castle he would overhear some kind of plot. Perhaps in this place everyone schemed so much it was actually commonplace. Perhaps corruption ran rampant and "someone in a position of leadership whom he could trust" did not exist.

Or it could be that God was placing him as a chess piece, a way to become ingratiated into the castle so he could do his mission better. Or even worse, what if the so-called gods in the old man's prophecy were setting him up? He shivered and drifted into an uneasy sleep, made difficult from the damp mist that began to settle.

CHAPTER 17
Offensive Clothing

The following day, Jason grabbed some hard biscuits from the kitchen and ventured out of the castle, hoping he could get back in without too much trouble. Without giving it much thought, he wandered toward the dock district. Perhaps he wanted to see the boats again.

After an uneventful morning, he returned to the castle and the same guard who was still on duty recognized him and let him in. He arrived in the garden in time to help Amanie with her lessons. He found her sitting hunched over a tablet mouthing out words. Scat, the white and black cat, sat upon her lap. She looked up as Jason walked over. "Oh, there you are. Could you test me on these words?"

"Of course," said Jason. "I'll point at the word and you tell me what it is, then you will spell it for me as you look at it, then do it again without looking." In this way, he began learning how to read and write without his young tutor knowing. At noon, they returned to the apartment to help Lady Killensdale with the sewing. Amanie's mother looked surprised to see the young lad accompanying her daughter but was behind in her orders and impatiently shooed the boy out.

That afternoon, Jason went to the barracks carrying his backpack, bedroll, and weapons. One section was set aside for squires and pages made up mostly of older boys.

He went over to the oldest boy. "I need to get a bed here."

The boy looked at Jason disdainfully. "Aren't you a little young to be a page? Who is your sponsor?"

"I have not been sponsored yet, but I have been commissioned by Lady Killensdale to be an errand boy. But since they only have two daughters, it is not seemly to stay with them, so I must sleep here," he explained.

"Okay," said the boy, "but since you are not a page or a squire, I cannot let you have a bed. But you may sleep in the loft. Try to stay out of the way and out of our sight as much as you can."

"Thank you," said Jason with a bow and was directed to some wooden boards nailed to the wall to make a rough ladder climbing the wall to a hole in the ceiling. Some of the other boys present snickered as he climbed it to discover a dark and dusty crawl space with some boards laid out. This was poor accommodations by their thinking, but for Jason, it was perfect. The dust showed that no one ever came up here. He and his things would not be disturbed, and compared to sleeping in the cold, this was heaven.

Sweeping the dust aside with his coat, he laid out his blanket to make his bed. He found a cubbyhole in the wall behind a loose board to store his money and gems. He left his bow and arrows beside his bed. He would find or buy more bedding to make it more comfortable, but this would be his home for the winter if God didn't move him on before then. Where he would go in the spring or how to fulfill his mission for God, he did not know.

Not knowing what else to do, he climbed down and returned to the garden. There were many children there this time, boys and girls playing hide and seek and running in the maze. Several ladies with their attendants held light conversations while sipping tea.

Feeling the tug of being a kid again, he joyfully joined the hide-and-seek game in the maze, becoming the seeker about halfway through the game. After some time, an entourage, led by a girl of about twelve, whom Jason recognized from the evening meal prior as a young princess by her extravagant gown and tiara- like crown, entered the garden. Five girls followed the princess of which Nelda, Amanie's sister, was a part. Following them was an older lady, dressed like a nun in a blue habit, looking rather bored, then three middle-aged men with stringed instruments.

All play in the garden stopped, and the entourage waited for the children to line up. Jason lined up beside Amanie. As the princess walked down the line, the girls curtsied and the princess offered her hand for the boys to kiss.

"What is the princess's name?" Jason whispered to Amanie.

Amanie shook her head and rolled her eyes and whispered back, "It is Princess Kuari."

Jason stifled a laugh since it reminded him of a term in a Brazilian native language where Kuari sounded identical to a poison called curare used by natives in the Amazon for warfare and to hunt monkeys.

Amanie curtsied to Princess Kuari ahead of Jason. Jason felt uncomfortable and tried to copy the movements of the other boys, as the princess held out her hand to him. Princess Kuari's eyes narrowed as she addressed Jason. "You are new here. What is your name?"

"Jason," he murmured, feeling it wise not to say too much and to act like a shy ten-year-old.

"Well, Jason, your clothing is not proper for my court. Your coat is covered with dust, and your pants are far too baggy," said Princess Kuari angrily.

"I am sorry," he offered in a little voice, trying to look ashamed while looking down.

Princess Kuari stuck her nose in the air with a harrumph while advancing to the next person.

After finishing her tour of the line, Princess Kuari said, "I want to dance. Musicians, a tune." She held her hand out to one of the oldest boys of about twelve, who took it with a bow. The musicians broke into a classical-sounding tune. The other boys tried to make themselves scarce, while most of the girls joined the princess's dance.

He followed the younger boys into the courtyard where several wooden swords appeared. Those who didn't have swords cheered on the combatants who were none too gentle with their strikes. Some of the guards took interest and cheered as well, a diversion from what was otherwise probably very boring duty.

Suddenly, the oldest boy who had been dancing with Princess Kuari entered the courtyard with three other older boys. He marched straight over to Jason and pushed him up against the wall.

"You displeased the princess. I will teach a lesson you will remember!" the outraged boy exclaimed as he swung at Jason's face. Even though the boy was larger by about thirty pounds and much stronger, Jason knew he could easily beat him with his martial art skills. However, that would be far too unusual and could cause an adult to investigate his presence, which could in turn jeopardize his stay. So he decided he must lose this fight and try to fade into obscurity again.

Jason sloughed the first punch by turning with it and stepping, making the blow appear more effective than it was. The blow still hurt, bringing tears to his eyes, but despite that, it was he who was in control of the situation. He turned slowly to face the boy with his own hands upraised in fists. Of course, since his hands were too high, he predicted the next blow would be to his stomach and readied himself. He collapsed with it, letting the bigger boy throw him back to the wall.

The other boys groaned with sympathy at the supposed punishment he was taking. Jason stood hunched over, apparently helpless from pain. The bully could have left him then, but he wasn't through yet. He cruelly kicked Jason between the legs. Reacting to the kick ahead of time, he snapped his thighs together, trapping the foot before it reached its target, then jumped as if the kick had lifted him into the air, then allowed his attacker to withdraw his foot.

Jason poised, teetering on the brink of collapse. "Thank you for the lesson, kind sir," he croaked as he toppled over. He laid there and watched with half-closed eyes as the older boy with his fellow hooligans strutted out the courtyard back to the garden. She might hear about it, but he was glad Amanie didn't see this altercation with her champion. As he lay there, the other boys gathered around and helped him to a sitting position.

"Ouch, that must have hurt!" exclaimed one of the boys.

"That is one of the worst beatings I have ever seen!" shouted another.

"But you took it like a man, even thanking that mean old Gunther for the beating!"

"So that's his name!" Jason bellowed as he stood up, brushing the dust off himself. "Did you guys see how I blocked his punch with my eye and nearly broke his fist with my stomach?"

The boys roared in laughter.

"By the way, does anyone know someplace where I can purchase appropriate attire, so I do not offend the princess in the future?" asked Jason.

One boy offered a suggestion. "Try Lady Killensdale. She's the best seamstress in the keep, but she is also the most expensive."

"You lads wouldn't happen to have an extra set of clothes around I could buy?" asked Jason.

All shook their heads no. He left them to return to the barracks, a slight limp to his stride to finish the show.

He climbed the loft to gather a few silver crowns to buy clothes and bedding, then found the Killensdale apartment. Lady Killensdale was supervising several other seamstresses. "I have come to purchase proper court clothes, milady," he replied to Lady Killensdale's inquiry.

Lady Killensdale asked bemusedly, "Do you have enough money to purchase them?"

"I believe so. I would leave it up to your good judgment as to the style and colors, but please use the proper materials," he answered, remembering Princess Kuari's admonishment.

"Jason, I have noticed you in Amanie's company, and she has told me you are her champion. What are your intentions toward my daughter?"

Feeling a little on the spot, he looked steadily into Lady Killensdale's eyes and replied, "I assure you my intentions are honorable. She is teaching me to read and write, though she doesn't know it."

Lady Killensdale laughed. "That is a fair exchange, Jason. However, it will not do for my daughter's champion to be dressed improperly. Do you have proper payment?"

Jason held out the coins in his hand, hoping they would be enough.

The noble woman's eyes widened, surprised to see that the ragged-looking boy actually had something to offer.

Noticing her response, he asked, "Is this not enough?"

"Actually, Jason, that is more than enough. If you would like, I could make you several sets of clothes for this."

"Yes, please do," replied Jason, smiling.

Lady Killensdale summoned another seamstress to take his measurements and lay out the cloth.

Afterward, he found Amanie in the garden playing with Scat and three younger girls. The princess and most of her entourage were gone, but Nelda was still in the garden reading a book, overseeing her sister's play. Nelda looked up from her book as Jason approached. "Are you okay?" she asked.

"What do you mean?" asked Jason.

"I mean, Gunther beating you," she replied.

Jason shook his head. He had completely forgotten. "Yes, I am okay, and your mother is making me some clothes, so I don't foresee any more problems with the princess or Gunther, for that matter."

"I wouldn't count on that," said Nelda. "Gunther is a mean one."

"Then it seems strange that Princess Kuari would favor him," mused Jason.

"That wouldn't seem so strange if you knew the Princess," supplied Nelda. "She has a cruelness that is more subtle."

"Then why do you accompany her?" he asked.

Nelda looked about uncomfortably and whispered, "I must. It is my station, and you don't know the things that can happen to someone who doesn't fit in."

"I think I just did experience it," he replied ruefully.

Nelda drew Jason to the bench and sat him down beside her.

"Listen. You stay away from Gunther and Princess Kuari. They are poison."

"You don't say," said Jason, thinking that Princess Kuari lived up to her name.

"They both pretend to worship Axialla, the mistress of the dark who accepts child sacrifices," said Nelda with some anxiety.

"Is this allowed?" asked Jason, somewhat surprised.

"Of course not," Nelda retorted. "But it is rumored that even King Beldane worships her for the powers and insights she provides."

"Just the king and not the queen?" queried Jason.

"I believe the queen is pure. She was forced into the marriage and is as kind and understanding as the king is cruel. I would also say that Princess Kuari's older sister, Princess Merinda, also has nothing to do with it."

"I see," said Jason. "You must be very careful to whom you tell these feelings of yours. But who is it among the court you know without a doubt you can trust?"

"I can trust my dad. He is a good and honest man and anguishes over the deceit he sees in the kingdom daily. I am not even sure why I trust you. I just don't want to see you hurt anymore. If I were you, I would go back where you came from."

"I really wish I could go back, but there are some things I must do first."

"What is that?" she asked almost absentmindedly. Jason looked at Nelda thoughtfully. "First, I must fulfill a prophecy, but I am not sure what I must do or how..."

She started to say something, with an incredulous look on her face, when just at that moment a servant called for dinner, and the children made their way toward their proper feasting halls. When Jason was seated between Amanie and Nelda, he bowed his head to give thanks silently. Nelda, unsure what Jason was doing, momentarily slipped her hand in his. When he finished, he squeezed her hand appreciatively and began helping Amanie with her dinner and ate heartily himself, after filling her plate.

The next day, he slept in, feeling comfortably warm for the first time in weeks. Being late, he missed breakfast and went directly to the garden to meet Amanie. A light sprinkling of rain had begun, so no one was in the garden. From there, he ventured to look for Amanie at the Killensdale apartment.

The tutor was just leaving when he arrived. Amanie welcomed him and set him up with her lessons in front of the fireplace. He found himself pushing Amanie to learn more quickly since he himself was learning at a faster pace.

When it came time for sewing, Lady Killensdale chased him out again. As he was leaving, she spoke, "Thank you for your help with Amanie's schooling, Jason. Do come by earlier for the tutor."

"Whee. Krucinda will love having you help us," Amanie gushed as she gave him a hug. Nelda looked up from her sewing and smiled. Even Scat seemed to approve, licking its paws contentedly.

"Mother," Amanie asked, "can we invite Jason for lunch with Nelda and I?"

"I guess so," she said distractedly as she went to correct one of the seamstresses.

Turning back to Jason, Amanie curtsied. "My champion, your presence in the parlor is requested at noon."

Jason laughed. "I will be there, milady."

At noon, Lord Killensdale also came to the apartment for a quick lunch. Lady Killensdale brought him into the parlor to dine with Jason and the girls, who were set up with a small table of their own and with what looked like fancy toy dishes. Nelda was humoring her younger sister and acting like a princess.

Since time was of the essence and seemingly through providence he was given access to Lord Killensdale, he decided to tell him about the conspiracy he had overheard in the darkness of the garden.

Jason boldly marched over to the table where Lord and Lady Killensdale sat. Lord Killensdale grinned at Jason, then said severely, "I was wondering when the champion of my daughter would come introduce himself."

"I am Jason Bristol, sir, and would gladly tell you of myself, but there is a matter of great urgency that is for your ears only."

"My, this does sound serious. What troubles can a little boy have that can warrant the attention of a lord?" he asked jovially.

"I overheard a conversation between two men that they would not want made known," he replied.

"Business follows me, even in my private chambers." Lord Killensdale sighed as he looked to his wife. "Would you pardon us a moment, dear?" he said as he stood, bowed graciously and led Jason to his study.

Jason then related the conversation he had overheard in the garden that night, omitting his reason for being there.

"Well, this is serious, indeed. While I know of no one by the name of Lord Griffon. It could be a code name or someone from outside the court. The council referred to is where we will vote to go to war with a neighboring country, to become their allies, or to simply remain neutral. I will start an investigation covertly, so please do not tell anyone else. The fact that you have been able to keep a secret so far shows I can trust your discretion. If you hear anything else or even suspect anything, let me know right away."

Jason promised he would, still hoping he had done the right thing.

The only thing he was sure of was that Lord Killensdale's voice did not match either of the men he heard talking that night. He then had the idea that if he just wandered around listening, he might recognize one of the voices of the men he heard, so he wandered around corridors and into rooms as unobtrusively as possible.

After about forty-five minutes, tired of sleuthing, he joined the children at play. He reasoned he must play the part of a child to fit in and not arouse suspicion, but in fact, he did enjoy his new found energy.

The rest of the evening, including dinner, was uneventful. He performed his evening ritual of praying in the garden before retiring to his room in the loft. The next morning, he returned early enough to take part in the lessons given by Krucinda.

Despite her youth, perhaps mid-twenties, Krucinda seemed worn out and forlorn. She probably would have been more attractive if she did not always seem so sad. She was unmarried, which for this society was a disastrous thing for a young woman, yet she probably could have been married if she did not carry the bitterness of not yet being married. It was one of those circular thinking things, but Krucinda did have a knack for languages and was a good teacher.

After classes, Lady Killensdale called him into the sewing room where he was pleased to see two new sets of clothes for him. Lady Killensdale could not wait for him to try them on. They were a perfect fit, and he warmly showed his appreciation, though inwardly, he grimaced a little to be wearing the tight- fitting pants, which looked a lot like girls' leotards. The clothes were also too bright for his sensibilities, but that was the style of the court, and now he fit in better.

CHAPTER 18
The Champion Fights

A few days later, while Jason was in the garden working on his own lessons the tutor had assigned, Amanie came running, crying "Help. Jason, help." Jason was up in an instant.

"What is wrong, Amanie?"

"It is Scat. They are going to hurt Scat."

"Show me," he said, following Amanie on the run. They ran past guards into the castle. It amused Jason that Amanie came to him instead of the guards, but perhaps she did, and none thought a cat worth their trouble. Also, Amanie was proud to have her own champion, and the opportunity to use him was something she would not miss. He regretted he did not have his dagger on him because he did not know who or what he might be facing, although with Amanie involved it must not be that serious.

Amanie led them down a dark stair he had not yet explored. There was a light down below from a room at the end of a short corridor. Slowing, they stealthily approached the room. He could hear chanting. He whispered to Amanie, "Wait here. If you hear me cry, 'Run, cat!' Then you run and tell the first guard you see that someone is being killed."

"Okay." She wrung her hands.

Stepping into the room, he saw a wine cellar; wine jars and bottles lined the shelves and casks of beer or ale lined the floor. In the center was a table and stone bench. Princess Kuari chanted and writhed about sensuously, with black makeup smeared under her eyes.

Gunther was the only other one there, standing like a statue with both hands over his head, holding a knife pointing downward over the stone bench. Tied spread-eagle on its back on the bench was Scat.

The cat couldn't move and was in obvious pain. It spotted Jason first and gave a pleading mew. Gunther turned, following the gaze of the cat. His first reaction, a guilty look of surprise, quickly turned to a sneer when he recognized the young boy he had pounded only a few days before.

"Let the cat go," Jason stated flatly. Kuari stopped dancing.

"You have seen nothing. Do you understand?" Gunther said disdainfully, still holding the dagger in position.

"Let the cat go," he repeated, stepping closer.

"We are not going to hurt the poor kitty. We are just playing," purred Princess Kuari.

"You are already hurting it." Jason moved closer to the bench.

"Leave," commanded Gunther, "or I will teach you another lesson."

Jason responded evenly and in complete control, "I choose the lesson. Are you so afraid of me you need a knife?"

"I am afraid of no one, least of all you," Gunther hissed as he flung the knife onto the table. Without warning, he then threw a wide, rounded punch at Jason's head while leaping over both the bench and cat.

Jason, not totally caught off guard, lightly blended with the arm with both hands and pulled, weighting Gunther's arm and spinning within the circle of the punch. Gunther flew off balance across the room, falling hard on the flagstone floor.

Taking this opportunity, Jason leaped across the bench, snatched up the knife, and quickly cut all four straps holding the cat down. The cat bolted like a rocket out the door into the dark hallway.

Gunther recovered, stood, and looked at Jason holding the knife.

"You have ruined our fun!" cried the princess. She then hissed to Gunther, "Get him."

Gunther said shakily, "But he has the knife."

Jason tucked the knife into his belt. "Let no one accuse me of threatening you with this."

The princess pointed at Jason and again commanded, "Get him now!"

Gunther rushed as Jason lightly hopped up and sat on the table, making it difficult for Gunther again to get past the stone bench. When Gunther was in range, Jason launched into a back roll, swinging a foot through Gunther's chin along the way. Gunther's head whipped back, and he spun backward through the air, falling heavily to the floor. There he stayed, unmoving.

The completion of Jason's back roll launched him off the table and near to Princess Kuari, who fled from him and ran to the unconscious boy. She looked at Jason spitefully and spat, "You will regret what you have done here. My father will—"

"Your father will do nothing," interrupted Amanie, moving from the shadow of the door. "Jason acted as my champion, and I will tell everything if you try to hurt him."

"There is nothing to say. We were only playing a game. Out of my way," commanded the princess.

"Before you leave, you had better wipe your face," Amanie admonished, offering Princess Kuari a silk handkerchief. Princess Kuari wiped off the incriminating makeup, then dropped the handkerchief. With a stiff back and not another word, Princess Kuari strode out the door.

Amanie picked up the handkerchief and held it for Jason to see. "Evidence," Amanie remarked gleefully as she carefully folded and tucked it into her pocket. Jason bent over Gunther and gently slapped his face, bringing him around. Gunther groaned as he helped him up, then kept him from falling again when he stumbled.

He helped Gunther up the stairs. "Remember this kindness. I won't tell, if you and Princess Kuari won't," he said, mainly in an attempt to keep his martial arts ability secret for now.

Once they were away from Gunther, Amanie exclaimed, "You were wonderful, Jason!"

"Thanks," he said.

Amanie went on, "I heard that Gunther beat you, but I didn't believe it!"

He confessed, "Yes, Gunther beat me the first time, but I allowed it so as not to draw attention to myself."

"But why?" asked Amanie.

"Because I do not really belong here. I am from a distant country, trying to find my way home," replied Jason.

"Then I will have my father take you home," said Amanie with finality.

"If it were only that easy," Jason said. "I do not know where my country is or even how to get there."

"Then, we can hire a diviner for you. They can find anything and the way to it if you pay them enough."

"That may be true," said Jason, "but I cannot go home even if I knew how. I cannot go until I have completed the unknown task my God, the Creator, has sent me to accomplish."

"Who is the Creator?" asked Amanie.

"He is the God who created all the stars, the worlds, and everything in them," he replied.

"Then you are a holy warrior on a mission!" exclaimed Amanie wonderingly, then continued, "I knew you were different from other boys, somehow bigger inside. When will you leave?"

"I never know what plans the Creator has for me."

They reached the Killensdale room and Scat was waiting outside the door. Amanie scooped him up and said to Jason, "Wherever you go, you will be missed, my champion."

Upon that remark, she kissed Jason's cheek and rushed through the door.

Jason thought to himself, Hey, you can't do that. I'm a married man! He walked back to his barrack loft, smiling.

CHAPTER 19
The Mysterious Swordsman

Princess Kuari and Gunther became a lot scarcer after that. Jason was told by the other children that Gunther, on coming of age and being the son of a lord, was exempt from the normal training for squires. However, Gunther's own special training had begun in earnest, from schooling in reading, writing, and history, as well as combat, under elite tutors.

At the castle, the date for the war conference rapidly approached. Jason learned that Lord Killensdale and a few others preferred to align themselves with the neighbor to the northeast, Harvella, which was, coincidentally, the country from which Jason had come. It seems that Harvella, in danger of being taken over by another country further east, needed allies and sent a request to King Beldane.

Jason overheard Lord Killensdale mention to Lady Killensdale that although it wasn't well known, there were some councilmen who wanted Chanderlon to attack Harvella in its moment of weakness while its attentions were focused on defending itself from the other invader. Lord Killensdale viewed this betrayal of friendship with their neighboring country not only immoral but impractical since Harvella made a good buffer between them and the aggressive country of Samyria.

Jason thought about the conspiracy. Who would benefit most going to war? The arms makers are too obvious. Sure, an army does travel on its stomach, but they don't eat much more food afar as they do near. Once an army succeeds in conquering a territory, it occupies the land. Whoever is put in charge of overseeing, especially the initial person in charge, can greatly abuse his position for a while and amass great wealth. It would be someone greatly favored by the king, but who that person was, he did not know.

A page stuck his head through the opening to Jason's attic, disturbing his thoughts. "Boy, this is a mess up here."

"Yes, but it is usually very private," countered Jason pointedly.

"Ah, yes. The Lord Killensdale would like to see you right away." The page exited down the rickety ladder.

Jason hurried to the Killensdale quarters and was seen into the parlor where Lord Killensdale awaited with another man. "Jason. Please come in," welcomed Lord Killensdale. He gestured to the man in the room. "And this, Sir Tadden, is the young boy of whom I spoke."

Jason stood before them, bowing deeply.

"Jason, we need to know if you have heard anything else. The leads you gave us have turned up dry. There is no one named Griffon, and there is nothing at Smitty's Hollow." Jason looked at the man beside Lord Killensdale, then looked down. "It's okay to speak in front of Sir Tadden. He is one of my investigators." Jason still kept looking down, not moving. Something about the man gave him an uneasy feeling.

"Okay, let's get on with it, boy," urged Sir Tadden. Jason remained still, barely breathing. Something about the man's voice seemed familiar in an unsettling way.

"Jason, you have made some very serious charges, and we need more information," said Sir Tadden, suddenly becoming impatient. Could this be one of the men at the meeting? Jason wondered to himself. The voice was similar, but he could not be sure. Also, the man's impatience irritated him, so he decided to continue to play the shy kid and looked down at his feet.

Sir Tadden raved on angrily for a few minutes asking questions to which Jason made no reply.

Finally, Lord Killensdale dismissed Sir Tadden. Turning to Jason, he admonished, "You came very close to insulting a knight, my boy."

"I am sorry for my behavior, sir, but this man's voice sounded similar to the one I heard." said Jason, suddenly breaking his silence. "How many investigators do you have?"

"I don't really see how that is your business," said Lord Killensdale indignantly. Again, Jason remained silent and looked at his feet, beginning to wonder if going to Lord Killensdale was a mistake. "There are five," admitted Lord Killensdale.

"Are they all your own men or are they on loan?" asked Jason.

"Why, they are all on loan. I do not have any investigators or any men purely at my disposal," answered Lord Killensdale.

"Who loaned them to you?" he asked.

Lord Killensdale started to look a little uneasy as he replied, "They belong to Lord Krogan, King Beldane's most trusted adviser."

Jason continued his line of questioning. "And if you go to war and win over Harvella, who is the most likely person to oversee the conquered lands?"

"Why, Lord Krogan, of course," said Lord Killensdale as if awakening from a stupor. "Jason, have I been played for a fool?" Lord Killensdale asked in despair. "Surly Lord Krogan would not stoop so low as to sabotage the council!"

"We do not know anything yet, sir, but tomorrow, I will go to Smitty's Hollow myself, while you search the court records on Lord Krogan, especially looking for any relationship to the name Griffon."

"My family and I were supposed to go to town tomorrow, but yes, Jason, I think that's a good plan, except that you are so young!" said Lord Killensdale.

"I am good at taking care of myself and I have some help from my god." replied Jason with a wink as he left by way of the balcony. He expected Sir Tadden to be waiting for him outside the front door for his own interrogation. Because it was dark outside when he climbed down the vines, he was sure he had not been seen. But as he headed to his barracks, on a long shot, he quietly detoured through the garden. If Sir Tadden wanted him, then the barracks would be the next place he would look.

The garden was empty, and all was quiet. He waited in the maze for about fifteen minutes and was about to go when he realized he had been hearing the distant ching of sword on sword for a while, but it had not registered. Swordplay, at this time of night?

Curious, he headed in the direction of the sound and came to a wall. Climbing a tree by the wall, he leaped to the top. Below was another garden with several fish ponds. It was the royal family's private courtyard, dimly lit with torches along the wall.

A flash of light caught his eye. He saw the lone silhouette of a swordsman practicing his moves, a kata of sorts. The man had two blades, one in each hand, the style Jason himself favored. Occasionally, the swords made a soft chinging sound as they brushed against each other. He admired the flowing moves that were so different and so graceful compared to the common soldiers he had seen so far.

After a few minutes, he was about to leave when a commotion in the first garden caught his attention. It was Sir Tadden with ten men, and they were searching the garden—presumably for him.

He immediately flattened along the top of the wall. For the moment, he was hidden by the tree he had just climbed, but with it being late fall, all the leaves were nearly gone. When the men got close enough, they would see him silhouetted against the night sky if they were any good, and he bet they were experts.

He hung over the side of the royal garden. He didn't know the penalty for being caught in the royal garden, but it didn't matter.

The result might be the same. He could be handed over to Sir Tadden or Lord Krogan, and he doubted either of the men's interrogation methods pleasant.

Knowing he would be seen if he just hung there, he let himself drop, landing noisily in a bush on his back. He continued to lie there quietly, hoping against hope that somehow he was not heard.

Silently, a slim blade came through the bushes, pointed at his throat.

"Who is there?" hissed a voice at the other end of the sword.

"I am Jason, sire," he said, assuming he was about to meet the king.

"A boy? Come out." The voice sounded strangely feminine.

He slowly emerged from the bush to see a young woman, perhaps eighteen or nineteen with her hair tied back, dressed in close fitting leather armor. A light sword rested in each hand with one, of course, still pointed at his throat.

He blinked, still trying to rectify the image of the woman before him with his expectations of a man and blurted, "Who are you?" in his bewilderment. But he knew who she must be. She must be Princess Merinda, the scarcely seen older sister of Princess Kuari.

The young woman laughed bitterly and stated like a curse, "I am the disbeliever. Now, young Jason, you must tell me why you are here, and your story had better be a good one."

Jason spoke low, "I can only tell you the truth. Whether the story is good or bad, I don't know. I fell here while fleeing interrogation by Sir Tadden. His intentions may be good, but I fear his methods, and I have no more new information to give. I do not know where his loyalties lay concerning a conspiracy I overheard."

"Conspiracy?" the swords woman was suddenly curious.

"Yes," he said, "it is an attempt to sway the vote at the upcoming council by kidnapping certain family members of certain lords. I do not trust Sir Tadden."

The princess interrupted, "And you trust me?"

"I do not know who to trust, but I tend to be very forthright to a person with a sword at my throat."

She looked at her sword then back at Jason, whipped the threatening tip away with a flourish and stowed her blades into place in their scabbards. "I guess it is safe to say you are not an assassin. Sir Tadden is the lackey of Lord Krogan, who is perhaps the only man more vile than my father."

Jason was taken aback by her bluntness and asked, "So you are Princess Merinda?"

She ignored his question and asked softly, "What are your plans now, little boy?"

"I must go tonight and visit a place called Smitty's Hollow, a place where the hostages were meant to be held. I think it is likely the kidnappers were warned and have moved the location, but perhaps I will find a clue."

"It would be difficult for you to leave the castle tonight. The gates are locked, and the walls are high, and you are being searched for, not to mention the vile things that come out at night in the moat. So do you have a plan for all that?" asked the princess, half smiling.

"Well, no," he confessed.

"A child like yourself has no business running around at night, trying to solve conspiracies. Come, I will find a safe place for you while I find others who can more appropriately deal with this problem."

Jason shook his head. "Do you know who to trust? I think I am probably safer facing the moat than staying here in the castle." The princess paused and turned her head away, then back to him. "You have a point. This place has a semblance of order but is rotten at the core."

After deciding, she grabbed his hand, a habit of adults around him with which he was still quite unaccustomed. The princess went on, "I am going out tonight and will take you out of the castle with me."

Princess Merinda went to the door and retrieved a heavily laden backpack. "I have done this many times," she confessed, "so stay close to me and be very quiet. If the royal guard ever found out, they would put an end to it."

She grabbed a torch and led Jason down a dark corridor to a blank wall. She motioned Jason quiet as she pushed a stone protuberance, then placed her hand on the wall as the concealed stone door swung inward, noiselessly.

Having explored most of the castle by now, it was a revelation to Jason that there might be another whole side to the castle he had not seen. In fact, he had not even considered secret passageways and rooms that might be anywhere and everywhere throughout this old castle.

She closed the door and after negotiating several connecting passageways, Princess Merinda said, "We can talk now. There are many secret passageways known only to the royal family for emergency escapes."

"Wow, I had no idea there were so many. Are there lots more secret passageways?"

Princess Merinda shrugged. Catching sight of her sheath, he then queried on his favorite subject, "Where did you learn your sword work?"

Princess Merinda replied, "My mother taught me at first, and then, I learned more from... From the townsfolk."

"Your sword work is very good," he said admiringly.

"Thank you. I have been working on it secretly for some time now, anticipating this day."

"And what is so important about this day?" he asked.

But the princess did not answer and continued leading deeper into the dark dungeons.

Eventually, they came to a stair leading up to a door of stone. It opened toward them to reveal the shaft of a well, with water below and rungs concealed in the stone leading up. Princess Merinda snuffed the torch and leaned it against the wall.

She motioned to Jason to go up and she followed, closing the door behind them. They climbed out in a poor area of town near the castle. The streets were dark with no one about. Only a dim light shone from the occasional window.

Jason faced the princess. "You are not going back, are you?"

"No," she said simply.

He continued, "When we met, you said you are the disbeliever. What does that mean?"

Her face was like stone. The bitterness in her voice could not be hidden as she said, "You are too young to know about such things. It is better if you never know."

Jason recognized the bitter desperation as something he had felt once as a young adult. It was at a time when he questioned his faith and even thought he had lost it. To his shame, he almost did not survive the ordeal, thinking once he had lost his faith he had lost everything. Depression followed years of searching, a burning desire to know the truth about God. He found the truth but at great personal cost and effort. He recognized a fellow truth-seeker in the princess.

"Princess, I think you are the disbeliever but only because you are still searching for something to believe in, the one thing you can point at and say, 'This is true.'"

"You are wrong, Jason," countered Princess Merinda. "I have searched and nothing... Nothing is true. There is nothing left to believe in."

Jason felt full of sympathy toward her. "Most would have said there is nothing to believe in except themselves—but you know that truth, don't you? You can't even trust yourself."

Tears started from the corners of her eyes as she stammered, "How... how did you know?"

Jason said flatly, "I've been there and done that."

"You? In your short life?" Princess Merinda said incredulously.

"I am older than I look, Princess Merinda, but disillusionment knows no age. If you can set your fierce pride aside, you will drop the last veil of illusion and see the full truth."

"And what is the full truth?" spat Princess Merinda bitterly.

"You may not believe me, princess, but the truth is so deep that aged scholars can't fathom it yet shallow enough for young children to play in it safely."

"What is it?" interrupted Princess Merinda impatiently, although with wonder at the words coming from this young boy's mouth.

Jason paused for emphasis. "It is the Creator's love for you," he said at last.

"Who...who is the Creator, Jason? I have never heard anyone speak of him," Princess Merinda asked skeptically.

"He is the one who brought everything, and I do mean everything, into existence. All illusions are contrived by created beings, but only clarity is found and given as a gift by the Creator.

Come and talk with me awhile and escort me to Smitty's Hollow. Speaking of which, do you know the way?"

Princess Merinda laughed. "Jason, you are out to save the world, and you are more lost than the rest of us. Come, I will show you the way."

CHAPTER 20
Champion of Children

A young woman and boy walked through town, chatting of the deeper meanings of life. More than once, men with evil intent approached, but some deep instinct warned them away, knowing in their heart it would mean their death to molest these two. There was something too sure, too confident about them despite their vulnerable appearance. Also, if they looked closely, the two blades in the young woman's scabbards with worn handles testified their owner knew how to use them.

He and Princess Merinda crossed the river bridge, exited the other side of town, and took a dirt road to the west following the river. They came to a low area, a reed-covered spit jutting into the river at the base of the ruins of a short tower. There were neither lights nor any indication of anyone there. However, the potentially present conspirators could be simply asleep with or without someone on watch.

Jason bid Princess Merinda wait at the edge of the copse, while he scouted ahead.

"No, you are too young and unarmed. I will go, and despite being a princess, I do know how to fight," said Merinda sharply. But Jason held firm. "I am a hunter, and being smaller and lighter, I am like a ghost. No one will see me."

Not waiting for approval, he took off. Keeping close to the ground, he followed along the brush to the ruins to avoid detection. When he reached the outer wall, he paused and listened, his young hearing exceptionally keen, then peered over the wall into the darkness. Seeing an opening with signs of being recently cleared, he swung over a low break and made his way cautiously to the hole.

Still no signs of life. He had no desire to stumble around in the dark so he returned to the outer wall and waved to Princess Merinda. When both were at the opening, Princess Merinda produced a flint and steel from her backpack and lit an impromptu torch made from brush.

The torch burned feebly but revealed several chambers recently cleaned of debris. With obviously no one about, they felt free to talk.

"What are we looking for?" asked Princess Merinda.

"Some clue to identify who was here or where they might have moved their operations. Look for anything—a track, a piece of cloth, or even a hand print," he said.

The place had been swept clean by an expert, so they took their search outside. He searched around the wall while the princess walked to the river. Soon, she called him over.

"Look Jason, over here." She showed him a footprint in the mud just below the bank. "Is it the print of a bear?"

Jason shook his head and sighed. "Too skinny. It's more like a man's, and the rough claw marks indicate a creature with which I am well acquainted."

"What is it?" she whispered.

"It is several days old. It is the print of a troll," he said.

Trombul, still looking for him? Or perhaps some other troll, he thought hopefully. If it was Trombul, then that troll really needed to get a life.

Jason walked out on the spit of land jutting into the river. At one time, it may have been a stone dock but now, it was deteriorated, covered with mud and brush. Midway to the end was a V mark in the mud and tracks of men.

"Bring your torch over here," he called to Princess Merinda. "Stay back on the rocks so you don't mess up the tracks." With the light overhead, he examined them closely. Though silt was starting to cover them, the tracks told him that three men, one dressed in armor, helped push the medium-sized barge back into the water. He then waded into the water with Princess Merinda's torch, examining the river. The barge had at least four sets of poles and left recently, probably that day.

He came back. "We need to make a larger torch, so I can see underwater. I want to know which direction the boat went." So Princess Merinda added brush to the torches and had a bright blaze, which she held high and waded out deep into the water to give him light. He submerged in the cold river and followed the pole marks. They headed directly across the river.

Coming out of the water, shivering, he huddled up next to the pile of burning brush set down by the princess.

"Can you see anything across the river?" he asked. Princess Merinda walked to the point of the spit to peer across the dark river.

She called back, "I just see a building...a farmhouse, perhaps."

He ran over to her. "Do you see any boats?"

"No," she replied.

"Let's get out of here," he said suddenly, feeling unsafe.

"Agreed," said Princess Merinda.

Someone must have warned the kidnappers of the investigation, and they swept the area clean of clues. There was not even any dust inside the rock-built rooms. But who gave the warning? Lord Krogan? Sir Tadden? Or was it someone whom they had innocently told? By now, a large number of people could know, and the possibilities were endless.

The only clues were the underwater tracks left by a barge going across the river. Even this could be happenstance, but on the morrow, he would hike down the other side of the river to check out the underwater tracks and possibly that farm house.

They walked up the road, very tired. When they got to town, Princess Merinda led them to a tavern. It was dark, and the princess beckoned him inside. The dim glow of a sputtering lamp lit the commons area; other patrons were barely visible, sleeping at tables with drinks still in their hands or lying on the floor.

Quietly, she led them up a stair to a room and produced a key. Without a word she unlocked and pushed the door closed behind them again, locking it. There was a single, fat, stubby candle set on a table beside a pitcher showing a bed and a bucket on the floor with a lid. She motioned Jason to the bed, shushing his silent protestations. He was asleep before he even lay down. Princess Merinda pulled the blanket up around him, then pulled another blanket for herself from her backpack and fell asleep alongside him.

Jason awoke late morning when Princess Merinda returned with breakfast. It consisted of hard bread, strips of ham, and a bottle of wine to wash it down. Figuring the wine would wreak havoc with his smaller body, he drank water from the pitcher.

The princess addressed him, "I have rented the room till the end of the week, not knowing specifically when I could get away. You may stay here for the duration of that. The affairs of the kingdom are no longer my concern, for I intend to take a ship out of town this very morning."

Jason felt a little disappointed, hoping that talking with her about God and his need for her help to prevent a crime against children would be enough for her to stay. But in fact, what reasons did he really have to stay? After all, it was even less of his fight than the princess's. There was a similar urge for him to leave town, and it was tempting to ask if he could go along with her.

"Thank you, Princess," he replied, "but think of the children. They are innocent pawns in this affair, and we must do what we can to help them."

Her eyes were moist, while the rest of her countenance was harsh. "Things like this have been going on for a long time, and it is always the children who suffer. I am sorry, Jason, but I don't want to see it anymore. Please don't tell anyone you have seen me. You have been the one bright spot in this whole affair, but one day, you will grow up and become as cynical as me."

Breakfast finished, she turned to leave. "Farewell, young dreamer."

"Farewell, disbeliever," he said gently as he watched her close the door.

Finishing the leftovers from breakfast, he wondered if the people looking for him had started looking in town yet. Somehow, he would have to get word to Lord Killensdale without going into the castle. He would have to wait until after the council before he could return safely and perhaps not even then.

What he needed was a messenger who could easily pass security at the gates. Leaving the inn, he wandered the market squares, looking for someone he could possibly hire for the job. He spotted a man he had seen working one of the smithies in the castle and was working his way through the crowd towards him when he heard a woman despairingly calling Amanie.

Amanie was here and is now missing? He felt a little confused since he knew that Lord Killensdale had postponed his family's trip into town so he could work on the investigation. Searching faces in the crowd, he ran to find Lady Killensdale and Nelda nearly in tears.

"What's wrong?" he asked.

Lady Killensdale grabbed his hands and shook them as she spoke, "Oh, Jason, I am so glad you are here. Is Amanie with you?"

"No, she is not. Is Lord Killensdale with you?" he asked in return.

"He had paperwork to do for his investigation, so we came to town on our own. We desperately needed more silk," she said.

"Did not Lord Killensdale tell you what the investigation was about?" queried Jason. She shook her head no. Jason commanded, "Find a town official and have him begin a search, then go to Lord Killensdale and tell him what happened. Also, tell him that Smitty's Hollow was clean—too clean—but the house across the river from it is suspect. Meanwhile, I will search for Amanie."

He left the two standing there as he took off on a trot. As he left, he heard Nelda call after him, "Go with the strength of the Creator, Jason!"

He thought, Now what made her think to say that?

Running through the crowd, he felt like calling Amanie's name but knew it would be useless. He felt so foolish. It was obvious to him now that Lord Killensdale's children would be a high priority in the kidnapper's objective. They needed to stifle the investigation as well as put pressure on his vote in the war council.

He did not know where Amanie was, but he did have an idea where they might be taking her. He ran through the streets, dodging carts and people, toward the river. There would be a road along the river to the farmhouse he and the princess discovered the night before across from Smitty's Hollow.

He did not relish a three- or four-mile run before possibly encountering kidnappers and kept an eye out for a likely cart he could catch a ride on or some other means of transportation available.

As he approached the docks, he could see a ship just pulling away. It would go downriver and pass the farmhouse. He was tired from running through town but put out a final sprint to leap the distance separating ship from shore.

He landed on the deck and collapsed, his lungs heaving desperately. The ship's crew paused from their work in surprise.

"What's the matter, Jason?" came a familiar voice. It was Princess Merinda.

"I think the youngest daughter of Lord Killensdale has just been kidnapped." Jason was out of breath.

The captain appeared and frowned to see a new passenger boarded without permission. After an introduction and short explanation from the princess, the captain replied in a choppy accent, "Aye, we will take you downriver, lad. To imagine cowards that would prey on young children makes my blood boil. You sit right there and catch yer breath. I will get us there in short time."

The captain used all his skill to speed their journey along the river. Captain Seldwick, a trader with a cargo of linen to take up north, chatted amiably with Jason, but Jason was preoccupied wondering what he was going to do when he got to the farmhouse. He assumed he would jump ship and swim to shore undetected when the time was near.

When the building and small barn came into view, they could see two men on the main house roof with hammers, supposedly repairing it, but looking very intently down the road toward town. They hardly glanced at the small trading ship.

He was about to jump when Captain Seldwick stopped him. Puzzled, Jason looked around and waited.

As they went by the first building, they could see armed men inside through the windows. At the backside of the house, the ground was freshly disturbed in three places, just the right size for three graves. Probably those of the previous owners, surmised Jason. As they went by the barn, two carriages unlike what a farmer would use were parked, horses still hitched. The horses looked lathered as if they had just finished a hard run.

The ship seemed to draw no alarm from the occupants, and after rounding a bend in the river, the captain grounded it as close to shore as possible. Two of the crew jumped into the waist- deep water and pulled a grapple to hook it on a rooty mass on the bank.

Jason thanked the captain, who again stopped him. "Leave those kidnappers to us, lad. Wait here. I see no reason to endanger one child while trying to rescue others."

Jason interrupted, "Captain Seldwick, I am the champion protector of one of the hostages and am a far better fighter than I appear. I would rather save my energies for the kidnappers rather than proving it to you. I welcome you and your crew's help, but this is my fight."

"And it is my fight too," came a voice from behind. Princess Merinda, still dressed in her black leather fighting suit, waved a cocked crossbow she had found. She had a quiver of bolts tied to her belt.

The captain shrugged. "Aye, aye, 'tis a crew of fools we all are, playing hero against a band of professional killers. May the gods smile on our folly."

Jason responded, "There is only one God sufficient to our needs, and he favors those willing to trust him. Follow me."

The captain and crew, with swords and clubs, followed Jason and Princess Merinda to a small group of trees just beyond the barn and carriages.

"Captain, could you send a discrete member of your crew to that riverbank by the window, so he can signal you if I am in trouble?"

Captain Seldwick nodded and sent one of his lither crew members, who crept stealthily into position.

"What do you want me to do, Jason?" asked Princess Merinda, almost skeptically.

"Take out the men on the roof with your crossbow, then Captain Seldwick can lead the charge. But it's very important you give me time to get in position to protect the hostages. Keep well hidden until I have been inside the house for about five minutes."

The captain looked dubiously at Jason. "I admire your heart, boy, but this is a job for a man."

"I am a man." Jason boldly stood and strode to the farmhouse in plain view.

No one from within the house or the roof noticed his approach, being intent on anyone coming from the city. He went to the front door and with a kiai (the yell for generating focus) kicked the door open and stepped inside. The men inside froze, surprise on their faces.

"Who are you?" asked one man.

"I am Jason, son of Lord Bristol and commander of the army outside. I have followed you traitors to your lair and now command you to drop your weapons if you wish to be spared," Jason stood, hands on hips, feet parted.

"Uh...any of you guys see an army outside?"

"No," came from the men all around.

"Check with the watch on the roof," said a man obviously in charge.

"I don't need an army to deal with you scallywags," retorted Jason as he kicked the first man on the shin. The man just looked at Jason and grinned. Another man approached Jason from behind and grabbed him. Jason was careful to kick and fight ineffectively. He didn't want to put up too much of a fight to cause the crewman watching the window to signal too soon. Jason stiffened and folded his arms defiantly.

"What shall we do with him?" the man holding Jason asked. The leader replied, "The boy is the son of Lord Bristol? I have never heard of Lord Bristol, but the boy is wearing court clothing. I would say the gods have just given a bonus. We can ransom him when our job here is done. Put him down with the others."

"You will regret this!" cried Jason.

They opened a trapdoor in the floor and carried him down a steep stair, almost a ladder, and deposited him on the floor. He stood and looked around as the man climbed the stair and shut the door. There was a single lamp and three small beds in what used to be the farm's root cellar. Three small children stood away from him, the oldest being Amanie.

"Oh, Jason, I knew you would come!" cried Amanie when she recognized him. She ran and hugged him tightly. Jason took note of the other two, a girl of maybe six or seven and a small boy of about five, wearing court clothing of red leggings and a green coat. They appeared unharmed, and since there were only three beds, there were probably no more hostages coming.

When Amanie stopped hugging him, she turned to the others. "This is Jason, my champion. He is here to rescue us, so no more crying, okay?"

The two children nodded, rubbing tears from their eyes.

Jason immediately went to work. He first tested the trap door.

It rose up a little, then made a clunking noise as it hit against a padlock. He could hear the men snicker. He slammed it up hard several more times before he stopped, making the men roar with laughter at his feeble attempt. Jason then found a small board he used to break apart the hand railing to gain a longer lever.

Jason talked to the children as he worked. "When I break out of here, I want you to follow me and stay close to me. Do you understand?"

They nodded.

"Good," said Jason. He double-looped his sword belt through the rafter near the locked trap door and buckled it. Then he stuck the hand rail through the belt making a kind of a teeter totter hanging from the ceiling.

When he pulled down on one side, the other side pushed up against the trap door. Since the fulcrum (the point where the rail hung from the belt) was close to the door, a great deal of power could be generated by pulling down on the longer end. Jason figured the lock could not withstand the hundreds of pounds of pressure generated by pulling down on the lever.

His responsibility was to keep the kids safe, and he figured the best way to do that was to get them out of there once the battle started. That way no matter who won, the kids would be safe.

With lever in place, he waited, listening for the battle he knew would ensue shortly. Amanie and the other two watched Jason with anticipation. The noise of the battle would also cover the noise of the lock breaking.

Back outside, Princess Merinda and the rest of the ship's crew had watched Jason kick in the door and heard him yelling his defiance. Some of the crew quietly snickered and shook their heads at the boy's audacity. Then all quieted, as their eyes transfixed upon the guards atop the roof, who looked extra alert.

Soon, the guards relaxed, and the crew watched for any signal their own lookout might give. After a few minutes, the look out gave his thumbs-up sign, and Princess Merinda went into action. She took the cocked crossbow and sighted in on one of the roof lookouts. She took a breath and smoothly squeezed the trigger.

The bolt whizzed through the air but struck a foot below her intended target who was lying on the roof looking again toward town. He heard the noise and was examining the thatch in the roof near him as Merinda desperately tried to recock the crossbow. His eyes widened as he found the partially buried feathers in the matted straw beside him.

He tried to follow the bolt's trajectory with his eyes as he opened his mouth to warn his colleague. But no sound came as the next bolt, course corrected, impaled deeply in his throat. The man reached for his throat as he fell back onto the roof, losing consciousness.

Merinda again raced to cock her bow, straining with the tight string cutting into her fingers. This bow was not as sophisticated as the good ones her own palace guards had, with a lever that pulled the string back for them. On this one she had to stand on a stirrup and pull the string up manually by hand.

She pulled up and aimed at the second watchman just as he noticed his comrade sliding down the roof. The man yelled, "Attackers!" as he tried to flip over to the other side of the roof to get out of the line of fire. She cursed inwardly as she fired, knowing their opportunity for surprise was ruined. This shot caught the man in the ribs just before he disappeared.

Already, the sailors were on the run with Captain Seldwick in the lead. Throwing down the crossbow, she sprinted to catch up. Back inside the farmhouse, one of the men said, "Hey, did you hear that?"

"Yeah," said another. "It sounded like the watch."

"Well, don't just stand there. Draw your weapons and guard the door!"

The leader then turned to a burly, dark-haired man, "Macken, check it out!"

Through the window, the hoodlum named Macken saw a body slide off the roof and fall to the ground.

"Look!" he said, pointing. Outside the window, the charging crew of sailors could now be clearly seen.

"There are too many. You rutters hold 'em off while I grab a hostage. A knife to that little girl's throat should do the trick." The kidnapper's leader moved toward the trapdoor.

Suddenly, through the entry door burst two of the sailors who took out the two men guarding it. Another sailor joined them in engaging the henchmen.

Down in the root cellar, Jason was awaiting the noise of battle to cover the sound of his breaking the lock. Upon hearing the door burst open and battle cries, he leaped to put his weight on the lever and the door slammed up, but to his disappointment, it did not move more than the slack the lock had allowed.

"I need more weight. Grab my legs," he said to the other children.

All three grabbed onto him and pulled down. Again, nothing happened; the lock was too strong. He had to change tactics— and quick—if his plan was to work.

"Let go," he ordered. When free, he hurriedly pulled the rail loose from the belt. He carried the pole to the stair and intended to use it as a battering ram. In the meantime, the stomping noise of fighting men above covered the noise of the trap door being unlocked. He heaved the handrail with all his might at the stubborn door just as it was flung open by the kidnapper's leader.

Thrown off balance by the unexpected lack of resistance, Jason fell forward as the rail veered and hit the outlaw square in the chest. Momentarily stunned, the man stood there trying to catch his breath, but Jason recovered quicker. Taking his heavy pole, he aimed again and rammed it into the man's throat, sending him flying onto his back.

Suddenly, Jason realized his error. This band of desperate men were now wanting to use one of these children to make their attackers back off. The odds of sneaking past them in the chaos of battle was low. He ran over to a bed and flipped it on its side.

"All of you hide behind this. Don't make a sound or come out no matter what you hear or how horrible the sounds are above you. Don't worry. Hide here to help our rescuers win!" he instructed.

With the children hidden and without considering that he too was a child who could be used by the kidnappers, he ran up the stairs and crouched with his head just sticking out above the floor. The leader lay unmoving before the stair on the floor. The sailors were bottle-necked at the door, surrounded by eight outlaws wielding clubs and swords.

Two more were just behind with spears, looking for a gap to push their weapons past the defenders and stab the rescuers. An exceptionally stout third man held a huge morning star, a club with spikes driven into it. He, too, was awaiting an opening.

Two sailors were on the floor either dead or dying. Some kidnappers showed nicks, but no wound bad enough to stop them. The defender's strategy was good; there was a chance they could kill those at the door and drive the advance back.

One of the spear men glanced back and saw Jason and their fallen leader. His face full of surprise, he started toward Jason. Jason jumped over the body blocking the stair and pulled the leader's short sword and knife.

The sword was more like a heavy machete and very unbalanced. Instantly, Jason knew he could not wield it effectively, but being weighted at the tip made this blade ideal for throwing. As the spear man approached, he flung the blade in a graceful arch. At a range of ten feet, he couldn't miss. However, in an effort to avoid the blade, the man turned, and the blade landed closer to the man's armpit rather than the center of his chest.

Still, the man moaned and fell heavily, attracting the attention of the other spear man. Someone yelled, "Get the young cur before he kills us all from behind!"

The burly kidnapper, Macken, turned and took in the scene of two downed men in surprise. Without pause, he charged Jason with a snarl, his massive club held before him. Jason was moving to snatch up his last victim's spear, but the advancing angry bull of a man made him dive under a nearby table instead.

The huge club smashed down on the table, crushing it with one blow. One of the spikes gashed Jason's shoulder as he dodged to the side of the collapsing table. He still held the bandit leader's knife and scooted under a chair. Leaping up, he propelled the chair at the attacker's face, following it with his knife ready. Dodging around behind the man as he flung the chair, Jason struck at the man's kidney region with a quick stab and continued his move to grab the fallen spear. His hurried thrust did not stab deeply and the bear of a man whirled with a roar, his morning star flying around with the impetus.

Jason dove to evade the swing and snatched up the spear as he rolled onto his back. He held the butt end of the spear on the floor as the charging kidnapper impaled himself on the spear's tip, driving the point deeply into the chest from the villain's own momentum. He then rolled to the side to avoid getting smashed as the huge man fell.

Pulling hard, bracing his foot against the corpse's chest, he removed the blood-drenched spear. Captain Seldwick was wounded but still fighting fiercely. The spear man from behind was scoring, the point of his spear bloody. So absorbed in their own battle and presuming Macken had taken care of things, they paid no heed to Jason.

Jason ran with the spear to aid the sailors who seemed to be tiring under the relentless blows. About to stab the criminal from behind, it suddenly seemed to him a cowardly attack. Being in a child's body, he should not have thought this way, but his sense of honor was not based on his size.

Instead, he flipped the spear around and struck with the butt end into the base of the man's skull. He dropped like a piece of chopped firewood. This relieved a sailor to now attack another, but also alerted the spear man who now thrust at Jason instead.

Jason tried to dodge, but the spear bit like a snake into his shoulder and knocked him to the floor. Angry at being caught by the surprise attack while sparring the man's comrade, Jason flung the knife he held in his left hand at the man's face. It was not a skilled throw as both shoulders were wounded, and he was lying on the floor, but a throw out of desperation, for the kidnapper was already poising his spear for a killing thrust.

The knife hit with its hilt in the man's eye. It did not badly hurt but was enough to stymie the attack. Jason did not have time to reverse the spear in order to use its point but came to one knee, driving the blunt end into the man's groin. Gasping, the man crumpled into a ball on his side on the floor.

Taking this opportunity, Jason charged and stomped heavily on the man's head, bouncing it off the floor. The man was probably going to awaken with quite a headache, assuming the brain was not damaged so much it hemorrhaged.

Turning to face the remaining combatants, he could see the fight was in control of the rescuers and went back over to guard the trap door, bloody spear in hand.

The kidnappers were pressed away from the door. More sailors poured in, fresh for the fight. Within moments, the remaining outlaws surrendered, laying down their arms.

As the princess approached him, Jason yelled down to the cellar, "You can come out now. We have won the fight."

"Jason, you are wounded," Princess Merinda said as she led him to a seat.

"Oh, it's just a scratch," Jason replied as he sat down. He then made the mistake of looking at his wounds, and that was the last he remembered. He had passed out.

CHAPTER 21
Deologue 4

"Ah, there you are, Axialla." Xan Rukkah addressed the dark- haired woman floating among bubbles on the ceiling.

"You have been looking for me, my king?" the woman crooned as she blew a bubble across the room. It crashed into another and, as it popped, revealed a small creature trapped inside, which screamed shrilly as it fell from the height of what appeared to be a medieval chapel.

The giant god Xan Rukkah casually reached out and caught the creature before it plunged to its death. He examined a dark- skinned lizard-like creature, part human, cowering in his hand. "Yes, I came to see if you knew the latest development of the Creator's child hero. I believe his name is Jason?"

"I see you have been watching him. It is good you are taking this threat seriously. In less time than a mortal child could do, he has gone from total obscurity to a major player in the affairs of a human kingdom."

"Were these kidnappers the boy defeated some of your minions?"

"They are mine, yet they acted on the scheme of another named Lord Griffon."

"A pity you could not foresee that Jason would fall into your hands, so you could have instructed your followers to kill him."

"I have many kingdoms to rule. Chanderlon is but one. However, I do see one opportunity. There are some followers of the assassin god visiting the area. Perhaps you could ask Dontevile to have one of his followers slit the boy's throat."

The huge titan shrugged, a motion that set the little creature in his hand screaming again. The giant blew at it gently and the creature stopped. "Dontevile is currently fighting with Scoron and won't be available for a while."

"Surely they are not fighting in person?" asked Axialla incredulously.

"No, no, of course not. It would be senseless for two immortals to actually fight. No, they fight with their mortal bodies in the form of their followers. Dontevile's martial artists and assassins will win, so I don't know why Scoron even tries."

"He thinks like the rest of the lesser gods who do our bidding. Instead, we should be working together to combat the Creator and the prophecy."

"My followers have killed the prophecy. It is now dead and will no longer bother us."

"Once uttered in the presence of others, a prophecy does not die until it is fulfilled," countered Axialla.

"True. Then, we will fulfill it in our own way, or make it false by stopping the Juggernaut. Keep your troll on him, but perhaps the champion will run afoul of Dontevile's assassins anyway," said Xan Rukkah thoughtfully.

Axialla popped another bubble and watched as another small creature fell screaming. As this one fell past Xan Rukkah, he let it fall, and it made a little black and red spot on the floor, amid many other similarly colored splotches.

Xan Rukkah held up the tiny creature still in his hand and examined it again, "Hey, I like this quasiling. May I have it? I will trade you one of mine."

"Of course, my lord."

"Who was it?"

"Oh, she was a young virgin named Loyah who was sacrificed upon one of my altars. Very beautiful."

"I like that," he said enthusiastically. "Hey, little one, you and I will have great sport together."

As the big god turned to go, the little creature squirmed from his grip and leaped to its death. Momentarily stunned, the giant gingerly picked up its crumpled form. "Ah, what a shame. It was beautiful, right?"

"Yes," said Axialla. And smart, too, she added to herself.

CHAPTER 22
The Challenge of the Princess

Jason awoke and found himself in a bed in the Killensdale sewing room. There was a fresh dressing over his wounded arm. Light streaming in the window told him it was morning. He could hear the tutor giving the girls their morning lessons.

Although this was the sewing room, most of the materials had been moved aside to accommodate him. He had bandages on both sides of his shoulders. He checked under the front bandage. It was as he figured. There was a crust of blood over the top, but the purple scar tissue underneath had already begun to disappear. He didn't need it but kept the bandage on to hide his abnormal rate of healing.

He wondered if he were killed, would he regenerate like a troll does in the legends? It was one theory he would not like to test. One thing he vowed was not to feel too cocky about his gift. In some ways, this could make him fearless in taking chances, but he also had no idea if this gift would be lost over time. He also knew God was displeased with proud people.

Lady Killensdale entered the room, grabbed a bolt of cloth, and glanced at him on the way out. "Oh, you are awake," she said with a smile.

"I hope you are not cleaning out this room on my account," he said, sitting up.

"As a matter of fact, we are. I am moving to a larger workspace we are renting across the hall."

"But I don't belong here," he sputtered.

"You do now, at least for a little while. We searched the whole castle for your parents, that is, until Amanie told us who you really are, you poor lost child. So now this is your room until we can find a way to get you home. We are so grateful for all you have done, we would not have it any other way, so make yourself at home. I will have Nelda bring in a tray. I have much work to do," she exclaimed as she bustled out of the room in a hurry.

In a few minutes, Nelda came into the room carrying a tray holding a silver pitcher of milk, rolls, and some mixed fruit and berries. She sat it on a small table by his bed. "Amanie and Princess Merinda told us everything.

You were very brave. I... I changed your bandage this morning. I hope it is okay."

"You did a wonderful job. I will probably heal twice as fast now," he said encouragingly.

He ate some food while the dark-haired girl sat and watched him. "Where is your father?" he asked.

"He is in session at the war council," she answered.

"Then we will know soon what the decision will be?" he asked.

"Yes," she said. "It will be announced at the general assembly at noon."

Just then, Amanie burst into the room and ran over to give Jason a hug. A beautiful woman in a flowing gown followed her, slightly out of breath. It was Princess Merinda.

Princess Merinda flushed slightly when Jason blurted out, "Princess Merinda, you are so beautiful."

Blushing, she said, "It is the new dress Lady Killensdale made for me."

He shook his head and declared, "It's not just the gown. There is an inward glow about you."

The princess looked straight at Jason. "I am beginning to have an appreciation for the Creator. I was amazed last night when my father took you to the healers at the temple of Xan Rukkah. Not only did they refuse to heal you but were so terrified of you, they closed the temple down, barring the gates and doors. Then I checked your wound myself. It was healing before my eyes. When a ten-year-old boy can terrify the followers of the greatest god of our world, then his god, your God, went ahead and started healing you. He must be far greater."

"Yes, he is. I had an encounter with the priests when I first came here. Their chief priest by the name of Varigold decided to become a follower of the Creator, then the rest of the priests killed him," replied Jason.

"You were there when Father Varigold died?" asked Princess Merinda.

Jason nodded, "Yes, the other priests didn't know it, but I was just outside the window when it happened."

"I will get someone to investigate. We were told Father Varigold died of natural causes. We all loved that old priest, and if he followed the Creator, then many of us would have, too. But I wonder why they got so upset? After all, there are so many gods. What is the problem with one more?" asked the princess.

Jason replied, "The Creator is not just another god. He is the God. He created all the gods and angels to begin with, and because the Creator granted these beings free will, his is tolerant of their rebellion. Their rebellion has spilled over to mankind as well, although I don't understand how much it has affected men on this world yet."

"Amanie told us you are a holy warrior for the Creator. I guess that explains you taking down five of the kidnappers all by yourself. Three of them were killed by you, which defies all reason for any young boy to do, unless empowered by the Creator," said Princess Merinda.

"Empowerment is for more than being a warrior. It comes from becoming God's child and the special favors he bestows."

"Could I become a warrior for the Creator?" she asked.

"The three of us," Amanie and Nelda affirmed together.

"It would be great if all of you decide to follow the Creator, but to truly receive the power means a special dedication, a special rite of passage," he said.

"What is this special rite?" asked the princess.

"It is a rite that emulates the Creator's death, burial, and resurrection."

Just then, Lady Killensdale called to her daughters. She needed assistance in the sewing room. Nelda and Amanie excused themselves quickly.

Princess Merinda also turned to leave. "I will talk to you more about this rite later. Now I must take my place in the general assembly with my family."

He stopped her. "Have you changed your mind about leaving the castle?"

She paused. "I was fleeing the illusions, the illusions that stole my free will. I was powerless to my station and powerless to my father. I am betrothed to a man I loathe and would be forced to marry, but now, those illusions are gone. Even if I fail and am thrown out into the streets, I am not a woman without means or without power, thanks to you and the Creator."

He nodded and mused to himself as he watched her go. Freedom truly was a state of mind and not the circumstances in which we find ourselves.

At noon, the assembly in the main hall gathered, with all the lords and ladies in attendance as well as the town officials. The large tables that dominated the hall for meals had been removed, and a long red rug ran down the middle. The padded chairs used by select lords at mealtime were set on either side of the throne. Jason stood with Lady Killensdale and her daughters close to the front of the crowd near the throne. Everyone made sure not to stand on the long rug leading to the elevated floor of the thrones. There were guards lining the walls to each side of the crowd.

The crowd hushed as a line of priests representing the various temples entered the room. The procession was led by two priests of Xan Rukkah—the high priests Father Dorrian and Brother Mussan holding censors on long poles. They used these to light the other censors behind the throne and then the entire procession lined up behind the chairs.

The royal family minus the king entered from the side— Queen Overa, Princess Merinda, Princess Kuari, and eight women attendants. These stopped, standing behind the chairs on the right side. The castellan, whom Jason didn't recognize, came from the opposite side of the room and seated Queen Overa next to the king's throne. He then produced a scroll and announced the date and purpose of the assembly. The lords on the war council then entered the room, walking woodenly, and sat on the chairs on either side of the throne.

Finally, the castellan announced King Beldane, who entered the room with two bodyguards from the left side. The king walked to the throne while the two guards took their stations at attention on either side of the rug at the bottom of the stair. The king bowed to the queen, who nodded in return, then sat on his elevated throne.

The castellan then proclaimed that Lord Krogan, head of the war council, was to read the verdict handed down by its members. Lord Krogan, a powerfully built man with a gray beard stood, walked over to the king and knelt in obeisance. The king gestured and Lord Krogan stood and turned to take the scroll from the castellan. Unrolling it, he solemnly held it up before the audience.

"We the members of the king's council have thoroughly explored the request of King Goshen of Harvella for aid and succor against their enemy, the Samyrites, and have found that we are in sympathy with the Samyrites. It is hereby the recommendation of the council to proactively and without reserve declare war." Lord Krogan turned to the king. "War, sire, war!"

Although this was the first time Jason heard Lord Krogan speak, he sounded familiar. Perhaps he was one of the men he heard in the garden? Lord Killensdale looked ashen, unhappy with the pronouncement.

King Beldane stood, walked forward, and with a firm voice, declared, "I have heard your counsel and have considered this matter in my heart. My trusted council members and advisors, I embrace your decision." The king drew his ceremonial sword and thrust it above his head into the air. "War!" he shouted.

"War!" echoed the soldiers in the room. Immediately, the people were in an uproar. Jason felt like he was about to get knocked down by the sudden pushing and shoving of excited people. War was such a powerful word and drew a myriad of emotions, and the crowd expressed them all. Although the king and the council members all stood like statues on the announcement, the priests and the royal court also seemed abuzz with their own opinions.

After several minutes, the king sheathed his sword, turned, and motioned to an attendant who brought forward a small ornate box. The king then took it into his own hands.

He stood with the box held before the assembly. The assembly quieted. When it was sufficiently quiet, he said loudly, "There was a plot to destroy the integrity of the council and to affect the outcome. Several children of council members were kidnapped. I am proud to say this plot was uncovered, and the children rescued by courageous subjects of our realm."

King Beldane turned to Lord Krogan who gave him the box, allowing the king to open it and withdraw a medal with a ribbon attached. The king turned back to the assembly. "Will Captain Seldwick come forward and accept this token of our appreciation on behalf of himself and his crew!"

The captain broke through the crowd and, red-faced and beaming, made his way to the king, bowing from side to side, then knelt before the king. A bandage on his shoulder was visible. The king placed the ribbon over the man's head to the cheering and clapping of the assembly.

As the crowd quieted, the king said, "We appreciate your sacrifice and the loss of one of your crew in the rescue. Our hearts share in your grief at the loss of the hero, Borgis Sanbalat who died in your service, and we declare all of your crew heroes as well." The clapping continued as the captain returned to his seat.

The king withdrew the next medal. "It is with much personal pride that I present this next medal. Often the royal family is accused of being a figurehead with no real power of its own or even real concern for its subjects. For her role in saving the hostages and acting above and beyond the call of duty, I am proud to call my daughter Princess Merinda to receive this badge of courage."

Princess Merinda came from her place behind the throne and stood before her father, proud and unbending. If King Beldane disapproved of this lack of respect, he did not show it. He graciously placed the medal over Princess Merinda's head, again to the enthusiastic cheers and applause of the crowd. The king turned to the audience and held up his hands for them to quiet. "This apparent breach of etiquette from my daughter is assuredly appropriate, for I would like to take this opportunity to announce that she is soon to be a queen in her own right."

The king motioned to a foppish-looking young man with dark skin, a ridiculously large yellow feather in his hat, who grinned from ear to ear as he approached Princess Merinda and the king. The young man boldly walked up to Princess Merinda and grabbed her around the waist with one hand and faced the assembly.

The king continued, "I am pleased to give my blessing to the engagement of Prince Dunaibi of the southern kingdom of Kudalon, to my daughter Princess Merinda."

Again, there were cheers and applause and ladies portraying

congratulations. Princess Merinda nodded solemnly, graciously acknowledging them. The two stepped back behind the king. King Beldane went to the box Lord Krogan was still holding and took out another medal and held it up, again waiting for silence.

"This is the most unusual honor I have ever given," announced the king, "for the recipient of this medal is a young boy. This boy has proven that valor and courage knows no age. This boy not only uncovered the plot against our council members but spearheaded the rescue of their children. I call forth the hero of Chanderlon, Jason Bristol."

The crowd broke into applause and spontaneous cheering, even before Jason moved. Despite himself, he felt a lump in his throat as he walked up to receive the honor. It felt like his feet wouldn't move right. He managed the steps without tripping or falling and knelt before the king.

"Stay kneeling, Jason," whispered King Beldane as he placed the award around his neck. When Jason did not stand as expected, the crowd grew quiet. The king continued in a loud voice, "Even though you are a boy, you have fought as valiantly as any man and have even been wounded in service to the kingdom. Your actions deserve more than a mere medal of courage. Therefore I, King Beldane, do hereby bestow on you the additional honor of knighthood in my court."

The king drew his sword and touched each of Jason's shoulders lightly. "Arise, Sir Jason Bristol, Knight of Chanderlon!"

Jason stood to thunderous applause while soldiers clashed their weapons and, as if on signal, snapped to a salute for the new knight of Chanderlon. He turned, bowed to the assembly as it seemed the thing to do, and started down the steps.

Over the din, he barely heard Princess Merinda say, "Jason, wait."

Jason froze in place and turned to face King Beldane. Jason looked past him evenly at Princess Merinda. Her lower lip quivered a little and Jason, feeling himself again, smiled at her encouragingly.

Princess Merinda galvanized herself, shook off the hold of Prince Dunaibi, and stepped forward to face her father. Jason could see Queen Overa in the background stand from her chair and look proudly at her daughter.

"Father," Princess Merinda said strongly, "as a princess, I have a right to place a challenge before all suitors. Therefore, I will not accept the betrothal to Prince Dunaibi until my challenge is met. My challenge to all suitors is to face my selected champion in combat, who must be defeated before I will consider engagement."

Prince Dunaibi appeared visibly shaken and angry to have been put off and stiffly stepped forward. Jason suspected what was coming next.

The king also looked angry but kept his composure. "My daughter," he spoke softly. "You have the right to a challenge as you say, but you don't have to be difficult. Consider the welfare of the kingdom."

Princess Merinda stood unmoved. She stared fiercely at her father. After a moment, he nodded wearily. "Very well, Merinda," he spoke loudly. "Choose your champion."

Princess Merinda looked squarely at Jason. "I choose the new hero of Chanderlon, Sir Jason Bristol." The audience gasped and murmured.

"Surely not this boy," Prince Dunaibi spoke with disbelief in his thick accent. "Sir Jason may be good, but the boy will get hurt. He is no match for a skilled fighter."

"I have a right to choose Sir Jason Bristol. Not only is he a knight and a hero, but I have seen him in action and he is able enough," declared Princess Merinda.

Jason felt trapped, but something inside him wanted to rise to the challenge. Jason stepped up to the raised floor. "I beg your pardon, Princess Merinda. I greatly desire to be your champion, but I am already in the service of Lady Killensdale, commissioned to be her daughter Amanie's champion."

Lady Killensdale immediately stood, holding Amanie's hand, and said loudly, with dignity, "Then I release you, Sir Jason."

"Thank you, Lady Killensdale," he said with a bow. He turned again to the Princess. "Princess Merinda, I would be proud to be your champion, take on any and all suitors and any who threaten your safety."

The prince had a sneer on his face as he looked at Jason, then turned to the princess. "I do not know what game you are playing, but there is no honor in defeating your champion. Yet for your hand, I will meet him on the field of open combat tomorrow at mid afternoon." The prince turned angrily and stomped out. The crowd was immediately in an uproar. Jason smiled to himself how the momentous announcement of war could so easily be forgotten and similarly, how politicians of his own world likewise took advantage of situations to draw scrutiny away from perhaps an unwise decision.

King Beldane turned to the castellan. "A dismissal is in order."

The castellan turned to the chaotic mass and cried, "You are all dismissed." The assembly immediately broke in all directions, eager to voice their opinions to their neighbors and spread the gossip.

Princess Merinda placed her hand on Jason and said lightly, "Thank you, Sir Jason."

"It will be my honor to serve," he replied.

Queen Overa was instantly there. How she did it without running Jason did not know—perhaps she did run. "Merinda, I have never been prouder of you than today. Do have your champion come to our parlor. I would love to get to know him."

Amanie was the next to appear, giving Jason a bear hug. "Oh, Jason, this is so wonderful, though I am sad to lose you as my champion."

"You have not lost me as your champion yet, and I will always be your friend, Amanie. That is far better than a champion," he promised. Amanie gave him another hug.

Princess Merinda left Jason to face the deluge of well wishers and advice givers. He had not had this much attention since the day in his other life when he got married. Many of the young boys felt they knew Jason well, but Jason couldn't remember most of their names. It didn't matter. It was as if they shared his moment of glory and reveled in it. Even some of the pages and squires from the barracks gave their congratulations. To skip the long path to knighthood as Jason had them envious.

Making his way to the royal quarters, the guards immediately allowed him through. He mused on how he tried to be obscure and in less than two weeks since arriving had become one of the best-known figures in the kingdom. He was sure God's hand was in this.

He was shown to the parlor where sat Queen Overa. "Greetings, Sir Bristol. It is good of you to come," said Queen Overa.

Bowing deeply, he replied, "It is an honor, Queen Overa."

"Merinda will join us shortly, but it is good I can speak to you privately first. I have tried to train both my daughters to be more than myself and felt I failed until today. The new hope Merinda has, I see, came from you. The change I now see in her is even more than I could hope for." The queen then spoke more cautiously. "However, she has set herself up for failure. If you fail her, she will lose her faith in you and everything you represent and will become like me. Perhaps even worse."

Jason replied, "The Creator moves in mysterious ways, but one thing I do know is that no matter what happens it will be for Princess Merinda's good."

"But how do you know?" asked the queen.

"It is simple. The Creator loves her," he spoke sincerely.

Just then, Princess Merinda floated into the room on tip toes as if gravity no longer existed. "Mother. Jason. I see you two have been getting acquainted."

"Yes, dear, Jason has been telling me about this Creator you are so excited about."

"Mother, isn't it wonderful?" Princess Merinda interrupted.

"But I don't want you hurt," Queen Overa said worriedly.

Princess Merinda interjected, "I won't be hurt. The Creator wants us to have free will and can empower us. It is with his help that Jason can defeat Prince Dunaibi. The Creator wants us to trust him instead of our own strength, our own cleverness, or even magic. That is what makes Jason the perfect choice as my champion."

"Well, I fear that trust is misplaced. I asked Kuari, who knows Jason much better than you, and she told me the boy, Gunther, easily beat up him when he first arrived," said the princess's mother.

"Is this true?" Princess Merinda asked him.

Jason wished he could relate the second incident but kept his word, "Yes, it is true...sort of. This may seem unlikely, but I let him win."

Queen Overa gave Princess Merinda a meaningful look and then interrupted, "Jason was lucky at the farmhouse and even then was nearly killed. Don't you care that Jason could die?"

Princess Merinda shook her head. "What I said about the Creator empowering us still stands. Come to the garden with me, Jason, and I will teach you what I know about swordplay with dual swords."

As they walked to the royal garden, Princess Merinda said, "Now that you are my champion, we will be working closely together, so in private, please drop the princess and just call me Merinda."

"Certainly, Merinda," he replied.

In the royal garden, she showed him some sword movements and then let him try. She corrected him and then did more movements. After about an hour, she called for a break.

She said wonderingly, "I feel you should be teaching me. I show you a move and you then perform it better than me."

"I am no stranger to many types of weapons. Merinda, do I have to kill the prince?"

"No," she replied, "just defeat him. He may surrender or leave the field, but otherwise, you fight until you or he can fight no more. Jason, there is something I want you to know... If you feel you are about to die, please surrender. I do not want your death on my conscience."

"Merinda, if I do die, please know that I am finally going home. Perhaps the Creator will send me to my home world, back to my family, or he will bring me to himself, but either way, I will go home."

"Amanie alluded that you were from someplace else, a different world. What world are you from?" she asked.

"A world very similar to this one, except it has not yet forgotten the Creator, at least not completely."

"You will have to tell me more about your world someday, but now there is little time. Let's get back to training."

They practiced until dinner time, then walked to the main hall. On the way, Jason asked worriedly, "If I win, am I expected to marry you?"

Princess Merinda laughed. "Of course not, Jason. Besides the fact you are too young, a champion is not necessarily a suitor. Two suitors can fight for a lady's hand, while a champion merely fights in place of one who is placing the challenge. In fact, both in a contest may have a stand in to fight for them. This is common when neither party is in physical condition to fight due to illness or injury. Me being a princess, it is tradition to have a champion rather than fight myself. Although, as you know, I am very capable of fighting. However, the difficulties increase if a marriage ensues, and either party is wounded by the other."

"I see," said Jason. "That relieves me because on my world, I am already married, and I look forward to seeing my wife and family again."

"Jason!" exclaimed Merinda, then laughed. "If I didn't know better, I would call you a liar. I see that I have much to learn about you. Come tell me about yourself over dinner."

When they reached the dinner table, Merinda made room for Jason to sit by her. Nearly all eyes were on them when they bowed their heads to pray and give thanks. Less noticeable were two little girls who followed suit.

At the head of the table as an honored guest, beside King Beldane, sat Prince Dunaibi. Prince Dunaibi stared at Jason in an effort to unnerve him. Jason frustrated him by smiling and nodding, then looked elsewhere as though the prince was no different from any other guest.

CHAPTER 23
Visitors in the Night

After dinner, Jason went to the barracks where again he received a warm welcome by the pages and squires. He had not had a chance to check on his things since before trying to escape the castle. His bed was thrown across the dusty rafters, his backpack dumped and his arrows scattered. Someone, presumably Sir Tadden, had rifled through his equipment searching for clues while searching for him.

He checked his secret stash of gems and coins and noted with relief they had not been discovered. He repacked his things, rolled his bedding, and tied it to his backpack—no telling when he might need them again. He carried them back with him and stashed them in the wardrobe of his new room at the Killensdale's.

The Killensdales, also preparing for bed, wished him a good night. Remembering his nightly ritual of prayer, he slipped out to the balcony in the night air and climbed down the shrubbery along the wall. He walked to the garden to be alone and pray but, after about fifteen minutes, Jason became aware that he was not alone. He felt the person rather than saw or heard. Cautiously, he turned to face the silent shadow of a large man who seemed to float in his direction.

As the man came closer, Jason could see a muscular, dark- skinned man dressed in silk robes and funny hat with a tall feather in it like Prince Dunaibi's. He spoke in a heavy foreign accent like the prince's. "Are you Sir Jason Bristol?"

"Yes," he answered.

"I am Maudid Guboh. You are a smaller boy than I imagined. I am here to ask you to do like so many boys do, and that is to be unreliable, get distracted, and go do something fun, so you miss your appointment with death tomorrow."

Jason said nothing, so Maudid continued, "It would be a strong and good union if our countries became united in this marriage. Free trade and military support would be an added benefit. Also, it is a shameful thing for a fighting man such as the prince to fight a little boy. If the prince wins by hurting or killing you, it is not a victory but a cowardly act. If, by some miracle or trickery, he loses, that is also shameful for a man to lose a physical contest to a child. Either way, it is an insult."

Jason stood on a bench to look at the man on more equal terms and said, "Then perhaps the prince should leave."

"He cannot do that either, for he cannot appear to be rebuffed by a woman or to be afraid of a child," said Maudid reasonably.

"I suppose you are here to make sure I do not make my appointment tomorrow?" asked Jason.

"No," said Maudid slowly as if considering the possibility. "Two can play at Princess Merinda's game. I am here to give you fair warning that Prince Dunaibi has another option to save face and that is to appoint a champion to take his place. He considered getting another child to face you, but this fight is representative of our kingdoms and to not put our best fighter forward is not in our best interest."

Jason queried, "I presume you are Prince Dunaibi's champion?"

"Yes," he replied. "I get to bear the humility and shame for my prince. I do not wish to kill you, boy, and be shamed. If you will disappear, I offer you a thousand gold crowns."

"Maudid Guboh, I believe you are sincere, but what is at stake here is more than an alliance and a trade agreement. It is the freedom that is promised by the Creator to all of mankind, including women and children—"

Maudid interrupted him, "I have heard that you are loyal to your god, but I only believe in this." Maudid showed his fists, then lifted Jason off the bench. With a roar, he slammed both fists down and smashed the stone bench into pieces. Jason was glad he was not still standing on the stone bench when the huge man slammed it.

Maudid left the boy standing there, looking at his own small hands. Even in his adult body, he could not have matched the force of this man. Jason felt doubt creep into his soul. He walked to another stone bench and looked at it. He calmed his breathing and focused himself. He had broken boards and stone before but never this thick.

After about two minutes, he released a loud kiai and smashed at the bench with his right hand. The bench didn't break or even move. Instead, he felt incredible pain. He looked at his hand, which turned involuntarily into a deformed claw. He had broken his hand. He knelt and bowed over the bench to pray with earnest sobs.

After a couple of minutes, a small squeaky voice said, "Your martial arts skills won't help you this time, Jason."

It was the demon Akari. The two-foot-tall creature leaped upon the bench to look Jason in the eye.

"Your timing is excellent, Akari," he said woefully.

"You will lose, Jason. If I were you, I would take the money and run," said Akari wisely.

"You have been watching my progress." Jason sat on the bench, nursing his broken hand. "Akari, I think I am beginning to understand at least one of the reasons the Creator sent me. He sent me for you."

"For me?" cried Akari, astonished.

"Yes, you," said Jason adamantly.

"Me? A demon? To imagine God would care anything about me is ludicrous. I am a demon. I am accursed. I am what I am, and I cannot change."

"Nonsense," said Jason. "Only God never changes. The Bible from my world mentions that all of creation waits, groaning in anticipation for the redemption of the righteous. You are a part of creation, Akari, a created being. God loves you, too, especially if you started doing good things, right things. Do you think God would still punish you if you became a creature on the side of light? Do you know what God did for the evil nation of Nineveh in my world after they repented when they heard Jonah's message? God hadn't promised them anything good, but he still showed them mercy."

"Bah," said Akari. "You will see. You will see tomorrow when you realize that your god just set things in motion to run its own course without his interference. God only helps those who help themselves, but for you, there is no help, even with your skills. Maudid serves the god of combat— Dontevile the Killer. Even Prince Dunaibi is a martial artist who surpasses anyone from your planet, and Maudid is his teacher. Maudid killed Nog, a stone giant, with his bare hands. It was nice knowing you Jason. Run. Run while you can!" Akari jumped up and down, waving his hands.

Jason had a sudden thought. "How many times have the gods of this realm sent their champions against me?" he asked.

"Many times," said Akari, "but you were lucky, Jason. Your god was not there helping you. It was just dumb luck, and he will not help you tomorrow. This time, the odds against you are too great. You do not have a chance. Listen to me. I can see the future, and I see your grave."

"Akari, do demons like to bet?" asked Jason, wondering if he was about to commit a sacrilege.

"Of course we do. We live for gambling. In fact, we are all betting on tomorrow's outcome," said Akari, enthusiastically rubbing his hands together.

"Then if I lose tomorrow, I will do the deed you wanted me to do earlier. But if I win, you will do one good deed for God."

"Well," said the little demon in concerned thought. "No good. There is no way to collect from the dead. Mark my words. I see your grave," Akari warned ominously as he disappeared in a puff of smoke.

Jason smiled to himself. At least, he had gotten the attention of the little demon. Who knows what might come of this? He felt more comfort and encouragement from the little demon and his dismal prediction than he might have from any angel of light God could have sent. When it comes to challenging God, as Maudid did, or to doubting God's caring, as Akari did, historically God has moved into action in proving the doubter wrong. Plus, he remembered the prophecy said the juggernaut could not be stopped. He didn't know how, but Jason felt confident he could not lose, for this was not about him, or even the princess, anymore.

He thanked God for sending him the little demon, who unwittingly served God's purpose. He then returned to his room in the Killensdale apartment. His hand had already begun to mend as he slept peacefully.

CHAPTER 24
The Message of the Trees

Next morning dawned a beautiful fall day. With the exception of his aching hand, Jason felt well and ready to visit the kitchen per his normal routine but found his breakfast waiting on a small table beside his bed. It bothered him a little he had never heard the person who brought it. Being waited on in the Killensdale apartment was something he would have to get used to. There was a basin to wash and a covered bucket to do his other business.

After breakfast, he wandered the living quarters, seeing only a servant woman cleaning the fireplace in the main living room. He left the apartment with part of his treasure to make some needed purchases, particularly a good sword. He might find a suitable one in the armory, but the type of sword he wanted was more suitable to a thief than a soldier. When he reached the courtyard, he saw a flurry of activity. Soldiers and craftsmen were loading wagons with tents and wood structures.

Jason asked Sir Tadden, who seemed to be in charge, "Is this preparation for war?"

Sir Tadden looked at Jason with sympathy in his eyes and said, "No, boy, this is for you. We are setting up the pavilions at Golgon's field. A large crowd is expecting to see you torn asunder. Prince Dunaibi is a renowned fighter in his own country. No knights here would be eager to trade places with you."

Jason nodded solemnly and continued on his way through the gate and into town. Evidently, the announcement he was to actually fight Maudid instead had not yet been given. Perhaps that had changed, but it was not his place to make such an announcement.

To his relief, no one in town recognized him by sight yet, although he heard his name mentioned many times on his way to the dock.

It seemed like everyone in town was preparing for a picnic or a fair. Merchants were packing tents and wares into carts. Families loaded themselves into wagons or prepared packs of food to carry to the field. Others were decorating their inns and preparing food for the anticipated celebration following. Overall the mood was festive.

Once at the dock, he searched for Captain Seldwick, whose ship was now back at the dock, still laden with its undelivered cargo. The crew welcomed him on the ship warmly and Captain Seldwick came out on deck.

"What is it you be needing, young hero of Chanderlon?" asked the captain graciously.

"I need you to teach me the value of these coins and gems before I use them to make some purchases," said Jason as he proffered his handful of valuables.

"Ach. Come over to the side of the cabin so we are not so visible. You have a grand wealth there, boy, but very old. The coins come from several eras of kingships and lost treasures. How did you come by them?"

"I found them in a bird's nest, on the edge of the plains on my way here to Chanderlon."

"Aye, birds fancy shiny baubles, they do. This large dark coin with the hole in it could buy my whole ship, cargo and all. It is worth at least a thousand crowns, for it is made from a rare metal called marillion. The others are gold and are worth about one hundred crowns apiece. The gems are garnets, opals, and emeralds. A jeweler could tell you their value more precisely. You should convert them into coin instead of using them to purchase things, for most assuredly, they'd be worth a hundred times more than what some merchant will trade for."

"I do not have a lot of time to do that today. I need to purchase a good sword."

Princess Merinda walked around the corner wearing a dark riding cloak. "I hoped I would find you here. I am worried sick, and you are acting like this is just another exciting day in your life."

He smiled at her. "And you sound just like my mother. If it is any comfort, I was trying to purchase some weapons, so rest assured, I have not forgotten our commitment for this afternoon."

Princess Merinda took off her sword belt and handed it to Jason. "There is no need for that. You will use mine. They are light and sharp, and you will not find a finer set anywhere."

Without thinking, Jason reached out with his right hand, forgetting his injury. Surprisingly, it was only sore, healing very quickly. "All right," he said buckling on the swords. "Thank you, Princess Merinda. I am honored to use them in your service."

The two returned to the castle. He didn't want to tell Merinda about the possibility Prince Dunaibi had his own champion, Maudid, since she was already worried. Instead, they talked about everything except what actually occupied their minds. Back at the castle, Princess Merinda took him to her private quarters and tried to fit her armor to him, but it was too big and cumbersome. He returned to his room at the Killensdale's to ready himself. Taking his backpack containing all his weapons, clothes, and money, he repacked it to include a bottle of water and loaf of bread.

He wanted to be ready for anything and wasn't sure if for some reason he might not be allowed to come back. Or perhaps he was still giving himself the option of running away. He wasn't completely sure himself. He grabbed his bow and quiver of arrows and carried them all with him as he left. Too bad he didn't have his plastic bag; it had a zillion survival uses.

Going to the room rented by the Killensdale's for their sewing, he found the family busily preparing for the outing, Lady Killensdale fussing over the girls as he entered.

"Jason, you look splendid." Lady Killensdale observed him in his court clothing. "But look, I have made you a cape appropriate for a hero of Chanderlon." It was blue trimmed in black, and she helped him put it on. "Oh my, don't you look dashing. After everyone sees you in this, they will be wanting one too." She smiled.

Amanie ran over and hugged him, sobbing, "You are not going to die, are you, Jason?"

Nelda was also fighting back tears.

Lady Killensdale spoke, "Normally, Jason, I would not allow the girls to see this sort of thing, but if I do not allow them to watch you and something happened, they would never forgive me."

Jason looked at them and smiled. "We must trust the Creator. He says that all things work for the good of those who love him and serve him. Who knows? Perhaps this event is what the Creator has brought me here for and once it is completed, he may send me home."

"Or you will come back home with us," said Nelda assertively.

"That would be good too," he said. "So, no matter what happens, it is good, so do not fret."

Lady Killensdale interjected, "Jason, I cannot fault your reasoning, but I pray the Creator will return you to us."

He spied a medium-sized green silk bag with drawstrings containing scrap pieces of cloth. "May I have this bag?" he asked.

"Of course." Lady Killensdale shook out the contents and handed it to him. It may not be as useful as a plastic bag, but it would work better than a leather one for some things.

The procession began a little past noon in the courtyard.

Mounted soldiers and knights guarded the line of carriages containing the royal family and lords with their families.

A whole carriage was given to Jason and Princess Merinda alone.

Although he would have preferred to ride on top with the driver, he contented himself with conversation inside the coach with the princess. They discussed strategies of what he would most likely face in combat that day, but he knew, despite all his skill, only God could give the victory. His martial arts skill, although good, was like a finger plugging a hole in a dam against the raw power of Maudid.

The conversation died to quiet contemplation as the procession left the city and followed the country road to the field of Golgon. Jason watched the trees in their fall colors and realized that if he died he would miss the beauty of these. It was as if he tried to drink them in with his eyes. He peered at the trees as if they could tell him the secret of how to live through the upcoming trial.

The trees took their nourishment from the light, just as his soul did from the light of God. The trees grew to be strong and the birds would make their nests in them for safety. He could see the variety of birds in the trees and even a squirrel or two. Then there were the insects that live in trees as well. There were ants, aphids, butterflies, and bees. He even spied a hornet's nest. He reflected that as a spiritual tree he was the strength for others to live in the light as well.

He remembered a time as a kid in Alaska, when he had learned how to handle a hornet's nest and how to destroy them. In Alaska, they have a larger type of hornet called a yellow jacket. The smaller hornets such as he just saw in these trees were quicker and more vicious when it came to defending their nests. What could he learn from the hornets? How could he fight like a hornet against a man four times his size without getting slapped?

Suddenly, Jason had an idea and turned to Princess Merinda. "I have just thought of something I need to do. I will meet you at the field." He quickly grabbed his backpack and jumped out the door.

"But, Jason, we are almost there!" said Princess Merinda in alarm.

Jason called back, "Don't worry. I'll be back before you know it."

No one paid much attention to a boy darting to the side. As Merinda had said, indeed, the procession was almost to the field, for he could see the tents and pavilions in the opening just ahead.

CHAPTER 25
Chi Master

Tents had been set up by soldiers and a pavilion faced the field. The field was actually a valley with low grassy hills, yellow in its fall colors, which the crowds from the city could climb to watch the events. The valley also had a small stream running through it at one side. On the side of the tents and pavilion was a flat plain, perfect for jousting tournaments and short horse races. A few trees dotted the hills, giving shade and adventuresome children a place to play.

The royal family had just been seated at the pavilion when Jason came trotting up with his backpack over his shoulder, dodging hawkers and vendors trying to sell their goods to the townsfolk streaming from the road and making their way to a spot by the pavilion or on the hill. Two small tents were set up at either end of the field, and he saw Princess Merinda standing outside one talking to a knight and his squire.

He jogged over to join them. "There you are!" Princess Merinda exclaimed, relieved, then turned to introduce Jason to the knight. "I am not sure if you have met him yet, but this is Sir Quineas and his squire, Torin. They have requested to assist you in your preparations."

"I do not need any assistance at the moment, but I do welcome your company," said Jason graciously.

"Sir Bristol, we have been impressed with your composure, and no matter what happens, you have inspired us to imitate your courage," said Sir Quineas. His squire, Torin, nodded in agreement.

"Thank you, but it is not so much courage as it is faith, for it is my God who will win the day," said Jason.

Sir Quineas looked over at Torin. "I believe the gods favor those who are prepared."

Jason looked at him critically. "Preparation is important, but do you believe I could ever prepare enough to meet the match I am to face today?"

"Well, no," said the knight honestly.

"Thus, faith," said the boy simply.

"Jason, I need to take my spot at the pavilion, and these two will advise you in etiquette and when to come out. And, Jason, please remember, if you feel like you are about to die, please surrender." She turned to leave.

"I will remember."

Two mounted knights in full armor and decorations, holding large lances, approached each end of the field.

"What are these knights for?" Jason asked Sir Quineas.

"It is an exhibition jousting tournament. The people love it, and it is tradition."

The knights took their positions, facing each other about a hundred yards apart and saluted. Trumpets blared as they charged each other at full speed. Their lances hit their opposing shields with a loud crashing noise. Both men rocked in their saddles as they went by and fought to stay upright. One knight's lance was cracked and broken on impact. The crowd cheered wildly. They continued to the other side and wheeled their chargers.

Their squires gave them both fresh lances, and they charged again. This time one of them was unseated in the clash and fell heavily to the ground. Jason smiled as he watched the man slap vigorously at the ground to help absorb his impact as he fell. If he had challenged any of his students on his home world to fall like that from a six-foot-height they would have thought him crazy.

Within a few seconds, the fallen knight rolled to his stomach and rose by going to his knees first. He stood and waved to the crowd to show he was all right, and the victor rode to the pavilion to accept a wreath from Queen Overa. After the ovation, he had his horse kneel to the queen, then to the crowd, and then rode off to the congratulations of comrades and friends.

Finally, it was Jason's turn. Jason instructed the knight and squire attending him. "Be ready to bring me my weapons and backpack."

Jason strode and stood in front of the pavilion. He saluted the king with one of Merinda's swords, hoping this wasn't an offensive move, bowed to Princess Merinda, then waved at Lady Killensdale, seated with Nelda and Amanie. Lady Killensdale had convinced a whole row of ladies to wave their handkerchiefs to show support. Lord Killensdale and the rest of the lords with their ladies were quite embarrassed by the outlandish display and tried to look aloof.

Jason remained standing before Princess Merinda and turned to face the two men coming from the opposing tent at the other end of the field. It was Prince Dunaibi and the giant man, Maudid.

Both men saluted the king and bowed to Princess Merinda.

"Who is this man, Prince Dunaibi? Your second?" asked Princess Merinda.

"No, princess. Just as you have your champion, I have mine.

This is Maudid Guboh. He has been my undefeated champion for many years. He is general of my armies and a powerful fighter, defeating even Nog the stone giant with his bare hands," said Prince Dunaibi smugly.

"This cannot be! It is not fair!" she cried despairingly.

"It never was fair, not for me or for Sir Jason. But you, Princess Merinda, are the one who put us in this impossible situation when you chose a little boy to be your champion. All that has changed is that my champion, whose only vow is to protect me, will bear the brunt of this insult instead of me, and he will not be as forgiving as I. Honor demands this be a match to the death; the boy will die."

"Jason, I... I—" stammered Princess Miranda, ghastly pale.

Jason whirled and interrupted her, "No. Do not even think it.

Everyone is wondering if the Creator will aid me. Although you do not yet realize it, the Creator already has given us the victory. We have only to act our part."

Maudid stepped forward and sneered, "Brave words from a foolish child. I have arranged to give you a demonstration in hopes both of you will change your minds before we enter the field of battle. For once I begin, I will not leave until I kill the boy and one other man to fill my need to avenge my honor. Maudid clapped his hands and two servants appeared, each carrying a heavy iron club. Prince Dunaibi took a seat with the royal family, though opposite of Princess Merinda.

Maudid removed his silk shirt, revealing solid muscle under dark skin. The man stood nearly seven feet tall and weighed a lean 350 pounds. Maudid handed his shirt to one of the servants as he took the clubs.

Jason had seen an Indian wrestler use iron clubs to develop arm and hand strength, but as Maudid whipped through his routine, he made it look easy. Despite his bulk, the huge man moved quick and lithe as a cat. The crowd clapped. He returned his clubs to the servants while two other servants led a large cow on a tether and stopped in front of him. The cow stood dumbly chewing her cud as the servant backed away. He stood in front of the cow and clenched his fists. With a sudden kiai, he leaped into the air and came crashing down with a huge fist onto the cow's head. The cow fell instantly over onto its back, stiff-legged. It shuddered once and was still. A murmur of awe could be heard throughout the masses on the hillside.

Maudid then flexed his muscles, faced the crowd, and bellowed his outrage. "You have insulted my prince, my country, and me. I defy you all. After I tear that young whelp apart, you had better have a real man ready to face me, or I will kill the next man of this country who crosses my path." At that, he flexed his muscles again, roaring at the people and the royal family. The crowd went wild with angry shouts and jeers. Some of the soldiers and guards fidgeted with their weapons.

Jason was not planning on showing anything of his skills so that surprise would be on his side, but he was sure the large stand-in was about to hurt someone. Indeed, just then, a woman from the crowd stepped forward and screamed at Maudid with just as much ferocity. Although he was over twenty feet away, he spun and thrust his palm at her, and she fell down unconscious, as though he had hit her. Jason had seen so-called chi masters on his world, but this seemed to be the genuine thing.

Jason walked calmly to the center of the field. He signaled Torin to bring his bow and quiver. With bow in hand and the quiver on his belt, the boy turned to face the crowd with a hand upraised. The crowd and Maudid silenced and watched in anticipation. He knew how to project his voice from many years of addressing audiences, both in martial arts classes, demonstrations and also from the pulpit.

Despite his little boy voice, he was able to manage nicely as he said loudly, "Maudid and Prince Dunaibi, listen to me. Princess Merinda has not insulted you nor has the government of Chanderlon. Princess Merinda has chosen me, a hero of Chanderlon, to represent her. I have been chosen a hero not because the people of Chanderlon are small, but because my God, who is the Creator, stands beside me and he is larger than all."

At that, Jason drew an arrow and shot in a high arc so it would land in the field in front of him. Although he had never tried this before, he knew he must not lose sight of the arrow if this was going to work, so without looking down, he grabbed another arrow and notched it. It no longer mattered to him if he succeeded or not since he had already accomplished his purpose in calming the crowd.

As the first arrow descended, he judged its rate. He drew and fired in one smooth motion and shot the other arrow out of the sky. The crowd murmured in awe at what they saw, then cheered wildly.

Laying down the bow and quiver, he then drew the two swords. He bowed toward the audience and began a sword kata called Ninto, which means invisible blade. It starts off with the blades hidden from sight, and throughout the kata, the blades are hidden at various intervals.

The blue cloak flowed behind him as the graceful and powerful motions sent the crowd cheering again. Just as he gave the finishing bow, he heard the raucous cry of a woman's voice screaming, "Kill him, Jason." He had to smile because it was the voice of the normally demure and proper Lady Killensdale.

Maudid looked disdainfully at Jason as he stalked over to the small tent at the other end of the field with his entourage of servants. Jason returned to his tent as a mule-drawn wagon came onto the field to haul the dead cow away.

CHAPTER 26

Oh Sting, Where Is Thy Death?

Sir Quineas slapped Jason on the back, nearly knocking him down, and pushed him into the tent. "Good show, my boy. If nothing else, the crowd is on your side."

"Sir Quineas," Jason said, "what are the rules concerning the combat?" He had asked this question of Merinda but wanted to be sure of his options.

"There are very few and poorly defined. Even if one of you surrenders, that does not have to be accepted," replied the knight. Jason shook his head. "I was wondering what type of fighting strategies are allowed. For instance, may I use my bow and arrows?" "Yes, of course," Sir Quineas assured him. "In fact, after your display, it is expected. But as far as other things: gas, fire, acid, poison, or even magic is acceptable as long as you do not receive outside aid."

"Thank you, Sir Quineas," Jason replied.

"One more thing... Both of you will be given a table to set your weapons on for convenient use. While it is proper that the other person's weapons on the table are off limits, it doesn't mean they cannot be used by the opponent, and frequently, they are. It is wise not to put your most powerful weapon on the table, or if you do, do not leave it unguarded. The table itself may also be used, and fighters in the past have used it as a shield from archers."

Torin suddenly spoke up, "Sir Bristol, until I saw your display, I did not think it possible for you to win. Do you really have a chance against such a monster?"

He looked at Torin thoughtfully and answered slowly, "There is more going on here than what you can see. There are demons gambling on the outcome. The gods of this world are focusing their powers against the Creator, and there are souls in the balance. This is more than a simple fight. It is the representation of a clash of powers in an unknown realm. I represent the Creator, for which anything is possible except failure. Though the Creator does not always define success the same as we might."

Sir Quineas cut in, "I have heard people speak of the Creator in these last few days. Why has no one heard of him before?"

"It is because mankind on this world long ago chose to forget, but now the Creator has sent me to refresh everyone's memory. I can hear from the crowds that Maudid is ready."

Indeed, the sound of boos and hisses echoed throughout the valley. Jason removed his blue cape and replaced it with the old worn jacket from his backpack. He tied his sword belt around the jacket in reminiscence of his karate gi. Then, grabbing his bows, arrows, and backpack, he stepped out of the tent.

Maudid was already in the middle of the field, wearing tight-fitting black trousers that ended at calf height. They were trimmed with gold with short slits on either side of the calves. Over this, he wore a purple cloth sash as a belt. His bare upper torso glistened from oil rubbed onto his skin. Without his hat and the ridiculous feather, he now revealed a nearly bald head with a narrow strip of black hair from the back of his head to the middle of his back, tied with cord at intervals.

Several bundles were on Maudid's table set part way into the field. Like a dark-skinned gladiator, he held a long black spear and a small net.

Jason placed his items on a similar table set for him, then notched an arrow onto his bowstring. Trumpets sounded and the crowd cheered. So it has begun, thought Jason without moving.

Maudid held the net and stalked toward him. It was a black colored combat net made of wire with little hooks sewn into it. "Little boy, I am going to trap you like a fish, so you can't run away," taunted the giant man loudly.

Jason experimentally fired an arrow at Maudid's body. Maudid turned aside and let the arrow fly past, but he was already firing another arrow. This one Maudid batted aside with his spear. Maudid charged while Jason calmly fitted another arrow and drew. This time, Jason aimed for the head. Maudid slapped it out of the air with his net. That told Jason all he needed to know. He did indeed face a superb martial artist, one way better than he.

In another moment, Maudid would be upon him, so he dropped his quiver and bow and drew one of Princess Merinda's swords. The Kuladonian was in the process of throwing his net when the irony of the situation occurred to Jason. As a set net fisherman with a lifetime experience with nets, someone was trying to catch him in one.

No way, Jose, thought Jason as he stepped aside.

Maudid threw the net with his spear ready to follow up for an easy victory. Jason instantly dodged to the right, grabbed the edge of the weighted net while it was still airborne, and pulled hard as he spun backward to redirect the net back onto Maudid.

The net came around in a complete circle, just as Maudid stabbed at him with the spear. The spear was caught in the net as the rest of the net slapped against Maudid's body, not quite entangling him, but some of the barbs sunk into his exposed flesh. The big man cursed as he ripped the net off, causing gashes on his skin, while Jason took the opportunity to cut Maudid's entangled spear shaft with his sword. The spear shaft cut cleanly under his blow, attesting to the sharpness of Princess Merinda's blades.

The powerful foreigner quickly recovered, and dropping the spear shaft, he stepped in and struck Jason's hand with the edge of his hand, knocking the sword from the boy's grip and numbing the nearly healed hand. This he followed with a quick backhand to Jason's face. Jason's world exploded into stars as he flew through the air and landed on his side. He should have rolled when he fell, but he did not seem able to move. The warlord pounced like a cat with a mouse, grabbing his throat and lifting him high into the air. Jason countered despite the pain and kicked himself away, releasing the man's grip.

Falling to the ground again, he didn't give himself the luxury of recovering. He was hurt and not sure exactly where he was hurt, but if he didn't do something fast, he would be dead. Rolling back to his feet, he kicked at a target between the man's legs but was too slow. Maudid swept his foot with one hand and was lifting it to dump him on his back.

Jason knew several counters to this move but chose the most aggressive one. He sprang forward off one foot and drove his captured leg down into Maudid's grip so that his knee was held instead of his foot. Then, he grabbed around the warrior's head and rammed his forehead into the man's face, smashing the fighter's nose painfully. He attempted to press his thumbs into Maudid's eyes to blind him, but the big man shook his head, preventing this, so Jason, still holding the bullet-shaped head, launched himself backward, pulling Maudid off balance. As they both went down, Jason added impetus by pressing with the once held foot up against the groin to help the unfortunate assailant on his way. Maudid flipped and landed heavily on the ground several feet away.

The roaring crowd was on their feet.

Jason beat the giant to his feet as the two faced each other.

Like a mad dog, the big man snarled, "That was a good trick, but it ends here." Blood ran from his nose.

Like an angry bull, the man roared and charged at Jason, swinging his fist in a downward chop, meaning to crush him with his most deadly blow. As the gargantuan fist came down, it looked to the crowd that Jason stopped the blow with his forearm, but actually, he redirected it, deflected it, and gave way at the same time, slowing the fist while absorbing little of the energy. He then counter-attacked with a high elbow strike to the hulking man's solar plexus.

Maudid staggered back, gasping, trying to catch his breath. Jason was vaguely aware of the cheering of the crowds. What he had done seemed impossible. He had disarmed the seemingly invincible Maudid, withstood the steamroller's strongest attacks, and as the two faced each other, only the large man was staggering, bleeding from his face and shoulders. Jason was probably staggering too but much less noticeable due to his diminutive size.

Maudid clumsily swung again with a roundhouse aimed at the boy's face, but this, Jason also intercepted with his forearm as he spun inside the circle, weighting the committed arm. Again, the fierce warrior was brought off balance and slung to the ground.

Drawing his other sword with his left hand and using a backward-facing grip, Jason advanced on the recovering man. Maudid narrowed his eyes, "Jason, you are far more skilled than I could have imagined and you have fought bravely, but it cannot save you."

Like a holy man, Maudid placed his hands together and bowed his head as if in prayer, in intense concentration. Jason could feel the power building as the titanic warrior then pulled his arm back as if coiling a heavy spring and punched his palm forward, even though Jason was about fifteen feet away. He felt nothing physically but did feel the extension of the man's soul as it sought a vulnerable spot in his own. Maudid blinked in surprise, for there was no vulnerable spot within him that had not already been assaulted from many spiritual battles in the past and strengthened by the years of experience of a much older man. Perhaps some protection from God was involved, as well. The chi attack was stymied.

Moving quickly, the big man sprinted away toward his own table where his weapons were laid, instead of charging like Jason expected. Jason took this momentary pause in battle to catch his breath.

This was a mistake. Suddenly, he felt all the pain he should have been feeling all along. He felt the bruised shoulders, arms, and welts stinging his face. His right forearm was still numb from the earlier vicious chop. He felt like limping even though his legs were not yet injured. He slowly backed toward where he had dropped Merinda's first sword, watching his opponent's actions.

Maudid picked up a weapon wrapped in yellow linen and unwound it while Jason dizzily scooped up the sword which had been knocked from his hands. He then continued back to his own side and opened the backpack on the table. Meanwhile, the dark-skinned warrior unwrapped an enormous, golden-looking scimitar, probably an alloy of some metal stronger than steel with a bejeweled handle that flashed in the sunlight.

Maudid swirled it over his head and behind his back in an amazing display of swordsmanship. The blade seemed to pulsate light as he held it, probably magical. He finished in a low stance with the blade behind his back and one hand pointing at Jason, his finger pointing upward.

"Feel honored, Jason. I have saved this blade for a worthy foe. No one who has faced this blade has ever lived to tell about it. You are about to experience the wrath of the Sun Blade!" shouted the warrior, now about seventy-five feet away. He then began slowly approaching Jason like a panther stalking his prey.

Sheathing his swords, Jason responded, "I too have a weapon I have been saving." He took the green silk sack Lady Killensdale had given him and loosened the strings tied at the top. The contents filled the bag like a small pillow. He walked toward Maudid partway and set the bag on the ground. As he bent over to set it down, the stalking man lunged with incredible speed, the scimitar swinging in a low arc. The light it emitted was like the sun, effectively blinding Jason.

Jason sprung backward causing the blow to miss. He could tell the blade radiated heat as it waved past him, and he purposely fell backward as the scimitar's back swing nearly caught him. He continued the fall into a back roll and came up in time to see a crazed strike from overhead, threatening to split him into two.

Whipping both blades out simultaneously to meet the scimitar, he was dismayed to see the golden sword cut right through his swords as if they were butter. Only his quick jump back again saved his life, leaving him holding two worthless sword handles. His eyes were partially blinded, seeing red and blue streaks when he blinked.

Now with Jason disarmed, Maudid lunged, recklessly stabbing at the adolescent's throat. Leaping back and to the side, not knowing he was now on the edge of the stream's sloped embankment, Jason lost his balance and did a back roll again, dropping the sword handles and landing in the stream.

Maudid laughed cruelly. He was standing between Jason and the green silk bag. Standing ankle deep in the stream, Jason thrust desperately into his coat pockets, looking for a knife or something he could use as a weapon. He felt a wad of leather wrapped with string. It was his forgotten sling, the one at which he had no skill.

The sling immediately brought to mind the biblical story of the boy David killing the giant Goliath. It would be great irony if God helped him defeat Maudid the same way. He pulled out the sling and snatched up five stones from the stream like David had done.

"You are going to kill me by slinging rocks?" the champion of Prince Dunaibi asked incredulously.

"No," replied Jason. "I'll kill you by the power of God. But first, I will give you a chance to surrender."

"Your god can't help you now," scoffed the man darkly.

With that, Jason quickly let loose a stone, hurling it full force, missing the incredulous warrior by about ten feet as it flew across the field. He felt embarrassed. He was as bad a shot with the sling as he ever was. Maudid blinked in surprise as the stone flew by and broke into laughter. "Try again, little one. Your god may be powerful, but he is not very accurate," he mocked.

Jason hurled another stone. It misfired, shooting straight up into the air. Now Maudid's laughter was uncontrollable. Looking for an opportunity, Jason seized upon the laughter as a chance of rushing Maudid and perhaps getting by him to his bag or disarming him.

Bounding into action, he fairly flew up the bank with a low side kick to the man's knee. But the martial champion merely sidestepped and slapped the boy down with the flat side of his scimitar. While falling on his back, Jason suddenly saw the stone he had just thrown so horribly, returning to earth. From his angle, it appeared to be right in line to hit Maudid on the head.

The scimitar was at his throat, and he held his breath as he watched. Surely the stone couldn't hit the big man hard enough to hurt him much, but the distraction could help him get away. His heart sank as he watched the stone fall past his attacker's head, landing somewhere behind with a whack that did not quite sound right for hitting the ground. Maudid didn't seem to notice the sound or how close he had come to being struck.

The big man was talking again. "Hah. I have you now, Jason. Even if you try to surrender, I will not listen. I want you to know that Prince Dunaibi has many wives, and when they do not please him, he gives them to me, and I make them disappear forever. The prince has promised Princess Merinda to me, when he is through with her, and her death will be a long and distasteful one, I promise you." The fiend hissed as he broke into maniacal laughter.

Suddenly, Maudid stopped and slapped himself. "Ouch," he said and slapped again. Jason kicked the blade aside, then kicked straight into Maudid's knee, making him stumble backward. Maudid tried to back-pedal to catch himself but fell near the now open green bag. The bag, having been struck by Jason's wayward stone, exposed a large nest full of mad hornets. The nest broke the rest of the way open as the foreign general's arm hit it on his backward fall. The hornets immediately attacked in a vicious buzzing cloud.

Jason, who by now had gained his feet, sprinted to his bow and arrows, snatching them from where he had dropped them and turned, kneeling.

Some hornets, attracted by his movements, swarmed at him. He froze in place, focusing on the now screaming giant. A hornet stung him, and it felt like being stabbed by a hot poker, but still he didn't move.

Screaming, the desperate combatant ran toward the stream, shaking his head like a mad man. The stream had no pools in this stretch big enough to protect such a large man. Maudid was frantic, with hornets all over him. Standing, his sword held forgotten in his hand, he swatted with one hand and shook his head back and forth, crying out with pain. Jason slowly notched an arrow and waited. Even that little movement caused three more hornets to hit him. Hornets landed and crawled on him, but still he remained frozen in spot, letting one of the angry hornets sting him again, while carefully watching the pain-crazed fighter.

He could have shot at that moment before the man looked back at him, but he felt that a coward's move. He then realized that if he failed to stop the man, Maudid had promised to kill him no matter what and then kill the first man from this country whom he came across, which would probably be Sir Quinias or Torin, and he also promised to eventually torture, rape, and kill Princess Merinda.

God wanted him to love his enemies, but this enemy was intent on harm, and even if he were not a Knight of Chanderlon, he had a duty to prevent this evil, or he would be accessory to it. Thus, he reasoned honor in this case was to kill this creature who went beyond man and had become monster.

He released the arrow and braced himself for another hornet sting, which did not come. Maudid was only about fifty feet away, and his arrow hit true, although the man's convulsive movements in trying to kill the bees brought his arm up right at that moment and the arrow struck his forearm.

The pain of the arrow shocked him back to the present situation, and as a true martial artist, Maudid stopped and recentered his thoughts and focused himself to his task. As he looked back up at Jason, one eye almost swollen shut, he broke off the arrow haft close to his arm.

Jason quickly fired again, hoping to keep the man off balanced, but on reflex, the agonized man swatted that arrow away with the golden looking scimitar. Jason was refitting another arrow when, suddenly, Maudid thrust the sword into the air and a bright light flashed from it. The brilliant light was like that of the sun, and an intense heat radiated from it.

Jason shielded his eyes. Feeling the heat, he was glad he was no closer to the source. He was not injured, but the hornets in the air fell with little tendrils of smoke while those crawling on Maudid's skin vaporized. Maudid was, of course, protected from the heat by the sword's magic.

Eyes still dazzled from the light, Jason fired blindly. A groan from the man showed he scored a hit, and as his eyes cleared, he could see he hit the man in the thigh.

Maudid did not attempt to remove the arrow in his leg, but with intense concentration, the mountain of a warrior readied his glowing scimitar and stalked toward him, weaving his head from side to side in an attempt to gain depth perception with his one good eye. The Sun Blade pulsed with light in an ascending frequency as though gathering power. Jason anticipated a magical attack from the blade. He figured he probably could not evade a magical attack by purely reacting, so he anticipated the man's motion or signal that would release the energies. Although Maudid was still twenty feet away, he made a thrusting motion with the sword toward Jason.

Jason dropped flat on the ground and closed his eyes. He heard a dull roar and felt searing heat scorch his back. The brilliance nearly blinded him even with his eyes closed. He sensed the bulk of the attack missed him, but he felt like he had more than a sunburn on any exposed skin.

Hoping the light blinded Maudid as well, he rolled to the left and was going to try to close the distance when he heard the sword strike the ground where he had lain just a moment before. Maudid was taking no more chances and had moved in quickly for the kill.

Opening his eyes, Jason saw he was beside Maudid on his blind side and his would-be killer was down on one knee holding a half buried sword. The roll on the ground had dumped half his remaining arrows. One of these he snatched as he lunged toward the man in hopes of hitting him before he could pull the sword from the ground.

Maudid, unable to see him, nevertheless sensed the attack and raised one hand to block but was too slow. The tip of the razor-sharp arrowhead slashed the side of his neck as he threw the young boy off like a rag doll. As a warrior, he knew the trouble of his wounds, especially this last one. As he lost blood, he would tire and perhaps die. The hornet poisons also continued their work. He needed to act quick, or indeed, he could lose.

He was angry before, but now, he let go of his discipline and allowed the beastal rage within to consume him. No more holding back. No more refined moves and combat tricks, just pure raw power and speed—something this little boy was no match for.

He jerked the sword out of the ground with a beastal scream, louder than that used to intimidate the crowd earlier. Dirt and smoke fell off the blade reflecting his rage and like a madman he charged, hacking from side to side, creating a wall of death before him.

Jason had just regained his feet with bow in one hand and a broken arrow with its head in the other, useless for shooting without the feathered side. He had no time to think as Maudid charged like an angry bear. He reacted as he had the last time he'd found himself in this situation with the cannibal.

He dropped his bow and charged underneath the swings of the sword, right between the giant's legs. Diving low to avoid being hit by the running knees, he rolled to a standing position behind the man. This move had broken and crushed the remaining arrows in his quiver, but he was rewarded by the sight of more blood streaming from the other leg of his attacker through the black pants. Blood dripped off his broken arrow tip.

Maudid whirled and charged again, though unsteadily, the Sun Blade blazing. Jason was a little boy facing a nearly unstoppable berserker with only a frail, broken shaft with a short blade attached at the end. Even he saw the impossibility of his situation and wondered if he was going to die.

The words of Princess Merinda echoed in his head, "Jason, remember, if you feel like you are about to die, please surrender." To surrender to Maudid at this point was to surrender to death. He could try to run, but even in his weakened state, Maudid was faster. The little weapon in his hand was no protection against what was coming so he risked nothing in a desperation move of throwing it.

He threw the arrowhead with all his might at the charging bull just a sword's width away from ending his life. He intended to throw it at the man's eye, but in this extreme situation, he was not accurate, and the shafted arrowhead sunk into the man's throat. The wound gave the man pause, and with a gargled cry, he struck at Jason.

Again, Jason jumped back but was cut across the chest, cutting his jacket and into his chest a little, giving a burning sensation.

He didn't have time to examine his wound, but if it were a long one, he knew there was danger of going into shock. Well, what happens, happens; for now, he was dodging for his life as other blows rained down upon him.

Again, his training was to move in close upon a weapon wielder, inside the range of the long blade. Then he intended to jab the man's good eye but was too short to reach such a target. Maudid's blood was flowing freely and smeared over Jason as he contacted the man's body. As he tried to circle around behind while clinging to the man's legs, Maudid was trying to whack Jason without hitting himself.

He was where he wanted to be but without a weapon was at a loss as to what he could do to take this man down. He then remembered the broken arrows still rattling around in his quiver. Snatching one, he repositioned his grip and slammed this one into the man's kidney. The shape of the arrowhead made it hard to withdraw, so he scrambled for another.

Content that Maudid would die no matter what happened to him, Jason went on the offensive himself. Holding the next arrow close to the head, he went on a slashing spree. He was not out of control as he tried to make every cut count, concentrating on the tendons in the back of the knee and below the man's calf.

Maudid knew he was going down and tried to fall on Jason. But being this close, Jason could feel the man's move and dove away, again rolling to a standing position. Maudid got back to his knees, unable to stand. It was only a matter of time now, and all Jason had to do was keep away from him.

Turning his back on Jason, the ultimate sign of disrespect, Maudid set the hilt of the sword on the ground. Knowing what this meant, Jason shouted, "Stop, don't do this!"

The man mumbled, "I will not be killed by a child."

"Wait! There is another option. Surrender to God! There is no shame in this."

"I alone control my destiny. I am my own god. You cannot stop me," the big man gurgled, with blood trickling from his mouth.

Before Jason could say another word, Maudid fell upon his blade. The magically sharp scimitar slipped through him and stuck out his back.

Maudid fell on his side, his one good eye fixed upon him. "I have won." He gasped, then closed his eyes. Jason just shook his head. From his perspective, the man's last act was a shame, defiant and willful to the end.

It seemed to be over too soon. At the same time, it seemed he'd been engaged in battle for hours. No theatrics, no drama, just a sudden silence. Though it was not silent, really. It was then that he became aware of the roar of the crowds. Now he realized that even he had never really believed he would prevail, even with God's help, and felt humbled.

He stood and waved toward the pavilion. At that moment, the trumpets sounded and someone loudly announced, "Maudid Guboh is defeated! Sir Jason Bristol is victor!"

Several servants from Maudid's tent rushed to tend to their master's body as Jason walked back toward the pavilion. Sir Quineas and Torin ran to meet him with their congratulations and wet rags to clean him up. As Jason neared the pavilion, the crowd jumped the pole fence barricade and stormed toward the heroic little boy.

Jason considered running, but instead, he spread his arms as if to embrace them all. Many were blessing him in the name of the Creator. They grabbed his legs, lifted him high into the air, and carried him before the royal family and the king. The crowd set Jason before the king and quieted. Princess Merinda stood beside the king, exuberantly smiling with tears in her eyes. Prince Dunaibi was nowhere to be seen.

"Sir Jason Bristol," orated King Beldane. "Today, we have witnessed valiant combat the likes of which we have never before seen. More than that, we have witnessed a miracle, an exhibition of the power of the god you serve. In honor of this event, I declare a victory celebration tonight. May the Creator bless you and may the Creator bless Chanderlon!"

The crowd gave another rousing cheer and began dispersing to prepare for the coming celebration. After a while, Jason was able to break away from the commotion and went to his tent.

Princess Merinda caught up with him there. "Jason, are you okay?" she asked with some concern.

"Other than some cuts, bruises, burns, and some bee stings, yeah, I'm fantastic!" he said happily.

Princess Merinda smiled, relieved. "You took some pretty good hits. I simply couldn't believe my eyes, seeing you throw Maudid around. Jason, I thank you, and I thank the Creator for what you did for me. I feel humbled he would care for me so much."

"You're welcome, Merinda. We both do care for you very much."

He took his bow and quiver, retrieved his backpack from Torin, and the now empty green bag.

As he shook out the green bag, he warned, "Stay back, Merinda, just in case some hornets are still stuck in here."

Two hornets came whizzing out but took off for the fields immediately. Sir Quineas came in from the field bearing the Sun Blade and presented it to Jason. "As victor in the field of combat the sword of the vanquished now belongs to you."

Jason accepted the hilt proffered him and touched the blade. It still felt hot but not so much as to burn. First the Moon Blade and now the Sun Blade. Was there a Star Blade somewhere too? Despite himself, he thought, those who live by the sword shall die by the sword, words of Jesus. He wanted the blade, but it represented as much a danger as the other did. He would find a way to dispose of it too.

By now, the crowd was thinning. "You go on back. I need to personally give thanks to God." He turned. "I will find my own way back to the castle. See you there."

"Jason, first let Sir Quineas and Torin attend to your wounds." Jason nodded, and as she watched him walk away, Princess

Merinda murmured to herself, "I am the Disbeliever no longer. You are strange, Jason, but strange in a wonderful way."

After tending his wounds, Sir Quineas and Torin followed at a distance as Jason climbed the hill behind the field and rested under a tree, the pain of his wounds abating with his unnatural healing. He felt exhausted. He'd consumed the bread and water in his backpack but needed more. Nevertheless, he knelt and began his prayers of thanks. That is when he noticed a little straw basket left by one of the townsfolk who had come to watch.

Opening it, he discovered a flask jar of wine, a hunk of bread, and some cheese. He smiled to himself. God provides. When finished, he left a small silver coin in the basket, just in case someone went through the effort to return for it.

With his strength restored somewhat, he prayed for about twenty minutes. The violence of the battle left him in deep need of spiritual healing as well. Again, remembering his family, he finished by praying for them.

When done, he realized it was getting late, so he joined the knight and his squire. He still had the Sun Blade with him. Should he bury this like he did the other? He bid the two escorts to go on ahead of him since he wanted to walk alone for a while and promised to catch up before they made it to town. With reluctance, they mounted their steeds and proceeded ahead.

A fine horse was also waiting for him, though Jason just led it. Soon, he spied a large boulder with brush growing on top and hid the scimitar underneath on the far side in a natural hole, which he covered with more rocks. He thought about riding the horse but did not think this the best time to learn since he had enough bumps and bruises as it was and continued trotting back to town, leading the horse at his pace. When he caught up with Sir Quineas and Torin, he mounted and let them lead his horse for him.

CHAPTER 27
Deologue 5

The combatants vigorously rolled in the mud of a forest stream bed, splashing water and debris with every move. Suddenly, one pushed the other away with a mighty kick, sending the other flying through the air until he hit heavily against a tree. As the mud-covered man slid down the tree, he flung three black daggers, appearing out of nowhere, in rapid succession.

The other mud-covered fighter was just standing when he saw the harbingers of death flying at him. With a quick motion of his hand, as if by magic, he raised a wall of muck and water to stop the deadly assault. Satisfaction showed on his face as the three blades stuck in the impromptu wall, halted in place. Unexpectedly, the other brawler burst through the watery wall with his fist leading, striking the surprised man in the chest, knocking him back into the water.

In an explosion of spray, both wrestled again, churning the once beautiful stream into a polluted drainage ditch. Then, as if the forest caught on fire, a bright light filled the area.

"Scoron and Dontevile, stop!" came the command that sounded as loud as thunder.

Stunned, both petty gods stood and looked around. Glowing with a bright light the giant titan Xan Rukkah stomped toward them, while a waif-like Axialla floated alongside on black moth wings sprouting from her back.

"You two know better than any how futile it is to actually fight in person."

"Yes." Dontevile smiled. "But smashing the nose on Scoron's face is so satisfying, even if it does not hurt him very much."

"You fool," hissed Axialla. "While you have been indulging yourself, your champion has been defeated by a child!"

"What?" asked Dontevile in surprise as he wiped mud from his face.

"It is true. Maudid Guboh has been defeated and killed by a child named Jason in single combat."

"Impossible," blurted the astonished god. "He could not have done it without divine help. Who would have dared?"

"The Creator," responded both Axialla and Xan Rukkah together.

Scoron sprayed both himself and Dontevile with water from his palm, and the mud melted off.

Scoron asked, "What does the Creator care? Have we not made this world vile enough to make the Creator not want it? Has not enough of mankind forgotten him for him to abandon them?"

Axialla responded, "This boy has reminded them. Already, people in Chanderlon are starting to call upon the Creator instead of us. This is a danger greater than those obscure prophets and seers who have been touched in their dreams by the Creator but have no idea what they are talking about. This boy knows things that go beyond this world. We have discovered he is from the prime world."

"Then he must be stopped," declared Dontevile.

"That is where we had hoped you would help us, though it may be too late," said Xan Rukkah.

Scoron interrupted, "The boy is in your realm, Xan Rukkah, in your power. Can you not stop him?"

"Our struggle is in our followers against the Creator's followers, and that pesky thing called free will granted to mankind. Could you imagine what would happen if you, or I, showed up in person and somehow Jason, with the help of the Creator, got the better of us? Even if we killed him it would invigorate martyrs for the cause."

"If he were in my realm, I would have no problem disposing of him, for the dead of the sea tell no tales," boasted Scoron.

Axialla interjected, "I hope you are right, Scoron, but bear in mind, the Creator claims all realms as his. We must work together against this common enemy if we are to succeed."

"Agreed," shouted Dontevile. "I will work with you because I have a personal score to settle with this boy and his protector. I will get the rest of the gods to help as well. Together, we will defeat them!"

With that, the four gods placed their hands together to seal the pact, then all vanished in a clap of thunder, leaving the forest stream in its ruined state.

CHAPTER 28
The Secret Room

Upon returning to Chanderlon, Jason found the celebration in full swing. Revelers were drinking, eating, and dancing in the streets. Jason's small band, in the dark, passed unnoticed until a group of carousing soldiers spotted him. They insisted on carrying him to the castle gates. With permission from his guardians, he dismounted and joined the soldiers. The night guard readily allowed them in, and he was ushered to the main hall.

The leftovers of a full banquet spread over the table. It appeared he was late for the main activities, and only a few lords and ladies remained dancing to the hired musicians. Princess Merinda was talking with several ladies when he walked in, and she rushed over to him. Seeing he was near exhaustion, Princess Merinda took charge of her small champion and saw to it that he ate well.

As he finished eating, the knights of Chanderlon entered the room and goblets of wine were distributed by servants to everyone. The knights then surrounded Jason's table. Sir Quineas bid Jason to stand on the table, then raised his goblet and spoke in a loud voice to the general audience, "Young Jason was appointed by the king to be a member of our rank. Many of us doubted the wisdom of that promotion, and although we loved the lad, we did not consider him our equal. Traditionally, a new knight is given initiation into our order, but many of us felt he would not be ready for such an initiation until he was much older.

"But Princess Merinda, through her faith in him and the Creator, offered the lad an initiation through combat that would cause the hearts of even the stoutest knight to fail. If Jason knew fear, he never showed it. I and my squire were with him in his tent today, and indeed, it was he who gave us comfort and encouragement.

"To my brothers in arms and to the royalty present, I lift my cup to Jason and do hereby declare that through the trial of combat, Jason is fully initiated and one of us, a full-fledged Knight of Chanderlon!"

The pronouncement was met by hurrah's of approval as the knights toasted Jason.

Then Princess Merinda stood on the table with Jason. When the room hushed, she said, "It is my privilege to toast my champion, who defended my honor today. When Jason came to me, I was running away from my obligations and duties, but he showed me what true faithfulness was and inspired me to face my own trials against overwhelming odds. Jason showed me that true freedom is a matter of the heart and the burden of love is the most freeing of all. Because of Jason's faithfulness, I now accept the Creator as my only God.

"I did not wish the union with Prince Dunaibi as I knew he did not follow our customs and had many wives. I also wanted the freedom to choose my own husband. I knew of Prince Dunaibi's reputation as a fighter and that with his foreign skills he was an equal match to any knight in Chanderlon.

"So what I needed was an edge, a champion who was just as foreign, just as surprising as Prince Dunaibi himself, and what better choice could I make than to choose the Creator's own chosen champion, Jason Bristol. When Prince Dunaibi made Maudid his champion, a fighter even more renowned and powerful, my heart quailed within me. But it was Jason's courage and faith in the Creator that carried us through.

"Jason, I know you give all the glory and honor for this victory to the Creator, but allow me to say that your faith is to your credit and is an example for all of us. With only the body of a small boy, you fought with the courage and strength that exceeded your physical limitations. Jason, with all my heart and on behalf of Chanderlon, I say—we say—thank you."

Princess Merinda gave him a hug, and everyone crowded around to congratulate. Afterward, he lumbered to his room at the Killensdale's, who offered their own congratulations and, seeing his exhaustion, mercifully allowed him to go to bed.

After breakfast and a bath the next morning, Princess Merinda entered the room and asked cheerfully, "How is our heroic champion this morning?"

"I think I am healed and ready for my next adventure," he returned, just as cheerful.

"Well, in that case, follow me," she said mysteriously, with a twinkle in her eye.

To his wonderment, she led him out of the Killensdale apartment and down the corridor toward the royal quarters. She stopped just one door short of her family's guarded apartment and opened it.

The princess spoke as she showed the room to him, "I know this isn't much, but I had the servants clean out this old storeroom and set a bed, wardrobe, and dresser for you. Come look at the balcony. It has a view of the royal gardens."

"It is perfect, Merinda, but isn't this a bit much? I mean, does this obligate me to the king or something?" he asked worriedly.

"Don't worry, Jason. Obligation goes both ways, and we of Chanderlon are already obligated to you for what you have done for us. You are free to leave whenever you wish, but as long as you stay here, we simply expect you to continue to do as you have always done."

"And what is it I do?" he asked, puzzled.

"The job of any Knight of Chanderlon—to be a hero." Princess Merinda beamed. "Jason, you don't want to be tied down, but you have shown me what true loyalty is. From what I have seen, you are more loyal than any of the knights or lords at their best. Most are self-serving and would switch loyalties in a moment if it were in their favor. Not you, Jason. Your loyalty is first to God, and because of God's love, you are as loyal as they come."

As Jason looked around the room, he noticed a small chime hanging on the wall and asked her about it.

"Well," she said, looking a bit sheepish, "I have never had my own champion before, and I want to be able to call on you day or night, for you see, my bedroom is on the other side of this wall. That chime is connected through a crack in the wall stones. I will pull on it and ring if I need you. If you need me, there is a chime on the other side as well. Pull on it, and I will be here in a heartbeat."

"That is a very good idea," he said.

"The castellan will be by to schedule the servants. Don't be bashful. Order cleaning, baths, meals, extra blankets, or any other decorations or accommodations you like."

Princess Merinda swept cheerfully from the room as though she were his fairy godmother and left him to organize things as he saw fit. He looked at his new surroundings. He never expected to get his very own room.

First, he went onto the balcony. It overlooked the royal garden, still beautiful in its fall colors. The wall that divided the royal garden from the common garden was fairly close, close enough that he could jump to it in an emergency. Princess Merinda's balcony was also about the same distance on the other side.

He went back inside the room and tested the bed. It felt softer than any bed he'd ever had before, even in his own world. Before he knew it, he was asleep. The fight had taken a lot of energy out of him, and he discovered he could use the extra rest.

A bit later, there was a knock on the door. He let the castellan in and set a schedule for a maid to clean in the mornings. He also requested a table, chair, and tapestry for covering the balcony door to insulate it from winter drafts.

He lay back on the bed and studied the high ceiling. All the castle rooms had incredibly high ceilings. A waste of room, but he supposed they were purposely high to be cooler in the summer and also to support taller ramparts on the fortifications. But something seemed strange about the ceiling in this room. It did not seem as high as the others. He thought about it. This used to be a storage room, which explained why there was no fireplace, but then, why would there be a balcony? Perhaps it had been a guard's station before it became a storeroom. He examined the walls with his eyes. Although rough stone, it was still too smooth for climbing. But wait! There were several small holes about a half inch in diameter spaced several feet apart—a place for attaching a ladder?

Near the holes in the wall on the ceiling between the rafters the boards ran opposite of the rest of the ceiling boards.

Aha, a trapdoor, he thought. Now curious, he studied the wall and found more ladder anchor holes filled with soft mortar.

The ceiling was about sixteen feet in height, so he needed some sort of rope or ladder to reach. To get a ladder tall enough would draw attention to his discovery, which he wanted to keep a secret for now. The holes in the wall were too far apart to climb with pegs and the rafters were supporting the boards above, so there was no space to throw a rope through or hook with some sort of grapple. He got his rope out but still didn't have any ideas. Even if he stood his bed on end atop the dresser and wardrobe, it would still be too short for him to balance upon and reach the trap door.

He decided to go to town and shop. He paused at the castle courtyard and considered where he might purchase the things he needed. Besides the barracks and stables there were small shops for repair and maintenance, such as a smithy and wood shop, an armory, and a small warehouse for dry goods and military items. He figured the unusual nature of the items he wanted might draw too much attention here at the keep.

Being a knight, the regular soldiers on duty were required to salute him as he departed. He did his best to imitate and salute back solemnly, wanting to make friends.

The first shop he visited was the weapon makers which Princess Merinda had recommended. He ordered a blade similar to a katana to fit his size and two straight ninja-like blades, painted black with scabbards.

At a furniture shop, he commissioned a rope ladder for which they were happy to provide and added the wooden pegs at no cost. They immediately started work on the ladder for him and finished while he waited. It was all he could do to keep them from giving it to him, for they wanted to play a role in what they imagined to be part of some heroic venture or rescue.

It was dinnertime when he returned, and after depositing his pegs and ladder in his new room, he took his spot beside Princess Merinda. She enthusiastically gave Jason the report of how the investigation was going into Father Varigold's death. Of course, the priests themselves stymied all questions regarding their role in the venerable man's death, but an exhumation of the corpse revealed a smashed skull.

Since Jason did not actually see the murder take place, the investigators advised caution in pressing any charges as yet and were hoping to bribe some lower priests into turning over evidence. They were also looking for any bystander testimony.

The dinner itself was beginning to wear on Jason. Of course, the food was good, but it hardly varied from one dinner to the next. What he wanted was something from his own world. He was not much of a cook himself, but if he could find the right spices which tasted like those from his home world, he thought he might introduce this world to the delicacies called spaghetti or pizza.

After dinner, he returned to his room. He pushed the dresser in place and stood on it to place the pegs where the last ladder anchors used to be. He hung his rope ladder on these, carefully climbed and inserted more pegs. In this fashion, he made it to the ceiling.

Pressing on the trap door, which was heavier than he expected, the door swung open up and inward on ancient hinges. Dust immediately wafted over him as he tried to stare into the dark room. Since it was too dark to see, he climbed back down for a lamp and carefully carried it back up to the dark chamber. There was a wooden ladder attached to the wall which started at the floor of the upper room and went a few feet up. He grabbed its lower rung and hoisted himself up into the room. Ancient spider webs thick with dust impeded his way as he surveyed the area.

The room had a low ceiling with several wood benches and a trough containing hundreds of ancient but usable arrows. They stood on end, so they could be quickly snatched for shooting. A large stone basin weighing probably a hundred pounds stood on a pedestal. There were cross-shaped slits cut into the outer stone wall. They were called murder slits in his home world. These were cut into the stone wall at a downward angle, providing a good view of the garden below, but virtually invisible from outside. Everything was covered in a half inch of dust, undisturbed for probably fifty years or more.

A short stout door was located in the back wall, which he opened and was immediately met by a draft from some sort of chimney but no suet or smell of smoke. Peering into the dark, Jason could see a shaft going both up and down with the barest rays of light from above. Iron rungs were affixed to the wall of the shaft, forming a ladder.

Because his lamp couldn't be tilted much, he could not see very far down. Perhaps it went to a well or some dungeon below the castle. He would explore it in time, but first, he wanted to see where the chimney went up above.

Taking his rope and lamp, he climbed up. It came to an opening that angled down through an outside wall, providing a view of the upper roof and battlements. From this height, he presumed he was on a tower wall. The opening was too small for him to use as an exit, though it was also comforting that no one else could use it to get to his room, but the passageway into the dark bowels of the castle made him feel uneasy.

He wanted to drop something down into the inky blackness below but had nothing on him he wanted to give up, so he ventured to climb down the shaft. It felt like going into a well, and he hoped the rungs would not suddenly break, dropping him to a watery grave.

He counted the rungs as he went down and at fifty, his feet could feel no more rungs, nor could they feel anything but open expanse. Climbing back to stand on the lowest rung, he tried to shine the lamp to see what was down below. Despite the glare of the uncovered lamp in his own eyes, he discovered himself in a hole in the ceiling of another passageway below with a floor he could walk on. Tying his rope to the lower rung, he slid the last ten feet to the floor.

His dim light showed no dust on the rough cut stones, and he could feel the dampness of the dungeon. He surmised the passageway went both directions, into and away from the castle. It was probably an escape route similar to what Princess Merinda took him through that first time he met her.

He decided to leave the exploration of the passageway leaving the castle for some other time. First, he wanted to see where it opened inside the castle. Perhaps there would be a stairwell going back up to tie into some hidden passageway or cellar. For all he knew, he could be in a sewer, although there was no particular smell other than damp stone.

In the light of his lamp, he followed the passage to where the walls narrowed and the ceiling lowered, forcing him to hunch. His passage came to a large cave-like room, which opened part way up the wall. A natural protrusion hid the opening from below, creating an alcove where he had a good view yet could remain unseen.

There was already a dim light in the room, and he held his lamp aloft to light the room better. Dimly, he could see a large black stone idol of a woman holding an orb. The orb glowed steadily, lighting a blood-stained altar just below it. No one else was there. He expected to at least see a ghost in these spooky surroundings, but he saw none.

Despite the beauty of the woman depicted in the stone work, it was almost like he could feel an evil presence from the image. He felt like destroying the statue despite its possible politically correct cultural and historical value. He could feel its evil purposes and vowed to return and cleanse the place sometime.

Returning to his secret attic, he climbed to his bedroom to search for some cleaning equipment in the castle. He borrowed a broom, a bucket, and a thin board used as a dust pan and set about the task of cleaning his new hiding spot. After a couple of hours, it was bearable, and he closed the trapdoor and took the pegs down with him. He would rig a way to use his rope ladder, so it couldn't be seen. With winter on the way and no good source of heat, the loft might be warmer for sleeping.

That night, he wrestled with his prayers. The image of the statue and the blood-stained altar kept coming to mind. He prayed for guidance and wisdom concerning this and the prophecy. What exactly was his mission? He wondered if it was his duty to inform the local authorities. Perhaps he would be committing a crime by not reporting it. He should let the castle guards go about the case as they saw fit, to set up surveillance and catch the cult members or not, but that was their responsibility, not his. But something inside told him that was the wrong thing to do. He was also now one of those very authorities in this kingdom. He could set up the sting operation himself and it would be proper.

But he also was here on a mission for God and if the prophecy meant anything, then he must take that into consideration first. Who could be affected and caught by this? Was King Beldane involved? Could this idol be the rumored Axialla? If so, then there could be many prominent citizens and court officials involved, too. Would they be condemned to death for involvement or would it be swept under the rug or, forbid the thought, establish legitimacy for another evil cult?

He prayed longer this night than usual. Then suddenly, he remembered a statement Jesus had made, "I came not to condemn the world, but to save it."

Jason considered this. When Jesus made this statement, the world was already condemned. But Jesus's mission was to save the world. Yes, someday there will be judgment and condemnation for those who do not accept salvation, but when Jesus first came, condemnation was not his mission.

If Jesus were physically on this world, would not his mission be the same here as when he first walked the region of Israel as a man? And as Jesus's representative, would not he have a similar mission?

The prophecy identified him as bringing light into this world. What was that light? It would be the message that God loves the men of this world. On his home world, God loved mankind, even while they were his enemies. So like a missionary sent to a foreign land, he too was sent.

Feeling more comfort about his decision and a little more clarity, he slept peacefully that night. He dreamed of the whole kingdom repenting, even the villain in the shadows, represented by Lord Krogan.

The next morning, Jason continued to explore the town. He visited several spice shops looking for ingredients for pizza, particularly anything that tasted like oregano. He bought several small bags of spurgen, which smelled and tasted just like it.

Back at the keep, he kept his daily appointment with the tutor at the Killensdale's apartment and visited a little with Amanie before heading to the kitchen to try his "new" idea. Rounding a corner, he ran square into Gunther, the older bully.

With a mean look, Gunther backed up, fists ready, then looked down, and said, more subdued, "I have been looking for you, Sir Jason."

"Why, Gunther?" he asked.

"It is Princess Kuari. She wants to meet you in the royal garden alone. Just go there. They will let you in, and she will find you."

Gunther did not seem to be himself, which seemed to Jason to be a good thing, yet he had to ask, "Gunther, are you okay?"

"Yeah, but I have to go to my lessons, and they are really hard... especially the combat ones because I am the smallest one there," said Gunther uncomfortably.

Jason looked at Gunther sympathetically. "Remember these feelings, Gunther, and treat those smaller than you the way you would like to be treated."

"You are right, Sir Jason," he said. "There are some bullies among the other lords' sons. They are out to hurt me or anyone they can." After a moment, he blurted, "Sir Jason, can you teach me how to fight? I fought you twice and after watching you fight Maudid, I realize how nice you were to me. Even though you are just a kid, you could have killed me anytime you wanted."

Jason considered the question thoughtfully. This was not what he was here for, or was it? In some ways, he never stopped preaching, even when he taught martial arts, and it would be nice to train with someone regularly.

"Come to my apartment after dinner, and I will see what kind of student you are."

"Thank you, Sir Jason. You will not regret it." The boy bowed to Jason before departing.

He smiled to himself. What other surprises awaited him at the royal gardens? It was cool out, so he stopped by his room to don his new blue cloak made for him by Lady Killensdale. Then he went to the guarded hallway that allowed admittance to the royal gardens.

The guard passed him through, and he found a bench in front of a fountain. As he waited, he looked around the garden. All the flowers were dying, their leaves falling and remnants of this morning's ice at the edges of the fountain.

After a few minutes, Princess Kuari came onto her balcony and waved at him, then went back inside to come down. Upon her arrival, he stood and bowed. She offered her hand, and he lightly kissed it.

"Sir Bristol," Princess Kuari said with an air, "you are dressed impeccably, and your manners are excellent."

"Thank you, milady," he replied. "It was an excellent suggestion you gave concerning my attire."

The princess blushed a little. "Sir Jason, I feel we have had a bad start, and I wish to make amends."

Jason interrupted, "It is not necessary, Princess, but forgive me if I find it hard to trust you."

"You are right, Sir Jason. I wanted to hurt you as well as Amanie's cat. What I wanted was the power, the magic that my father has." Princess Kuari paused, hesitating.

He asked, "Is that where you saw the ceremony?"

Princess Kuari nodded, tears forming in her eyes. "Merinda wouldn't have anything to do with it. I thought she was afraid and weak, but I was wrong. I have never seen anyone stronger than she is now, except maybe you."

"So, Princess, do you want to become more like your sister?" he asked.

"Yes," she nodded emphatically, "but I don't expect you to believe me, so I have brought you something as a peace offering." Princess Kuari grabbed him suddenly and pulled him near, "There was a kindly old man asking about you today. There have been others, but they are just excited fans of yours. This man, though, was asking the children more specific things such as your schedule, where you go and where you sleep. Although he didn't talk to me, I am familiar with castle intrigue and could tell the man was a fake, so I followed him as he was leaving. The old man went behind a wagon and emerged a young man, stuffing a fake wig and beard into a pouch. Jason, I think someone has hired an assassin to kill you."

Jason nodded. "I have had the uneasy feeling I am being watched, but when I quickly turn to look, everyone is watching." "Don't joke about this, Sir Jason." Princess Kuari was gravely serious. "Your life is in danger. I would ask my father to assign a guard and start an investigation, except I think he is among those who might like to see you disappear."

"Really?" Jason was taken aback. "Are there others?"

"Why yes, of course." Princess Kuari rolled her eyes at Jason's naivety. "Prince Dunaibi for starters and whoever was behind the kidnapping of the lord's children may be after you as well. Even knights and lords in the castle jealous of your advancement may want to kill you. And don't forget, the priests of nearly every sect feel threatened by you. It is well-known that the priests of Xan Rukkah have closed their doors to you. That has never happened before in the history of Chanderlon!"

"Thank you for the warning and insight, Princess Kuari." He bowed.

The princess curtsied, and before making her way to her quarters, she warned, "You are very good at taking care of yourself, but these assassins don't fight fair, so please watch your back, Sir Jason."

As he watched her go, he thought it ironic that not too long ago she might have hired an assassin to kill him. He decided to be extra vigilant, especially at night.

CHAPTER 29
Assassin's Honor

Although the staff let Jason make his pizza, he self-admittedly was not good in the kitchen, especially one not equipped with a microwave, and enlisted help from some of the cooks. He instructed the baker to roll the bread dough flat and all watched as he applied the toppings. After a careful baking, it turned out very good, and the aroma made the cooks beg to try it. It was simple yet very tasty, and the head chef changed that evening's menu to include the pizza along with everything else.

He then went by Lady Killensdale's new sewing shop and picked up a spool of black silk thread. Back at his room, he climbed to the loft to reset the rope ladder. He made a bed using the two benches side by side and spread his bed roll over it. A silent alarm was made for both doors using string and pieces of wood which would fall on him and wake him up as he slept on the benches. The tapestry he requested had been delivered but not yet set up, rolled up on one side of the room. Jason was glad it wasn't up yet; it would give an assassin a potential hiding spot.

At dinner that evening, the pizza was placed as a side dish but quickly became the main dish as the diners asked for more. Evidently, the kitchen staff was cooking pizza for themselves because the second rounds came out almost immediately upon request. Amanie, Nelda, and the rest of the children could not get enough.

After dinner, he cleared away evidence of the secret bedroom and waited for Gunther. In the meantime, he made a mark on the door frame to measure his height. Someday, he would check it again and see how much he had grown and perhaps determine how long his new childhood would last. That is, assuming he was not killed by an assassin.

He thought of the assassin. It occurred to him he could hide and watch from the hole in the ceiling and shoot the assassin as it attacked a decoy made of pillows in his bed, but then, he wouldn't learn who had hired him. Even if he trapped the assassin alive, the assassin may not talk or even know.

Also, he didn't want to get blood all over his bed if he could help it, so trapping the assassin alive with a rope trap would be the better course of action. He daydreamed of using a big bear spring trap just under the blankets; it would break bones and potentially kill the assassin, but he doubted he had the strength to set one anyway.

The solution settled upon was a rope snare using the heavy pedestal washbasin already in the loft as a counterweight. He would set it after Gunther left. Someone knocked on the door. Jason cautiously asked who it was before opening. It was Gunther. Jason invited him in.

Gunther stepped in and smiled sheepishly, not knowing what to do or say, so Jason began, "Gunther, I know you and I have seen you at your worst, but now you have an opportunity to show me your best. I will teach you some basics for now and we will see what you do with that."

Jason then taught Gunther the basics on punching, kicking, and how to use leverage to escape from almost any hold. Later, if his new student was up to it, he would teach Gunther some throws but would need more than the one thin rug in his room.

After Gunther left, he set his trap. He made a noose with a slip knot and hid it under the rug at the side of the bed, ran the rope under the covers over to the wall by the dresser, then brought it up the wall and through a hole in the rafter of the loft. The hole was bored there purposely by someone before, probably for a pulley to easily haul things up. He tied the other end to the stone washbasin, which he moved close to the edge, so he could push it off at the right time.

He wondered if it might be too obvious but supposed in the dark, it would hardly be noticeable. When he went to sleep on the benches in his hidden loft, he felt confident that not only was he safe, but he could catch the assassin, assuming one existed.

Instead of going to the garden, he went out onto his balcony to pray instead. While praying, his conversation with Gunther about fighting and killing came back to him. It occurred to him that he had spilled a lot of blood since arriving here: a cannibal, bandits, goblins, kidnappers, Maudid, and now possibly, an assassin. He had only been here less than six months and had never killed anyone before that. What was he doing wrong? Was it his pride?

He then recounted each one of the killings and, in no instance, could see that pride played any part. Feeling better, he finished his prayers and returned to his room. He did not plan to kill an assassin tonight anyway. If the man died, well, that would be of his own making. Perhaps he was taking too big of a risk by not intending to kill a thug who intended to kill him.

Lying down to sleep in the upper chamber's bench, he tried to get comfortable. At first, he thought he may not be able to sleep until he recalled a song called "Anywhere with Jesus," especially the verse, "Anywhere with Jesus I can go to sleep, when the darkening shadows 'round about me creep." He sung the song to himself a few times and drifted off without really knowing it.

In the middle of the night, he felt the thump on his leg from the wooden block on his alarm for the balcony door. He lay there listening, his heart racing, but there was no sound. The assassin was good at his job, probably even oiled the hinges. He crept out of his bedroll, stalked to the trapdoor, and peered over the edge, trying to keep his breathing under control and quiet.

The bed down below appeared as he had left it, with the decoy of pillows under the blankets untouched. He surveyed the rest of the room, but no one was there. The balcony door was open, so perhaps the assassin discovered his trap and already fled.

He was just about to go down and close the door again when suddenly, a man appeared out of thin air and stabbed the pillow with a sharp dagger several times. Feathers flew into the air instead of the expected sight of blood, and the assassin froze in spot, aware he had been tricked.

After a long pause, the killer cautiously looked about the room, expecting someone to leap out at him. When no one appeared, he relaxed a little and cautiously backed away from the bed, stepping to the center of the rug. That is when Jason pushed the washbasin over the edge.

As the basin fell, taking up the slack in the rope and gaining momentum, it jerked the rug up around the man's knees and tightened there. The man was pulled off his feet, and the rope pulled him and the rug viciously upside down and into the stone wall. While the man was heavier than the washbasin, there was so much friction over the wood rafter that neither moved for a moment, swinging against each other.

The assassin had lost his knife when jerked off his feet, but he pulled another knife hidden on his person and slashed the rope around the rug on his legs. The knife cut the rope, dropping the assassin onto his back as the stone basin dropped too. The assassin tried to roll out of the way but was too late, and the washbasin struck him on the shoulder and side of his head and he lay there, unmoving.

Fearing the assassin was killed, Jason hurried down. As he checked the man's pulse, suddenly the assassin slashed, knife still in hand. Although not totally unprepared, the sudden move caught him before he could leap out of range. The knife bit a nasty deep gash in his arm, going all the way to the bone.

There was no time to chide himself for not taking care of the man's knife first, for the thug was already sawing at the rope between his feet, although getting around the rug to do so was slowing him down. Jason dove in at the knife, hoping to wrest it out of the stealthy killer's hands before it could be used on him again. However, the hoodlum intercepted him with his other hand and with his greater strength, hurled Jason across the room, and finished cutting his bond.

Standing, the professional slayer stepped out of the ropes, with a gash along his head from the stone basin and breathing heavily, but Jason was already at him again. Knowing the man would thrust his knife to meet his incoming charge, he changed course at the last second and turned sideways, to make the assassin miss his target. He then lightly grabbed the killer's hand and followed it back to its chambered position by the man's chest.

This time, however, he fooled the attacker into believing his intentions were to disarm him again with a grip now firmly on the knife hand. So instead, using his other hand, he jabbed into the eyes. Jason had hoped to at least partially blind the killer, so he could get away if he needed to.

The invader reeled back in pain, his other hand going to his eyes. Taking this opportunity, the boy switched his focus back to the knife hand, which he still held in a firm grip. Spinning his body to the outside and taking the assassin's hand with it, he completed one rotation and then bowed. The man followed his torqued hand and painfully flipped through the air, the knife falling harmlessly to the floor.

The night stalker landed hard on the floor on his back, knocked unconscious. Jason considered going ahead and killing his assailant, but now, it seemed more like murder since the man was unconscious; at least, he hoped he was out and not faking it again. Hastily putting the knives in a dresser drawer, he searched the body for more weapons. Finding none, he took a moment to bind his own wound and then dragged the assassin onto the balcony, shutting the door behind them.

After a few minutes, the cool night air brought the cutthroat to his senses. He was surprised to see Jason sitting across from him and that he was untied. With a groan, he sat up and gingerly felt his head and shoulder. Jason didn't say a word, just silently sat there, watching the would-be murderer. Finally, the man cautiously stood and looked around.

"Is this another trap?" he asked.

"Yes," replied Jason, "you are free to go."

"Then how is this a trap?" asked the assassin, truly puzzled.

"You will come after me again, won't you?" Jason countered.

"Yes, it is a matter of professional pride," said the assassin.

"Then that is the trap because I am protected by my God and you will die. If you did not see it, you probably heard about the defeat of the foreign champion, Maudid. That proves what I say is true."

"Yes," said the assassin. "What do you suggest I do?"

"Make another attempt," said Jason, smiling, with a little taunt in his voice.

"Why do you not try to make me reveal my employer?" the assassin, inquired suddenly suspicious.

"Would you tell me?" asked Jason.

"No," said the assassin, "it is a matter of professional pride."

"A profession is a way to make a living, but since now it will be earning your death, I suggest you change. It is your own pride that will kill you. However, since you have such great pride and professional honor, keep in mind that I have given you your life and freedom back, so you do owe me something."

The assassin nodded, stood on the rail of the balcony, and grabbed two hooks hanging from cracks in the wall and used them to crawl along the stones to the garden wall and then whispered, "Lord Krogan" over his shoulder and disappeared into the night.

Jason turned to go back into his room but was surprised to see Princess Merinda standing on her balcony in a nightgown, bow in hand. Princess Merinda spoke as if offended, "Jason, do keep in mind my room is next to yours, so if you can keep the noise down a little, I would appreciate it."

A bit shocked, Jason simply said, "Will do, Princess," as he faced her and bowed deeply.

They both returned to their rooms, and Jason felt a little chagrined by not alerting the princess or ringing the little chimes she provided. She was, after all, his confidant and had already placed such great trust in him. Could he not do the same for her? Perhaps the princess already knew about the upper room since royalty were privy to the secret escape routes.

Nevertheless, he wanted to keep the secret room a secret, at least for now. He set to work removing evidences of the trap and closed the door to the hidden bedroom. He couldn't get the basin back into the loft by himself, so decided it would be a great addition to his balcony as a bird bath.

Returning to his room, he then put on a fresh shirt and slept in his bed the remainder of the night, after locking both doors and leaning some arrows against the door so the noise of them clattering on the stone floor would wake him if someone did manage to open it again.

Several days later, he revisited the passage connected to his secret loft. This time, he went the other way, following the tunnel that led out of the castle. It became damper, the rock walls wet and besotted with moss or algae, while the floor had occasional slick spots and puddles.

After winding a half mile through a single dark passage, it began to dry out and ended in steps leading up to a square hole in a blank ceiling. The ceiling did not push up as he expected, but after some experimentation, it slid backward away from the steps in a smooth, gliding fashion.

Pushing his lamp ahead, he found himself climbing out of a sarcophagus with writing on it. He was inside a tomb. By now, he was literate enough to understand some runes. "Here lies King... King...the name undecipherable. Violators will be cursed," he read. A good way to keep people from messing with it, at least here where people took curses seriously. On his home world, this would have been the first tomb raided.

Wading through cobwebs and dust, he then went to the stone door of the tomb and, with some effort, opened it. He looked out to see a graveyard on a hill and nearly scared himself to death when he turned and saw a stone gargoyle perched above the door like a guardian. The gargoyle was a caricature of a winged beast, perhaps a lion. Was this a griffon? Perhaps this tomb held a clue to who Lord Griffon was.

Going back in, he examined the runes closely and tried to memorize the runes of the name of the person supposedly buried here since he had nothing to write on. Runes tended to be very specific and often represented whole words rather than components of words, such as our alphabet. He would need to be able to reproduce this and then find someone who could recognize it.

Experimentally, he closed the lid to the sarcophagus. It closed and opened, sliding smoothly from the outside if you knew which direction to initially push. Going back inside made him feel like he was entering a grave. Though his lamp pushed away the darkness, he could not help but get a sense of finality as he closed the lid back over the top of him.

The feeling subsided once he started going back through the stone lined hall toward the castle. Although he walked softly, almost every movement made a little noise that seemed to echo ahead of him. Perhaps that is why he did not see any rats, or perhaps there was a reason more sinister. The thought made him feel uncomfortable.

Before climbing his rope back up to the iron ladder, he also checked on the room containing the idol to see if anything had changed. The idol was just as he had left it, with no apparent signs of use. He was still unsure what to do about it. To try to monitor this place closely would be a waste of time. This place was probably used only at certain times of the year; he needed to figure out when that would be.

Although he found it distasteful, he considered the prospect of educating himself on the local religions as he climbed back to his room. Since Xan Rukkah's clerics and some of the other religious groups viewed him as a threat, it was not a great idea to go to them. Perhaps Princess Kuari knew more about the cult of Axialla. As he became her friend, he would ask her about it.

On the third day of training Gunther, Jason sat him down Japanese style with his legs folded under him. It was a painful tradition that had little to do with real fighting but did help develop self-discipline.

He sat the same way across from the older boy and asked, "Gunther, you are training very diligently and are an excellent student, but how does it feel to be taught by someone younger than you?"

Gunther shrugged. "I don't know. I kind of thought it weird at first, but when I realized you have something I badly want, I guess I respect your knowledge more than anything else. Now that I have worked with you, even though you are smaller than me, you do not talk or act like a kid. You speak like you are used to having authority, but you do not lord it, so I now respect you even more."

Jason nodded and said, "The time has come for us to make a decision. You now know a little of what I expect from you, but you once were a bully and I want to make sure you do not take the things I show you and abuse them."

Gunther was uncomfortable with the sitting position but did not dare squirm. Knowing he was being evaluated very closely, he replied carefully, "I am willing to make any vow to show my commitment."

Jason looked at the reformed bully firmly, "Gunther, not only am I a knight of Chanderlon, but I am a holy warrior on a mission for the Creator. Understand that a vow to me carries more weight than just to a ten-year-old kid. With such power and skill carries great responsibility. Do you promise to be kind to all—even your enemies?"

He asked wonderingly, "Even my enemies? I thought I was supposed to hate them enough to kill them and be happy about it." Jason patiently replied, "Enemies may attack, but with the superior skill you will have, it behooves you to be merciful and graceful and let them live if at all possible. When I say to be kind to all, it includes children, women, animals, and lesser beings."

Gunther was puzzled. "If I am kind to my enemies, does that mean I can never fight?"

"No," said Jason, "we cannot keep people from choosing to be our enemies, but we can choose to rise above. Justice is considered noble and is the cause for much fighting because that is the thinking of small people. Justice is described in the law as an eye for an eye and a tooth for a tooth, but that is equality at a very low level. Only out of superiority can we exhibit mercy. Only a superior fighter, one who has the advantage, one with the choice to kill or not, can show mercy to his enemies, a kindness that goes beyond rational thinking and even the concept of justice.

"We who are superior fighters train and sharpen our skills not so we can kill easier, but so we can be more merciful and forgiving. Sometimes, we can't afford to be merciful, but it is always on our minds and is our greatest goal. We train by forgiving and being kind to those lesser than ourselves, from the smallest to the greatest of offenses.

"The strongest of us strive for peace, even to the extent of accepting a wrong, because this is mercy shown in advance.

Mercy triumphs over justice because it is far stronger and the nobler of the two."

"But you killed three of the kidnappers and Maudid," pointed out Gunther.

"Yes, there is a time to kill, and because of our own weakness, we cannot always save someone from themselves. Even the Creator does not forcefully save someone who refuses to be saved. There are times to distribute justice, especially when you are in a position of authority, but even then, look for ways to be fair and creative so justice may be served while still showing mercy. Restitution and restoration are ways of applying justice while still helping everyone. As far as the kidnappers went, we spared the lives of the rest of them because we were able to."

Gunther allowed himself one little squirm and looked into Jason's eye and asked hopefully, "Will I become a holy warrior too?"

"Perhaps, but that requires a different vow to the Creator. I will teach you about the Creator, if you wish, along with your regular training."

The youth leaned over and set his hand on the apparently younger boy's shoulder and solemnly stated, "I, Gunther Birchhill, promise to Sir Jason Bristol, that I will practice kindness to my enemies and to all creatures and peoples both great and small."

Jason nodded in approval. "Very good. You may keep coming and we will train for one hour each night."

He and Gunther made a traditional bow toward each other and ended the session. He felt it good to have made a friend out of someone who once was his enemy, although he reminded himself that it was all from Gunther's efforts. Here was someone who had the ability to set his own jealousies aside and to think outside of the typical pattern. Gunther had great potential not only as a martial artist but as a leader.

The next week was relatively uneventful. There were no more assassination attempts on his life. The weather continued to get colder and the last leaves all blew off in one day during a small windstorm. Jason made it a practice to visit the town every day. With harvest season over, the market squares were all but abandoned, but the dock always had some sort of activity, and so he often found himself down at the river front.

He replicated the rune he saw in the tomb on a sheet of parchment and inquired of Krucinda, the Killensdale's tutor. She did not recognize it and recommended he visit a historian in one of the temples. She added the best historians were in the temple of Xan Rukkah. Well, so much that for that, unless he could get someone to ask for him.

One gray late fall morning, Princess Merinda was waiting for him as he started his usual jaunt into town. She was in the hall just outside his door, wearing a fashionable riding outfit with a cloak trimmed in silver fox fur. Smugly, she greeted Jason, "I have a surprise for you this morning, Jason. Wear something warm."

He retrieved his coat and put on several shirts, then rejoined the princess. She led him to the castle courtyard. In front of the stable were two saddled horses held by squires.

"We are going riding this morning. Which would you like?"

"I am sure it doesn't matter," he said, "because both seem to have a look in their eye that they would like to kill me." Princess Merinda laughed. "Jason, take the red horse. He is the gentlest. He will even let Kuari ride him."

It was his turn to laugh. "That is a fine endorsement. I will gladly be killed by the gentle one. Lead on, Merinda."

Jason had only ridden a horse a few times in his life and that was when he was about six years old. The last time he had slipped off and broken his forearm. Then his folks moved before he got a chance to "get back on the horse that threw him." He knew that "being relaxed" and "in command, yet gentle" were key to controlling a horse. You do not "drive" a horse. You let it do generally the things it wants to do and go in the same general direction you want it to go at your prodding and encouragement. At least, he hoped those were the right principles.

They mounted and Princess Merinda led the way. He gave the horse its head and allowed it to follow the princess's horse. They rode through town, then out of the city along the river to the west.

As they left the city, Princess Merinda looked back and noticed a lone horseman riding hard to catch them. They pulled up and waited. Soon, they could make out the figure of a girl on the horse. It was Princess Kuari.

"Are you two trying to sneak a ride without me?" exclaimed Princess Kuari breathlessly as she came abreast.

Princess Merinda laughed. "Welcome along, little sister. Did you let anyone know where you were going?"

"Did you?" countered Kuari, sticking her tongue out at Merinda.

"No, I guess I didn't, not with my champion along," Merinda smiled at her mischievously.

The trio rode along, merrily chatting and enjoying the scenery. They went past the farmhouse where the hostages were once held. Smoke wisped from the chimney, cattle grazed the field, and a man was throwing hay into the barn.

They went another mile, and on a rise, they could see the ocean and a small coastal village perhaps ten miles from the city. As they neared, they could see it was a fishing village with poles along the beach holding nets to dry.

This reminded Jason of his set net site in Alaska. He and his family fished using gill nets, anchored between two buoys close to shore. Red salmon would get caught as they swam by on their way to their coastal river to spawn. Since his nylon nets didn't rot, they didn't hang them to dry like these. In fact, they had to be covered to protect from deterioration due to the sun.

The three riders skirted the village, then galloped along the beach to play in the surf. Jason tried to relax in the saddle while Princess Merinda gave him pointers on how to ride. A gentle breeze blew, but it was too cold to do anything but wade.

Princess Kuari, especially, enjoyed riding her horse into the water. Meanwhile Princess Merinda pulled a loaf of bread and some cheese with a few bottles of wine out of her saddlebag for lunch. Finding a grassy area to sit away from the sand, they held their picnic and enjoyed each others' company.

Later that afternoon, Princess Merinda found a trail going up the bluff that a horse could climb, so they went to the top. From there, they could see the wide flood plain of the river and the hilly area around Chanderlon. There was a large mountain maybe ten miles behind the town, mostly hidden by clouds.

While they watched, a cloud from the north rolled in and obscured their sight of Chanderlon and half the plain. Despite this, Princess Merinda took a course straight across the plains toward Chanderlon. Jason felt uneasy, especially since more clouds and fog began to roll in and the sun was not visible at all. If they got caught in the fog, they may have trouble navigating. He followed behind Princess Kuari.

After traveling about fifteen minutes, it started to snow lightly and progressively their whole world became shades of white and gray. The two princesses were thrilled.

"Oh, Jason, the snow is so beautiful," said Princess Kuari, noticing he was less than merry.

"Yes, the snow is beautiful, but we need to be careful since there are absolutely no landmarks," he said warily.

Princess Merinda replied, "Never fear, Sir Jason, I have never been lost in my life. Follow me." With a whoop, she set her horse into a cheerful gallop. Three quarters of an hour later, they came across another set of tracks almost obscured by the snow. Jason dismounted and led his horse to take a look. "Three horsemen riding hard."

"What a coincidence that three other people are out here riding today," said Princess Kuari merrily.

"It is no coincidence," said Jason gloomily. "Those tracks are ours." The snow was coming down heavier with a little breeze so even the tracks they had just made were starting to disappear.

"They can't be ours!" Princess Merinda exclaimed but already knew the truth of it. "What do we do now, Jason?"

"There are three safe options and a fourth that isn't so safe, as I see it," replied Jason. "First, we can try to follow our own tracks back to the coast, then back to the village and up the river."

"But that will take hours," complained Kuari.

"Or," continued Jason, "we can try to follow the slope of the land which will lead to a stream, which in turn will lead to the river." He was met by frowns from both girls. "Or the last safe thing we can do is make camp right here and wait for the storm to lift."

Princess Merinda screwed up her nose. "That may take even longer, and we could freeze to death out here. What is the unsafe option?"

He hesitated. "I do not know much about horses, but many animals have an innate sense of direction, or perhaps their sense of smell and hearing are so much better they never seem to get lost, but if we let our horses have their heads, perhaps they will lead us home. Or not."

Princesses Merinda and Kuari conferred and announced their decision. "We will trust our horses," they said in unison. They got the horses walking, then let them go where they willed. After milling about for a while, Princess Kuari's black horse took off, and the others galloped to catch up, then all slowed to a brisk walk. Within an hour, they made it to the outskirts of Chanderlon. They dismounted and led their horses to prevent them from falling on the slick cobblestone with four inches of wet snow on top. It was dark in Chanderlon, and very few people were on the streets.

When they reached the castle, stable hands appeared to take care of their horses. Meanwhile the gate guards sent dispatches to inform the castle of their return. The castellan and a small group of handmaidens and ladies-in-waiting met them at the door, relieved to see they were okay. When the children had not shown up for dinner, they were all concerned and had begun efforts to search for them. The princesses invited Jason to sup with them, since none of them had anything to eat since their shared picnic, but Jason requested a delay since he had an appointment with Gunther to keep.

Gunther was waiting for him outside his door. Going in, they reviewed the lesson of the previous day, then added to it. Afterward, he made his way to the royal quarters.

The king was sipping wine in front of the fire while the queen read aloud from a book of history. They directed Jason to the parlor where the princesses awaited him. The dinner leftovers were spread on the table before them. Unfortunately, pizza was not among them. He was surprised the girls had not yet eaten and had waited for him.

"If you could wait, then we could wait too," was their reply.

Princess Merinda asked Jason to pray aloud, blessing their food. His simple prayer gave thanks for their food and their rescue.

They all ate ravenously, not speaking much until their hunger was somewhat satisfied. Princess Kuari broached a topic. "Jason, what is it you are doing with Gunther that is more important than eating?"

Between mouthfuls Jason responded, "Gunther has asked me to teach him my style of fighting."

"And you agreed? After everything Gunther tried to do to you?" asked Kuari incredulously.

Jason replied, "Gunther has promised to change. Bullying is an abuse of power to compensate for a weakness elsewhere. If there is no need to compensate, there is no need to bully."

"You are not afraid he will use it against you?" Kuari asked.

"The full skill takes several years to develop, so hopefully, not only will Gunther's heart be revealed to me, but he will have truly changed for the better."

"Perhaps," said Princess Kuari, then shyly, "Do you think I can change, Jason?"

"You have already changed, but I wonder if you will continue in this new direction or revert back to the old? Many people have decided to follow the Creator halfheartedly or on their own terms. These people never really discover the power of the Creator nor have the courage to face the Creator's enemies. They return to their old ways for many reasons. Choose to be a person whose roots are deep, who cannot be moved, and then I will say, yes, you have truly changed."

Princess Merinda chimed in and said to Kuari, "It is good to see you so cheerful and carefree. I feel I got my sister back."

She beamed in return. "I am back, sister, and I mean to stay."

Later that evening in a dark room at the corner of a temple sat five clerics in their white robes on several stone benches facing a darkly robed figure wearing a gold mask.

The man in the mask laughed. "Your attempts at clandestine are pathetic. We meet in a darkened room in your very own temple. What? Are you afraid other clerics will see?"

The lead cleric squirmed uncomfortably. "We did this for you, Lord Griffon, assuming you would not want your visit here known."

"For those who would want to know, we could not hide it anyway. Let's get on with it. Why have you clerics of Xan Rukkah summoned me?"

"We have a problem we would like removed, and we have heard you are the one who can do it."

Lord Griffon laughed again. "You mean the little boy, Jason?"

"Yes. We will pay you ten thousand crowns."

"Woo hoo," crowed the dark man. "That is a king's ransom. Any petty assassin around here would do it for two hundred. Why me?"

"That is our own business," snapped the leader.

The leader of thieves wagged his finger at them. "Tsk, tsk. I come in good will, and as you know, I am not an assassin for hire. Perhaps I will wait until Father Dorrian himself speaks with me."

The leader abruptly stood. "No. We are to insulate him from this sordid affair. Very well, we shall tell you. The little boy brings a new god whom he claims is older than all the rest. This god requires that all other gods be renounced as imposters. If that happened, Chanderlon would be thrown into chaos and a war of the gods. It could mean our country's doom."

Lord Griffon spoke carefully, "And I bet that is not all that concerns you. Besides losing your court influence, you have a long tradition of ordaining the new kings with the passing of the sword of Xan Rukkah to the new leader. You help to validate the kingship."

"That is correct," replied the priest.

"Keep your money, for I do not promise to remove Jason right away. However, when he is removed, this is what I want from you. I want you to ordain me as the new king."

The priest gasped. "But what of King Beldane?"

"I doubt he will be in a position to object," replied Lord Griffon.

With that and a swoop from his cloak, the dark lord vanished from their sight, causing the rest of the clerics to rise in wonder.

One of them said to the lead cleric, "Brother Mussan, did we just make a deal with the devil?"

The older cleric just shook his head. "I do not know. Perhaps we are about to pay for our sin of murdering Father Varigold."

CHAPTER 30
Sledding Party

The snow continued to fall over the next several weeks, turning the town into a different world. Sounds were muffled, and the busy marketplace slowed to a comfortable pace. Although it wasn't the deep cold of winter, the older people acted like it, while children frolicked with snowball fights and snow forts built to withstand sieges from other children.

Gunther memorized a moral guide to his martial arts training. "If it is possible, as far as it depends on me, I will live at peace with everyone." Gunther was quite pleased with himself because he walked away from a challenge to fight from another lord's sons, even though he knew he was clearly superior. He was even called a coward by the lad. He responded with, "There is a difference between fear and stupidity. Someday, you will thank me for the grace I have just given you." He then turned and walked away.

Meanwhile, Jason improved his method of getting to his secret attic bedroom, using hidden cords with pulleys to open and close the trapdoor. A similar system was used to raise and lower the rope ladder. No one else had tried to kill him, but he doubted that was the end of it.

The straight blades he had commissioned were finished but the small katana, a high-quality blade, would take more time. He commissioned the furniture maker to construct six toboggans and asked Lady Killensdale for a warm fur coat, hat, and mittens for himself. He hired a cobbler to make a pair of warm boots.

When all was ready, he hired a teamster to haul a wagon load of kids, toboggans, and blankets several miles toward the mountains, where he was told of a particularly good sledding hill by some of the more adventuresome kids in town.

It was a beautiful snowy day, and he was able to rouse about fifteen children from the castle to accompany him. Two mounted soldiers rode guard and to chaperone.

Jason sat in back with the children and tried to get them to sing winter or sledding songs, but to his surprise, they did not know any. He was sitting between Amanie and Nelda and asked if they knew any songs at all.

"Oh yes," said Nelda. "I know the love ballads of Syra and Jakim."

"Does anyone else know them?" asked Jason.

"I doubt it," said Amanie making a turned-up face. "Most of us like more exciting songs."

"Like what?" he asked.

She thought a second. "'Piddlesome Bread' and 'We're off to Slay a Dragon,'" she proffered brightly.

"What is piddlesome bread?" he asked.

"Oh, you know, it is a silly song about crumbled bread mixed with milk and berries for breakfast."

"The other one sounds perfect. Could you lead everyone in 'We're off to Slay a Dragon'?"

"Of course," she said with a sparkle in her eye.

She waved to get the other children's attention and sang in her cute baritone voice that sounded a lot like Shirley Temple, "We're off to slay a dragon...A beast bigger than a wagon," and so on, not rhyming well in English. Jason joined in as he could, but that got them going and silliness prevailed. When they reached the hill they could see signs of its popularity with runs, jumps, and evidence of many wipe outs.

The troupe of children climbed to the top of the hill while the driver and two soldiers started a fire to roast nuts and heat water for tea. Jason wished they had hot cocoa and marshmallows, but otherwise, it looked perfect.

The top of the hill was flat, and he surveyed the area while the eager children lined themselves up two or three to a sled. Nelda and Amanie claimed a sled and saved a spot for him while he took his time, soaking in the beauty of the scene. The backside of the hill sloped and ended in a small cliff not so great for sledding, but the mountain view was magnificent.

"Come on, Jason," cried Amanie, sitting on the sled with Nelda. The slope was perfect, not too steep nor too tame. He pushed on the back of the sled and with a run plopped onto the end on his knees as it came up to speed. The girls squealed with delight, mixed with a little fear, as he expertly guided the sled around the wrecks of other children and hit the small jump.

The jump gave only a little height, but for the castle kids, most of whom had never done this before, it was a grand sight to behold, and they all headed back up the hill at a dead run to be the first to do it the way Jason did. The two girls were laughing and giggling by the time they reached bottom. They stood and brushed snow off themselves while Jason turned the sled to begin hauling it uphill.

Nelda mischievously threw a snowball at him. Okay. In kids' terms, this meant war. He prepared to throw one back. He found that along with his youthful body, there also came all the extra energy of youth, and he enjoyed playing. Being an Alaskan veteran of many snowball fights as a kid, he knew how to rain snowballs—three or four to every one of Nelda's, with deadly accuracy. Of course, Amanie had to get in the action with a snowball or two of her own.

With shrieks of laughter, Nelda surrendered. Of course, the victor of any snowball fight is expected to whitewash the loser, so Jason flung Nelda to the ground, for which she went down far easier than he expected. As he was about to finish her off with a handful of snow, Nelda arched into his arm and dramatically exclaimed, "Kiss me, sir knight." She closed her eyes and pursed her lips, face thrust up to his. Jason was glad he was in the body of a ten-year-old boy. She would never understand why he would refuse her otherwise.

"Yes, Snow Princess, your Snow Knight will oblige you." With that, he let her have it—a face full of snow. He hated to do it. He really wished he could fulfill her dreams and grow into a lord or even a king, and she could be his queen. He forced a gleeful laugh as he raced uphill, pulling the sled.

He looked back and found she reacted just the way he had hoped, sputtering mad and vowing vengeance, in a good-natured way, as she and Amanie raced up the hill after him. He purposely slipped, fell and rolled between the two girls, allowing them to pelt him with snow. He lay there while they grabbed the sled and marched up the hill indignantly without him.

He rolled up to a sitting position and observed the fire with the three men around it, drinking hot toddy from their mugs. Just beyond them, Jason's eye caught something moving in the woods.

A deer? he wondered. He had brought his weapons, currently stashed in the wagon rolled in a blanket.

Not bothering to second-guess himself, he walked the rest of the way down the hill, climbed into the wagon and unrolled the blanket with his new swords and bow. While belting his swords, he watched the woods closely, an arrow notched.

He tried to get the attention of the men by calling quietly to them, but they didn't hear, so he watched a little longer and scanned the rest of the area before hopping out and walking over to those by the fire. The guards looked up in surprise to see Jason carrying his weapons as he approached. "I saw something move in the woods. I think I will check it out."

"I'll go with you," one of the guards replied, pulling out his sword.

Stalking to the trees, Jason didn't see anything, so he checked for tracks. There were some fresh deer tracks, which he pointed out to the guard, who visibly relaxed, but there was something else odd just beyond it. The snow had been brushed off a tree higher than just a deer passing, and there were some strange depressions in the snow, too large for deer tracks, just beyond it.

Suddenly, to the right, a deer moved into a clearing. Jason ignored it but heard the guard say, "Ah, it is just a deer."

How foolish, thought Jason. If there was a perfect time for something to attack, it was now at the moment of distraction. As a precaution, he hurled himself against the tree ahead of him and spun, drawing his bow from a low position, keeping the tree to his back.

But instead of the ambush he expected, he saw a large dark figure running through the woods behind and away from the dumbfounded guard. He pointed, but by the time the man turned, the creature was gone. Going over to the area, he closely examined the tracks. They appeared to be of a giant human with elongated nails but very messed up from running. Was it a yeti or a troll? He'd nearly forgotten about Trombul.

"Those tracks are huge, but whatever it was is gone now!" exclaimed the guard.

Well, this was going to ruin the outing, thought Jason gloomily. Then to the guard, he said, "We had better call the rest of the children and head home, just to be safe."

"Pedong and I can handle whatever this beast is. You kids just enjoy your outing," said the guard, slapping the flat of his blade against the leather armor on his chest.

Great, thought Jason as he responded dubiously, "I am glad to hear that, but we probably should leave anyway, for if these kids even see a threatening animal, it could jeopardize future trips."

"Yes, sir, you are in charge, Sir Jason, but I think it is a shame to cut your fun short. As a soldier, I know nothing is ever absolutely safe, and if we always tried to play it completely safe, we would never do anything."

Jason had to admit the soldier had a point. "Okay, we will let Pedong decide, for as guards, it is your lives that are mainly at risk, and if the creature returns and attacks, it is your job to at least delay it long enough for us to get away."

The hired protector nodded somberly. They returned to the fire and presented the choice to the other soldier. Pedong was in agreement with the first soldier, and Jason hoped they did not have to earn their pay.

Jason then played and roasted nuts with the children for about another hour and was about to admit to himself the guards were right when a deep-throated, eerie howl broke from the forest. It seemed to form the words.

"Jaaasooon."

The children gathered around the fire, looking all around.

Jason called for everyone to load up, and this time, the guards were quite willing.

As the driver turned the team of draft horses around, the two guards mounted their own horses and rode on either side of the wagon. They had not gotten up to speed yet when out of the woods, to the right, loped an ugly giant creature. It stood about eight feet tall even hunched over. Jason recognized it in a heartbeat. It was Trombul.

Trombul's skin seemed paler and less green than normal from the cold. It had also tried to cover itself with a variety of raw animal skins, interwoven with the tattered bloody remains of human clothing. The troll was covering the snowy ground quickly. Both guards rode toward it to block its way, swords drawn.

The driver shook the reins to encourage the draft horses but found it unnecessary. They had spotted the troll and were already running full out. The children fearfully huddled down in the bed of the wagon as Jason pulled out his bow and positioned himself in the back with an arrow notched, ready to fire.

The monster giant slowed as it approached the men and stopped before them. The guards stopped too, about thirty feet away, not eager to test their skill against a nearly unstoppable brute.

Again, it howled, "Jaaasooon."

Jason felt the hair rise on the back of his neck. He was not afraid, he told himself, and gave his own little growl as he steadied the bow in the back of the jerky, bouncing wagon. Quickly, the wagon went over the rise, and as the view disappeared, he could have sworn he saw the beast ripping at its own flesh with its claws. What did this odd behavior mean?

Soon, the guards caught up, their horses wild-eyed and prancing.

"We are safe for now. The monster returned to the woods," said Pedong, as they sheathed their swords.

Jason wanted to ask them more about what they saw, but for the sake of the children, he decided to wait until afterward. After about two miles, they slowed and continued at a less brisk pace the rest of the way to town and eventually to the castle.

Seeing the children safely to the castle, he returned to the guards awaiting him.

One of the guards spoke first. "It seems the giant was looking for you, Sir Jason."

"Yes, I have met the creature several times," he replied.

The guards exchanged uncomfortable looks, and Jason continued without acknowledging it. "Did you notice anything odd about the creature?"

"Besides it being a troll?" The other laughed. "Yes, it had an odd crawling to its skin, as if many large worms crawled under it. It also seemed to be in pain, for the monster tore at those worms with its claws, and as we watched, even those wounds seemed to heal before our eyes. I have heard the only way to kill a troll is to burn it."

Jason paid the men a bonus, dismissed them, and returned to his quarters to ready himself for dinner. So Trombul had not given up, even with some parasite eating away at him. Or maybe it was because of the worms the troll had not given up. Haglar had some sort of power over the troll, and he doubted it was because the fiend loved her like a mother.

Some sort of magic or curse kept the troll to its task. It's possible the worms were related. He needed to do some research and ask among the soldiers and rural folks for strategies on how to evade, reason with or kill trolls. It seemed inevitable he would have to deal with it again, so he needed to prepare himself.

CHAPTER 31
Skiing Adventure

The weather grew colder and the snow deeper as winter wore on. It was the worst winter anyone in Chanderlon could remember. To the Alaskan, however, it was mild, even enjoyable, and he determined to make the most of it. He commissioned the furniture shop to make a pair of Nordic style cross-country skis and poles. As these were a novelty, he had to draw up designs and explain to the wood worker the theory of wax-able skis, so they would have the proper camber for his weight.

His katana was finished. Though perhaps not done in the traditional Japanese manner, it was a serviceable sword with very good balance. He used it for his own practice after the training sessions with Gunther, creating his own style of iaijutsu, as well as continuing to practice the two-sword fighting method Merinda had shown him.

When his skis were completed, he visited candle shops, tested various waxes, and eventually came up with some adequate ski waxes. Wax, through friction, warms up the snow to the point that it becomes a thin layer of water so the skis slip easily through the snow. Other waxes, called kicker wax, allow the skis to grip the snow, sticking to provide forward thrust. The camber helps the stickier wax to disengage, and if skis are waxed right, they are a very efficient means of traveling, usually exceeding what a man could do on foot over dry ground.

At practice that night, Jason told Gunther he would require a service of him the following day at noon. Gunther took it as a solemn charge and promised to be there—no matter what. Jason did not think his surprise would be that big of a deal, but had problems sleeping because of his excitement. He found he missed skiing. As a boy, it had been one of his passions.

Around noon, he had a horse ready for Gunther when they met in the courtyard. There was a long rope tied to the saddle, and his skis were leaning against the wall of the stable.

"Gunther, I want you to ride this horse," he said.

"Sure, but where is your horse? Aren't you riding with me?" asked the puzzled teen.

In response, Jason said, "I do not need a horse because you are going to tow me."

A puzzled Gunther mounted the horse and turned to watch Jason put on his skis, buckling the leather strap bindings to his boots. Then he grabbed the end of the rope and hollered, "Gunther, I hear you like to ride fast. Let it rip."

"Let it rip?" Gunther puzzled, then smiled a broad grin of understanding as he let out a whoop and they were off, the younger boy flying behind Gunther on his skis. Everyone in the courtyard stopped to stare, having never seen skis before. The guards at the gate didn't even have time to salute as they tried to clear themselves and everyone else on the drawbridge out of the way.

Gunther was a good horseman and took Jason on a wild ride around the frozen castle moat and then went tearing through the narrow, winding streets toward the closest edge of town. Suddenly, they came around a corner where a wagon had slid sideways on the other side, nearly covering the whole street. The horse just made it past a narrow opening in front of the team of oxen pulling it, but Jason slid too wide.

With a yell of anticipation, he let go of the rope and fell to his side while still trying to cut the edge of his skis into the packed snow enough to guide him between the wheels. He had hoped he could slide under the cart and come up on the other side in time to grab the rope again. However, the skis did not grip enough, and he slid between the spokes of the back wheels, pinned underneath.

Gunther stopped and returned for him. "Jason, are you still alive?"

Jason had to laugh at the concern he heard in his friend's voice. "No, I am in heaven. I haven't had this much fun since I rode hanging onto the side of a bison."

Gunther dismounted and helped him untangle himself. "Should I go slower, Sir Jason?"

"No way, Gunther. Even if I got hurt, it would be worth it." For a moment, he considered if his quick healing was making him reckless, but then thought, naw, I'd be reckless anyway.

Gunther grinned again, and they sped off as fast as the horse dared in the semi-busy streets. When they reached the hilly area north of town, he really let it fly with Jason swerving from side to side, taking small jumps as opportunity afforded.

At last, the spirited horse was winded and came to a halt, breathing hard. Gunther sat and watched wonderingly as Jason climbed up some hills and skied down, dodging the occasional tree and flying over bumps, obviously enjoying himself.

When he came skiing up to Gunther with a sideways stop, throwing a wall of snow over him, Gunther said, "Wow, Jason! You make that look really easy. May I try?"

"Sure thing," he said as helped Gunther get set up. Once he had the skis on, the first thing Gunther did was fall down.

"This is harder than it looks," said Gunther. "How do you do it?"

He gave Gunther a few short lessons on how to walk, slide, turn, and stop. After the boy got a good grasp of the fundamentals, Jason towed him at a slow pace, which the horse appreciated as well.

When they had just circled a large hill, they spotted a troop of mounted horsemen headed their way, returning to the castle. Their horses, walking at a tired pace, had just finished practicing battle maneuvers all morning. Lord Krogan led them.

The men were also tired but still amused to see Gunther being towed on skis. Lord Krogan, as dignified as ever, tried to ignore them, but Jason matched his horse to go beside Lord Krogan's, a move which incidentally swung Gunther into the line of knights. The knights scrambled their horses to avoid a collision with the out-of-control youngster.

Without looking back, Lord Krogan said, "Sir Bristol, your contraption is spoiling my column of knights."

"Then let us ride further in advance of the column, so it is no longer spoiled," Jason replied as he urged his horse forward. Lord Krogan seemed irritated as his presumption but matched his speed anyway and rode beside him.

"Now what is this about, young man?" Lord Krogan sounded indignant.

Jason noticed the general did not use the proper title in addressing him—not that he cared, but it did show an attitude. "I overheard something about you having a grudge against me," Jason began, and Lord Krogan made a harrumph sound. "So, I just wanted to make it clear that even if I could identify the voice in the garden I heard as being yours or connect you to the kidnapping or murdered farm family, or even prove you hired an assassin to kill me, I want you to know I am not coming after you."

"I am offended at your implications, though if you believed all that, why wouldn't you try to do something about it?" asked Lord Krogan, genuinely surprised.

"Because the mission the Creator sent me to do is not to clean out the corruption of every kingdom, but to change the hearts of mankind, so they will remember who they are and the purpose God has for them."

"Does not the corruption of this kingdom concern the Creator?"

"Yes, of course, it does," said Jason. "But the corruption is so deep that if it were rooted out completely there would be little left of the kingdom or even of this whole world."

Lord Krogan turned to Jason and asked, "What is it the Creator wants?"

"To save it," said Jason "To save it for the sake of the people in it, to save it for himself."

"That is hard to believe, especially coming from a child," said Lord Krogan.

"Yes, but it is true." Jason spurred his horse on again, launching ahead of the cavalcade and leaving Lord Krogan behind.

"Slow down," Gunther screamed as he went whizzing past Lord Krogan, causing the general's horse to rear. The men all laughed heartily until Lord Krogan regained control. Jason did not slow until after the next bend, then switched places with the now exhausted boy for the remainder of the ride to the castle.

Lord Krogan, however, was not amused. After regaining the proper somber discipline among his cavalry, he sulkily contemplated the impudent young boy's visit. He was guilty of all of the boy's charges and more. He would have had Sir Tadden kill the boy that night after the interview with Lord Killensdale, except the boy had vanished from the castle.

It seemed the boy lived a charmed life. He was shot with luck. When Jason found the kidnapper's hideout, he became an instant hero—a knight even. King Beldane was too gracious, perhaps because he hoped to mollify his daughter into accepting the marriage and her role as a diplomat. Or perhaps it was merely to distract everyone from the fact that he had just declared war on Harvella.

He did not dare move against Jason right then but felt he did not need to. With the foolish child accepting the challenge to fight Prince Dunaibi, his death was nearly guaranteed. When Maudid promised to kill the boy, he was overjoyed. How could it fail?

Then there was the dirty trick with the bees. Although it was not against the rules, it was not an honorable thing to do. A bad guy just does not get a break. He even hired an assassin to finish the job, an especially wicked man who had never failed him before. Although he never found out what exactly happened, the man never returned to him. He worried about that loose end, too.

And now, of all the cursed things, the little brat is close friends with the royal family. Princess Merinda had especially taken a fondness to him. The fortunate circumstances surrounding Jason were too unbelievable. His best laid plans were almost ruined by this boy. Could there really be a god helping him?

Now the boy comes and tells him he is onto his schemes but is not going to undo him. What does that mean? Well, it did not matter since the boy knows too much to live. Jason must die, but how? If Jason is helped by a god, then a god is needed to help him kill the boy. He hated Jason but should take care, lest his hate cause him to make a false move. Perhaps Lord Griffon would have an idea.

CHAPTER 32
The Crooked Little Stick

Although the weather grew colder, Jason continued to make his early morning trips around town. The river had not yet frozen but was beautiful bordered by snow. Sometimes, he was able to convince Princess Merinda to join him, and they would discuss the Creator as they walked along the river banks. Sometimes, they would also discuss the upcoming war in the spring. Surprisingly nobody, not even the townsfolk, seemed overly concerned.

Princess Merinda explained it once. "War is a frequent occurrence and often kingdoms rise and fall around the townsfolk and peasants, but they hardly notice the difference. They are still taxed and still provide essential services. If anything, they believe war invigorates the economy and is therefore a good thing."

"Aren't they worried about dying or the loved ones they may lose?"

"Yes, but most flee an approaching enemy, and those who are fit to fight relish the opportunity to take part in the plunder, if there is any. They find the risks well worth it.

He wondered if, as a knight, he was to play a role in this war. He figured when spring came, a better time for travel, the Lord would send him on, so he could begin his mission of spreading the light to this world and then go home. But then again, he may already be exactly where God wanted him. He felt like a little more direct guidance, similar to what the prophets of old experienced would be helpful.

Then again, Christ had already given him his mission to teach the good news about the gift of life to every living creature. Did he need a specific invitation to do it here? Maybe the whole point was to just be himself or rather, just be his Christian self as an example.

One night, he did have a dream. He did not know for sure if it was from God or not, but he relived the day just before he fought Maudid and dreamed again of shooting an arrow out of the sky.

Suddenly, his son appeared and handed him a blindfold. "Here, Dad, put this on and do it again."

"But I need to keep my eye on the arrow or I will miss."

"No, Dad," he responded. "You did not hit it the first time because you kept your eye on it. You hit it because you trusted God."

Jason put on the blindfold and shot again and then tried to shoot that arrow out of the air without being able to see it. It was weird dreaming you could not see, but then his son shouted, 'Hurray', and, taking off his blindfold, he saw he had shot the arrow again.

His dream ended with a statement from his son. "When you are unsure of your target, close your eyes and trust the Lord."

He awoke afterward and thanked God for the dream, hoping it to be a promise to him, for otherwise, just shooting blindly could get him into a lot of trouble. Perhaps it actually had nothing to do with shooting, but he was too groggy to contemplate any deeper, more philosophical meanings.

On another morning as both he and Princess Merinda made their way to the dock district, they walked past an empty market square and saw a young boy shivering in the cold, sitting on the icy ground with a crooked, gnarled walking stick beside him.

"Are you okay?" asked Jason.

The boy, who appeared about eight years old, held an empty basket to him and pleaded, "Can you give me something?"

Jason went to one knee to look at the boy more closely. "What is your name?"

"Chaney," said the boy.

"Who sent you out here?" asked Jason.

"My mother. She is sick and can no longer work."

"And what was her work?"

"She goes to taverns and men give her money for being their friend."

Jason felt very sad for the boy but said, "I do not just give things away. I am sorry. But may I look at your stick?"

The boy nodded and handed it to Jason. It was very twisted and beautiful in its own way, with a small carving of a horse's head at one end. He commented to the crippled lad, "I am a carver too, and I recognize good work when I see it. How much?" The boy shook his head wonderingly. "I will give you two gold crowns for it," offered Jason, "and if you carve another, I would like to see it." The boy took the money, overjoyed, and hobbled away with his lame foot.

"That was very kind of you, Jason," said Princess Merinda admiringly.

"No, I collect sticks as a hobby. This stick is a rare find," he replied solemnly.

They continued their way to the river park. This morning seemed darker and drearier than the day before. The days were getting shorter as winter solstice approached. The priests at the temples seemed to be up early, busily cleaning and sweeping snow off the temple steps and porches.

As they rounded a corner, they could see several hundred yards though the buildings down to the dock. However, this morning, the docks were all lit up, throwing a reddish haze into the fog over the river. At the end of the docks, they could see the masts of what looked like a huge ship, seemingly too large to have come up the river.

Jason and Princess Merinda hurried forward and joined a crowd of dock workers and longshoremen standing around gawking.

"It is a beauty," commented a merchant near them, and it was. The ship was made of dark wood with its battened sails rolled up on the masts. Decorated with flags, banners, streamers, and paper lanterns, it reminded Jason of a very exotic Chinese dragon ship. Having recently been at sea, the rest of the rigging was covered with ice. Icicles hung down, making the ropes look as if they were made of glass, which lent a fairy tale–like quality. Another dock worker spoke in awe, echoing his thoughts, "They must have some navigator to get it up the river through ice flows in the dark."

Jason walked onto the dock to get a closer look and hailed some crew securing the gangplank. They had an exotic look about them, with even the lowliest crew hand dressed in brightly colored silk of various colors. One of them tried answering him, but their language was foreign, and both just ended up smiling and nodding to each other. As he stood there watching, to all appearances he was just a little boy with a beggar's stick in hand, so it is understandable that in the following event he was not treated appropriately as a Knight of Chanderlon.

Ten soldiers wearing painted, lacquered armor of wood and leather marched out on deck wearing swords and holding long- poled halberds. The armor was a shiny dark brown with a gold insignia of a dragon stamped on the chest. Their bronze helmets came gracefully to a point from which a blue silk tassel flowed. They formed two lines and waited at attention.

Soon, a door to the main cabin burst open, and a girl with black hair in simple yellow clothing came stumbling out, shrieking and crying, followed closely by a domineering man, perhaps thirty, in a flowing white robe tied with a wide black belt at the waist with an upraised staff in hand. He had one long braided strand coming from the back of his cleanly shaved head. His blue eyes blazed with anger, and he moved with the lithe movements of a skilled fighter, daring any to stand before his wrath. The soldiers quickly gave way to make room for their master.

The girl lay on the deck, crying for mercy. The man struck a hard blow with his staff that smashed her upraised arm, then kicked her as she lay in a sobbing heap holding her injured, possibly broken arm. The man then seemed to notice where he was and walked to the head of the column as it reassembled. He stood and impatiently shouted a command, and more men and women came streaming out of the cabin, all carrying bundles or ornate wooden boxes. With the slaves lined up behind the column, the man strode boldly forward with an air of importance down the ramp, his entourage following.

Jason stood quietly to the side. The man briefly glanced at the boy and brushed past. As the soldiers went by, one purposely kicked him down. Not wanting to draw attention, he lay there until the last slave passed. Then, without permission, he rose and darted up the gangplank onto the ship. The crew made no move to stop him, even though he had no real right to be there.

The girl still lay there sobbing, shivering miserably from the cold and pain. He put his coat over the girl. She was probably fifteen and quivering while holding her injured arm with her other hand. He examined it and verified it was broken. Sitting the girl up, he looked for something with which to splint her arm.

Suddenly, Princess Merinda appeared. "Let's get her inside," she said as she went on to stand the girl up. They made a move towards the cabin and one of the crew, who seemed to be dressed even better than the rest, moved as if to stop them, but a glare from the princess caused him to suddenly bob his head and instead open the door for them.

They brought the girl into the brightly lit room. The room felt like a blast furnace compared to the cold outside. The inside looked like a Chinese curio shop, with bizarre colors and interesting instruments. A small cast iron wood stove covered with black ceramic heated the place. They took the girl to a chair beside a table. He had no trouble finding something to make a splint, using a piece of wooden armor that was meant to protect the forearm. Merinda poured some hot tea for the girl while Jason worked securing the splint with its own black silk cords.

The girl stopped crying and tried to speak, but they couldn't understand her. The girl smiled her gratitude, then went over to a couch and lay on it, covering herself with a blanket. Not knowing what more they could do, they left her to care for herself.

The crew continued to ignore them when they left the ship. On the dock, Merinda knelt and prayed silently. Touched, Jason said when she finished, "Don't worry, Merinda. The girl will be okay."

"I wasn't praying for her," she said. "I was praying for myself, praying that this arrogant leader, whoever he is, is not here for me because he is just the type my father would like. Rich and powerful. If he is a prince, my father would have me marry him in a heartbeat."

He nodded. "It looks like he brought enough to buy the whole kingdom, undoubtedly some sort of dowry."

They both walked in silence back to the castle. The guards at the gate seemed more formal than usual as they saluted the two. Jason, out of habit, returned their salute solemnly.

"Why do you do that, Jason? You know it is not expected of you."

"I do it to remind myself that I am no better than anyone else, and that all men are deserving of respect, no matter how lowly their station or duty."

"Jason, you will make a great leader someday," she prophesied.

They could see the castellan running across the courtyard toward them. "Here it comes," muttered Merinda, but to her surprise, he ran to Jason.

"Sir Jason," the castellan said breathlessly, "your presence is requested in the main hall immediately."

Jason turned to Princess Merinda and laughed. "You are wrong, Merinda. It seems the man wants to marry me instead."

He trotted along beside the castellan and arrived at the main hall to see the king in conversation with the man from the ship. His soldiers stood behind him, still armed, and the slaves knelt beside their burdens. A large audience from the curious lords and ladies in the castle filled the room. He felt small and insignificant as he approached and bowed before the king.

King Beldane began, "Sir Bristol, Master Kaishek has traveled a long way to speak with you."

Jason faced the man. If Master Kaishek or any of the soldiers recognized him from the dock they gave no indication. "I am Jason Bristol," he said to them simply.

Master Kaishek bowed low to Jason and said, with very little accent, "I am Wuzon Kaishek of the Miza Province of Pautang and have brought you many gifts." He paused as he vigorously motioned to the servants, who came running forward, bowing and opening their bags and chests presenting jewels, fine clothes, incense, spices, dried fruits, and nuts. There were many wonderful carvings in jade and ivory, as well as bejeweled weapons, rods, and tools. Mechanical eggs opened automatically and displayed other strange looking devices with mysterious purposes. Perhaps the most intriguing was a small cage that, when uncovered, revealed a small dragon.

The foreign prince continued, "Master Bristol, I have brought all this for you." He fell to the floor, bowing, as did all his servants and guards. Master Kaishek said humbly, "I have heard how you, a mere boy, defeated Master Maudid Duboh, reputed to have the greatest martial ability. I beg you, Master Bristol, please take me as your student."

Jason felt overwhelmed by the attention but also felt a little irritated at a man who fully expected to get his way no matter what. He motioned for Master Kaishek to stand and replied, "Actually, Maudid was defeated by the will of God."

"I have heard that you, a mere boy, stood up to Maudid's greatest attacks and that it was you who threw him onto the bee's nest. All feats that not even the greatest warriors could have done. Again, I humbly ask to be your student."

"I am sorry. I already have a student."

At that, the entire court gasped at his audacity. Jason saw Gunther, in the audience, flush and straighten with pride. Master Kaishek raised his staff to emphasize his words. "Then I will fight your student to show I am of more worth." This challenge made Jason angry, and he stepped forward to confront the man towering over him. "Tell me, Master Kaishek, why are you called master?"

Master Kaishek twirled his staff and planted the end on the floor with pride, almost between Jason's feet. "I am master of the staff, undefeated in more than two hundred tournaments and awarded the title Master by the Battle Priests of Dushan in the province of Xing Xang."

"But Master Kaishek, have you used your skill in actual combat?" asked Jason.

"Why, yes, of course," said Master Kaishek, puzzled, rubbing his nearly bald head.

"I saw your battle this morning, and you are no master," Jason said forcefully, pointing at the warrior. Anger clouded the oriental lord's face, and again gasps could be heard from the crowd at the young boy's impetuousness.

"I fought no battles this morning. You are mistaken, Master," he said sternly. There was a warning in his voice.

"Yes, you fought a battle with yourself this morning and lost. You struck an unarmed slave girl and broke her arm with your staff. You have no discipline and no self-control. You know nothing about the staff or how to fight with it," Jason said as he stamped his crooked walking stick for emphasis.

Master Kaishek replied, "On the contrary, Master, that slave girl deserved death, and I controlled myself by only punishing her a little. Here, I will show you my skill."

Master Kaishek stepped back, motioned for his guards and servants to give room, and began to whirl his staff through a kata. He jumped and rolled, striking and blocking invisible attackers with power and precision. His white robe floated and accentuated his every move.

Jason was impressed in spite of himself; he had never seen a finer display. When Master Kaishek finished, he looked at Jason, trying to hide his defiance, the crowd murmuring in awed approval. He felt a little inadequate at this challenge. This man was a superb martial artist yet lacked character. He felt the crooked little stick in his hand and imagined the contrast between him and this elegant warrior. The stick gave him an idea.

He was reminded of a tale of a boy who wanted to go to a calligraphy school in Japan, so his parents sent him to one of his teachers to get a reference. The teacher, instead of getting out his paints, grabbed a crayon, and merely signed his name to a piece of paper using the calligraphy style.

Although the parents were ashamed, they presented their boy to the college with the reference. When the curator saw it, he was so overcome by the elegance done with a simple crayon that he accepted the boy immediately. He said only a master could have drawn that well with simply a crayon.

With this story in mind, he walked over to the proud warrior as he spoke more gently, "That was a beautiful display of your skill. Is that your staff?"

"Yes, it was given to me by the great teacher Wubushi Manniah himself, and it is perfect, with no flaw. It is my most prized possession," the martial artist proudly proclaimed.

"Here, take this stick, Master Kaishek," he responded as he thrust the crooked walking stick at him, which was about a third shorter than the man's staff. "Do your demonstration again, but use this."

Master Kaishek looked at it incredulously, "That is not a weapon. It is just a stick. It will not function right nor work with my forms as it is way too short."

Jason didn't say a word, just continued to hold the stick before the man. Finally, Master Kaishek gave his staff to one of his soldiers and angrily snatched the stick from Jason's hands.

The oriental lord shook the stick with both hands as if to straighten it and clumsily began the same kata he did before. The crooked stick caught in his sleeves and snagged his flowing robes. It would not slide through his hands or strike where he wanted. Halfway through his routine, Master Kaishek threw the stick down in disgust.

"This is not a weapon!" he cried.

Jason walked over and picked up the stick. "Your straight stick is flawless. That is why it is not the weapon of a master. It has no spirit. It has no character which you can take advantage of ... Allow me to demonstrate with this stick, which I have never used before today. Princess Merinda can verify that I bought this stick just this morning from a beggar child named Chaney. Note the loving care this child used in carving a horse's head in the end. This stick carries the dreams of a little crippled boy as a knight riding a charger, yet I tell you this stick is more powerful than the mightiest sword."

Jason raised the stick in emphasis and brought it down into a powerful arc, spinning with the direction of the stick. Originally, he had planned to do a staff kata he himself was familiar with, but instead found himself letting the stick corkscrew in a bizarre fashion as it slid through his hands on his first move, then stood as still as a statue emphasizing the first strike.

Only a master could use a toy such as this stick in such a way as to make it a deadly weapon. Could he, Jason, do this? This brought to mind his own son who, while playing in his imagination, would be transformed into a miraculous ninja fighter, fighting with sticks even more crooked than this to defeat imaginary foes that would make grown men tremble if faced in real life. Although only play, it was a wonder to behold, gracefully smooth and effortless. Who better than a kid to bring a toy to life!

On intuition, he let go of his adultness, his experience, his knowledge of martial arts, and submitted to what his body and even his mind wanted to do. He released all restraint and allowed himself to go into his imagination—into that world where kids go without fear. He glinted his eyes like he had seen Bruce Lee do in a movie, looked around, and did a fierce kiai in a theatrical manner as he would never do as an adult and sprang into action with a quick twirling strike. Then, as if holding an invisible warrior at bay, he slowly swept the stick across the room. Appearing out of nowhere, he saw in his mind's eye the cannibal who attacked him when he first arrived. The cannibal attacked suddenly, only this time with his big barbarian two-handed sword.

A chill went through him. It was as if this stick actually was a magical weapon, helping to control his movements, helping to strike terror into his massive enemies, or was it the Holy Spirit? He did not know but just went with the flow of power coursing through him and around him. It was as if the cannibal himself was really there, not only providing targets but also an element of danger.

Ducking to the side, he then sprang forward, striking into the armpit of the barbarian cannibal's upraised arm. Sweeping through, he snagged the tribesman's feet with the crooked end of the stick. Pulling hard, he jerked the barbarian off balance, so he fell. He finished the imaginary opponent with another kiai, and an audible crunch to the larynx that sounded throughout the hall.

But his kata wasn't through yet. Suddenly, he could see the goblins ahead attacking the poor farmhouse, only this time, he didn't have his bow and arrows or a magical sword. He only had this stick. In his anger at the injustice of it, he took on the whole hoard, fighting with the same vengeance and desperation that drove him that night. Jumping, diving, rolling, and even aerial flips were accented with strikes and blocks. He was so absorbed in his fantasy he forgot the roomful of spectators. He was filled with an odd joy, an exultation he had not felt for many years— something a child would simply describe as fun—and he didn't want to quit. Though breathing hard, he was on what could only be described as a runner's high. With a kiai, he swept his foe and finished its life with a crushing blow to its skull. As the last goblin fell, the battle ended. The sound of the powerful smash echoed throughout the room as the end of the stick hit the floor, bringing him out of his dream battle.

His fiercely glinted eyes roamed the room. He was frozen in the position of his last blow, not even sure himself what all he had done. Now that reality came back to him all that was left to do was stand and bow, which he did slowly and deliberately, then looked at the crowd.

The court broke into wild applause and cheers. Even King Beldane smiled. Although he dearly would have loved to examine the young dragon, Jason bowed to Master Kaishek, then to the king and walked out of the hall. Master Kaishek angrily waved to his entourage and marched out with all the gifts.

Master Kaishek returned to his ship but did not leave port right away, perhaps hoping Jason would change his mind. In the following days, Jason saw the ship every morning as he wandered the town, but it was rare anyone was on deck. The river ice floes increased even more over the next few days.

CHAPTER 33
Who's the Master?

The poor crippled boy named Chaney suddenly found a little notoriety when a few nobles sought him out with orders for his sticks and carvings. Jason visited him a few days later. The boy now had a little stand with wood carvings all over the table and a barrel with various walking sticks capped with carved animal heads. A few people were standing around looking at his things.

Chaney smiled when he recognized his benefactor. "Sir Jason, I couldn't believe it when someone told me it was you who had bought my stick!"

Jason returned the smile. "Hi, Chaney. I have come to look at more of your carvings."

"Did you really beat a staff master with my stick?" asked Chaney eagerly.

"I guess I did, in a manner of speaking. Your stick has the unusual ability to bring out the worst in some people and the best in others. Has business been good?" he went on to ask.

"I have sold three for more money than I have ever dreamed!" The young boy beamed, then asked, "I hope it's okay I tell people that you use my sticks."

"Of course," replied Jason, realizing his celebrity status endorsement would help the boy. "Hey, how much is that walking stick with the eagle's head?"

"Four gold crowns."

"Four gold crowns?" asked Jason, astonished. "I bought the other stick for two."

The boy quickly said, "But only two for you, of course."

Jason fished out and paid four crowns.

Just then a man, whom he recognized as a dock worker, appeared, "Master Kaishek wishes to see you on his ship." Thanking the man, Jason left immediately, swinging his new stick.

When he arrived at the docks, the river had a slushy, sluggish look to it. It should be freezing soon, he thought to himself. The dragon ship was still at its moor, but a flurry of activity told him it would be leaving soon. He was brought on deck and shown into Master Kaishek's quarters.

After greetings, Master Kaishek began, "Master Bristol, I did not know you were also a master of the staff and upon reflection, I have learned several lessons from you. One is that a weapon does not define or make a master and the other is that a master is someone who is always in control of himself."

Jason nodded. "You have learned some good lessons, but perhaps missed the most important one of all."

Surprised, the staff master asked, "What is that?"

Jason grabbed a cluster of grapes at the table and began popping them into his mouth one at a time, then replied slowly, "I will tell you, but you will not believe it. You probably won't believe it until you are very old."

"Yes, yes, what is it?" Master Kaishek asked impatiently.

"The secret is that all mastery is merely an illusion. It is a comparison. To slugs, a butterfly is a master at flight. To a butterfly, a chicken is a master at flight. To a chicken, an eagle is a master at flight. But all are deceived by the illusion that the other is the ultimate in ability. In reality, there is always something better. Striving for mastery is vanity, it is an illusion we set for ourselves."

"That cannot be," said the man incredulously, then pointed at the eagle on Jason's stick. "There is nothing that is master over the eagle, and that is what I want to be."

Jason smiled, thinking of airplanes, but instead twirled his stick and said, "The angels are masters over the eagles, and the Creator is master over all."

"Then I shall be my own god, my own creator. I shall be undefeatable," Kaishek said adamantly.

"Then tell me," demanded Jason, "why do you think Maudid lost in his fight against me?"

"It is obvious," replied Master Kaishek. "You were better than him. You know the secret ways and used a strategy with the hornets that gave you an advantage—"

"No," interrupted Jason. "Maudid was a superior martial artist, superior in every way except one. I was not the greater master, as you believe. Yes, I know some things, and I know some secret ways, but there is only one reason I overcame Maudid."

"What was that?" asked the oriental curiously.

"Maudid and those he served challenged the Creator. And the Creator squashed him."

"The Creator?" Master Kaishek repeated in disbelief.

"Yes. He sent me to give the world a chance to shed its slavery to the petty gods and to stand up as men again."

"You...a child...you serve the Creator, and he granted you the ability to defeat Maudid?" he repeated with obvious disbelief. "No, the Creator used me as an excuse to show his power and took my feeble attempts and amplified them. The real question is, whose side will you choose? Will you be one of those people who will return to the one true God?"

Master Kaishek was indignant. "I serve no man or god. I serve only myself."

"Then you are the worst slave of all because you serve no higher ideals, no higher purpose than your own stomach when you are hungry, your own skin when it is cold, and your own sexual desires when you are aroused. This is no different from a goat. You are a slave to your created nature and created flesh, and in the end, all end up serving the cruelest master—and that is death. The only one who can truly free you from death is the Creator himself, who not only made life to begin with, but can renew it eternally."

"Bah, who wants to live forever?" exclaimed the warlord boorishly.

Jason shook his head sadly. "You do, I think, otherwise why search for mastery? You do it for self-preservation, for power, and for real life. Think on this, Master Kaishek, for your life is like this ship which is about to get trapped in this ice. You better move on to the open sea before it is too late. Good-bye, Master Kaishek."

Jason retrieved his new walking stick with the eagle's head and left Master Kaishek staring at his goblet of wine. When the boy left, Kaishek sat a little while longer, thinking. Suddenly, he reached out and poured the wine on the table and set the goblet upside down. The wine looked like blood running down the table. Master Kaishek went on deck and ordered the captain to depart. The ship was so large, it could not turn around without grounding itself, so they had to shift the rudder to the other end and guide it out to sea backward.

The oriental overlord watched as the riverbank passed and saw a group of children playing in the snow. He saw one boy with a beggar's stick standing apart from the rest of the group, whirling in mimicry of Jason's moves. Master Kaishek could see the castle above the city with a garrison of barely two hundred fighting men. Sure, they could rouse a much larger force from within the city, but if he wished, he could return with not even a quarter of his fleet and crush it.

There would not be much wealth here to be gained, but he would have the satisfaction of defeating Jason. Jason? A little boy? He shook his head at the thought of sending his military might to crush one little boy. Looking to the shore through the mist, he could envision himself returning with his fleet and there, standing on the shore to greet him, would be a little boy with a crooked stick.

He would send the signal and beach his landing crafts. His army would then storm the shore, and all would fall before his military might, except... Except that one little boy.

Here his vision got out of control. Jason, twirling his stick, became a tornado and like martial arts legends of old, swept through the army toward him, men flying away like chaff before a wind. When the child finally stood before him, he had the fierce countenance of a man.

Master Kaishek imagined fighting the diminutive boy with his magical staff, which helped him move like a master.

He shuddered to himself as he thought, who is the real master here, me or my staff? If it was the staff, then he was its slave and his title a sham.

His warrior spirit could envision Jason defending against his attacks, the little stick curling around his straight staff to strike him over and over. He would lose. He saw himself throw his staff down and it turn into a snake to fight for him, but Jason threw his little crooked stick down, and it too turned into a smaller snake but wriggled with a vitality his own snake couldn't match and Jason's snake ate his. That is where he stopped the vision, not bearing to see more.

He returned to his quarters and picked up his staff. It resonated with power to his touch. He swung the staff in some quick jabs and strikes with precision and power no one could possibly match, but it felt hollow and empty. The pride he felt before was not there. He felt the futility of it as if he were only flailing in the wind and then the moment would be gone with nothing left to show for it. The little boy had more than he did.

Suddenly, Master Kaishek grabbed his staff at both ends and could feel the magical power coursing through it that he alone could wield. Or was he deceived? Did it really wield him? If he was a real master, it wouldn't matter what he held in his hands. This stick was robbing him of the chance to become a true master. This staff, instead of being a mighty weapon in his hands, was a crutch upon which to lean his ego.

Now he felt his own rage surge, a power mightier than the magic in the staff, and he pulled hard on the ends, bending it, then quickly and decisively broke it over his knee. The magical energies stored in the staff exploded, sending Master Kaishek backward over the table and ruining his room. Master Kaishek stood, his robe burnt, torn, and ruined, but he was laughing. He was staff master no more...and for the first time in his life, he felt free.

CHAPTER 34
The Demon Contract

Later that afternoon, Jason was invited to celebrate winter solstice with the royal family. King Beldane had pressing business preparing for the upcoming war, so Jason spent the evening entertaining and socializing with the queen and princesses and some of their closest friends. Princess Merinda invited some of her friends from town and a swarthy-looking man, perhaps in his late twenties, Yaveen Quantrel, whom she introduced to Jason as her sword instructor. The instructor seemed a little embarrassed to be in the presence of nobility and felt much more comfortable talking to the young Jason. Jason found himself liking the man.

Princess Kuari had her usual entourage of girls, which included Nelda. The princess seemed unusually tense and twittery. At midnight, everyone climbed the parapets to view the town, and although the city was usually dark this time of night, it was now alive and well-lit. Suddenly, fireworks erupted from various locations in the town and shouts of revelry could be heard ringing in the cold, rarefied air.

The castle, not to be outdone, launched its own fireworks, reminding him of the castle at Disneyland. The difference being that Tinkerbell could really exist here, adding the finishing touch to the fireworks with her wand. He had presumed fireworks a precursor to the invention of firearms but instead found that fireworks were considered a magical item bought from oriental traders, and none in Chanderlon knew how to make them.

Well after midnight, the party guests left and Yaveen, the princess's sword instructor, gave a particular invitation for Jason to visit him at his shop in town. Jason thanked him for the invitation, and the man walked out of the hall to make his way home.

Just as the man approached the main doors, from a side corridor he heard a "pssst." Turning, he was beckoned by a shadowy figure. Without saying a word, both went down the hall to an open chamber by a window.

"What is it you want?" asked Yaveen. In the light of the night sky, he could see the silver in the man's sharp, pointed beard.

"Did you get my message?"

"That Jason needs to die?"

"Yes, he knows too much."

"Well, the fact that he did not reveal you may play to our advantage. Make no move against him for now. He may make the perfect stooge for when I make my move. Hopefully by then, you will be ruling the kingdom of Harvella."

"But what if he reveals me to the king before then?"

"That boy is more than what he appears. I think he can't reveal you without revealing himself."

"Then what is he?"

"I don't know, but I hope to find out."

"Then, perhaps, I should have him arrested and tortured until he confesses."

"No, too many ears. Only in secrecy do we gain an advantage. Go back and wait until I direct you further."

Lord Krogan smiled to himself as he watched the shadowy figure leave. His own sources told him much more than what Yaveen revealed. Yaveen was the offspring of a young and wild Prince Beldane's tryst on foreign soil. Raised by a commoner, he was indentured as a servant into the court of Kuladon. Yaveen became trained as a fighter and in the ways of magic. The young man was especially gifted in both, and as a master of intrigue, he later ventured to his father's kingdom with the intent to claim his rightful place. Upon his arrival, however, he discovered magic was distrusted by the inhabitants and his skills and motives would be suspect. He joined a band of outlaws and became known as Lord Griffon. He had even captured and trained a real live griffon to help lend to his notoriety.

Lord Krogan felt confident he knew all about the king's illegitimate son, but still he felt a danger he could not put his finger on. Perhaps it was the man's ways with magic. As of yet, he had not seen the man use any of that power. He had no problem with the use of magic himself. Why, it was well known that even the king carried an enchanted sword. Maybe it was more the uncomfortable feeling that he was actually expendable to Yaveen's plans. Yes, that was it. That was the uncomfortable feeling. Well, perhaps he would find an opportunity to betray Lord Griffon before Lord Griffon expended him, but for now, he must wait.

The next morning, Jason awoke with a start. The previous night was the winter solstice, and it suddenly occurred to him that ominous night has great significance to the arcane and religious cults. He felt so stupid to have missed it. He hurriedly made his way to the room with the idol in it. Sure enough, on the altar was fresh blood. He was too late. He felt guilty for not exposing it so it could be destroyed but also knew that wouldn't save any lives. The cult members would just hold their ceremonies elsewhere.

He needed to catch them in the act and expose the members if he was going to have any effect. Perhaps that was why Princess Kuari was so tense, knowing something was happening. He needed to befriend the youngest princess, so she would come to him the next time the cult was about to perform a ceremony. He hoped he could do that without becoming her chosen consort. The princess, being the same age as Nelda, was too close to his apparent age for comfort.

The following month of winter proved uneventful. He talked to everyone individually about the Creator as opportunity arose. It became a part of his normal routine, and he felt fairly content, sometimes forgetting he was anything but a little boy in a medieval castle. He still missed his family terribly and hoped to leave in early spring before the kingdom tore itself apart waging war on its neighbor. Perhaps the Lord would send him home even before then.

He also learned from Lord Killensdale that the war council actually had little choice but to choose war. Harvella, though weak in military might, was strong in magic.

Harvella was making overtures to expanding its borders, so nearby countries wanted to strike before its magical preparations were complete. Chanderlon also felt vulnerable and wished to join forces with the other countries before Harvella became too powerful and no one could stop them. It seemed to Jason that magic was this world's equivalent to his home world's nuclear powers. A balance of powers was desired even here.

The investigation into Father Varigold's death brought no results. No other witnesses outside of the clergy of Xan Rukkah could be found, and the clerics themselves were not talking. Since it was not a formal inquisition, methods to make the clerics talk could not be used, so the investigation was stymied and eventually faded into obscurity.

The interrogations from the surviving kidnappers brought no new evidence. The kidnappers did not know who they worked for but took orders from a shadowy figure known as Lord Griffon, who only came to them in the dark and was never seen clearly. Sir Tadden's methods were extreme, and some of the kidnappers did not survive the interrogation.

Jason did take up Yaveen's offer to visit him and was taken to admire his rich collection of swords and various weapons. Yaveen seemed very interested in everything about the boy and confessed he was a little jealous the princess had chosen Jason over him as champion. But upon witnessing the battle with Maudid, everything had worked out for the best. Jason was invited to visit again, and perhaps Yaveen would test his swordsmanship against his.

Gunther was doing well with his lessons, now probably the equivalent of a green belt at his home world dojo. They made some mats out of several layers of thick rugs so they could practice throws.

One of the bigger boys had forced Gunther into a fight, and Gunther threw him and beat him soundly, but let the boy go before he was seriously injured. That is when the arms master discovered his tutelage under Jason. Through Gunther, the arms master sent Jason an invitation to teach the hand-to-hand portion of the training. Jason had not responded yet when Gunther surprised him with an unusual request. After practice that night, Gunther came to Jason, went to one knee and said, "Jason, it is time for me to enter the service of the Creator and to become a holy warrior too."

"Do you know how to do that and what will be required of you?"

"Yes," replied Gunther, "you have told me how the Creator became a human named Jesus, so he could experience death and how, by that death, he paid the price to free us from slavery. When Jesus came back to life, he showed that even death had no power over him. Then Jesus made a ritual for those who have chosen to follow him, emulating what he experienced, as a way to adopt us into his family. Those adopted into his family must then live a life that makes the Father proud to call us his children. His children are the priests, the holy warriors, the princes and princesses of a kingdom far greater than any on this world. Jason, I want to experience that ritual. Will you bury me in water, so I may rise out of it a new person?"

Jason smiled. "There is one more thing that will allow you to complete the ritual."

"What is that?" queried Gunther eagerly.

"You must precede the ritual by publicly announcing you will follow the Creator by proclaiming his human name," said Jason.

"Jesus, my Lord and my God," declared Gunther.

That made Jason smile again, because those were the exact words Jesus's apostle used, the one who came to be known as doubting Thomas.

Gunther later surprised everyone by announcing at dinner the following evening that he had decided to become a servant of Jesus and invited all to watch Jason bury him by immersing him in water. A murmur arose, as everyone wondered about this Jesus.

"Jesus is the name of the Creator when he became a man," Gunther announced proudly. Everyone then wanted to know what being immersed in water had to do with anything. Gunther went on to tell them, and Jason was proud of him for, as far as he knew, the reformed bully preached the first gospel message to an audience on this planet.

Afterward, Princess Merinda, Nelda, and Amanie ran and hugged Gunther, announcing that they, too, believed in Jesus and wanted Jason to immerse them as well. Many of the lords and their families came to watch, including the royal family. After their baptism in a tub of warm water Gunther had arranged, Nelda sang a song she had adapted from a love song and dedicated it to Jesus, substituting his name where appropriate. Gunther led a prayer and thanked everyone for coming.

Jason smiled before drifting off to sleep that night. He often thought of his family at this time, but now, he didn't feel so lonely because he had family here too—his brothers and sisters in the Creator's family.

The next day, Gunther, Princess Merinda, Nelda, and Amanie were waiting for Jason when he arose from bed. They had some servants bring breakfast for everyone and ate in his room. After breakfast, Princess Merinda asked him, "Could you write down the things we must know about the Creator and how to worship him?"

He replied, "In my world, there is a book called the Bible, which contains the history of how God dealt with mankind and what God wishes for our lives, but I think this world may have to trust the Holy Spirit to guide it and provide either myself or someone else to write something. Perhaps in the future a Bible will be provided.

"You are now in God's family, just as I am. He will teach you through many means and inspire you to write as he sees fit. Right now, I have one more ritual to teach you. It is where we copy, to some degree, Jesus's last supper before mankind killed him, in order to remind ourselves of his sacrifice."

The small group held what was probably that world's first church service in a long time and continued to meet once a week. Jason taught as much as he could of the teachings of Jesus and the deeper mysteries of the nature of God and the relationship of the Father and the Son.

One cold morning, the queen came in from the balcony after watching her children at play with Jason and some of their friends. The days were getting longer and brighter and the children, even Princess Merinda, were out playing in the snow building a large snow castle.

It was good her daughters had such friends, for they will help when the news finally comes. Princess Juggerinda had proven she can take care of herself, while Princess Kuari was the apple of her father's eye. They would be okay.

The king was in the hall and for a little while she had time to herself. She would have liked to have gone to a remote part of the castle, perhaps a tower, but if she set one foot outside their royal apartments, the guards would have called her ladies and an escort to accompany her. If she forbid it, then they would follow themselves in order to "protect" her.

Only here did she have any privacy, so closing the curtains and going into her bedroom and closing the door so she could not be heard outside, she called aloud, "Donjoni. Donjoni. I summon you. Come, Donjoni."

Almost instantly, a candle fizzled and went out. The smoke that swirled up from the dying flame carried the stench of evil and soon became thick columns of black vapor, as if from hell itself, to create a scene of a crude underground palace. From its center came a billowy cloud moving as if it were a living beast trying to escape the realms of horror. Then a black foot stepped out from it and down into the room. Following it came the body of a tall lanky black figure, perhaps seven feet tall, towering over the queen who was boldly facing it. Its eyes glowed an unearthly orange that seemed to drink all living things into their depths.

It had small black bull's horns sticking out of the sides of its head, and when it smiled, it disclosed a set of startling white fangs. Its barbed tail twitched about like a cat's in readiness to pounce. Its clawed fingertips had a manicured look and its bare flesh, visible from beyond a chain mail waist cloth, was well muscled under black skin.

The dark creature of evil beckoned elegantly. "Ah, Queen Overa, it is you who are summoning me. I trust you have the rest of your payment in readiness?"

The queen bent over by her bed and pulled out a black cloth bag, full of heavy coin. "Yes, I have two thousand more crowns as we discussed. Do you have a hero who can rescue me?"

"Yes, Queeny. You can rest assured one is on his way, though he may be here as late as this fall."

"What?" cried the queen, suddenly drawing the bag of money behind her. "I asked you over a year ago to find a hero, and now, I will have to wait another half a year?"

"Well, remember, to us immortals time is a trifling thing, but in this case, it is actually necessary. My minions have scoured the world looking for a hero who would take on this task and we have not found one until recently."

"Can't you just wave your hand and send me someplace?"

The demon rolled its eyes and continued on patiently, "I could spirit you away to my realm right now, if you wished, but for traveling in this mundane world you need mundane transportation. And to go to a realm beyond where your husband can simply retrieve you requires a lengthy voyage. Your hero might be here sooner if he has fair sailing."

Mollified, the queen handed the demon fiend the money. "I am sorry, Donjoni. I will be patient. The hero is sufficient."

"Thank you, Overa," said the evil spirit, weighing the bag in its hand.

"Now that you have fulfilled your end of the contract, rest assured I will fulfill mine. Until then."

It disappeared in another puff of smoke.

"Until then," said the woman with a half smile.

Amanie's birthday fell in the spring as the weather just started to warm. Jason carved her a wooden dragon that cracked nuts in its jaws. Amanie was very proud of this unique gift. He had also found a common interest with Kuari in playing chess. He made her a chess set with a monster army facing an army of elves. They would play and talk for about an hour each day.

He made sure to take time to talk to soldiers and other knights as well. He asked about open field battle tactics and their experiences with war, which they generally were glad to tell.

Preparations for war began in earnest now, with the armor and weapon makers in full swing for equipping the troops that would be conscripted after the spring breakup. Most of the castle troops were training themselves to manage and command these new soldiers drafted from the city and countryside among the common folk.

One project for himself was to make a troll destroying kit with a bottle of very flammable oil with a flint striker attached, put in a pouch to be always carried on his belt. He had done his research, and all agreed this was the best way. Some had suggested acid, but the amount was always in question as to how much would be enough, for acid dilutes fairly quickly.

The recommended strategy was to some way immobilize the troll, then pour oil over it and set it on fire. This was the only way to stop it from regenerating. It seemed that burning it completely to the bone was not necessary and even a small amount of oil was adequate as long as there was enough to douse the whole beast.

Even though he doubted his vial of oil itself was adequate, he figured he could add brush and other flammable material that may be available. The creature still haunted his dreams, for he knew it was out there waiting for him. He almost welcomed the opportunity to confront the troll for his own peace of mind.

The fledgling church in Chanderlon grew, with Lord and Lady Killensdale the next converts. Gunther now began another group outside the castle, using a local warehouse in the mornings one day a week. At first, Gunther appealed to kids, but adults soon followed.

Jason checked the mark on the door frame indicating his height when he first moved into his apartment and measured his height now after five months of winter. He had not grown at all. He had suspected as much since even Amanie was catching up to him in size.

He considered this. Either the effect of his transfer here had not worn off yet, or he was growing so slowly it was not measurable. Only time would tell. Being ten again was great if you would then grow normally. But if he had to choose one age to be stuck at, it would have been preferable to be somewhere between twenty-five or thirty.

Why would God want a child to lead this world to the light? He mused on a verse talking about a time when the lion will lay down with the lamb and a child will lead them. But he was not a child—not really. Then again, he remembered in his own world how people would describe him as a kid at heart. Did that mean he was actually in a body that now matched his heart? Even as it was, he seemed to have a hard time remembering what he used to look like as a man.

CHAPTER 35
Eye of a Goddess

The blooming of the royal and common gardens marked that spring had truly sprung. After such a hard winter, everyone appreciated the beauty and warmth. Princess Kuari invited Jason to an afternoon chess match in the royal garden. Jason had the board set up as he waited for her.

The pink apple blossoms were beautiful on the tree over the bench where he sat. Princess Kuari entered the garden but did not greet him with her usual smile. He watched her. She had grown taller too. She had a grace and beauty that more than hinted at the beautiful woman she would soon become.

"Jason, thanks for coming, but I do not feel like playing today."

"Why?" he asked. "Are you feeling ill?"

"No, I am more depressed than anything. Today, they have set the tents on the plains and started conscripting for the army."

"But I thought you were in favor of the war. Why does this depress you?" he asked.

"Yes, I am in favor of this war, but I know many will die for the good of the kingdom. The burden falls heavily on the royal family. I wish to be alone right now. We can play tomorrow. I will be in a much better mood then, but today, I wish to mourn."

"Very well, Princess, tomorrow it is." He put away the chess set and returned to his room. Princess Kuari won't be as depressed tomorrow, even though the conscription will continue for weeks to come. Does that mean there is something particular happening today which she is depressed about? Princess Kuari was depressed about people dying, so was someone about to die? Was this the break concerning the castle cult he had been waiting for? He had hoped Kuari would confide in him and come right out and tell him.

Not knowing what to expect, he donned his double swords, bow and quiver, and stashed his treasures into the upper room, pulling up the rope ladder and closing the trap door so no one would discover its existence. If he had to fight, it would be in close quarters where the shorter swords would be more useful, so he purposefully left his katana on the dresser, just so the curious would not look around so much if for some reason he did not immediately make it back.

He made his way to the secret chamber, setting his lamp down before readying his bow and sneaking to the hidden alcove. Low, chanting voices could be heard before he reached the sacrificial chamber. When he arrived, it seemed like the glowing orb was brighter. In the dim light, he saw the chamber filled with silhouetted figures in the dark. He also heard the muffled cries of a little girl who was tied down and stretched across the altar. A woman outlined in darkness stood over the altar, knife upraised, while chanters ringed the room and dancers writhed around the altar. Underneath the statue of the goddess holding the glowing orb stood the only person whose face was visible in its light— King Beldane.

At the crescendo of the chant, all stopped and the dancers lay prostrate. The voice of the priestess rang through the room. "Axialla, mother of dark and magic, we have gathered to show our loyalty and to worship your greatness. We have summoned your power with many sacrifices and seek your favor with this final sacrifice to bestow your full ability to your chosen vessel."

Jason knew he had better do something soon, or this woman would kill the child. He aimed for the woman's heart. That would stop her, but was there another way? He then remembered his dream where his son told him that if he was in doubt as to the target, then he was to let God do the aiming for him. He prayed, closed his eyes, and released the arrow. He just made sure he was high enough to miss the child.

He had heard some practitioners of the Japanese archery style Kyudo were able to hit their target blindfolded, but this was different because he did not even know what the target should be. He opened his eyes as the woman screamed. It was a nearly impossible shot, but the arrow transfixed both her hands, and she dropped the knife involuntarily at her feet.

All he knew then was he had to do something to save the girl. To run into the midst of these crazed worshipers would be madness, but in complete darkness, he had a chance. His next arrow hit the glowing orb. The orb shattered as though made of glass, sending the room into total darkness.

He dropped his bow and arrows to one side and jumped over the edge into the darkness, relying on his memory of the layout of the room. To his own surprise, he landed on a man with force. The man cried out in pain, which added to the uproar caused by the cries of the priestess.

In both worlds, he had often trained to fight blindfolded, which helped him to not become confused amidst the chaos of the milling people. He raced to the altar and felt for the girl's wrists and ankles, pulled his knife, and cut the bonds. He felt some clothing at his feet which he scooped with one hand as he helped the girl with the other and led her, weaving through the agitated throng to the hidden alcove. As he did, he could hear the king's strong voice chanting an incantation.

Reaching the alcove, he quickly lifted the girl up into it and climbed up after her. He didn't spare the time to remove the girl's gag but shoved the clothes into her arms and pushed her down the hallway towards the dim glow of his own lamp set on the floor.

"Take the lamp," Jason whispered into little girl's ear. "Go to the end of the passageway and push on the ceiling so it slides backward." He figured that was safer than having her attempt to climb his dangling rope.

As the girl ran, he turned in time to see a red light spring into existence, coming from a large red eye, about three feet in diameter with blood-red tentacles writhing about as it floated before the king.

"The eye of Axialla!" someone screamed fearfully.

The large eye resembled a giant glowing beach ball with what looked like the orange-colored arms of a squid or octopus popping out of its pale, watery surface in various places. Each was about eight to ten feet long. It would have looked ridiculous, except for the way it seemed to quiver in anticipation at finding someone to devour. It was accompanied by a strange sucking noise, and evil seemed to radiate from it along with its soft glowing light.

A bright red beam came from the pupil of the eye as it searched for a sacrificial victim. Seeing at first only the priestess kneeling before it with an arrow transfixing her hands, the eye darted forward as the tentacles grabbed her, pulling the struggling priestess to it, and she entered the eye as if it were made of gelatin, her scream cut short by the horrid gurgling that enveloped her.

The mass undulated wildly with the struggles of the victim within, then suddenly stilled. The eye left her about two seconds later, a standing bloody mass with all her skin and most of her flesh ripped off. She toppled to the floor a writhing, dying, skeletal mass. In the dim light, it just looked like she had melted into a red waxy pile on the floor. The other worshipers recoiled in terror, while the king began another incantation.

The worshipers ducked away as the beam from the eye now searched for the intruder. Jason knew he should run before it discovered him, but he didn't want to leave his bow, so he first snatched up that and the quiver. The eye stopped and focused its beam to the right of him and shot across the room in that direction. He heard a cry of terror and looked to where the eye was suddenly focused. In another hidden alcove, transfixed by the glow, stood Princess Kuari.

Horrified, King Beldane shouted, "No! Run, Kuari! Run!"

But the eye was too fast and reached Princess Kuari in a heartbeat. Without thinking, Jason fired as a tentacle grabbed Kuari's arm.

"Stop, I command you!" cried the king futilely.

The arrow sank deep into the gelatinous glob, and the eye instantly released Kuari while turning to search for its attacker. Princess Kuari then ran, vanishing into the dark passageway. Jason shot another arrow, striking dead-center in the pupil as it darted toward him. He dove into his hole just as the eye darted a tentacle forward, wrapping it around his foot far faster than he thought possible. The eye was too big to fit through the narrow passageway and hit the walls, jamming itself into place.

The tentacle was stronger than he, jerking him off his feet and dragging him back down the corridor toward the eye. He caught the edge of a crack in a stone with one hand and grabbed for his sword with the other hand. Bathed in the red light of the eye, he let go and struck at the tentacle around his foot at the same time, but it pulled him next to the eye before being severed. More tentacles were trying to squeeze past, and he knew he did not have much time.

Making a quick slash at the eye next to the arrow, he rolled backward to avoid another tentacle that had just squeezed through. Once out of range, he grabbed his bow again and began to fill the eye with arrows. After the seventh arrow, the eye burst, and he leaped back to avoid the spewing bloody ichors. A piece of tentacle flew past him and seemed to begin boiling as it dissolved, while the spot where the eye had been became a glowing pool of boiling ooze as it too began to evaporate into nothingness.

He was filled with disgust at the stench it made and fled with his hand over his mouth. Not knowing if he was being pursued or not, he sped down the passageway in the dark, using his bow to feel the wall. He paused as he reached his rope, and while he listened, he flung the end high up in the rungs in hopes that a pursuer would not find it. He couldn't hear any pursuit but ran on down the tunnel anyway to see if the girl needed help.

After a little time, he could see the dim glow of the lamp ahead. When he caught up with the young girl, she was dressed and at the stair leading up to the concealed doorway in the ceiling. The lamp was on the floor, and the girl was pushing and shoving on the slab, unable to open it. The girl was perhaps five or six with stringy brown hair. He did not recognize her as being from the keep.

"Here, let me open that for you," he said. The girl turned with a look of terror but relaxed to see the boy who rescued her. "My name is Jason. What is yours?" he said as he went by her to the top of the stair.

"I am Marigold," she replied. "You...you are Jason?"

"Yes, I am Jason."

"Jason, I prayed to the Creator that you would come and you did!" Marigold exclaimed.

"Do you know the Creator?" he asked as he opened the lid to the sarcophagus.

Marigold confessed, "Not very well, but my parents have started praying to the Creator because they say he is stronger than all the other gods. They told me if I am in trouble to pray to the Creator."

They climbed into the tomb, and since a little light came from the partially opened door of the tomb, he snuffed out the lamp and put it back into the passageway for future use. Then he slid the lid back over the sarcophagus. Then, opening the door to the tomb the rest of the way, he said, "Come, Marigold, I will get you out of this graveyard and take you home. Where do you live?"

"I live on a farm from up the river," she replied.

The graveyard looked different without the snow. But what caught his eye was a freshly dug grave. It did not look right. Curious, he walked over to it. The ground looked as if some animal had clawed it open. He could see it had a new headstone, but when he looked into the hole, there was a broken coffin with rags and bones strewn about as if something had fed upon the corpse.

Turning to hide the view from Marigold, he saw standing behind her and towering over both of them was Trombul. The fiend had chosen this very graveyard to hide in during the day while searching for him. The giant's bristly gray and black hair stood out from his head like a thinning porcupine.

Trombul would have attacked the little girl immediately, except it was so surprised to see Jason it stood in shock for a moment—but only for a moment. Jason grabbed for the girl, who had not yet seen the troll, and jerked her out of the way just as a huge clawed hand swung down. He was pushing her further away as a second clawed hand swept him from his feet.

He hit the ground hard and rolled, feeling the rips in his back and shoulder from the troll's dirty claw-like nails.

"Run, Marigold!" he cried as he regained his feet. Pulling both swords, he desperately tried to ward off the frenzied onslaught that followed but the monstrous beast, whose only interest now was in the prey he had sought for so long, was not taking any chances. The giant backhanded him across the face and he felt the impact registering to his brain like a flash of light. He had the sensation of flying through the air, then utter darkness.

CHAPTER 36
Transport by Troll-y

When Jason finally became conscious, it was to a world of utter pain. His face, head, and lacerated shoulder hurt, to be sure, but what hurt most were his legs below the knees. They were broken. Evidently, Trombul had seen it as a simple way to keep him from escaping. He felt sick to his stomach because the whole world was moving.

Trombul was carrying him in a large, rough hemp bag that smelled of feed grain and hemp. He was cramped inside the bag and desperately wanted fresh air and a way to ease his pain. From the way the bag was bouncing and jerking, the huge troll must be running and each jostle caused immense pain to radiate from his broken bones. He struggled to get more upright so he could breathe better, but his ruined legs were useless.

Almost too abruptly, the great troll stopped and slung the bag to the ground. The impact and jarring of his broken bones almost made him pass out again. Lying there, his body busted and bleeding, he could hear the chattering of a squirrel and the sound of a brook. Suddenly, he realized how thirsty he was. The dust and chaff of the bag combined with his injuries had resulted in a powerful thirst that threatened to choke him worse than the claustrophobic atmosphere of his cloth prison. He also had no idea how long he had been unconscious. Given the extent of his injuries, he could have been out for a day or longer.

He took inventory to see what Trombul had left him. His weapons and daggers were gone, but the items in his coat pockets were still there—his sling and some coins. He felt his belt and the small pouch that held his anti-troll kit was still there (a bottle of oil and flint striker).

Painfully, he crawled out of the bag his captor had failed to tie shut. It was midday, and he was in a wooded clearing by a small stream. The troll was drinking noisily from the creek. A bump raised under the troll's skin and moved across its back. The troll stood and tried to claw at the place but could not reach it. It then backed against a tree and scratched its back on the rough bark violently, leaving a visible greenish red rash as it turned back to drinking again.

Noticing the boy's movements, it stood, still in the creek, to watch as its captive crawled painfully toward the stream. The troll, satisfied of his prey's inability to escape, made no motion to stop Jason from slacking his thirst.

Suddenly, with the speed and voracity of a cat, the troll snatched a small wiggling fish out of the water and stuffed it in his mouth, swallowing it in one gulp. Jason kept crawling, his thirst driving him toward the cool water with an urgency that overpowered the agonizing pain in his crippled legs.

Trombul moved toward him, smiling—if you could call it that—with blood and scales in its teeth. The squirrel chattered again, and the troll stopped, turning toward the sound, then was off on the hunt, leaving Jason to fend for himself.

After taking a long drink of water, he considered his options. The troll was the ultimate survivalist. He had better learn from the troll if he was going to live to make it to his destination. He figured his accelerated healing needed fuel to work and food was probably something the troll may not think to provide.

Seeing the flash of another small fish, he did not take time to think about it and thrust a hand into the water for it. Years of commercial fishing had taught him well how to hold a slippery fish with his bare hands, though the feat was more difficult with his kid-sized hands. He doubted he had time to make a fire, or if he did, the troll may come back and take his food away and eat it before he could. He must eat it now in the same manner as the troll.

With the fish wiggling in his hands, he needed to psyche himself up. As a kid, he often pretended he was a tiger or a lion and used that visualization to help him eat the occasional unsavory meals forced on him by his parents. Baring his fangs, he bit the head off the fish and spat it out, blood dripping from his mouth. He quickly ate the rest before he lost his resolve, finishing with a long drink of water to help keep it down. It felt like it was still wiggling inside him.

The troll was not back yet, but he could hear it crashing through the woods on a wild squirrel chase. He now determined he must reset the bones in his legs and splint them before his accelerated healing caused them to regrow deformed.

There were plenty of fallen branches here to make splints so he gathered four, breaking them to the right length. Then he crawled to two large rocks and caught one ankle between them. Pulling hard and in intense pain, he straightened his leg and tied the splints in place with the string from his sling.

He lay there panting from the pain, trying to psych himself up to face what he just experienced yet again. He considered waiting to see if his leg would straighten on its own or wait and see if there would be another opportunity to do the second leg later. Then, he visualized himself with a healed but bent leg. He would have to rebreak it, and without a doctor to help him set it properly, it may never be straight again. It had to be done now.

Gritting his teeth and growling to hide his cries, he splinted the other leg in a similar manner, using a rag stripped from the edge of his shirt to secure it in place. Then he lay there, waiting in utter exhaustion, hoping his accelerated healing was fast enough to start binding the bone in place as he waited for his captor to return.

Trombul eventually returned. Blood with bits of rabbit fur flecked its chest. It seemed to not notice Jason's new splints and roughly grabbed him by his neck and stuffed him back into the bag. He wanted to scream as his legs jostled heedlessly. Fearing his splints had loosened, he quickly checked their tightness and if his shins were still straight.

He was jolted on impact as the troll swung the bag up onto its shoulder. Soon, he was bouncing on the back of the troll again as it took off on a run, and with some effort he got himself upright. After a while, the pain in his legs subsided a bit, so perhaps they had started to heal. He did get some sleep, but only because he passed out again.

Later that night, he could hear the barking of dogs through the sack. As the pack closed in, he could hear the snarling and snapping of teeth just inches from the bag. The troll swung the bag around, dumping him on some brush, in order to fight off the dogs. The noise of the attack was horrendous, and Jason was buffeted several times by the legs and tails of several hounds as they circled around the troll, seeking a vulnerable spot for a bite.

Whatever harm the dogs had intended upon the troll befell them instead, and it was not long before their barks of attack turned to yips of fear as the huge humanoid quickly turned from hunted to hunter. Jason heard a thump, and a crack as one dog fell to Trombul's powerful feet. A piercing canine scream ended in a wet snap as another of the four-footed assailants came to an end. The terrifying mêlée was made all the more unnerving to Jason because he could see nothing from inside his sack prison.

Soon, the barking and growling faded as the survivors of the pack fled. Jason wasn't certain how many dogs the troll managed to kill, but the fight was a short one, and Trombul feasted well that evening. For the first time in three days (that Jason was aware of) the beast slept.

He took this opportunity to try and crawl away to make his escape. Slipping out of the sack, he wormed his way to an irrigation ditch by the road and rolled down the embankment. By the time he hit the bottom he himself was already asleep. It was the first good sleep since his ordeal began.

The food lodged in the swarthy, dark-haired thief's mouth. He was sitting at a table in a tavern eating dinner when the news came, and he stared in disbelief at the young man who had burst through the door, not even a town crier, shouting the news that Sir Jason had been killed and taken by some foul beast.

Although he was in shock, he knew the castle and royalty would be in greater shock at the loss of their beloved hero. The town would be in shock of a lesser degree, while the clerics of the various temples would secretly rejoice. He knew there were opportunities in this somewhere, and he needed to act quickly.

He finished chewing as he made his plans. Other people in the tavern were milling about now, some wanting to launch a monster hunt, but no one knew where to begin. They argued and shouted at each other, frustrated that they could do nothing. Many could not accept that Jason was dead, but it seemed a little girl witnessed the event and the remains of blood, and the boy's weapons verified her story. He noticed a transient hunter slip out of the room, unobserved by the rest of the crowd.

Yaveen smiled to himself, surmising the hunter was hoping to cash in on the reward for Jason's return, dead or alive. There were other schemers at this moment as well who, just like him, were examining the opportunities presented by people in shock and grief.

Casually standing so as not to draw attention, he worked his way through the crowd and out the door. He had to do two things right away. First, he had to find that hunter and promise a goodly sum for proof of Jason's death. Second, he needed to send a messenger with a note to the clerics of Xan Rukkah claiming credit for Jason's demise.

It was a small step for his ambitions, but it was a start. His ultimate goal was to be the new king of Chanderlon. He felt his time approaching, for he knew King Beldane planned to lead his own men into battle. Things happen on the field of combat even if the campaign is successful; the king could still die. He would be seen as a savior to a grieving kingdom.

Lost in visions of future grandeur, he headed toward the dock district where he knew some of his men would be in the midst of an early night's gambling. He would dispatch them to the clerics and to find the hunter. The hunter could be a problem finding, but was sure that if needed, he could search the huntsman from the air with his griffon. He might even find Jason himself if he was lucky.

To his dismay, Jason awoke later inside the bouncing bag again, this time bloody strips and chunks of meat from the dogs resided in the bag with him. He didn't know if Trombul was saving the meat for a snack later or if the troll intended it for him, but he forced himself to eat it just the same. Ravenous hunger managed to drive away queasiness for eating raw dog.

When his captor finally stopped, a day and a half later, it dumped him out and searched the bag disappointingly. The troll's intended snack was little more than gnawed bones. They were on the plains at the river with the border stones. Trombul left the boy at the river to fend for himself while it hunted.

Jason checked his legs. They were mending straight, but it was still too painful to walk. A vulture circled lazily over him. He thought he must look pretty bad if the buzzards were already eyeballing him as a meal.

"Tell me, vulture, am I more alive or dead?" he asked out loud.

The vulture seemed to hear his question, and by answer, it flew off, following the river. He then noticed many vultures, all of them following the river, almost like they were patrolling it for trespassers.

The troll came over the hill toward the bank on a run. It grabbed the bag and stuffed Jason in so violently it tore a hole in the side. Jason looked out of the new hole as Trombul noisily splashed across the river. Shadows, semi-transparent like ghosts, floated from the other bank several feet in the air over the water towards the two, even though it was broad daylight.

The giant monster roared, and the shadows backed off, allowing it to pass with its burden. As they went up the slope on the other side, he saw the reason for the troll's haste. A cavalry of at least twenty horsemen broke over the ridge with their flowing yellow and orange capes and plumed helmets.

"Help! Help! The troll's got me!" Jason hollered at the top of his voice, although he doubted they could hear him. The cavalry charged into the river in pursuit but halted midstream as the shadows appeared from the banks.

He couldn't see them anymore after the troll crested the hill, and it slowed its pace down to a ground-eating trot, no longer concerned about being chased.

At the next break, looking back toward the river, he saw something large flying in the distance toward them. At first, he thought it a large falcon similar to the one that had captured him, but it seemed odd in that there were either two heads or something was riding on its back. Apparently, it approached the river from the other side as the vultures swarmed it, driving it back and away.

During the aerial combat, it revealed another set of legs and seemed to have a body like that of a great cat. He watched with great interest, hoping that a rescue of some sort was on its way, but alas, it was overwhelmed by the number of vultures and he watched as it disappeared from sight.

During the stops, Jason noticed that the closer they got to their destination, the odd skin crawling characteristic became less apparent, and the troll had less fits of pain, although this did not make its nature any more appealing. The troll had an almost human look of malice in its eyes that told Jason that were it not for the spell, it would rather rip him apart limb from limb. Whenever he caught the troll looking at him, it gave him the creeps.

He was now able to more easily right himself as the troll would usually pick him up and stuff him into the bag head first. His cuts and wounds from the initial combat with the troll had healed, and even though his legs still hurt, they were now at a more tolerable level.

By the next morning, they made it to the woods. At mid afternoon when Trombul loped through a thicket, they disturbed a large bear. The giant troll roared at it to move along, but being a large bear, it rose to the challenge and roared back.

At that, Trombul dropped the sack with Jason in it and charged the insolent bruin. The two titanic creatures clashed with roars and bone-jarring strikes. Jason poked his head out of the sack to watch the fight.

With horrible grunts and roars that shook Jason to the core, the bear tore at Trombul with a fury and fierceness that drove the troll back toward Jason in the sack. Suddenly, both giants rolled on the ground almost on top of him, the bear's snapping jaws and yellow fangs momentarily just inches from Jason's face. He waddled, bag and all, around and behind a tree, then peeked out again. Fur flew and the troll's claws moved at an unbelievable speed, ripping through that wall of thick fur like a weed eater as it regained its feet.

The grizzly punished the troll for that offense by practically throwing it against a small tree and following closely. The combined weights broke the tree off at the base, toppling it with a crash.

For a while, with its superior strength, the bear was winning, biting and tearing viciously at the troll's flesh. Jason hoped the bear would knock the troll down for good, so he could finish it off with his burning oil.

He considered lighting it and just throwing the little bottle at them while they fought but was afraid the stout little bottle might not break, and if it did, it would probably not spread enough to completely kill the troll nor could he move well enough to add brush to it to finish the job. Also, the fire could scare the bear off before it could do enough damage.

The battling titans tore up the ground as they traded blow per blow and bite per bite. Trombul had a severe gash on his head, while the bear had blood matting down its shaggy coat. Even as they fought the troll regenerated quickly, healing its wounds. The unnatural endurance of the troll won out, and after one final fierce and bloody struggle, the bear ran off.

Trombul roared his defiance after the vanquished animal. During the intensity of watching the combat, suddenly, Jason realized he was standing. He quickly fell to the ground before Trombul could see. He expected the troll to rest after its ordeal, but instead, it seemed invigorated by the exchange, or perhaps it was just they were so close to their destination.

A short while later, they crossed the second river. By early the next morning, they reached the village by Haglar's house. The village Vorkana was a wreck with no one about. This was puzzling because Chanderlon had not mobilized any troops yet. No, this was most likely a raid from some other violent race to the north or perhaps Harvella's own style of recruitment for their troops.

The troll cut through the woods to Haglar's. Her place looked the way he had left it and she was feeding her chickens, the very picture of a kindly old lady lovingly caring for her place.

Trombul hauled him over to Haglar, dumping him unceremoniously in front of her. She ignored Jason and scolded Trombul, "Trombul, there you are. I called and called you all winter. I thought you were dead."

Trombul held out his palms and cried in the guttural gasps of troll language.

The old woman replied, "No, I will not release you from my service yet. There are big things happening, and I will need you. I will make the worms go dormant for a while, but come when I call or the worms will eat you alive. Now, what is it you have done to the boy?"

Again, the big troll grumbled and growled while pantomiming his actions. It finished with a moan while pointing at Jason's legs. Haglar yelled, "Broken legs! You dolt. Now the boy is worthless to me until he heals. Away from here, you miserable toad, and do not come back until I call you."

With that, the greenish monster loped off and the witch turned to Jason. Over the winter, she must have gotten worse about talking to herself out loud because she immediately exposed her thoughts to him as though he couldn't hear. "Ah, yes, Haglar must go, must go and help the wizard make his army. Can't be dragging this boy around. He must stay here and take care of chickens. How will I make him stay...worms, yes, pretty little worms like Trombul has...but worms might kill boy. He is not as tough as old Trombul, but they only kill if boy disobey. Well, rules are rules." Haglar strode over to Jason and with amazing strength grabbed him by the collar with one hand and dragged him into the cottage.

Inside, she propped him against some bags of dried herbs and nuts along the back wall. She took a bottle from a shelf and poured a little in a bowl and thrust it into his hands. "Here Jason, drink this," she commanded and then added. "It will help you heal."

Noticing Jason's surprise at calling his name, she said, "Don't be surprised. I divined your name and gave it to Trombul to help him look for you. You were a naughty boy for running off like that."

When she turned her back, Jason poured the foul concoction behind the sacks. Haglar started the fire and took another, larger bowl and went to a bag of grain. She scooped out a full bowl and sifted it through her fingers as she picked out the worms, putting them back into the first bowl.

She put a kettle of water on the fire and poured some oil from a jar in with the bowl of worms. When the water was warm, she this too she poured into the worm's bowl and then began her incantation.

Well, Jason sure didn't want worms of any sort, especially after seeing the torment Trombul went through. He knew he should run, but his legs were just barely strong enough to stand, so having no other plan, he stood.

The old hag glared at him severely and raised the tempo in her voice. He needed to stop the incantation before she finished. He opened the bag he was leaning against, looking for something to distract her. It was full of chestnuts. Not much of a weapon, but he picked one out and threw it anyway.

It hit her chest, and she winced but continued, waving her hands now. He threw another nut, as hard as he could, this time at her face. It hit her lip and spoiled her enunciation. She spat out a flurry of curses and began the incantation again. Throwing another, he hit her squarely in the eye. It bounced into the bowl. The bowl started steaming, and she cursed again and said, "Aaaargh. You have spoiled the spell."

"I must begin again, but first, I will bind you." While pursing her wrinkled lips, she grabbed a stout cord coiled on the wall and stalked over to the boy. He took a step back and stumbled. She grabbed his wrist and tried to put a loop around it. Even though she was stronger, he countered the grip with a painful wrist-pinning technique the Japanese call Nikyo.

The ancient oracle screamed her rage at the audacity of his counter and prepared to jerk out of his hold. Feeling her preparing for an all out effort, at the very moment she jerked to free herself, Jason let go of her wrist. Expecting full resistance, Haglar staggered across the room, trying to catch her balance.

She fell against the table, knocking it over. The oily worms and the jar of oil fell on the floor and splashed against the hearth. Fire sprang up, raging across the floor, igniting the dry bags of leaves, herbs, and tubers next to it. The bags made a poofing sound as their dry ingredients ignited explosively. Haglar grabbed a basin of water, desperate to extinguish the blaze.

Jason cried, "No, don't—"

But she flung it across the floor over the fire. It made the burning oil flare and flow everywhere and a choking smoke filled the room. Now two of the four walls were blazing and starting to catch the roof. Once that caught, the place would become an inferno.

Knowing this as well, the old witch cried out in fear and ran screaming through the fire and out the door, the dirty hem of her skirt becoming a ring of flame. He could hear her still screaming outside the cottage above the roar of flames, probably still on fire.

He considered running through the open door too. Running? At best, he would stumble and then would have to crawl through the burning oil on the floor. Once coated with burning oil, he would probably suffer the same fate he had originally intended for the troll.

Looking at the tiny window near him, he knew he would never be able to fit through it. If his legs were stronger, he could have climbed over the wall and through this part of the thatch roof, which had not yet caught fire. He looked at the window again. Wait a minute. He was thinking like an adult. In his little boy's body, he should be able to just barely squeeze through. He tore the oiled paper from the window and put his arms through.

The roof thatch made popping noises as it literally caught all at once. The wind from the back draft the inferno was creating was threatening to suck him back in as his body filled the window. He was beginning to feel the heat of the blaze on his back and legs as he inched his way through. Halfway, he felt hot cinders burn his neck as the roof above him caught fire, sending a shower of sparks into the night.

In desperation, he kicked his legs in the air to help drive him through the window, but the pain of his still healing, unsupported shins flinging around in the air nearly made him pass out. That, along with the sudden increase in temperature in the cottage room, made him wonder if his legs were already on fire.

With a final thrust, his legs painfully banged and twisted the rest of the way through the little window as he then fell to the ground outside and rolled away from the flaming shower. The building was now totally engulfed. The fierce heat and loud roar of the flames drove him away from the cabin. He continued rolling on the ground toward safety. It was an awesome sight to see the fire rise nearly a hundred feet into the sky.

He stood painfully and looked around. Not seeing the old woman anywhere, he presumed she ran to the river to cool her burns. He limped woodenly and slowly the opposite direction into the forest.

CHAPTER 37
The Dragon

Later, from the safety of the woods, Jason watched Haglar return to examine the charred remains of her home. She didn't even bother going inside. Her clothing was tattered and charred, and she wore salve and bandages on both her hands, which must have been burned in her efforts to extinguish herself. She circled the ruins of her home a few times, then went to the chicken pen and released all the chickens except two. These she killed, plucked, and cut open to examine their innards. Her divination finished, she cut the birds into pieces, wrapped them in her shawl and walked back toward the abandoned village.

With the crone gone, he slowly limped back to the burnt cottage. His minor burns were already healed. There were black mounds where the grain sacks had been. He dug into these and found grain that had been roasted and good enough to eat. He found the same with the nuts. At the bottom of these piles, the grain and nuts were still raw.

After some more digging toward the center of where the hut used to be, he found some butcher knives, their handles burned away, but still serviceable. He also found clay cups and bowls and an iron pot that had survived the fire. With the grain, he was able to coax the chickens back into their pen, catching one for dinner. Using his striker, he started a fire to roast the chicken, then used the bag the troll had carried him in as bedding and went right to sleep.

With some decent food and a good night's rest, he felt much better by morning. In fact, he could almost walk normally, though running was still out of the question. He checked for eggs and found five, which he boiled in his pot with water from the well, and roasted another chicken for breakfast, saving the leftovers for later. He then released the chickens and left for the village.

Around noon, he surreptitiously explored the village, searching for any sign of Haglar. After going through the whole village once and not finding her, he settled into a more thorough search for anything he could use. It had been ransacked and had less value than Haglar's burnt cottage, but he did find a smaller feed sack in which to carry the knives, pot, cups, and ax and could rid himself of the troll's smelly feed sack.

All the village river boats were gone. He thought of his stash with the gun nearby at the base of the cliff but did not feel he had the energy to retrieve them. He returned to Haglar's burnt plot and filled his pot with grain and nuts, then returned to the village and chose a house in decent condition to temporarily occupy.

While he rested, he began fashioning a new set of bow and arrows. That evening, he said his prayers in earnest. He was tired and wanted to go home. That night while lying on a cot, he felt like the little lost boy he now was. He tried to remind himself he was actually a fifty-year-old man, but that was like a dream. Did that life really exist or was it a figment of his imagination? And if it was true, did it really matter? He felt so small and alone. Should he just go back to his friends and try to lead as normal a life as he could?

He fell into a restless sleep. He dreamed he was still being helplessly carried away by the giant troll in the smelly feed sack. Again, he was so little and helpless, he curled up in a ball to cry. But instead of crying he growled, just as he had purposed to do when he first arrived here. He woke up growling. Sitting up, he contemplated his nightmare.

He hated the feeling of being a helpless victim. It then occurred to him that the troll represented everything corrupt in this world. This corruptness was a monster devouring everyone, taking their very souls.

That's why he was here. It was an emergency rescue, and he was saving lives. Even on his own world, he would have gladly given his life to save someone else, even knowing he would be leaving his own family permanently in this life. To God, spiritual death is far more dangerous than physical death.

What was the difference now? His family probably already considered him dead. He would still work toward getting home, but he had a mission. Perhaps not a specific one, but one to save a whole world. As God's representative he probably had a variety of small missions which tied into the main one. If, for some reason, he never made it home, it would not be for his lack of trying, but he also would not harbor feelings of regret.

Maybe he should just try to forget his previous life and wife and kids. But again, that would be easier if he knew there was no hope of going back. No, they were a part of him. He needed them to become whole again. He needed to be needed by them. He loved them. No matter what, he would remember them and be true to them, for in so doing he would be true to himself.

For now, he would be a man with a foot in both worlds. Despite his child-like appearance and youthful feelings, a man is what he is in his heart.

As a man he would live a life of honor, following his convictions. Perhaps he was tilting after windmills, but he would put God first and trust that God would reward him appropriately.

He spent the next day finishing his arrows, splitting and attaching chicken feathers he had saved as fletching. By the third day, he felt armed and as good as new. He converted the small feed bag into a backpack by tying some scrap rope he had found in the village around it.

He considered going straight back to Chanderlon or even hiking the few miles to find his cache, though now that he had a bow and arrows, he felt the nine millimeter gun with its eight shots would be worth the effort only if he could find a way to make more bullets. Of course, the gun would be a lot more effective against Trombul than these primitive tools, but then, the pleasant realization dawned that Trombul was no longer hunting him!

So, what did God want him to do, specifically, right now? God had sent him back here for a reason. Was God ready to send him home? Should he get the orb and try to find a way to use it? He doubted God sent him all this way just to aid in burning down the house of a wicked old witch and then turn around to go directly back to Chanderlon.

He made a quiver of birch bark and tied this to his pack as well. He packed his pot, bowl and clay cup, then placed the remaining grain and nuts into his homemade backpack and made his way to the edge of the village by the river.

Feeling adventuresome, he decided to explore the local area and found a wide shallow spot to cross the river. An old path showing some recent use headed east. He noted the tracks of game crossing the trail he was on as he followed it for several miles. Soon, the trail went up a steep embankment, cutting back and forth among the trees.

In trepidation, he faded into the woods and watched it awhile. Men always set ambushes where there are strategic advantages, and this hill had one. After a few minutes of not seeing anything, he ventured to walk carefully up the hill. Upon still seeing nothing of a trap, he wondered if he was becoming paranoid or too cautious.

From the top of the hill, he had a grand view. To the southeast, the general direction he was going, he could see a large lake surrounded by forest, and beyond that the plains. To his left (the northeast) were high mountains with steep cliffs and narrow canyons. The hills between him and the cliffs were steep and rugged.

Such wild land beckoned to his Alaskan pioneer spirit. He supposed he could see caves in the cliffs where shadows were more pronounced than others. As he started down the other side of the hill, he suddenly noticed the human tracks were gone. There were no side paths, and as he continued, the path became little more than a game trail.

He walked back up the hill, puzzled by this mystery. He scanned the area again, looking for signs of human habitation. This time he noticed a faint haze near the mountains, possibly indicating the smoke of a cooking fire filtered by the trees. Whoever these people were, they were good woodsmen and didn't want to be found. He examined the plain again for signs of human habitation.

There were stone columns reaching out of the plains. At first, he took them to be natural formations but then noticed they were too uniform in height and too evenly spaced to be natural phenomenon. He could see a faint haze over that direction too. While he watched, the plain at that distance rippled slowly with the movement of something. Was it herds moving or something else?

He considered his duty toward Chanderlon as well as caring about his friends. He was in enemy territory with a guarded crossing at the rivers. It could be he was the only eyes the Chanderlon army had before invading. Although he had no feelings toward the war itself, he cared about his friends walking into a trap. As a knight of Chanderlon, by rights, he should be fighting in it or at least serving in supportive duty. Although he had taken no formal oath, such as the other knights had, it was inferred since he did not refuse the honor.

God had placed him in this location for a reason, perhaps many reasons. Scouting out the enemy for Chanderlon may or may not be one of those reasons, but for now, it gave him a direction and purpose.

With a little more clarity, he decided to explore but was torn as to which to investigate first. Since he was closer, he decided to investigate the mountains first. He went back down the hill the way he had originally come and followed the trail to the east. After a quarter of a mile, he discovered tracks in the moss, probably not more than a day old. Soon, the tracks led to a path barely discernible headed towards the foothills.

Afterward, he found occasional human tracks, all going in the same direction. Soon other paths merged to join this one to run alongside a small stream flowing from the mountains before him. The stream continued to the east. Following the path upstream, it came to a small valley between the hills. At the side of the path was a wooden totem pole, perhaps a dozen feet tall. It was made of stylized animals and what looked like a dragon, its outstretched wings adorning the top. The carved animals had been painted in various colors, but time had faded it. However, the dragon was still a dark blue with gold gilt trim along its wings. Was it identification or a warning?

He backed away, circled to the left, and carefully made his way along the ridge, alert for whoever may be observing the path below. About halfway up the valley, he spied a guard station made of stone. Two women stationed there wore chain mail and helmets and held shields and spears. A large dog sat with them. They chatted in low tones, guarding a trail where almost no one would ever go.

He made his way toward them, climbing down the slope. He was so quiet even the dog was not aware of him. While he considered greeting them, the dog looked suddenly up to the other hillside, threw up his hackles, and emitted a low growl.

The guards and Jason looked in that direction. Even though it was large, it blended so well with the environment and stalked so slowly and carefully that Jason didn't notice it until it moved slightly and stopped. What he saw looked like a dragon with its wings pressed closely to its back. It was camouflaged so well as to be nearly invisible; its flesh a mottled gray and black to perfectly match its surroundings of shadow and leaves. It was probably there as he walked up the valley, but he had failed to notice.

In anticipation, he readied his bow, for although the two women looked, they couldn't see it because of the brush. He was about to cry out a warning when the dog suddenly charged, barking into the brush right at the dragon. The dragon pounced, flaring its wings as it sprung clear over the brush the dog was in, then gliding toward the women while emitting an awful, loud hiss. The creature was enormous, nearly twenty-five feet long with a body as large as a hippo.

Jason fired an arrow at its gaping maw, but so swift was the dragon's attack that the arrow missed and struck the neck instead, clattering off the hard scales harmlessly. The dragon's head snaked past the woman nearest to it and snatched the second woman's torso. The other woman thrust her spear at the dragon's chest, but the spearhead also slid on the scales causing no damage. The dragon's right claw knocked her weapon to the ground and pinned her underneath the great serpent's foot.

Jason was at a full run leaping down the slope, firing again at the dragon's body in mid leap. The arrow went through a wing membrane and struck the dragon's body with no force.

The scaly monster was now shaking the woman in its mouth like a rag doll while the dog burst back out of the brush with a noisy charge. Dodging the tail, it attacked the dragon's haunches. Jason dropped his bow and pulled the wood ax from his backpack. The dragon was turned sideways to him now, so he vaulted off the low stone wall and swung the ax as he landed on the wing's membrane, striking the brittle wrist joint that held the wing open like a hand, cutting it deeply. That got the dragon's attention, and it dropped the now unconscious woman and lifted its foot off the struggling female it had pinned in order to turn and attack the small boy who had dared to assault it.

Other than making a fearsome noise, the dog was having no effect on the dragon at all. Jason fell off the injured wing as the dragon spun to strike, mouth wide open. From his side on the ground, he rammed the head of the ax straight into the dragon's upper teeth, meeting the force of the attack. Although breaking one of the smaller fangs, the momentum of the head and muscle drove the boy back into the brush.

Miraculously, he still had a grip on the ax and quickly regained his feet. While the dragon pursued, he sprinted out of the brush and around one of the stone posts atop the wall. The dragon slammed the post to the side with its right leg, shattering the rock into pieces.

Turning again, Jason ran down the trail by the stream. The dragon launched itself into the air with a mighty jump and spread its wings, intending to fly over and past its fleeing prey, but instead, it fell head first into the stream as the left wing Jason damaged collapsed.

The dog followed, still viciously barking and trying to bite through the hard scales on the dragons hind legs. Jason, who was now also at the dragon's rear, saw his advantage and attacked the dragon's outstretched hind leg, smashing its foot with the ax. If he was his former adult self he might have severed the foot cleanly off but, as it was, he thought he heard the bone crunch some, though it left only a scratch on the scaly armor.

The dragon regained its footing but appeared wounded and stunned. The dog, attacking aggressively, was now more in its element. Angry and in pain, the dragon snapped at the dog, but the furry assailant bounced away expertly and charged again at the dragon's face. Jason was about to leap onto the dragon's back when the serpent's tail struck his legs, sweeping him off his feet. He rolled away from the hazardous tail, snapping like a whip.

Still facing the dog, the dragon arched its neck like a snake ready to strike, but in mid strike it spewed a clear, slimy substance instead. Although the animal tried to evade, the surprise of this form of attack was too much. The poor creature yelped in pain as the stream struck it on its side, and its yelp soon became a horrible cry as its flesh and hair dissolved in the powerful acid spray. The war dog fell, whimpering, then moved no more.

Upon seeing this, Jason ran back toward the women, hoping the two had the sense to run. The woman who had been pinned was wounded but still dragged her unconscious comrade up the trail. Looking back, he could see the dragon limping painfully, coming for them. The women would not be fast enough to get away.

Seeing their fallen spears and shield, he had an idea. If it didn't work, he and the women would probably die. Picking up the spear and wooden shield, he ran to a small pool about knee deep in the stream at the edge of the stone wall. If the dragon sprayed him, he would submerge himself in an attempt to dilute the wicked acid. He held the shield loosely in his hand, instead of putting his forearm through the handle for a secure grip.

The dragon lumbered to the wall and saw the little boy boldly standing in the pool. It looked at him, then at the two injured women and started for the easier meal instead, which happened to be the women. This was not part of Jason's plan, so he yelled and charged forward.

That changed its mind, as it turned back to snap at him. Continuing to leap forward, Jason met the wide-open maw of the dragon and jammed the narrow side of the shield into the teeth and let go. Jerking its head back, the dragon thrashed to and fro in an attempt to dislodge the shield from its mouth. Jason ducked under its wing and ran to one side.

The dragon's overlapping scales faced backward, making it nearly impervious to frontal attacks, but Jason reasoned it possible for a spear to be slipped into the scales from behind. He could imagine an experienced dragon-fighter advising to spear at the joints where the scales are smaller, but he could see this would not do much more than injure it and probably just make it madder. Even stabbing up through the armpit would not hit a vital organ. He gave a guess as to where the lungs and heart would be from his angle and dove in with all his might.

The spear tip went in, and the dragon whirled in rage. Using all of his weight, he forced the butt end of the spear down into the ground, which drove the spear in more deeply, breaking the haft of the spear off where it entered the scaly hide. The dragon continued to turn to strike at Jason despite the pain it must have felt and the splintering shield in its mouth.

Having nowhere to go with nothing but the broken shaft of wood in his hands, Jason felt like he was as good as dead. He fell back as the head struck him, sending him flying through the air. He hit the ground on the trail with a solid whack, wondering if he was still alive. He painfully sat up to see the draconian monster step toward him, but it looked like it was moving in slow motion and off balanced.

Quivering violently, the monster teetered and slumped forward, its terrible jaws just inches from his feet. The now crushed shield lay beside the head and death was glazing over its eyes. The spear evidently had done its work. The body quivered violently as the dragon fell stiffly on its side and started whipping around. Jason dove to the stream again to evade the dragon's death throes and waited until it was still.

Even after watching the dragon a few more minutes, he just could not believe he had actually just killed a dragon. It was not as huge as the one he had seen when he first arrived, but it was enormous compared to himself. He trotted over to help the woman, who had her unconscious companion around the corner of the path.

The woman looked at him, wide-eyed. "Boy, you just killed a black dragon," she said wonderingly. She was a rough-looking woman, her face bearing the marks of a hard life. "Help me get Kancha to the village," she pleaded.

He nodded and grabbed the unconscious woman's feet. She was bleeding from her chest and shoulder, but since she wore banded mail, the bite was not as severe as it might have been. At that moment, a band of women, dressed in plain shabby dresses and shawls rounded the corner carrying crude spears, pitchforks, and even a few brooms. A large husky woman in the lead spoke, "Isbeth, are you okay? We heard the noise. Did the dragon come?"

"Yes, but thanks to that child, it will never come again," replied Isbeth.

"You mean a child killed the dragon?" demanded the large woman, unbelieving.

"Yes," said the guard. "The beast attacked us, knocking me down and biting Kancha. But this boy appeared out of nowhere, attacked the dragon with a wood ax, and broke its wing. Then the dragon killed the dog with its breath. As the dragon came after us again, the boy attacked it with a spear, killing it. I would not have believed it if I had not seen it with my own eyes."

While several women took Kancha, the large woman turned to Jason and asked, "What is your name, child, and where are you from?"

He replied, "I am Jason. I am from far away."

"Then you are an orphan?" she asked.

Wary, as he figured orphaned children could be open game for slavery, he said carefully, "I am separated from my parents and am looking for them. Might they be here?"

"No," the large woman replied, "but we can help you find them after a little while."

He bowed and said, "Thank you, ma'am."

The woman replied, "What nice manners and fine clothing, even if they are dirty. Are you a king's son?"

"Not in the way that you mean," replied Jason.

"Well, anyway, let's go look at this dragon you killed. It has already killed two children and one woman. You have done us a great service."

A group of women stood around the dragon, afraid to get too close. The large woman said, "I am Klenellis, Jason, leader of the women here. We are refugees from the upcoming war. Since King Goshen has decided to win this war with sorcery, we pay the price in casualties before the war starts, in the form of human sacrifice. We hide here in the mountains to be safe from our own people. You are safe here with us too, Jason."

"But where are the men?" he asked.

"They have gone to fight, but our men have hid us here, so they have something to fight for. Not all the women and children can be sacrificed. But in the meantime, we are on our own. This dragon fed off us. Now it will save us by being food for us."

The women immediately set to butchering the dragon, cutting it into steaks for cooking and strips for drying and smoking. More women and children came from the village to gawk and carry meat.

He was mingling and talking with the children when Klenellis sought him out. "Tonight, Jason, you are our guest of honor, and if you could tell the story of how you came to us and how you slew the dragon, we would love to hear it."

"Very well," he said graciously, retrieved his weapons, and followed them to their hideout. The refugee village was very primitive, with a nearby stream and huts made of sticks and grass. Most had arrived recently and were still in the process of building their huts.

That night, dragon steaks were in abundance and surprisingly delicious, kind of like the dark meat of chicken. After dinner, Klenellis announced Jason to the group. He stood behind the fire and told an abbreviated version of his mission for the Creator and then the details of killing the dragon, with the guard Isbeth interjecting her details as well.

Afterward, he spoke long into the night answering questions about the Creator. Finally, Klenellis invited him to spend the night in her hut. As she made a bed for him, Jason asked, "Klenellis, to whom does King Goshen offer sacrifices?"

"Axialla," Klenellis said before turning over and going to sleep in her bed.

Now there is a twist, he thought. Both kings of opposing countries are trying to win the goddess's favor. King Beldane's sacrifices were miniscule compared to the outright slaughter done by King Goshen. The evil goddess would probably string King Beldane along with promises of power and magic, while leading him like a lamb unto the slaughter.

The next morning, he arose before dawn and left without anyone seeing him. He arrived at the hill on the main trail just as the sun broke over the distant mountains in the east.

Looking out on the plains, the rarefied morning air coupled with the angle of the sun showed a large group of white tents on the distant plain around the towering stone piers. The monoliths looked blood red in the sunrise, like bloody fingers of a huge hand sticking out of the earth.

This was most likely the gathering army that Chanderlon was to face and his enemy as well. It was too early for this to be King Beldane's force, so he figured he should at least get a rough count and see what his enemy looked like before heading back. Maybe there would be something he could do. Perhaps if he introduced them to the Creator, the whole war might be unnecessary.

However, his heart actually burned with anger, thinking of what the camp refugees told him. Killing their own women and children for the sake of a victory seemed a cowardly and obscene thing to do. No wonder in the Bible God was so incensed at idol worship and child sacrifice. Trading innocent human lives for what? For their own comfort or ambitions?

After getting his bearings as to where the stone monuments were, he made his way through the woods in that general direction without any path to follow, except the occasional small game trail that intercepted his direction.

CHAPTER 38
Thirteen Statues of Blood

Jason's encounter with the dragon made him extra wary, since he might not have seen it in time without the dog alerting him. Once, while strolling down a particularly wide trail, he heard a faint sound from behind. Not seeing anything, he quickly retreated into some bushes and waited, bow ready.

Soon, some men—giant men—came striding down the trail. They were huge, nearly twelve feet tall. Ducking under trees and walking carefully as hunters would, they carried huge clubs and spears and wore animal skins crudely stitched together. Quietly, they went by Jason's hiding place without seeing him. A few minutes later, he could still smell their lingering scent of smoke and rancid meat. What a basketball team they would make!

After seeing giants on that course, he took another path. Two days later, he came to the edge of a narrow plain. Instead of crossing the open space, he circled along the trees to the east, using them for cover. It took a couple of days to circle the expanse and reach the other side. He spent the night on a narrow peninsula of the forest that reached out into the sea of the plains. He was closer to where he could see the light of fires dotting the plains to the east. The fires lit up monolithic structures bright enough to where he could almost make out the details.

The next morning a rag-tag looking army of tribesmen passed by his hiding place, headed toward the camps to the east. Jason ventured to crawl through the grass to take a closer look. The men wore irregular armor with a homemade appearance, but in their midst, they herded around thirty women and children bound together with rope. Not close enough to see their faces, he could nevertheless see despair in their movement and posture.

Wanting to rescue them, he strained to think of some sort of strategy to release them and get them away without being hunted down himself by the fifty or so soldiers guarding them. Unable to think of anything he could do at the moment, he considered that perhaps under cover of night there might be opportunity, but many hostages did not appear to be in shape for much further travel.

Anyway, it verified to him that the tents he saw on the hill were indeed part of a war camp. From the hidden village of women, he had learned the army was involved with some religious or magical rite. The stone monoliths were probably considered sacred or perhaps a means to focus magic for their evil strategy.

He crawled back to the shelter of the woods and traveled most of the day to the east again, following the forest edge. It would be so much quicker to cross the open plain in the dark, so he made camp for a few hours to wait until nightfall.

While he waited, he shot a rabbit and cooked it for dinner over a very small fire. Again, as he did when he first arrived to this world, he roasted it for several hours over the smoke to give it flavor. It was dark by the time he started eating, so he only ate about a third and put the rest in his pack for later. Then he began the hike across the treeless plain with only the moon and stars for illumination.

He was most of the way across, nearing dark edge of the forest ahead, when he heard a howl behind him. It sounded like the howl of a wolf but deeper and throatier. He wondered what sort of creature could have made such a sound. Whatever it was, he had no desire to encounter it in the dark.

There were no other howls after that, which meant they were hunting and probably hunting him. He took off at a run, hoping to reach the safety of the trees before whatever it was caught him. In the open, there wasn't much he could do, especially if there were more than one of the mystery creatures.

About a quarter mile from the trees, he heard the panting of something running hard on his trail. He ran on, not daring to look back. In another minute, he would be in the trees, but he knew the wolf-thing was already close enough to catch him. He reached back quickly and pulled the remains of the rabbit from his pack and dropped it. He was rewarded with the sound of several beasts fighting over it. He hoped the ten seconds or so it bought him would be enough.

Now he could see individual trees and scanned them for one easy enough to climb. He sprinted toward a likely candidate. He could hear the creatures coming again. Something that appeared to be a huge wolf came in fast as he leaped for the first low branch of a pine tree. He grabbed it and allowed his momentum to spin him around the tree trunk instead of climbing it immediately. That move probably saved his life, as the wolf sprang at that moment and got hung up in the branches, falling painfully on its side.

He then climbed desperately as the wolf quickly recovered and lunged again, nearly biting his foot, except right at that moment he kicked backward, striking the monster under the jaw. The wolf reeled backward, falling to the ground with a heavy thud.

The rest of the wolves arrived at the tree and circled. He was so high in the tree by then, they didn't even bother trying to jump. A few sniffed the fallen wolf and sat down to study their treed prey. Jason did the same from his lofty perch.

At first, he thought the wolves just seemed bigger because it was dark, and he was a small boy, but soon, he realized they actually were bigger than a normal wolf, perhaps twice the size. The heads were more massive, larger in proportion to their body than a normal wolf.

The term direwolf came to mind as a type of extreme wolf now extinct on his home world. These wolves were not as fast runners as their smaller cousins. Otherwise, they probably would have caught him before he made it to the tree. It was an interesting thought that a boy his size could actually ride a wolf this big as though it were a pony.

The stunned wolf he had kicked arose and began pacing around the tree. Jason remained as still as he could, not even daring to watch. After a long while of pacing back and forth, they started to become distracted by other scents and sounds and soon began another hunt. He waited almost an hour before climbing from the tree. He found another tree with roots suitable for sleeping and finished out the night curled beneath them.

The next day, he cut through this next peninsula of forest that jutted out into the plain, knowing it to be a short distance to the other side. In the middle, he was surprised to discover a swampy lake, which he skirted. Strange birds roosted among the trees around it, a type he had never seen before. They had scaly bodies with tufts of colorful feathers. They were the size of a chicken with oversized talons and powerful hooked beaks. Several of the strange avians followed him noiselessly through the forest, giving him the creeps. Upon reaching the plain, the birds were distracted by a rabbit and followed it instead.

The plain looked similar to the others except for a road in the middle of it. A multitude of ox-drawn wagons filled with large stones moved southeast, while other wagons returned empty. The teamsters driving the wagons wore large floppy hats and heavy overcoats. Most of the drivers were big men with course black beards.

He thought he could sneak a ride, but the risk of discovery was too great. If children were routinely swept up for sacrifices, then he would stand out as an obvious target if discovered. It was better to ghost his way through the woods, even though it was slower.

Traveling along the edge of the forest, he came to a small hill that reached the tops of the trees, which he climbed to overlook the grassy expanse. From here, he had a clear view of the camp filled with soldiers and other activities. It was situated on both sides of a stream with a small shallow lake to the north. Among the bustle of activity huge bonfires burned, even during daylight. Spaced along the hills stood gigantic stone statues crudely shaped in the likeness of men, festooned with ladders and scaffolds.

The only creatures he could make out clearly at this distance were huge men—hairless, bald giants with gray skin that made the other giants he saw earlier in the forest seem like children. These gargantuans were climbing around working upon the nearly completed statues, with heads that reminded him of pictures he had seen of the statues on Easter Island. Smaller, normal-sized men, who seemed like ants, moved about camps and tents around the base of the statues.

He could make an estimation of the numbers of men from here, perhaps several thousand, but why were they and giants wasting time building statues the size of small sky scrapers? Were they idols? If so, why would they need so many? It just did not make any sense. He would need to get closer to see what he could learn.

He waited for evening before venturing on the plain toward the fires. After about an hour, he reached the outskirts of the camp. From his position downwind, the stench of human waste, sweat and blood filled his nostrils. Feeling nauseous, he climbed a hill hoping to get above the smell somewhat. That failing, he sat hidden in the grass and watched.

Construction on the statues continued nonstop. Giants used an odd pink-hued mortar to seal the stones they shaped with their bare hands into the constructs. Scores of men dressed in robes also surrounded each stone structure, setting up a constant drone with their spells and chants. In the middle of camp, stone altars stood before a large black idol that appeared to be a giant copy of the one he found under the castle in Chanderlon. It was of a woman holding a large crystal globe, probably the goddess Axialla. Each altar had troughs that drained into buckets.

The ceremony King Beldane performed back in Chanderlon was nothing compared to the massive rituals taking place here. Here, multiple human sacrifices were performed at once. Priests chanted while others danced and killed their victims, their blood running down the troughs into the buckets.

Women and children were kept in pens like animals waiting to be slaughtered. Servants of the priests would tie their victims down and then remove the grisly corpses after the sacrifice. The bodies were loaded into carts and hauled someplace out of his sight, while the buckets of blood were carried to the mortar troughs to be mixed with the aggregates for the cement the giants used.

He felt sick watching the abomination. Some sacrificial victims would proudly lie on the altars, seeing themselves as giving their lives to help their country, while others were strapped down screaming and begging. He wanted to help them, but of those he would attempt to rescue, some would betray his presence to the soldiers. Without taking on the whole army, he could see no way to help them.

His thoughts turned to sabotage. If there were some way to stop the project, the deaths would then be unnecessary. But even if he managed to destroy one statue, it wouldn't be enough. He counted thirteen statues. He had never felt so small and impotent.

He—Jason, the hero of Chanderlon, champion of princesses, slayer of dragons, and stomper of goblins—felt powerless to do anything about the atrocities before him. He found the giants particularly fascinating to watch. Their gray skin made them appear to be made out of stone themselves. Clad only with animal skins around their waists, their muscles seemed proportionally larger, like a bodybuilder's, rippling under their skin.

Perhaps his own faith wasn't strong enough to march down there with the might of his God and...do what? Kill everyone? How many of the sacrificial victims, once freed, would take up arms to fight him as well? Harvella did indeed pay the price of war ahead of time, their casualties beyond count even before war began, their magical weapon still a mystery.

He contemplated the statues. It was as if they were trying to infuse them with magic, with life. If so, what could these statues do? Could these magical powers somehow be released when the Chanderlon army approached? Would they shoot fire or lightning? Perhaps they could move...that thought gave him a chill. He did not even want to think about that.

"Juggernaut," he mused. He had once been called juggernaut because some had thought that as a martial artist he was unstoppable. Now here he was, a little boy pitted against barbarians, monsters, sorcery, and magic. He wasn't alone, of course, but sometimes, it is easy to forget when you can't see your spiritual allies and they seem to seldom give an encouraging word or advice.

He considered his next move. As a knight of Chanderlon, he should try to make it back and give warning. Though his duty to God superseded his knightly duties, he could not determine any other course of action.

Suddenly, Jason noticed a troop of perhaps twenty men running toward the hill he was sitting on. He could make out words like escape and sacrifice. That was enough to send him running. As a boy, he could not match the speed of an adult in an all out sprint, but he had a head start and meant to keep it.

The soldiers were closing in on him as he reached the forest. In the trees and the dark, he had a chance; being smaller, he could maneuver better through brush and trees. But when he actually made the dark woods, the soldiers paused. Scary things hid among the trees. One little boy escaping was not worth the risk of entering the dark woods. Perhaps he should have worried, too, but to him, this was a welcoming fortress.

Making his way through a tangled thicket, he found what seemed a good place to sleep through the rest of the night. After a quick prayer for the lost souls he had witnessed, and another for his family, he curled up among the roots of a large tree, using his rough sacks as a blanket.

He had only lain there a short while when he got the feeling he was not alone. Having learned to trust his intuition, he slowly notched an arrow as he quietly sat up. The shadow of a small creature came toward him ducking branches of the thicket, as quiet as a cat and with pointy ears like one, too. The eyes glowed in a soft greenish way. Was it a lynx or a fox? The size was about right.

Whatever it was, it knew he was here. He was in the mood to shoot first and ask questions later, so he pulled back to full draw, ready to release in a heartbeat.

"Stop! Don't fire!" came a squeaky but familiar voice. "It is I, Akari."

Jason eased the tension off his bowstring but kept the arrow notched, not feeling any reason to trust the little demon.

"All I see is your shadow, demon. Why can you not visit me in the daylight?" he asked.

"Because you may not live to see the daylight again," the little marauder said ominously, then continued, "Since I see you are about to die, I have come to give you one more chance to do a service for me."

"What makes you think I am about to die?" asked Jason curiously.

"I was just summoned by Haglar. She is in service to the priests of Axialla who noticed your little foray tonight. They determined you were not an escapee after all, since all their prisoners were accounted for, so they wanted to know about the snooping small creature who would dare death to approach the camp."

"So you told them?"

"Yes. They see you as a spy and blame Haglar for bringing you here. She has been put in charge of capturing and killing you and is on her way now with a whole bunch of soldiers."

"And you have come to warn me?" asked Jason.

"No, the warning will do you no good, for she is using a divination spell to track you. Your only way out is to do my task which, as I said before, is not a bad thing. Your current position in Chanderlon would make it even easier than before, and I will even send you home if you still want to go."

Jason shook his head. "First, you betray me, and then ask for my help?"

"Betraying is what I do," said Akari, apologetically raising his hands and shrugging his shoulders. "But I will give you some information to make up for that, to put us even. The giant statues you saw tonight are more than just mere idols. They are being prepared to become automatons, having a semblance to life. They will march right over your army. It is a bit of overkill, for just one is capable of taking out the entire army of Chanderlon."

"That is impossible," said Jason incredulously. "The energy it would take to move one would be enormous."

The shadow of the demon folded its arms. "That shows how little you know about magic. King Goshen's sorcerers have already stored more energy than what is needed to bring those cold stones to life. The secret is in the blood."

Jason shuddered as a Bible passage came to mind. "The life is in the blood," even the power of the blood of Jesus. This was a desecration to the inferred sanctity of blood in the Bible. He replied, "Okay, that makes us even, I suppose, but I still won't do your task. I have discovered God has a job for me to do here, and whether I go home or not is in his hands."

Jason continued while packing his rough sackcloth blanket, "I would love to stay and chitchat, but I think it wise to get as much of a head start as I can on Haglar."

"Bah. Jason, you are just plain stubborn. Listen to reason and live. You can't beat magic, for when it works, it works very well."

Jason called over his shoulder as he took off into the night. "I would trust in God over magic any day."

He thought of saying good-bye, but it did not feel right to wish anything good for the demon when all its motives were for the sake of evil. Stumbling on blindly, he used his bow to help feel his way and warn him of pitfalls.

He considered which way to run. It would be easier to run on the plains, but they would catch him faster there. In the forest, he would be harder to follow. He now had enough information to go back to Chanderlon, but if pursued, a circumventive route had the most merit.

While he traveled, he pondered what the little demon told him. In his home world, thirteen living stone juggernauts would be threatening, but not unstoppable. Small nuclear weapons and armor piercing shells would eventually pulverize them. He contemplated what was possible with this world's technology. Battering rams and boulders flung from catapults or trebuchets would eventually wear the juggernauts down, but most likely, the juggernauts would be unstoppable by primitive war craft.

Tripping might be effective, assuming it couldn't stand back up again. He surmised that even the heavy drawbridge chains from the castle at Chanderlon would probably break if tied around the feet of one of these monsters. Explosives? Even if he made a massive charge from all the fireworks at Chanderlon, it would not be concentrated enough to damage even a single juggernaut sufficiently.

It would take time to develop the technology to build cannons and produce gunpowder. However, if a juggernaut could be led into a huge canyon or deep quicksand...but no such place existed near these plains that he knew.

After traveling about an hour, he paused to rest and listen. He could hear men shouting in the distance to the right, and branches breaking. Suddenly, he heard something crashing through the brush toward him at tremendous speed.

If Haglar could summon a troll like Trombul, he dreaded to see what she might call up now. Running from something that could move that fast would be useless, so he examined the tree he was beside to see if it were climbable. He hoped that in the dark whatever it was would bypass him, but still it seemed the game was over.

As he started to climb, a large stag elk burst into view and darted by him, fear making the whites of its eyes show in the dim woods. Relieved it was not some sort of monster intent on finding him, he resumed his own flight. He would stop every hour or so to rest a few minutes, then continue on.

When the predawn light penetrated the woods, he was exhausted but could still hear the men, now closer. He came to where the plain cut into his path, carving a cove into the woods. Instead of circling it, he sprinted across the clearing. Upon reaching the other side, he slowed to catch his breath and look back.

Five men with spears appeared across the glen. One had three medium-sized dogs on a leash. Up to this point, there had been no baying or other sound to indicate dogs were in use. Looking further away, following where the plain met the forest, a small army of men followed with someone riding in a wagon drawn by draft horses. The squat and cowled figure could be none other than Haglar.

One of the men saw him at the edge of the wood and pointed while the man with the dogs released them as if launching missiles from a cannon. Still the dogs did not bark, but merely growled lowly as they sped toward him.

Jason fired a long shot from his bow and turned to run without waiting to see if he had scored a hit. Not hearing any whimper of pain from the beast told him he probably missed. So magic wasn't the only thing being used to track him.

Finding a good trail he could run on, he felt like he was pulling away from his human pursuers, but the dogs would be on him in only moments. After hopping over a fallen tree, he stopped and pulled out his ax and slammed the head into the wood so it would be easy to grab. Drawing his bow, he only had to hold it seconds before the first dog appeared.

It was a beautiful brown and white dog with thick fur, running full out with its head down. He regretted having to kill it, but fired at the base of the neck between the shoulder blades. At less than thirty feet, it dropped like a rock. The other two dogs appeared and charged before he could draw another arrow, so loosening the ax he stood upon the fallen tree and readied a swing.

As the next dog tried to jump at him, he caught it on the skull in midair. That dog too dropped, instantly still as in death. The third dog had better luck and snapped onto Jason's leg like a bear trap, making him lose his balance, falling off the tree backward. The dog's teeth felt like they hit bone, and his whole leg felt paralyzed by the pain. Now hung up in the branches with one leg held firmly, the dog worried it from side to side, trying to do more damage to his calf.

Pulling himself to standing with one leg, he took aim at the dog's neck and swung the ax. The blade sank deep into the neck in a spray of blood. He had intended to break the neck bones but had missed and hit the jugular. It was only a matter of moments before the dog let go and laid down as if asleep.

Now with an injured leg, Jason limped on down the path. The bite put holes in his calf but did not bleed freely. On the positive side, he did not leave a blood trail, though the chances for infection increased. It was likely that unless they were very good trackers, those hunting him did not know of his wound.

After a little while, he would be away from the plain altogether. Perhaps they would give up then, since the wagon would not be able to follow in the forest without a good trail or road. Just as he climbed a short hill, he thought he heard something strange and stopped to listen. It sounded like a shrill whistle, like an eagle calling. It made him shiver involuntarily.

It seemed like fog was rolling from the plain and covering over the tree tops, followed by a noticeable drop in temperature. Although he stared in wonder, he did not let himself stay too long and took off again. In the next few minutes, it started snowing! Had Haglar actually summoned up a snowstorm? He wondered at the scope of her magical power.

At first, it started light, making his tracks evident, which was probably the whole reason for the snow, but then, it came down heavily as if pushed off a roof. In fact, the snow came down so fast and hard it did not fall smoothly as normal snow would, but left rough clumps that fell off trees. He kept moving and almost instantly the snow covered his tracks. Soon, he was trudging through about a foot and a half of snow. Taking a divergent course, he hoped he might now indeed get away.

As time went on, his leg felt better, and he could no longer hear the sound of pursuit. A good tracker could follow him even in the snow, but it would take time—time he could use to get some needed distance. By noon, he was out of the snow, and the climate returned to its normal seasonal warmth. Now he desperately needed sleep but forced himself to travel a few more miles, getting him close to the foothills.

At the top of a small cliff, he sat on a comfortable mat of moss and checked his leg. It was much as he expected. The actual bite wound had a layer of fresh skin growing over a purplish bruise. He wondered what would happen if he ever got an infection. Perhaps he healed faster than infectious microbes could reproduce. He hoped so.

Allowing himself to only sleep a few hours, he was on the move again by mid afternoon and followed along the hills, cutting to the north. On one hill, he could see the plains, and less than a mile away the small troop of hunters mirrored his movements. He had not made as clean an escape as he had hoped. Obviously, they intended to intercept him when he made his move to return towards Chanderlon.

He shook his head in despair, knowing that it would be a while before he would be able to return to Chanderlon, and resolved to a pattern of only catnaps before moving on again. He thought perhaps he could sneak by if he swam down the river that flowed by Vorkana, Haglar's village. If they truly had some magical means of knowing his every movement, however, then it would be a futile effort.

Three days later, he found himself across the river from Haglar's abandoned village, just as he heard the distant sound of thunder from an approaching storm. It was late morning when he arrived and peered at the ransacked little town from the bushes.

It had changed. There was a rough rock and log barricade, more like a pile of rubble and brush thrown up to block access from the river side and another one blocking the dirt road at the other end. He could see the village beyond and the smoldering remains of a bonfire in the village center with an empty spit over it. It looked like its current inhabitants partied all night and were now sleeping it off.

There must be a watch or guard, and he studied the surroundings closely. Within the barricade, he noticed some movement. He saw what looked like a man sleeping under a broken table that had become part of the debris wall. He was dressed in furs similar to the hunters tracking him. It made sense that Haglar would guess this destination as one of his way points and send some men ahead to stop him.

He scanned his immediate surroundings on this side of the river to see if someone waited in ambush. He could not believe these men expected him to waltz into town and announce his presence. Another rumble of thunder stirred the sleeping sentinel who crawled out from under the table to look at the sky.

Suddenly, some men appeared at the far side of the village, climbing over the makeshift wall on the other side. They started to clear an opening for the wagon drawn by horses, upon which rode the oracle Haglar.

Not waiting to see more, he decided to head upriver toward his cache. Perhaps it was now time to go home to be with his wife and kids. He hoped he was not being presumptuous, but unless God showed him a way to get past his pursuers, then his mission here was probably done.

With the approaching electrical storm, he might be able to focus the power of a lightning strike to power the orb and send him home. The thought of seeing Molly again made him feel almost guilty he wanted his mission for God to end now.

A light sprinkling of rain started falling when he cautiously moved upriver to look for a way to cross. He found a narrow spot where a tree had fallen across, catching in the branches of another tree. He climbed across as lithe as a monkey. On the other side, he looked for a sheltering tree to wait out the rain as it had started to fall heavier.

A third crash of lightning sounded nearby, and the wind began to blow gustily. He found a huge tree on the edge of an ancient bank and ran under it, at the same time remembering some advice he had heard that in a lightning storm, you should never sit under a tree because it could attract a lightning bolt, especially a lone tree in a field.

Lightning storms in Alaska are comparatively rare, and Jason felt confused. He needed shelter from the downpour, yet he was supposed to stay away from trees. He decided that as a matter of probability, in a forest full of trees, the odds were in his favor this particular tree would not be struck by lightning.

Under the tree, the grass was tall, partially concealing an opening to a hollow or small cave. He parted the grass to see if he could use the hole for additional shelter, only to find himself staring into the smiling, grotesque face of Trombul. Jason didn't take time to marvel at the odds of picking the same hiding place as the troll. The ugly giant lunged to grab him, but Jason quickly jumped back as the troll tried to worm the rest of its way out of the comparatively small hole.

He was already running through the storm when Trombul finally emerged. The troll gave a howl of victory, since now, nothing would stop it from killing the object of its intense hatred, and then began a vigorous chase.

Weaving in and out of trees as the troll closed in on him, Jason disparagingly thought how almost everything on this planet could outrun him, and he was once a track star in high school. He ducked under a fallen tree, notched, and fired an arrow into the troll's thigh as it climbed over the tree. Jumping from the tree, Trombul's leg collapsed and sent him sprawling, giving Jason another good head start. With a howl of pain, Trombul ripped the arrow from his leg, got up, and limped after the small boy.

Jason broke out of the trees into a clearing only to see through the now heavy downpour a tall cliff towering above him on the other side of the clearing, blocking his escape. Almost in despair, he looked up the wall of the cliff to see a pinnacle of stone perched on top. It was the landmark for his stash.

He dashed to the lone sapling standing in the glen where his cache was hid. Almost frantically, he rolled away the stones. To his relief, the black plastic bag was still there. It had little holes from curious rodents, but the briefcase inside was still intact and held what he needed now.

Trombul broke into the clearing, no longer limping but charging at full speed. Jason quickly opened the briefcase and pulled out the loaded nine millimeter handgun. The heavy rain quickly made the gun slippery in his hands as he stood and fired pointblank into the troll's chest, back-peddling to buy time for more shots.

The green, rain-slicked beast hardly noticed the shock of the bullet and continued its charge, so he fired three more shots, one right after another. He was not sure where he hit or if he even hit at all, but the troll was nearly upon him when he shifted his aim to shoot between the eyes. Thunder accentuated his last shot as the bullet hit just above the monster's right eye. Blood sprayed out the back of the monster's head as half its brain was blown away.

The troll flopped on the ground convulsively. The storm thunderously rained down. Using burning oil to get rid of the troll for good was now out of the question. He stuffed the gun in his pocket and grabbed the old backpack with the orb inside. He ran around the lower edge of the cliff to climb the hill.

It took perhaps fifteen minutes for Jason to reach the top, and he turned to see what the troll was doing. The troll seemed able to regenerate three or four times faster than he, so he half expected to see the hardy creature already coming; however, Trombul was just getting up again. Could it be possible that with half its brain destroyed it might forget about him? Not a chance. The troll looked around, saw him, and the chase was on again.

It might be possible to lose the troll in the rain, but Trombul would eventually hunt him down. He had another idea on how to lose the unjolly green giant permanently. Lightning was striking all around this area, and he might not get another chance.

The troll ran lopsided as if the injured brain had not fully healed yet. It came along the base of the cliff toward the edge of the hill. With the orb securely tied to his impromptu backpack, he started to climb the pinnacle. The pinnacle, wet and slick from the rain, was nearly impossible to climb, especially coming back down, but he sincerely hoped he would not have to.

In the back of his mind, he wondered how using lightning to power the orb could work. Even if it did transport him somewhere, there was no reason to think it would send him home. This was not science. This was madness, almost as bad as trusting that something magical would happen. Probably he would just get fried by a zillion volts of electricity. But looking at his current alternatives, it was either that, torn to shreds by a troll, or offered as a sacrifice to an idol when the others caught up.

Well, you can't blame a guy for trying, he thought to himself.

As he neared the top, a glance told him Trombul was gaining quickly and already at the base of the pinnacle. When he finally pulled himself to the top, he suddenly felt afraid to move, especially to stand. The wind and rain whipped around, threatening to blow him off balance. His old fear of heights had returned.

But the troll was scooting up toward him like a squirrel climbing a tree, using its claw-like hands to good advantage. That gave Jason the impetus to pull the orb out of his pack and stand.

"Be patient, dear, I am coming," he said, thinking of his wife, Molly, hoping it to be the truth.

He held the orb high over his head as he prayed aloud, "Father, I am ready to go home. I have done your mission. I have brought light to this world, and you have a church here to do the rest of your work. Please, in the name of Jesus my king, I ask you, let me go home."

Just then, lightning struck the orb. The orb absorbed the energy, keeping him from the full brunt of the charge. But because of the angle he held it or perhaps because it could have been cracked from any number of things, the gray ray shot out of the orb not at Jason, but at the troll just now reaching the summit, ready to pounce.

"Nooo," cried Jason as the beam engulfed the troll instead of him. The troll vanished instantly as Jason lost consciousness from the deadly current of electricity surging through him.

CHAPTER 39
Deologue 6

"Ha, ha, ha, ha," laughed the brown-skinned primitive in war paint. "The little champion just killed himself trying to dimensionally teleport back home."

Axialla sat in the petals of a giant flower, looking at the crazy god as though he had lost his mind. "Jazeel, are you sure he is dead?"

"Of course. My hunters made sure of it. One arrow in the heart and one in each lung. Trust me, he is dead."

"Did my servant Haglar verify it?"

"Yes, but she was not happy because she wanted to keep the boy alive long enough to sacrifice him."

"The boy was too dangerous for that. You did well, Jazeel.

Between the two of us, we did what the great Xan Rukkah could not," she said as the flower lowered her down from her perch to the ground. It deposited her before a small table that held a chess board, surrounded by what looked like a giant garden, with huge flowers everywhere.

Jazeel folded his arms. "I would not celebrate just yet. The Creator is tricky. This boy was probably just a diversion while the real champion is fulfilling the prophecy elsewhere without us even realizing."

"You may be right. I want you and your minions to investigate that possibility. For a god who can't think clearly, you seem to have a knack for seeing through schemes," said Axialla, with some admiration.

"Of course," he replied proudly. "It is nice to finally be appreciated for my true capabilities."

"Report back as soon as possible, for if this truly was the Creator's champion, then this death would be an omen, a sign that defeating the Creator himself is possible. Such encouragement would greatly invigorate the whole pantheon."

"I will do that, Axialla," said the god, bowing. "But keep in mind I see through your schemes as well and fully intend to be rewarded appropriately when you make your move."

"I will remember your loyalty," she said as she watched the god of insanity leave. The bizarre god acted like he was crazy, but was not the fool the other gods thought him to be.

She walked over to the chess board and examined the pieces. They were in the shapes and forms of most of the major gods and goddesses in the pantheon.

Picking up the one that looked like a king holding a huge sword, she said, "Xan Rukkah, our battle is coming soon, and you do not know I have these." With a wave of her hand, the middle row contained thirteen game pieces of the statues made by King Goshen of Harvella.

"Go, kill, and destroy," she commanded.

The row of little statuettes came alive and marched across the board driving all the enemy pieces before them, pushing them off their half of the board. The statuettes stopped at the last row, claiming victory.

"Checkmate," Axialla said smugly to herself as she looked at the Xan Rukkah game piece, still in her hand, then smashed it violently to the ground.

CHAPTER 40

Battle Cry

Much later, when Jason began to regain consciousness, he could feel the warmth of the sun on his body. Before he opened his eyes, he could feel the gentle breeze on his skin and the smell of moss and grass. Opening his eyes, he sat up too quickly and immediately lay back down. He opened his eyes again and saw the pinnacle of stone standing above him.

He sat up slowly this time, feeling hungry and nauseous at the same time. He did not see evidence of the troll anywhere. He hoped he didn't send the troll to his own world or anyplace else that would be terrorized by the monster.

He examined the burn marks on his clothes and was surprised to find three barbed arrows stuck in his shirt. He pulled one out and noticed the head and first six inches covered in dried blood. The others were the same. Was it his blood on the arrows?

Opening his shirt, he saw his chest covered with dry black blood, heaviest where the arrows had made a hole in his shirt. Did his regeneration push the arrows out of his body? Did Haglar's men catch up with him, shoot him, and then leave him for dead? If so, then he might very well be free of them.

Now he examined the impression he left in the moss and grass. He must have lain there a long time barely alive, for the moss and grass had begun to yellow. Obviously, he fell from the top of the pinnacle after the lightning strike and was hurt. Many people survive lightning strikes but how could he, in addition, survive that great a fall and three arrow piercings? Could he have actually died, then regenerated?

He pulled the gun from his pocket. It had partially melted from the lightning strike, attesting to the intensity of the electricity that went through him. Although his pocket was scorched, he found no burn mark on his flesh. Worthless now, he threw the junk metal to the ground. He stood slowly and looked around. It was a beautiful summer's day about noon. How long had he lain there? A week? A month? He did not know.

A glint of light reflected from the ground near the base of the pinnacle. It was the remnants of the crystal orb shattered into pieces. He recalled a technician saying they needed a mirror to stabilize the beam. Even if he'd had a mirror, it may not have mattered anyway. But now the orb was gone.

"Well, Lord," he said, "I guess my work here is not done yet."

A squeaky voice interrupted his reverie, "Hey, neat trick making everyone think you were dead. You are still serving the Creator, even though he won't send you home?" It was Akari, the little demon.

"Akari," he answered wearily, "after serving the Creator so long, who else could I serve?"

"Well," said Akari, pushing some of the crystal shards with his toes, "you could serve me for only a little while, and I will send you home."

"I know my desire to go home may never be fulfilled, but I believe in the Creator's cause and would gladly die in his service." "The Creator's cause," spat the little devil contemptuously. "His cause is lost here, just like it is on your home world. Most men will die rejecting and cursing him. God has failed in his plan, and this feeble attempt of yours will, in the end, save no one. You might as well give up and let me send you home where you will be with your wife and kids. They need you."

Jason spoke thoughtfully, "Akari, you have a point. But even if I save one person, or even if I don't save any, that I was faithful is enough for me, because there is one thing you don't understand"— Akari made a pained look—"and that is love. I love the Creator because he first loved me. He even proved it once about two thousand years ago and then over and over again in my life. I must share his love with others. Tell me, Akari, did you lay any bets with the other demons on my contest with Maudid?"

"Yes," said the little demon, suddenly looking angry.

"Well, who did you bet on?"

Akari rolled his eyes. "On Maudid, of course. You would not have won, either, if you didn't cheat."

"On the contrary, I didn't win. The Creator did. However, before you pop out of existence, tell me, where did the troll Trombul get zapped?"

"To your home world, of course," said Akari as he disappeared in a puff of smoke.

He frowned, wondering if the demon lied. The greedy little Akari would have never given out free information unless it was a lie or, if it were the truth, then possibly not the whole truth.

Gathering his things into his backpack, he headed down the hill, making his way around the cliff to the clearing below. He looked into the hole of his cache and found his old bow. Rodents had chewed through the string, and the bow itself was probably starting to rot, so he left it there. He also left the spear since it was too cumbersome to carry. The arrows were still good, so he added them to his supply as well as the three barbed ones he had found piercing his shirt. He also took the blow gun with its darts.

If the demon was right and everyone thought him dead, he should have no more trouble making it back to Chanderlon. He had two thoughts. First, he was probably not going home for a long time, and he would just simply have to endure. That made him feel a little angry, but he purposed to distract himself with the second thought.

That thought was he might have actually died and either God resurrected him, or his uncanny healing ability made him nearly indestructible. If that was the case and if he could not age, then that would mean he was physically immortal. Was he now the same as what Jesus promised when he returned, a being changed so he could live forever? He did not know the implications of that, but felt a shiver at being given such a gift, and how he could be held before God with greater accountability because of it.

Thinking now of his next move, he decided he was fully committed to the upcoming battle and he needed to help Chanderlon anyway he could. As a knight, he could be assigned for any duty by the king or even the general, Lord Krogan. As long as this duty did not conflict with God's purposes and the moral guidelines set in the New Testament scriptures, he determined, for now at least, to submit to their leadership.

Taking his time, he avoided the villages of Harvella as he journeyed back to Chanderlon, using his recovered blowgun to hunt small game. After many days of travel through the forest and crossing the plains again, he came close to the border river. He climbed a hill to see ahead. The vultures still patrolled the river, and far downstream on the other side, he could see the tents and army of Chanderlon, camped along the banks.

As he approached the river, he could sense the shadow beings but not see them. They ignored him as he crossed, although he wasn't sure why. Perhaps he was deemed too insignificant and going a direction not forbidden, or perhaps he was protected somehow. Traveling just far enough away from the river to be safe, he walked downstream toward the camp.

There were several mounted patrols about, but they either didn't see him or simply weren't interested in one little boy playing soldier with his toys. He stopped on a hill overlooking the camp by the charred remains of the previous evening watch's fire. The camp seemed to be getting ready to move. Military tents neatly lined along the river were being broken down. However, the more colorful and rag tag tents of the camp followers and supply wagons did not seem to be in such a hurry.

He could see priests of the various deities lining the river bank. They were saying prayers and chants, presumably to remove the dark, ghostly shadows that guarded the border. They stepped into the river and the shadows fled. The priests did indeed wield the powers granted to them by their gods.

The priests led the way across the river, and the army followed with the mounted warriors first. The foot troops came next, then the conscripted men in their bright new equipment.

He ran to join the army, and as he neared, the mounted rear guard warned Jason back. Then one recognized him. "Why, Sir Bristol, we thought you dead. A little girl said you were killed and carried off by a troll. Our investigation found your weapons and verified her story."

Jason laughed. "And almost kill me it did. But I have an urgent message for the commanding officer." The rear guard offered Jason a hand to lift him onto his horse and said, "Lord Krogan is general, and King Beldane is with us, too. The royal family was particularly distressed at your disappearance. The king especially made a concerted effort to find you, deploying half the palace guards. The king will be so happy to see you."

I doubt it, thought Jason to himself as they rode through the banks crossing the river. There were five standard bearers in the forefront and the rear guardsmen rode toward the king's standard.

As they approached, some of the castle men recognized him and set up a cheer saying, "The hero of Chanderlon has returned!" The king, riding a magnificent white charger beside Lord Krogan, looked back to see about the commotion. Jason could read the shock in his body language, but he recovered nicely and extended Jason a warm welcome.

"Jason, my boy," King Beldane greeted, "I thought you lost to us. You need to tell me all about it."

He detected a note of warning in the king's voice, but to the king's relief, he replied, "It is a long story, and I will tell you later, but first I must report what I have seen in the country ahead of you. It is a matter of great urgency."

The king said, "You have been over there? Our scouts were not able to penetrate the border, but do not tell it here. Once the army is across the river, Lord Krogan and I will halt the army and hold council with all the officers and you can tell us then."

The king commanded the rear guardsman who had brought Jason forward to stay with him and keep him out of harm's way. After the army crossed and made room for the camp followers, Lord Krogan called the officers to meet at the top of a hill to hear Jason's report. The priests returned across the river and kept to their camp on the Chanderlon side of the border at the river crossing. Apparently, that was their only task at the moment and they stayed out of the actual fighting.

When the officers assembled, Lord Krogan inquired of Jason, "How is it you have preceded us across the border since it was tightly guarded by the shades?"

The child knight stood and replied, "I was taken across the river by a troll sent to retrieve me by Haglar the Watcher. I was able to escape and make a survey of the army we are coming against." He paused, knowing he had their rapt attention, then continued, "Some weeks ago, I am not sure how long for I was unconscious part of the time, the war camp of Harvella was about twenty miles from here to the southeast. It was of comparable size to ours, but not as well equipped, with no mounted troops. However, I did see about fifty gray-skinned giants, perhaps twenty feet tall, working on stone constructs in the shape of a human, each about one hundred feet tall. I was informed that by magic they can move and will fight for Harvella."

The officers looked concerned and one asked, "How many constructs were there?"

"Thirteen," replied Jason.

"Thirteen!" exploded an impatient-looking officer. "Impossible. Such magical constructs are costly and never have I heard of one being taller than fifty feet. The boy exaggerates."

Jason faced him squarely and said, "You are right to say that such constructs are costly and be assured, they paid the price. They paid it in the blood of their people. I know not what strategies we may use against them and prevail, but I suggest we turn to the Creator for help.

At that the officers broke into arguing among themselves. The king said to him, "Thank you for your report, Sir Bristol. You may leave now but do stay near, for we may need to ask more specific questions."

He walked down the hill and waited, watching the troops as they stamped impatiently, waiting to continue their march. After about an hour, one of the junior officers got his attention and led him back up the hill. The officers were all standing or sitting sullenly, not speaking a word. Lord Krogan looked angry and had his back turned to the group and would not even acknowledge Jason's presence. Only the king seemed to retain his composure.

The King spoke to Jason. "After much debate, Sir Bristol, the council has decided to ask the opinion of the champion of Chanderlon as to a strategy they might consider. Some of the members of the council have pointed out that you are well acquainted with going against superior forces and winning. Do you have some advice the council can consider?"

Jason looked at those men. Despite their pride, their faces told they were already defeated. He felt sorry for them as he spoke. "In a country far away, there is a word for strategy in dealing with a superior force. It is called Kazushi. It means using an enemy's own strength against him. If you can figure out how to do that, you will have a chance. If the Creator is on your side, you will win."

No one said a word, and Jason left their midst, thinking they should probably run. He wandered among the troops, and a short while later, the army was given orders to move. After a couple hours marching and six miles later, the army camped in a low valley with a small stream. Scouts and patrols were dispatched and that evening the scouts reported back.

After another strategy meeting, one of the minor officers found Jason. "The scouts have found the Harvellian army about five miles away. It is much the way you said, but there are no giants or magical constructs. The commanders are greatly encouraged. Perhaps the juggernauts have been deployed elsewhere, perhaps to meet the Samyrites—"

Jason interrupted, "You are very kind, but that is not what the commanders are saying about my report, is it?"

"No" he said. "The commanders think your imagination is over-active, and what you saw were only idols. Others think... they think you have been sent by the enemy to demoralize us, or as an attempt to convert us to the Creator. I think you should remain out of sight for a while."

"Thank you for your concern," he said as the man left. He considered, "Why would the enemy hide such awesome weapons? Perhaps they are not finished making them yet." He then took the officer's advice and moved to the back of the army.

He could see a second camp pitched a little ways off by the supporting townsfolk. Some rough-looking women painted themselves up to look pretty for soldiers with money who might visit them that night. Others were the village and castle craftsmen setting up temporary shops to help repair weapons, wagons, and the hostelry of the cavalry. Some merely hauled supplies of food, grain, and clothing.

This was the army's supply line, and as the stores were used, wagons would be coming and going back for more if necessary. Sometimes, an army could supply itself by living off the land and raiding enemy towns along the way, but this was difficult and only done when the army was deep in enemy territory under dire circumstances.

Jason wandered into this camp looking for a familiar face. Suddenly, someone called cheerfully, "Jason. I thought you were dead!"

Searching for the owner of the voice, Jason saw Yaveen, Princess Merinda's swarthy sword instructor, waving at him. He was sitting in a wagon drawn by horses, four other tough-looking men with him. Jason did not like the looks of the other men, but here in this world, looking tough was nearly as important to survival as being tough, so he did not think more about it.

"Hi, Yaveen," Jason called back as he trotted over to him.

Before he got there, Yaveen said something to the other men, and they got out of the wagon and went into a nearby tent. Jason noticed they were well armed with swords and cross bows and wore black leather armor. Yaveen did too, but on him, it did not seem so ominous.

Jumping off the wagon, the smiling Yaveen met Jason and gave him a warm handshake, "I knew you were too tough and skilled for a mere troll to have killed you. But tell me, how did you end up all the way out here?"

Jason returned the man's smile. "First, I alone without God's help, am no match for a troll, and it was that rascally beast that busted me up and carried me in a grain sack to the witch who had quested it to retrieve me." Jason considered telling more of his adventure and scouting out the enemy, but thought it not appropriate as the commanders might think it vital information on a need to know basis, so instead he said, "When that sorceress accidentally caught her own house on fire, I was able to escape and make my way back and was happy to discover the army at the river, so now I am here."

"It is so good to see you again. Surely the gods have smiled upon you. Now come. I was about to sup and you shall eat with me and tell me all about your adventures." Yaveen herded Jason toward his tent.

Mentally, Jason shrugged off Yaveen's words about the "gods smiling on him" and let himself be shown into the tent. He set his pack and weapons just inside the door and was surprised to see about twenty or so men circled about the tent while several rather attractive women, looking a little like gypsies with large hoop metal earrings, served them food and drink from a low table in the center.

Jason was given a spot on some cushions next to Yaveen, and the women began to serve him too.

Yaveen explained he was partial to the food from Kuladon and introduced Jason to a variety of melons and vegetables. Along with meat, the man tried to ply Jason with a variety of wines, which he politely declined. Finally, he had Jason try a concoction of goat milk and honey with a flavoring of berries. Jason liked it, for it tasted a little like a strawberry milkshake.

The sword instructor plied him with all sorts of questions, but he spoke mainly of his capture and journey with the troll. Jason also inquired of Yaveen as to why he was here and who were all of these men.

"Oh, I am here for two reasons. First, I have been hired by some of the lords to train their sons in the finer arts of sword work, and secondly, I want to see the sword work of military combat, so I can modify how I teach the lord's sons appropriately.

"And these men? They are protection for the camp followers. Sometimes the enemy, sometimes bandits prey on the noble people here serving the army. While the camp is near the army, the army is often too busy with their own problems to worry about us, so we must fend for ourselves."

"I see," said Jason. That explanation did a lot to alleviate his suspicions.

After dinner, they all laid out on mats and cushions in the tent, and as the fire died down, soon everyone was fast asleep, but Jason's tummy began to bother him. He had a gassy burp that tasted like goat's milk, bile, and something else he could not identify. He felt sick to his stomach and got up.

Yaveen was awake in an instant with his hand on his knife. "Are you okay, my brother Jason?"

"Uh yes, I think I ate something that doesn't agree with me. I will be back," he said as he stumbled through the dark, trying to pick his way among the sleeping men.

Yaveen lay back down.

When Jason made it outside, he felt so nauseous, he could not stand and made his way to a latrine trench and disgorged his meal. When he was through and about to bury it, he noticed blood mixed in with it. He spat some more and blood came out of his mouth. This was not good. The thought occurred to him that he might have been poisoned. He found a water pitcher and drank a long draught from a ladle.

He could not see his friend purposefully poisoning him, so he must have had an allergic reaction to some of the food. Still feeling too sick to return to the tent, he slept the rest of the night under a grain wagon. The next morning, he awoke feeling better and made his way back to Yaveen's tent. The whole area was covered with a dense fog. He was just about to enter the tent when he could hear the scouts at the other camp running as they shouted, "To arms, we are under attack!"

A trumpet sounded an alarm, almost immediately followed by the war cry from two thousand barbaric throats. Still being with the camp followers, he first thought everyone was running in terror, but it was only the camp followers scrambling to get clear of the battle.

He grabbed his bow and arrows, along with his ax and knives from just inside the tent and exited again. There was chaos within the army camp, so he ran toward the shadows fighting among the tents in the fog. The wet dew made the trampled grass between the tents slippery. The enemy warriors were an undisciplined horde dressed in war paint and patchwork armor. There was the fierce sound of metal against metal as swords and shields clashed.

He hid at a tent entrance and fired at the enemy as they went past. He shot at quite a few, but only three fell as the arrows found a vulnerable spot between the random plates of armor. One barbarian discovered his location and jumped through the opening with a horrible war cry and a double-edged war ax ready to swing. He shot the man in the face, striking him under the cheek bone as the ax came down in a vicious chop, but his arrow made only a glancing blow, cutting the mans rugged features with a wide gash.

Using his bow to help divert the chop, he stepped to the outside and pulled one of the butcher knives from Haglar's hut. Not bothering to attack at the man's armored torso, he slashed at the warrior's forearms as the man tried to pull the ax out of the ground where Jason once stood. The marauder wore heavy gloves that protected his wrists, but Jason went just past them from underneath, trying to cut both forearms at once.

The warrior, an experienced fighter, easily blocked the move by lowering the end of the handle on his war ax. Seeing that his adversary was only a small boy, the barbarian smiled at what he thought would be an easy kill. Blood running freely from the lacerated cheek made him look like some ghoulish monster. He slapped Jason away with a leather gauntlet while he pulled the ax free from the ground with his other hand.

Snatching up his bow again, Jason tried to circle, keeping his distance as he tried to pull another arrow from his quiver. Somewhere a horn sounded and the barbarian swung at him again with a frustrated grunt. Jason danced out of the path of the cleaving blow and notched his arrow.

The grizzled warrior stepped back toward the tent entrance and with a spit of disgust went out the door. Jason fired just as the man ducked out of the tent, but his aim at the head missed because of the barbarian's sudden movement. The surprise attack ended as quickly as it begun, and the horde disappeared into the fog as if they were never there.

Jason went to where the officers assembled and listened unnoticed outside the circle. When all the units reported, it was discovered there were sixteen dead and twenty-three wounded; of the enemy, thirty-five died. Not bad, considering the surprise of the attack. No one had noticed his efforts in repelling the attackers, which was fine with him.

The commanders took the failed surprise attack to be an act of desperation and ordered the troops to break camp and prepare to move. King Beldane and Lord Krogan seemed to be in much better moods than the day before now that they had actually engaged the enemy and repelled them successfully.

Later that morning, a breeze began from the northeast, and the sun burned off the fog, revealing a very hazy day. The army began to march ahead, while the camp followers stayed in relative safety several miles behind.

CHAPTER 41

The Monster Mash

Jason strolled behind the rear guard. Bored with the view and the slow pace, he swung to the left and trotted alongside the army up on the hills, which was precisely what some of the scouts were doing, holding horns to give signal if unexpectedly attacked from a different direction.

After marching for about an hour, the two armies met in a broad valley. Instead of facing them straight on, the Harvellian army angled to the left. When the army of Chanderlon squared up, the Harvellian army screamed taunts and made obscene gestures, trying to goad the Chanderlon army to attack. Lord Krogan sent the archers forward. They moved into range and began firing. Jason watched but did not let himself get too focused on the battle, instead scanning the horizon every so often. He felt uneasy and was sure there was more here than what met the eye.

The king, his bodyguard, and his standard bearer rode up to a hill near Jason to get a better view of the battle. The king's four guards on foot circled about him. There was also a scout between Jason and the King and two more on this side of the valley, five on the other side. While the battle escalated with several fake charges and several cavalry maneuvers, Jason scanned the plain from his hill.

He could see trails where troops and scouts made paths in the tall grass but noticed several trails leading up to the hills he hadn't noticed before. The fresh trails in the grass seem to come up to the hills but stopped just before reaching the summit. Jason checked his hill, and sure enough, a trail stopped about twenty feet away. He could faintly smell something familiar, like the rancid meat smell of the giants that had passed him in the woods.

A small songbird flying along suddenly veered when it came to the spot where the trail ended. Suspicious, he faced away from where the trail stopped and notched an arrow, then turned and fired about six feet above the spot. The arrow vanished, and he heard a grunt of pain. The sound came from higher than ten feet. He fired again at the ten-foot height and was rewarded by a roar as the trail in the grass sped toward him.

He dove to the side as the growing trail got close and yelled, "Invisible giants!" He heard a swish go by him and fired again at the gray-skinned giant clad in ragged animal skins, now suddenly visible. It held a long iron pole with a large curved blade at the end. He ran toward the nearest scout, now taking aim with his bow at the mighty giant chasing the boy. Other scouts blew their horns in warning.

Behind the scout and on the next hill where the king was, Jason saw the head of one of the bodyguards explode as a giant appeared, swinging a huge wooden club made of a tree trunk. He felt like he needed to protect the king, but both he and the scout had their hands full with this giant.

As he ran past the scout, he whirled and fired an arrow at the giant's chest but missed. However, fortunately or by the grace of God, the arrow sunk into one eye, and the giant clawed at it in pain. In a rage, it bellowed and flung its glaive, spinning like a helicopter's blade. The scout moved faster than Jason thought possible, diving into him as they both tumbled to the ground. The massive whirling missile grazed the grass just over their heads like scythe and stuck into the turf just beyond them.

But the titanic monster was not idle. While they regained their feet, it flung itself through the air with the intent of squishing them under its crushing stomp. This creature looked big and ponderous but moved surprisingly quick, with almost the same agility as a much smaller man. In fact, scientists from his world would have said the bone mass could not support such a maneuver.

Again, diving to either side, both the scout and Jason evaded certain death. The giant then made a tactical error, for which Jason often chided his own martial art students. The giant could have killed them if it had continued its attack, but instead reached for its weapon.

This gave both himself and the scout a chance to fire their bows again. Jason fired at the kidney area on the giant's back, since the giant was partially turned away from him, but the scout's next arrow went into its throat and the giant made a gurgling noise as it fell. Neither he nor the scout took time to make sure the downed gray giant was dead, but checked the others.

The other scouts were in similar straights, but being forewarned had a fighting chance. The king fared better than Jason had hoped. Two of his bodyguards were down, but the king had pulled his sword and had it pointed at the giant. The blade was glowing with an unearthly light. With a snap of thunder, a bolt of lightning shot forth from the tip of the blade, burning the giant's chest. The giant fell backwards as white and gray smoke rose from the wound and then it lay, unmoving.

He had heard that the king's sword was magical but had no idea it contained so much power. He was suddenly very curious about it. Did it need to recharge before firing again? Could the voltage be controlled? Was there a limit to it? If it took down a huge giant, could it take down a moving skyscraper? Even if it could not, was there a strategy where it could be used to help?

Seeing the king okay, both he and the scout assisted the other scouts, pouring a volley of deadly accurate shots into the next giant. That giant began to look somewhat like a porcupine and soon it, too, was down and the three ran to help the others in their life and death struggles.

After a few minutes, all the giants on this side were down, but the other side of the valley didn't fare so well. The scouts had all been killed in the surprise attack and now six giants moved in unison to meet the back of the Chanderlon army. Lord Krogan spotted them and sent a detachment of knights. The knights hit them at full charge with the lances. A couple of chargers were knocked aside, horse and all. Two giants also fell immediately, skewered by several lances, but the other four beat at the mounted men with their great weapons of various types made to accommodate their size.

Jason had to admire the knights' courage. These were Lord Krogan's handpicked men the general had trained personally and, although they had never before faced a giant in combat, it was apparent they were not unprepared. Their horses pranced aside, dodging blows while the armored men used their lances like spears, thrusting at the giant's vulnerable areas with the lance's greater reach of about fifteen feet.

As the huge monsters apparently sent the men before them to flight, they were at the same time being stabbed from the knights behind, and one by one went down. One last giant was surrounded, and on signal, all the knights charged at once. The huge man died standing up and did not fall until the knights backed their chargers out of the way. These men never showed fear and were an inspiration to the rest of the troops who cheered and rushed to help the two that fell in the mêlée.

The men had also seen the king take out a giant with a single stroke of lightning and felt confident in their advantage and pressed their attack, driving the Harvellians back. Jason wondered where the rest of the giants were and the juggernauts. He hoped they weren't invisible too.

Jason rested near the king with a couple scouts while the rest went over to check their comrades on the other side of the valley. He pondered the sword again. It was supposedly a gift from the clerics of Xan Rukkah and through years of tradition became a symbol of rule for Chanderlon.

While Jason pondered the king's sword, the king too was lost in thought. He glanced at the little boy he had knighted more as a political diversion, and it had come back to bite him. Although grateful the boy did not expose the events surrounding the abduction, that did not matter much since they were about to be exposed anyway by his own actions. No, there was another danger he could not quite discern.

The boy brought with him a new god which terrified the clerics of Xan Rukkah. His making Jason a hero was not to distract people from his announcement of war nor to help his daughter's mood about marriage, as many supposed.

No, it was deeper than that. What he sought was a balance of power. The clerics of Xan Rukkah were too powerful politically. In fact, this very war was their doing, although done secretly. They wanted to take over a territory controlled by the goddess of magic, Axialla, using him and the soldiers as their shock troops. This was a war between the gods and he did not like the powerless role he played.

Jason's appearance with a new god could not have been at a more opportune time. If Xan Rukkah clerics could be put in their place a little or become distracted by the child, then he might actually begin to regain some semblance of authority.

Speaking of power, he had an ace up his sleeve. Sure, his sword was fantastic, but it was only on loan from Xan Rukkah. It had become the symbol of rule in Chanderlon, which the clerics could take from him at anytime. He was a puppet to their whims, except he had become a follower of Axialla and had learned how to use magic to some degree.

Magic had never been in favor, a holdover from the barbaric roots of his people who distrusted anything they could not understand. The gods did as they willed, but magic was typified by evil outcasts hungry for power. But the people did not understand that magic was man's only way out from the tyranny of the gods—to wield the power the gods themselves used.

He was not afraid of King Goshen's magic, for he had magic of his own. He hoped when the people saw how useful magic could be, he might be able to hire a wizard as a counselor like many other kingdoms. But having just witnessed Jason's encounter with the giant made him wonder if his promoting the boy was a mistake.

One could just attribute the boy's successes to pure dumb luck, but the boy seemed protected somehow, as if he could do no wrong. Perhaps what protected the boy was too powerful. What if the boy's religion displaced all the others? The clerics of Xan Rukkah tolerated the clerics of other religions, but were very afraid of this one.

Perhaps he should have talked more with his daughter to discover what this new religion was about before he left. He did not mind her choosing her own god, but what if he, due to pressure from the clerics in Chanderlon, must make this religion illegal?

And just who was this Creator anyway? The god of artists? No, the princess had told him once, this god was the maker of all things, even the lesser gods themselves. The lesser gods? Perhaps that is why the other clerics seemed threatened.

He knew the princess had launched an investigation into Father Varigold's death. She charged the clerics of Xan Rukkah with murdering him for becoming a follower of the Creator. Evidently, because of some prophecy, the old man had changed his loyalty to the new god. The investigation came to nothing, so he had dismissed it but now thought he would like very much to hear that prophecy. Perhaps there was some advantage he could take of it.

Suddenly, he felt the ground shake with a deep vibration. He could see the men reacting to it too, looking about in wonder. The thumping vibration became strong, then audible. The king and his standard bearer, from their higher vantage point on the hill, were the first to see. The standard bearer cried, "Look, sire!"

Soon Jason too could see the heads of the juggernauts coming over the opposite side of the hill. Now it was time for the Harvellian army to cheer. Running from the south to further support the Harvellians were about forty more tall gray giants which joined their ranks. He heard one of the scouts call them stone giants. This is what Maudid defeated with his bare hands? If so, then the former champion of Prince Dunaibi truly was a great martial artist.

The juggernauts were now nearly to the top of the hill and their massive size was truly amazing, standing over one hundred feet above the hilltop. Just one falling down could take out a fifth of the army. There was a grating sound of stone against stone as joints rubbed together. Despite their semblance to life, there was no life in the statue's eyes, just dull gray stone.

Their movements were measured, paced, almost robotic. They seemed to have no volition of their own. The dispassion made them more terrifying for they did not, nor could not, care who or what they trampled. Anything too slow to get out of the way would simply die in their path, and the fact that there were so many would ensure that most would not be able to get out of the way without running into the path of another.

Jason and the scouts moved closer to King Beldane, who got off his horse and drew frantically on the ground with his rod, muttering an incantation.

Lord Krogan, realizing the danger of the army being crushed between the two forces, sounded a retreat. However, it was too late. The juggernauts were already coming down the hill from behind, cutting them off. They seemed to be moving in slow motion, but since each stride covered thirty feet, they moved faster than a man could run. Their footprint alone mashed an area the size of a Mack truck and sank two to three feet deep into the plain's soil. Each step threw up soil with it as the toes scoured through the earth.

The horses of the cavalry whinnied in terror, further eroding the morale of the troops. The king's own horse fled in terror, while the standard bearer fought to keep his mount under control. A few men near the rear of the army fell to their knees to entreat their own personal gods. They were the first to die when the juggernauts of destruction plowed into the first row of men.

Mens screams mingled with those of the horses. Those tread on were instantly silenced while others were kicked through the air on the way to the next step. The army was fluid now, trying to flee or avoid the onslaught. Archers shot and spear men flung their missiles in futility at the approaching wall of stone, only to see their arrows and spears bounce off, doing no damage.

The king finished his incantation. Sparks flew from his fingertips and the outline gave a little puff of smoke and then... nothing. Nothing. In disbelief, King Beldane dropped to his knees in despair. Seeing Jason with the scouts, he shouted, "You!"

Jason came forward. Pointing a finger at Jason, he shouted again, more angrily, "You! Because of you, the final ceremony back in Chanderlon was disrupted! Now my magic has failed, and my people will die!"

"No, King Beldane," Jason replied, stepping close. "You appealed to Axialla with numerous sacrifices, but King Goshen sacrificed hundreds to each one of yours. Who do you think Axialla would favor? Besides, she would rather see your kingdom fall into chaos than see Harvella fall under your law and order. Your only chance is to turn this battle over to the Creator by deciding to serve him."

The king stood and pointed to the juggernauts, just now reaching the army. "I do not believe that even the Creator can stop the likes of those. But, Jason, if you and the Creator can stop them, I will promise to serve the Creator."

"No!" shouted Jason. "Choose now whom you will serve. Faith that is conditional is no faith at all. If you show no faith when times are desperate, you will show no faith when times are easy."

By now, the cries of much of the army being stamped by the Juggernauts reached them. The Harvellian army stood back and watched, cutting down any who chose to flee their direction. The king fell to his knees and said, "Please, Jason, call on the Creator to save us."

Jason said patiently. "That is still not much on your part. This is your kingdom, and it is your responsibility toward them as well as to God. I could ask him but it would be far more effective if you addressed him yourself."

As they talked, Jason noticed that among the first to fall were the standard bearers. In fact, one juggernaut detached from the battle and now headed toward them.

Why would the brainless golum single them out? Was it the banner it was attracted to? If so, then perhaps this tendency could be exploited, he thought. It was as if they were programmed like some giant robot to only do certain things or perhaps in a certain order with the priorities to take out the leaders.

King Beldane looked in terror as his standard bearer cried, "One is coming for us!"

The king looked over at Jason, then at the sky and raised his hands in supplication, "Creator, God of the universe, I am nothing in your sight, and I have worked against you. Please forgive me and my people. From now on, no matter what happens, you are my king and commander, and I am your servant. We place ourselves and our destiny in your hands."

The king looked at Jason with a brave smile and nodded while Jason flew into action. "Get down," he commanded the standard bearer, whose horse was getting even more nervous with the approaching juggernaut. The standard bearer dismounted, held the horse for Jason, and gave him his banner. Jason instructed him to attach the banner to the holder in the saddle.

"God speed, Sir Jason," he said, and Jason charged the horse at the juggernaut, banner flying. He then veered the frantic horse to the left. To his relief the juggernaut followed. Fighting down his own panicky feelings, he reigned in the steed a little to ensure he did not lose the stone monster as it ponderously turned to chase him.

At a trot, flag waving, he led the behemoth back toward the battle. The Chanderlon army was in utter disarray, each man desperately trying to avoid being stamped. He knew he was taking a big chance and probably putting the hapless soldiers at greater risk, but if he was right, this was the only thing he could do to save them. He yelled a warning at a mass of men before him who had not seen his approach and they scattered upon the sight of the gargantuan rock figure behind him bearing down upon them.

He considered if he needed to blindfold the flag bearer's horse. He was not an expert rider but would need a trustworthy horse and more riding skill than he had for what he planned to do. Even if the horse wasn't normally terrified by such things as a walking castle-high statue, the animal could sense the terror of all those around him. Perhaps it would sense even the terror that dwelt in his own heart.

If only he could communicate to the horse. But God could do that for him, so he prayed, "Lord help us and help me to ride this mount, help us to be as one."

He rode into the fray, approaching another juggernaut. That juggernaut too focused on his banner and started stomping its way toward him. He stopped with two juggernauts bearing down on him from two different directions. Between the horse trembling, the ground shaking, and the sound of soldiers yelling, Jason felt disorientated, but miraculously, the horse held its position. Despite all this chaos, this situation seemed familiar, like he had been in this position not just once, but many times before and what he was doing was surprisingly simplistic.

He timed the steps carefully, then spurred the horse forward, charging it straight between the legs of the facing juggernaut. With the force of two mountains colliding, both juggernauts ran into each other and began crumbling as they sought to squash the one little boy holding the enemy flag. Like an avalanche, they began to tear each other apart as falling rocks and boulders rained down from them. Then it was as if whatever was holding them together suddenly came undone, and with a loud noise, they fell into a large, nondescriptive pile of rock.

Dust flew around Jason and the horse, and he had to take a moment to catch his breath and clear his eyes. As everything settled, he saw Lord Krogan before him, mounted on his own steed and holding a soiled banner as well. All the other flag bearers had either thrown down their flags in fear, or were crushed when they could not get out of the way in time.

"Sir Jason Bristol,"—this was the first time Lord Krogan had ever used that title for the boy—"I salute you." Then the gray- bearded veteran, with a brave smile, thrust his banner in the air and yelled, "Kazushi!"—the term to describe using an enemy's own strength against them, as he charged toward another juggernaut attempting to squish a knot of men nearby. The experienced warrior had instantly grasped Jason's strategy and now attempted to implement it himself.

Jason, elated he was not alone in this fight and his plan had worked, had little time to celebrate his victory as another of the massive rock beasts lumbered toward him and his mount. Allowing the masonry machine to get so close he could make out the sparkle of quartz in its rocky skin, he waited to make his move. Just as the war pony began to prance sideways, he urged the horse away from the moving mountain and toward enemy forces while practically dancing between the behemoth's stride.

Upon seeing the rocky horror now coming at them, the Harvellian forces gave way as he sped through their ranks. A few archers fired as he passed, attempting to skewer him or the horse but didn't come close, their spent arrows whizzing instead into the mass of their own troops. Men scrambled, trying to avoid Jason's horse and the juggernaut's crushing feet, running into each other and falling over themselves. His horse bounded over a tangled mass of living bodies fallen in his path and he heard behind him the awful cries of terror from men who knew they were going to die.

When he finally plowed through the enemy army with the death golem in tow, he gave the horse its head and allowed it to go into a full gallop, racing along the flanks of the enemy army and back around to the battle front. The juggernaut, unable to keep up with the speeding horse, took the shortest route to its target and again stomped its way through the enemy army.

The hapless Harvellians were too disorganized to realize it was Jason they needed to stop. As he rode alongside enemy troops, two more juggernauts targeted his banner and stomped through the Harvellian army to get to him, causing the enemy army to call a retreat.

When he was again between the two opposing forces, more juggernauts from the mass of Chanderlon's army had become aware of him and now changed direction to come for him. He slowed and rested the horse, speaking in low tones and patting its neck to soothe and calm it. It seemed incredible to him he was still alive, but he knew the worst was yet to come.

Lord Krogan spent his efforts leading the stone monsters away from the men of Chanderlon so some were able to make their escape back down the valley. In fact, his circling efforts had attracted four of the stone automatons but, as of yet, had not timed it so any of them had the misfortune of running into each other. To do that required a daring maneuver of dancing a horse between the feet of the juggernauts, and he had determined to do just that.

Taking position before one of these animations and attracting its attention, Lord Krogan led it to where another juggernaut was being diverted by his cavalry. The noise and vibration could be felt through his mount, and he prayed that it would not falter. This was not as easy as Jason made it look, feeling that any second could be his last. But not being one to give into his fear, he drove his mount between the stomping feet of the second monstrous statue ahead of him.

His mount held true and the general was rewarded with the sound of crashing rock behind him. As the mountains of slag fell behind him, he began to appreciate the courage of the little boy who threatened to turn the world as they knew it upside down. Despite his downing of two juggernauts, he knew the glory of this battle would go to Jason, and suddenly he did not mind. His shaking steed was a remarkable mount that he knew from birth, while the boy awkwardly rode the borrowed horse of a standard bearer. Despite this, Jason's courage and brilliant strategy did not convince Lord Krogan that some deity had anything to do with this. He turned to see what else he could do, but Jason was already on the move, attracting the attention of the nearest juggernauts to his position.

Jason waved his banner and yelled at the closest rocky behemoths. Yelling seemed to do no good, so he rode back and forth in front of the bloody mayhem. Two changed direction, not including the three still steamrolling their way through the enemy.

Like stiff robots, the massive rock statues came in from all directions, but most importantly, Jason positioned himself so they would all arrive at the same spot at about the same time. He felt trapped, wanting to just flee and be done with it. With so many bearing down on him at once the ground shook and rolled continuously.

If he failed to get out of their way in time, the juggernauts would make a mountain over him too deep for anyone to dig him out. It would he his tomb. Perhaps this was the time for him to go home. He felt a surprising calmness at the thought. The horse began prancing sideways again, and Jason gently calmed it, speaking softly with a calmness he genuinely felt. The tired horse sensed the peace that had come over its rider and relaxed, allowing itself to be at peace as well.

Suddenly, he had a remembrance of a method he used to train his students for fighting multiple attackers called a robot drill. One student would be in the middle while the rest of the class emulated robots with slow, stiff arm and leg motions. The slow and stilted approach gave the student time to formulate strategies and do a similar thing to what he was doing now. No wonder this battle seemed familiar.

Once again, he timed the giant footsteps and urged the horse between the legs of an approaching juggernaut. The valiant animal seemed to be moving in slow motion as they approached the moving monster, and as a house-sized foot sank into the trampled plain beside him, mud squirted, covering him on one side.

The unexpected mud spray caused the horse to shy to the side, throwing the inexperienced Jason from the saddle. He tried to grab a stirrup as he went down, but all he managed to hang on to was the banner of Chanderlon. Upon hitting the ground he rolled, then immediately flung himself into another diving roll, still holding the pole of the banner, to get clear of the juggernaut.

Then came the sound of the thundering impact like a thousand bowling pins being struck at once. It seemed as if the sound of cracking and grating boulders released a cry of spirits, perhaps trapped in the blood used for mortar. Since he fell outside the circle of destruction, he was not caught by the full brunt of the avalanche of falling debris that followed.

Rock and dust fell around him as the stone-binding magic came undone. In a matter of moments, the monolithic monsters turned into a huge hill of stone and gravel. Spitting dirt, the small boy strode out of the dust cloud dragging the flag, in stark contrast to the mass behind him. Seeing this victory was enough to inspire hope in the men of Chanderlon and provoke fear in the Harvellian army.

He circled and waved the standard, raising a cheer from the soldiers, although he was actually trying to attract the attention of the remaining juggernauts. He got the attention of three others, and in a show of bravery he did not feel, ran back and forth before them as they all bore down from one direction. This left a fourth one rampaging the ranks of Chanderlon.

However, the men were so scattered by now the juggernauts caused little damage, and taking a cue from Jason and Lord Krogan, a unit of horsemen diverted the remaining juggernaut by making themselves bait, protecting the rest of the army.

Not having a mount any longer, Jason was in trouble as the wall of death approached him. Could he be fast enough to escape between them? Just then, to his relief another knight, Sir Quineas, who was his second in the fight with Maudid, led his horse back to him. He was especially glad, because this horse and he had experience together. His chore done, Sir Quineas urged his horse to aid others still trying to vacate the area on foot.

Remounting the page's steed, Jason led the three juggernauts through what remained of the retreating Harvellian army, using their own weapon against them. The three juggernauts walked in a straight-line side by side, gradually getting closer together. By now, most of the Harvellian army had vacated the field, and the few stragglers left scrambled to get out of the way.

As they neared their intended prey, the stone monster's shoulders began grinding against each other with the sound of a great stone mill. Dust and rocks cracked from the impact and acted like mini-explosions, throwing a shower of dust and rock. Now Jason wheeled the horse and ran it right through the middle of them all. His borrowed steed seemed to know the score now, and even flying muck and falling debris did not deter it. The one on the outside edge turned inward and collided into the other two. However, they were so close that the effect on the others was almost immediate, and it threw the balance and stride off the one Jason had chosen to ride under.

Its descending foot suddenly changed direction to compensate and Jason was surprised to find a wall of stone coming at him from the side. It slammed into him with such force that it sent him, horse and all, flying through the air. He was separated from the horse in the air, still clinging to the flag.

He hit the ground and rolled as the group of living statues destroyed themselves, making another large pile and shaking the earth greatly. He rolled to his stomach and covered his head as again dust, dirt, and small pebbles rained down upon him. When the rain of stone stopped, he raised his head at the same time the stunned horse lying near him also raised its head.

He went over and helped the horse to its feet. It seemed okay, so he mounted it again and rode toward his home forces. He could see that the footmen had escaped and only Lord Krogan and a tired cavalry were taking turns harassing the remaining stone opponent.

With only one juggernaut left, Jason knew they had a problem. There were no other juggernauts to lead it into. He rode over to Lord Krogan, who was letting his horse rest. Like a relay team, the mounted knights would pass off the flag between themselves so the giant statue would target someone else.

Lord Krogan addressed him first. "Well done, lad. But we now have a problem, for the stone golem does not tire. We could lead it out on the plain and abandon it, but we do not know what it will do then. If it was commanded to go to Chanderlon after this, we cannot stop it."

Jason nodded. "The king has asked the Creator to help, but perhaps he is leaving the last one to us."

Lord Krogan made a harrumphing noise, then said, "Your strategy, although brilliant, was nothing more than clever tactics. With a little luck and courage, anyone could have pulled off the stunt you did, but I have yet to see your god's hand in this."

Jason nodded. "Point well taken. Then leave the last juggernaut to me and pull your troops back."

"Do you have a plan?" asked Lord Krogan incredulously.

"No, but God will provide," he said as he rode toward the present game of cat-and-mouse.

Lord Krogan blew a whistle commanding the cavalry to pull back as Jason wearily rode his horse to meet the monster. Both he and the horse were tired. Just the fear and excitement itself was draining. He reminded himself of his training that being relaxed, even from tiredness, was actually an asset in a fight.

This was his first chance to let his mind wander. Of course, his first thought was of his wife, her black curly hair tinged with silver and her slim figure. She was not a runway model but attractive none-the-less. He longed to be a man again and have her rush into his arms. Now he might die under the stomp of a moving statue and never see her again. It's odd how imminent death increases longing.

He then imagined his kids, Trevor and Cassandra, visiting his grave and reading the tombstone. "Here lies Jason the Juggernaut, the oldest child in history. Flattened by a bigger juggernaut. Thought he could do anything...

Guess not." He smiled a little at his joke, then refocused himself to the task at hand.

As the other horsemen got out of his way, it was easy to draw the attention of the remaining behemoth, and he guided it toward the largest pile of juggernaut remains. If he could make it run into or onto the rocky remnants of its compatriots, then perhaps it would fall and damage itself.

He thought he felt the ground trembling. It seemed the ground had never stopped quaking from the last crash of craggy monsters. In fact, the ground seemed to be shaking worse.

The juggernaut was coming and Jason's horse, tired as it was, stumbled and fell, throwing him to the ground. He lay only a moment and realized the horse had actually fallen into a deeper foot print of the gargantuan statue monsters. He rolled to his side to find himself face to face with a dead soldier, crushed and pressed into the ground.

He felt sick and quickly stood, with the standard lying beside him. The horse regained its feet and fled the approaching giant. He knew it was futile to try to outrun the juggernaut on foot, so he grabbed the standard and held it over his head, waving the flag high as he continued to run toward the largest pile of rubble. It was only then he realized the quaking he felt was not just from the steps of the juggernaut or the quivering of his fatigued legs. It was an actual earthquake.

He had felt earthquakes in Alaska before, but none of this intensity. The ground bucked and rolled like waves on a stormy lake, then grew in intensity until grass turf heaved around him. Suddenly, the solid ground underneath became a shifting and sliding maze of cracks and upheavals. The juggernaut weaved and swayed from side to side in an attempt to retain its footing and still came toward him. In the next moment, a large fracture opened in the ground between Jason and his stoney assailant. Unable to stop its forward momentum, the mass of living boulders stepped into the hole and, as if in slow motion, fell towards him. At the same time, the break in the ground opened wider.

He tried to leap out of the way of the expanding fissure and the falling behemoth, but the ground was too unstable for him to do anything more than stand. As hundreds of tons hit the ground, Jason too fell, and dirt flew over him from the impact of the juggernaut's fall. The ground continued to split as the juggernaut fell, forming a huge crevasse in the ground into which the golem fell.

Jason now managed to jump from one lump of shifting earth to another to avoid falling into the miniature canyons forming, some very deep. The juggernaut did not fare as well and could not climb out of the one huge fissure swallowing it. The ground closed in again, covering the juggernaut with earth and leaving a quarter mile area of muddy churned soil. All that was left was one upraised hand which froze into a towering monument, one stoney finger lifted as if pointing to heaven. The stillness contrasted markedly to the rumbling and crashing noises from before.

The Chanderlon army, which had retreated to the hills to watch this last battle between boy and monster, regained their feet, having been knocked down by the earthquake themselves. They could see Jason climbing through the rubble and mud filled valleys and broke into wild cheers. From them rose the chant, "Praise to the Creator and praise to Jason, the juggernaut killer."

He had to smile because it was King Beldane who led the chant. He could not see Lord Krogan anywhere, or the rest of the cavalry, but assumed they were cleaning up stragglers from the enemy army.

CHAPTER 42
Deologue 7

In a cavern, both god and goddess stood over the brightly lit warring pit in stunned silence. The pit had a copy of the valley where the battle took place and they watched the little game pieces of the army of Chanderlon withdraw from the pit, moving without help as though an unseen hand directed them.

Xan Rukkah shook his huge head as his deep voice rumbled like thunder. "We came thinking to fight each other and the game was stolen from us."

"I was robbed of my victory. Have you conspired to ally with the Creator?" Axialla, suddenly animated, hit both fists against the rim of the bowl-like pit.

"Nay, but I would have never guessed you could conjure so many juggernauts. And how could the Creator use the boy? You assured me he was dead."

"Dead? Yes, and double dead. Jazeel assured me this was so, and he is not one to be mistaken in this area."

"Then what can account for what we just saw? Could there be more than one?" thundered the questioning titan.

"Jazeel suggested as much, and I sent him to investigate, but we never thought there would be twins." She put her hand to her mouth. "What if there are many more? Perhaps hundreds were all hiding in the wilderness or other parts of the world, waiting to make their move."

"Then go," commanded the greater being. "We need information. We are gods, and yet we are stumbling around in the dark as if mere mortals."

Axialla bowed and swooped out of the cavern, gliding the long tresses of the black gown she chose for this occasion.

Xan Rukkah watched her go. She was beautiful to the eye, enough to make any man or god lust after her, but he remembered her original form. Something like a giant black spider. He shuddered at the thought of her. It had been centuries since he'd seen her look like that, but once seen, it was a sight hard to forget.

Her multiple eyes could detach and float around, trailing long sticky tentacles, moving to her will. She was creepy, even for a goddess, but it was she who first captured men's hearts with her gifts of magic. It was she who set the gods on the path of power, gaining followers. It was she who gave him the idea to defy the Creator.

Now he would have totally lost this battle if it were not for the Creator. If he had lost to her, would she have pressed her advantage to declare herself the supreme goddess? But now, she lost and is having to regroup. Unfortunately, they both lost to the Creator. The way the men cheered the Creator made him jealous. These should have been cheers and praises for him instead.

The Creator won, and they never even saw his presence. Early in the battle, he did not try to stop Jason since Axialla would have crushed him anyway with her monstrous automatons. At the time, he was not even worried about King Beldane accepting the Creator since he had the skeptical Lord Krogan on his side to help dissuade everyone that the Creator or any god had helped the boy.

But the destruction of the last automaton was simply a display of raw power. He could have not put on such a display without much preparation. The thought made him uneasy. He felt that soon he was about to lose much more.

CHAPTER 43

The Lord's Army

Three smaller aftershocks followed the earthquake that destroyed the last juggernaut. Jason now rode with King Beldane and Lord Krogan at the head of the army on a beautiful beige-colored pony purchased from the camp followers.

Jason had looked for Yaveen among the camp followers, but the sword instructor was nowhere to be found, and no one seemed to know where he and the men with him had gone. Perhaps with the main battle over, he simply returned home.

While the camps were being taken down for travel, the king summoned Jason. Since the king was on his horse on a hill overlooking the field, Jason mounted his new pony to go speak to him.

"Jason the Juggernaut, a boy they say cannot be stopped. Compared to the living statues, you are a juggernaut in miniature, but a juggernaut nonetheless," the king mused.

Jason shrugged. "God destroyed the last juggernaut and even the others, although not in such an obvious way."

"Yes, that is why I called you. I have sworn service to a god I know little about. What is this god's game? What are his end goals for his servants? Why is he meddling in our affairs now at this time?"

"I do not know why at this time," Jason confessed. "But I can tell you why. It is out of love."

"Really? All the other gods view us as beneath them, only fit to serve in some capacity or another, and in exchange, they occasionally throw us a bone."

"To the contrary, the Creator views us as his children, and we are destined to eventually rule with him. We are his servants, but we follow God's own example, in that he served us first. The serving we do now is toward each other, and in this way, we serve and worship him."

The king shook his head in wonder. "A god who actually cares about mankind? I like that. Tell me more, young Jason."

For the next hour, Jason told him about Jesus and a little of history preceding his coming. He also spoke of his own coming to this world and the prophecy that preceded himself.

When the time came to lead the army to the capitol town of Hundor, King Beldane rode in silence far enough ahead to be lost in his own thoughts. He reflected on what Jason had told him and his own recent experiences.

The fact that Jason was actually an alien from another world, a man in a boy's body, raised many questions but also explained a lot of things. Being a hero in the rescue of the children to being Princess Merinda's champion clearly set this boy apart. The fear of the clerics as well as Jason's talk of a strange god who helps him brought the king's thoughts back to his own problem.

He had tipped his hand during the Battle of the Juggernauts, as it was already coming to be known. He had violated the standing laws of Chanderlon by resorting to sorcery. He was accountable for the deaths of six sacrificial victims, and nearly a seventh, to do his failed performance. In fact, his own daughter had nearly become a victim. He felt like such a fool when Jason pointed out that his effort was greatly outdone anyway by King Goshen.

He would have preferred hiring a wizard who directly bent the forces of magic to his will, but the only sources of magic available in Chanderlon were the clerics of Axialla, who practiced in secrecy. Even though he was king, he could be tried and executed for what he had done and right now, he felt a little frightened at what he had done, even ashamed.

Perhaps Jason offered him a way out. Jason told him of the Creator's ability to forgive, and while that did not absolve him of full accountability, he could at least sleep with a clear conscience. His dreams were haunted by the screams of the children sacrificed.

They were small children terrified by their abduction, but he could see the relief on their faces when they saw him, for they believed for a moment they had been saved. Their protector had come. Then their look of horror as they realized he was the reason for their abduction in the first place. They depended on him, and their protector betrayed them.

Yes, he deserved to die. Could this god of Jason's really forgive him? This god was described as pure good, one who could not abide with evil. Yet this god sent a son, a being that was in essence his own self, to pay the ultimate penalty of all crimes in everyone's place. As the son, going by the name of Jesus, he experienced death as a human. Then he raised himself from the dead after three days.

His promise to mankind was that even the penalty of death was defeated. Would any other god do this for mankind? Also, this god was everywhere at once and knew all things. Imagine a god who listened to even your very thoughts and judged the heart. This was in itself scary and yet comforting at the same time.

A person who directly had a god's ear had no need of magic, for if they were in accordance to that god's wishes, they had the power of a god at their disposal. If what Jason said was true, then this god was sovereign over all the gods and in fact had no restrictions as to which realm he ruled.

Xan Rukkah was supposedly this now. He was the god of healing and vigor. But this came at a cost. Only the wealthy would be healed by the clerics. A sudden illness of a poor person meant death. Would this god he had chosen to follow do better? That was something to think about.

During the trip, Lord Krogan hardly said a word to Jason. Jason tried to engage him in conversation several times, but his efforts were rebuffed with a noncommittal harrumph.

Lord Krogan viewed himself as a hard but fair man. His strength was in his hardness, though some would call it stubbornness. To be fair, Jason had proved his god existed and had helped them that day of battle. Now he faced a bitterness that refused to allow him to concede Jason's victory. He was a proud man, proud enough to even defy the gods, and certainly Jason's god as well.

He resented supernatural interference. Why cannot the gods just leave mankind to its own devices, allow them to make their own way as they willed? When it is all over let the good be rewarded and the evil be damned.

Speaking of evil, the king did evil in acquiring magic. He should take the king into custody. Meanwhile, he would act as regent until he could have the clerics declare Lord Griffon or even himself as the new king. But the men would not support such an action yet. They are still too flush with victory from the battle and had heard that King Beldane now embraced Jason's god. He would have to bide his time for now.

Four days later, they rode into Hundor, Harvella's capitol city, as conquerors, while the city welcomed them with open arms. King Goshen fled before they arrived, so there was no resistance. When it became clear to the inhabitants that Chanderlon's army was not on the verge of razing the place, outright celebration broke out, though the lack of women and children was very noticeable.

Jason thought of the women and children hidden in the valley by the mountains and wondered if they had made it. They would probably stay hidden until their men came for them, which would probably be soon, at least for those who managed to escape the battle.

The plan now was for at least half the army to return home to Chanderlon, since it was discovered from some of the locals that Samyrite forces, which had invaded the badlands in the east over a week ago, had begun to withdraw upon the news of the defeat of King Goshen's army. It was still unclear if the Samyrites intended to continue their invasion or now return home.

The next day, the king conferred with Lord Krogan on the affairs of the country of Harvella. Half the castle regulars and half the conscripted men were to return to Chanderlon with the supply train and camp followers.

Lord Krogan would remain and employ people from the populace to care for the palace as well as recruit and train soldiers to bring order to the outlying areas. The plan was to later send the rest of the conscripted men home in a couple months time, to help with the fall harvests.

The following day, the king made ready to leave as Lord Krogan busily established his new command. The guards and soldiers saluted the parting troops as they rode out of town.

The king insisted Jason stay close to him on the return trip. King Beldane seemed afraid Jason might disappear if he took his eyes off him for too long, and Jason couldn't guarantee this wouldn't happen either, since he had no idea when or where God would send him next.

On the march, the king asked Jason as they rode, and in the nightly camps, men asked Jason to speak around the fires of this new god. Jason went on to speak to the men of Jesus and the sacrifice of his own life to save mankind. Otherwise, the march was uneventful until they reached the border river where the priests camped.

Crossing the river itself was uneventful as the evil shadows seemed to have fled and the magics that bound them and the vultures seemed to have been dispelled. Jason, riding upon the river bank on Chanderlon's side with the leaders, caught sight of the clerics' camp.

The pagan clerics had idols and altars set everywhere. Father Dorrian, with an entourage of priests of the various orders and religions, approached the king as they rode into the center of camp. The king and his men dismounted.

"Sire," said Father Dorrian, kneeling, "we have heard of your victory in Harvella and have set the appropriate altars to the gods to give your offerings of thanks for their aid in your battles—"

The king interrupted, "And what, Father Dorrian, gives you the impression it was the gods who gave me victories in my battles?"

Father Dorrian was taken aback. Recovering, he stood and admonished in a stern voice used to chastise beginning acolytes, "It is obvious you had the gods' help, O King, for without them, you could not have been victorious."

King Beldane replied, "Nay, Father Dorrian, I found myself fighting the gods, and I could not have won if it were not for the help of the Creator."

"The Creator!" exploded Father Dorrian, pointing to Jason. "That whelp has poisoned your mind with this Creator nonsense, for we know it was the gods who created our world. It was Xan Rukkah who made the rocks with his—"

"Wait," interrupted Jason. "Tell us Father Varigold's prophecy."

Father Dorrian shot daggers at Jason with his eyes. "That dream is only for the senior priests of our temple and none other."

Jason countered, "That prophecy concerns the whole world, does it not? The whole world has a right to know it."

"No. I will not tell it," responded Father Dorrian defiantly.

"If you do not tell it, I will, for Father Varigold told it to me just before he converted to the Creator, and you killed him for it."

"Those are serious charges, boy," warned Father Dorrian.

King Beldane reinserted his presence and spoke, "Father Dorrian, you will tell us the prophecy. I command it. And for every word you leave out, you will be lashed ten times."

Father Dorrian paled. "Yes, sire." The head priest looked around uncomfortably at the other clerics and armed men who had gathered around and began speaking. "About a year ago, Father Varigold called the elders together and told us the vision he had while walking along the river of Chanderlon. He thought he was transported to a place above the world. A bright shining winged man came to him and said, 'See what has happened and what will happen to your world.' Then he saw the gods and goddesses seated in the clouds over the world. Xan Rukkah addressed the pantheon..."

Father Dorrian continued, repeating fairly accurately the prophecy as Jason had heard it from Father Varigold. He told of how the beings that came to be known as gods were given charge of the world by the Creator, and decided to corrupt the world so much the Creator wouldn't want it. That would leave the men and creatures on it worshipers and playthings for the gods. He then told how the Creator sent a man with white hair, a hero from another place not of this world, and the hero was called the Juggernaut. The Juggernaut would dispel the darkness of sorcery and turn men's hearts back to the Creator.

"And then the creature with wings turned back to Father Varigold. 'The Juggernaut light is given strength by the light of others. Although the hero cannot be stopped, it is up to mankind to change.' The vision ends there. But, King Beldane, the vision is but a dream and a false one at that. I should know, because I spent three months on a quest for Father Varigold to verify the existence of the juggernaut, and no such man exists on our planet."

"How do you know?" inquired King Beldane.

"Because"—Father Dorrian hesitated a moment—"it was verified by

Haglar the Watcher, and that information came straight from a demon summoned by her."

The king and other priests looked surprised at Father Dorrian's admission he had dealt with a demon. The king voiced the sentiment. "I was not aware the priests of Xan Rukkah consorted with demons. However, Jason, what were you called before being brought to this world?"

Jason looked at him and replied, "I was known as Jason the Juggernaut Bristol for my martial arts abilities."

"Are you inferring his boy is the juggernaut?" asked Father Dorrian incredulously. "That is not possible, because the Juggernaut is a large, powerful, older man with white hair."

"What color was your hair?" the king asked Jason.

"It wasn't completely white, but it was getting there."

"I refuse to think this boy is the Juggernaut. He's clever, yes, but a clever liar as well." At this, the men surrounding the king murmured angrily. Father Dorrian continued, pulling out his ace card. "And you, O King, owe homage to Xan Rukkah, for I know you have used his sword and the power contained within it. Do you deny this?"

The king drew his sword, looked at it, sheathed it again, and unbuckled it. "The sword of Xan Rukkah passed down from king to king. No, I do not deny using it, but if this is what continues to make me a slave to Xan Rukkah, then I release myself and all future kings of Chanderlon by returning the sword. Here, take it, Father Dorrian."

The king thrust it sideways toward him. Father Dorrian took it automatically, then immediately began to protest, but the king cut in again. "Furthermore," he said, "you are all the same as the now outlawed cult of Axialla. Therefore I, King of Chanderlon, do hereby outlaw all religions and worship, except to the Creator."

"But," protested Father Dorrian, "we are the healers. What will the injured and sick do?"

"You heal for a price," retorted the king. "Besides the high price of an actual healing, you then continue to tax the healthy in the form of sacrifices. The real cost of your services is slavery to Xan Rukkah and the rest of the gods. If infirmities are the cost of our freedom, then so be it. If you and your elders are not out of Chanderlon by the end of the month, we will start another investigation into the mysterious death of Father Varigold. Do you understand?"

Father Dorrian nodded and said, "Yes, I understand." He turned away, but turned back again, with the sword of Xan Rukkah drawn and pointed at the king. "I understand now you were never worthy to be king. You have consorted with Axialla. Yes, we all know it, and you cannot deny it, and now you have a new false cult of the Creator. It is our priesthood that ordains kings and it is for our priesthood to remove them. You, King Beldane, are no longer worthy. Now you will feel the wrath of Xan Rukkah!"

Jason tried to step in front of the king, but the guard on the other side did so as well, knocking the smaller knight aside. The lightning bolt struck the man in the chest, burning a hole in his armor and flesh and exploding out the soles of his feet. A faint blue smoke lingered in the air above the fallen corpse, and the smell of ozone filled everyone's nostrils.

The king did not have to give the order. Father Dorrian and the priests with him who resisted were put to the sword by the angry soldiers. The rest of the clerics fled for their lives. They ran past their tents and out of sight into the forest on the other side of the clearing.

As the men returned, Jason knelt by the guard who had stepped in front of the king, his body quiet in death. It was the brave knight who had returned the flag bearer's horse to him in the midst of his combat with the juggernauts. He had been at every fireside chat about the Creator. The king knelt beside Jason in silence. Behind the group of men, a quiet voice whispered, "The Creator has power over everything, except death."

Jason was about to say this was not true, but a quiet voice inside said, "Show them."

He was not from a background of faith healers, but he did believe in the power of God to do anything he desired. Jason did not want a show to make the men think he was anything special so he stood, looked heavenward and said, "Father, in the name of your son Jesus, and for the glory of your name, may we please have this one back." Upon saying this, he turned and walked away.

He could hear the men marveling and exclaiming as they witnessed the flesh instantly knead back together and life pump back into the body. Jason paused and watched from a distance as the man sat up and asked what happened. The men and the king cheered and spontaneously praised God.

That evening, as soldiers buried the dead priests, Jason buried many of the living in the water of the river. Men announced their acceptance of Jesus as Lord and a desire to follow him, and Jason would immerse them in that name. When they arose from the water, they immediately told something they knew about Jesus.

He didn't understand it but knew that God's Spirit was teaching them. Over two hundred men were baptized that night and more the following day, though now others did the baptizing.

Chanderlon, watch out, thought Jason to himself. The sword of Xan Rukkah was buried with Father Dorrian in an unmarked grave in a secret place.

When the men were ready to move out, King Beldane ordered them to assemble by the river one more time. The king then asked Jason to bury him in baptism, and as they waded into the river, he addressed the assembly. "I dedicated my life and my kingdom to the service of the Creator at the Battle of the Juggernauts. We did not know it at the time, but Jason is a miniature Juggernaut. I cannot bestow a higher title than what the Creator has already given him. Even the prophecy of Father Varigold described Jason as an irresistible force; we ourselves experienced this to be true. Jason is the Juggernaut."

From the men rose a rousing cheer. When the sound died down, the king continued, "Now it is my time to be immersed because that is when Jesus seals us as his own, and we are born into his kingdom. In title, I am still your king, but in spirit, I am your brother. I now accept Jesus as my king and savior with all my heart. Jason, my older brother, will you now immerse me?" Jason then baptized the king who, without even drying off, left the river, mounted his horse and led the Lord's army back to Chanderlon.

CHAPTER 44

The Portal Visitors

The news of the appearance of Jason and the victory over the Harvellian army, as well as the juggernauts, preceded them to Chanderlon. A hero's welcome awaited them. Upon first receiving the news of Jason's death in the spring, much of Chanderlon had gone into mourning. Yet many simply refused to believe he was dead and felt vindicated at the news of the boy not only surviving, but destroying the juggernauts of Harvella.

As Jason rode beside the king, the crowd went wild at the sight of them, throwing hats and chanting, "Long live the king and Jason the Juggernaut." Women threw flowers before them and on them as opportunity afforded.

As they approached the castle ramparts, all flags and pennants were hoisted at full height, and suddenly, streamers rolled out of the windows and down the walls with the runes King Beldane and Sir Jason written on them. The palace guard welcomed them with full ceremony, and afterward, the King and Jason were mobbed by the royal family.

Somehow, Nelda and Amanie were with them too. Princess Kuari surprised Jason by giving him a kiss that was a little less than chaste. When the commotion died down, Gunther formally welcomed Jason back and then, informally, with a new martial arts throw he had just "invented," which looked suspiciously like a scissors throw. Jason went along with it, laughing.

They were then treated to a celebration meal featuring pizza, as well as a new flavor Princess Merinda took the initiative to invent she called dessert pizza, with cinnamon and apples.

He was given a seat of honor at dinner to the right of the king, which the king proclaimed to be Jason's permanent seat. After dinner, both princesses escorted him to his room and had him close his eyes as they opened the door. His room had a surprising new makeover with plush red carpet, a matching set of fine hardwood dresser, wardrobe, table, chair, and bed. Ornate scenic tapestries adorned the walls. The bed had high posts with draping curtains.

He was given a new balcony door with a window framed in stained glass and flowers everywhere. Even his katana and two ninja blades, which

Trombul had taken and discarded, were given a place of honor in their own stands atop the wardrobe.

Princess Merinda and Kuari were beside themselves to see his expression when he opened the door. He pretended to pass out several times and then exuberantly hugged them. They were very pleased he liked their surprise and when they left, both went skipping down the hallway holding hands.

Finally alone, he prepared for bed and even said his prayers, but found that he could not sleep. He had to do something about the evil idol in the depths of the castle, so he found his cords for opening the trap door hidden behind a tapestry. If anyone had discovered or used them, Jason could not tell, but he checked his upper room now and found everything the way he had left it, including the hidden stash of gems and coins he had taken from the giant falcon's nest.

Taking a lamp, he climbed down the air chute and noted his rope still there. He went back to the room with the temple. He heard the sound of hammer on stone and a light shown down the hall from the room. He set down his lamp and crept quietly to the hidden alcove. A strange-looking slime seemed to cover the passage walls where he had destroyed the eye of Axialla.

There in the chamber, in the light of a lamp, was the king. Princess Kuari was with him, and together, they were crushing the idol of Axialla with sledge hammers. He crept back, quietly smiling. The light of the Creator was indeed filling the darkness of this world, perhaps with a vitality missing in his own world. Maybe the Creator was training him to bring the light back to his home world as well.

He returned to his room and, though the royal sheets were tempting, instead slept in his loft on the crude hewn planks of the bench with his old bedroll. He did not feel in danger, he just wanted to remind himself he was still only a little boy in a strange world and needed a big God beside him.

The celebrating in Chanderlon lasted another two days, and Jason deemed it wise not to leave the castle during that time. Instead, he began building a compound bow. He was able to get a powerful bow from the armory and wheels and pulleys from the castle craftsmen to modify his new creation. With some trial and error, he produced a fair facsimile of a compound bow. Although a little hard for him to pull, it worked sufficiently.

His tests with it in the courtyard drew considerable interest from the guards on duty and a castle weaponsmith asked if he could study it. It was almost as powerful as a crossbow, yet it could be fired with the ease and speed of a long bow. Jason hoped the weaponsmith could do a better job than he, for he felt like the bow would tear itself apart after a few shots. He therefore gave the smith the bow, requesting he give him a better-made one.

On the third day, Gunther returned to Jason from town, shaking his head.

"What is the matter, Gunther?"

"Oh, nothing is wrong. We just had a church service in town at an inn this morning and had to take it out into the streets."

"Why?"

"Because," Gunther said, beaming, "we had over two thousand people there. I think the whole town came."

"What did you do? How did you handle it?"

"Well, I stood on a wagon and told the story of Jesus and the town criers stood on elevations and repeated segments of what I said. Jason, so many people wanted to be buried with Jesus. That is what they are all doing now at the river."

"That is wonderful!" he exclaimed.

"And that is not all. Some of the rich merchants are buying the temples of the outlawed religions and giving them to the church. Jason, how will we provide speakers and leaders for all these places?"

"Don't worry, Gunther, the Creator will provide."

"But Jason, how will we control what is taught, make sure it is right and not influenced by the meddling of the pantheon or demons?"

"Gunther, that is not our responsibility. That is mankind's responsibility. All we can do is encourage truth seeking, because the Lord promises that those who truly seek him will find him, even if the Lord must teach them himself. Definitely, there will be false teachers who will teach their own way of following the Creator. Even if it is not what the Creator desires, the Creator knows his own and we cannot see the heart the way he does. So even if false teachers and their congregations claim to follow the Creator, treat them as brothers and try to correct them gently, so the Creator is honored in everything we do."

"I wish I knew as much as you do, Jason. It would be so much easier."

"It is easy!" he exclaimed. "Just remember to seek the truth and teach others to do the same. Jesus says he is the way, the truth, and the life. So in searching for the truth, all roads lead to him."

"It would be so much easier if we had the Bible you talk about."

"Yes, it would. But the Creator has not seen fit to give into this world yet. I could try to write one, but He has not laid it upon my heart to do so. Perhaps one of you will write, as the Creator leads. Maybe it will be the same as the one from my world or perhaps it will be different; I do not know."

The next day, Princess Merinda and Kuari took Jason riding. First, they rode to the dock and were surprised to see Captain Seldwick's ship back in port. They greeted the crew but the captain was about on business, so the three continued a brisk ride along the banks of the river. They stopped at a park-like corner on the river and ate a basket lunch.

Both princesses were abuzz with the changes they had seen in their dad and how much happier he seemed. He even went with them to hear Gunther speak one Sunday. They were full of hope for better days ahead.

When they returned to the castle, he was met by Gunther and the weaponsmith. The weaponsmith presented him with a new compound bow of sturdier build. Jason tried it out. It worked perfectly and he praised the weaponsmith, asking what he owed. The master craftsman waved it off and asked permission to use this design for making others, which Jason gladly gave.

He now turned his attention to Gunther, who was a little impatient to tell his news. He was just promoted to teaching the hand-to-hand combat segment of training for the lord's sons. Jason was happy for his friend and to celebrate they both immediately went back to his room to train some more. Gunther was eager to learn how to disarm a weapon so he could pass it on to his new students.

One morning, a few days later, while riding with both princesses on the coast, west of Chanderlon, they saw a strange- looking ship. It was all dark wood with large, black lateen sails similar to an Arabian dhow, though several times larger than pictures Jason had seen of such vessels. They watched it sail in and anchor off about a mile from shore. The ship's crew furled the triangular sails, then all activity ceased.

Although it was a little far out, Jason expected a small row boat or something to ferry the passengers in, but none came.

He queried the princesses, but they had never seen anything like it. Although a mystery, it was totally forgotten by the time they returned to the castle. The knights were teaching some of their squires to joust. It seems the whole castle was there for the entertainment, and entertaining it was.

The young men clumsily tried to control their horses just using their legs while holding onto a heavy lance and shield. The lances had blunted tips wrapped in rags, a fortunate fact for the bystanders as well. The horses behaved poorly, and many squires were dumped. They were not charging each other, but a wooden dummy with a shield in one hand and a sandbag on a rope in the other. If the shield was hit, the dummy was constructed to pivot and hit the rider as he went by. This also taught the squire to use his shield. Many squires were knocked off by the dummy, to the merriment of all. None were really hurt, but all were much bruised, especially some egos.

Jason spent the afternoon in the garden with the children. The boys imitated the knights and squires, pretending to joust using brooms for horses and mops for lances. When it came time for fighting with wooden swords he joined in and found that besides being great fun, it was fair training.

That evening, Queen Overa was unusually talkative and caught the king up on events during his departure. She ran the government in his absence and was quite proud of how well she did. King Beldane did his best to pay attention, but his boredom showed through.

Even at that, Princess Merinda and Princess Kuari commented to Jason how much their father had changed since accepting Jesus, but their mother was still dubious. He considered the way the king behaved before and wondered if his cruelty had not been directed at Queen Overa. She was still beautiful and gracious, but seemed to hide a grievance and smiled infrequently.

That evening, he and Gunther worked new throws and explored how easily Gunther's new scissors throw could be countered, as well as the poor strategic position a failed throw would leave a person in, namely, lying on the floor. Gunther still liked his throw, but had to admit there were times it shouldn't be used.

After Gunther left, Jason practiced his Iaijutsu using his katana, then readied himself for bed. He had been sleeping in his plush royal bed for a week now and enjoyed it. After saying his nightly prayers, he walked onto the balcony hoping to see stars. As far as he knew, his home world could be circling around one of them. But this night the sky was dark and gusts of wind tore at him. Even darker clouds were rolling in from the north. A storm was approaching. In the distance sounded the roll of thunder.

Just before drifting off to sleep the rain hit, blowing against the stained glass window on his balcony door. He always liked the sound of rain, especially when he was warm and dry in a soft, warm bed. He slept deeply. So deeply, in fact, that with the noise of the storm he almost missed it—the soft jingle of chimes.

He awoke thinking he heard chimes but couldn't hear anything now. He got up and looked at them closely. They were swinging, perhaps a draft from the storm?

Surely, the princess would ring again if she needed help. Or perhaps she couldn't. On that thought, Jason sprang into action. Even if she didn't need him, she would forgive his intrusion. Quickly, he threw on his coat and belted his katana. He also swung his quiver over his shoulder and grabbed his new compound bow. First, he tried opening her bedroom door, but it was locked. Strangely, there was no guard in the hallway.

Returning to his room, he stepped onto the balcony and was glad he took the time to put on his coat, for the wind and rain brought an instant chill. At that moment, he questioned the wisdom of jumping to the other stone balcony as he could easily slip in this weather in the dark. Or was that the cautionary thinking of an old man? The young Jason would never hesitate.

He threw his bow across and then jumped off the rail. He caught the edge of the other balcony, scraping his knee on the wall, then climbed up.

There was a window in Princess Merinda's balcony door as well, and through it a dim gray light shown. He was surprised to see the light emanating not from a lamp but from a swirling misty circle that floated in her room vertically like a mirror, the light of sorcery.

Princess Merinda was barely visible, standing on her bed in her nightgown with a sword in each hand keeping three men at bay. While he watched, a fourth man stepped into the room out of the circle of light. The scimitar wielding men were large and muscular, wearing sailors' loose, light clothing and turbans. They moved like men experienced in battle and laughed at the game the girl offered.

Jason tried the door, but it was locked. This is where Jason bemoaned being a small boy, for normally such a door would not have slowed him down. He took the alternative of readying his bow and aimed at one of the sailors' image through the window. Normally he would have smashed the glass first, but the power of his new compound bow would go through it easily.

There was one man facing his direction, making a good target. The arrow easily shattered the window as the shot found its mark in the sailor's throat. Three remaining men turned to the window as his first victim fell. Seeing the men distracted, Princess Merinda leaped off the bed to deliver a wicked slash to a man's sword arm and her second blade bit into his neck. She leaped back before the man knew what happened.

The other two men quickly turned back to Princess Merinda and drove her to the wall as their companion fell. Jason shot another through the temple. He dropped without a sound. Upon seeing all his comrades down, the last man desperately turned to run toward the shining portal, but Princess Merinda was faster and cut him down before he could reach it.

Jason let himself in by reaching through the broken window and unlatching the door.

"What took you so long?" asked Princess Merinda breathlessly.

"I was sleeping and with the noise of the storm, I nearly missed your call," said Jason apologetically.

Sounds of battle were coming from the next room, so Jason quickly opened the door to the hallway, with Princess Merinda looking over his shoulder. The king called for guards as he battled two turbaned men while Princess Kuari huddled in a corner behind him.

Jason fired, striking one of the attackers through the ribs while Princess Merinda rushed into the fray. Seeing the odds suddenly against him, the last attacker ran into the other room while the king finished off the injured man.

Two guards burst into the room, and the king commanded, "To the other room, help the Queen!" All rushed into the other room in time to see the glowing portal in that room fading, with no sign of the attackers or the queen.

"I am sorry, my lord. We are too late. They have taken her!" one guard lamented.

Two more guards ran in and one announced, "Sire, there have been attacks all over the castle, and the treasury has been robbed." Jason was already running to the other portal when he heard the king cry out, "I don't care about the treasury! Someone rescue the queen!"

The portal was still there but fading fast. There was no time for any other course of action. Jason gave a war cry and leaped in. The king and Princess Merinda ran into the room upon hearing Jason's cry, but all they saw was the shimmering circle shrink and fade out.

"Father," Princess Merinda said woefully, "there goes our rescue team. One little boy to face an unknown foe."

"Nay," said the king. "You, of all people, should know better. Your champion is no mere little boy. He is a miniature juggernaut, and God help those who stand in his way."

CHAPTER 45

Dark Magic

Jason jumped through the portal, bow in hand, ready to immediately fight any who stood in his way. He landed in a place so unexpected, however, that he fell and rolled, almost losing his bow. He immediately met with a spray of cold salt water, and the heaving wooden deck of a ship in a storm.

In the darkness, water washed across the deck of the black Arabian dhow he had seen earlier that day. Losing his balance, he rolled again to a kneeling position as another wave washed across the deck, totally drenching him and threatening to wash him overboard. The sudden noise of wind and waves deafened him.

Almost no men were on deck except the helmsman on an elevated steering station at the back, and five men to the front fighting a small sail, which had broken its rope stay. The two main sails were furled, but a small lateen sail was set at the stern to drive the boat in the storm. The furled sail above his head needed to be lashed down as it whipped back and forth, a line along its length hanging loose, threatening to snag and throw anyone on that section of the deck into the ocean.

The helmsman, fighting two huge rudders using ropes and pulleys to aid him, yelled above the storm, "Get below deck, for all the good it will do you."

He considered his options. He expected a fight, but it appeared there was no one to fight. Perhaps all were below deck. Looking ahead of them in the waves, Jason could see the reason for the helmsman's despairing remark, for not far ahead, the white spray and foam indicated a rock just beneath the surface; the men were trying to fix the bow sail so they could steer around it.

In just moments, the ship was in danger of sinking; and if the queen were aboard, she was in more danger from that than anything else. He decided to help and looped his bow over his shoulder, so he wouldn't lose it.

Just then, one of the crew washed overboard. Jason quickly cut the hanging line on the spar above him and tied a knot so he could throw it to the man struggling in the water before the boat swept by. Knowing there wasn't time to pull the man in, he threw the rope, which the distraught sailor caught, and left the man to fend for himself as he raced up the bucking and heaving deck toward the bow.

The four men had wrestled the lower spar of the swinging sail and had pulled it in close but needed someone to tie it off. Jason saw the loose rope being washed around on deck, grabbed it, and made a slip knot, looping it over the outside end of the spar.

The crewmen then hurried to secure the rope, tightening it through a windlass. The sail pulled the bow to the side, turning the ship away from the rocks. He could now see rocks on both sides, and the ship just squeezed through the gap. He ran back to try to pull the man in the water back on board while wondering if this might be a good time to take over the ship, using the storm to his advantage. Another sailor ran to help him pull the man aboard.

No, now is not the time, he thought. The men were blown and washed about less than he.

Two sailors opened a hatch to below deck and shoved Jason in, jumping in behind him, the hatch slamming with a loud booming noise. The interior, dimly lit by swinging oil lamps, revealed the worried faces of the ship's general crew sitting around a table. The only happy faces were the two crewmen who followed Jason.

"Young boy, thank you for saving my life," said the nearly drowned man.

"Saving your life," interjected the second sailor. "He saved all our lives. That young lad ran up the deck, being washed from side to side and without a safety line, to catch fast the loose spar on the foresail, so we could steer past the rocks. And just in the nick of time too, I might add."

With that, one of the dour crew cheered and welcomed him to the table. Someone passed him a hot toddy made mostly of ale. Jason took a sip and held it down, despite the awful taste. The sailor who shared his spot noted this and slapped him on the back, calling him a smart boy. Three remaining sailors out in the storm entered soaking wet and attempted to dry off. Joining their fellows, they too expressed their gratitude for Jason's help.

A man wearing a greasy apron (obviously the ship's cook) entered the room and asked for volunteers to help organize the new stores. Several immediately volunteered, for any crew knows not to get the cook mad. Jason asked one of the sailors about it.

"The new stores are from the raid the soldiers did on the castle, at the orders of Vizier Keldokar, who used magic and the aid of a demon to pull it off. They got some treasure and some women as well, but I assumed you knew all this—what is your name, lad, and how did you come to be here?"

The crew grew quiet to hear his response.

"I am Jason, and I came to rescue the stolen women by jumping through the portal. If I defeat the wizard and his troops, would you boys mind sailing the ship back to Chanderlon?"

At that, the crew laughed heartily, and as the laughter died, one jovially said, "If you could defeat the wizard and his troops, we would have no choice but to go where you captained, but why should we believe a little boy like you would have that capability?"

"Look at yourselves already. Who was it in the last fifteen minutes who saved one of the crew from drowning and kept your ship from going down? If you have any more doubts, send one of your crew to the women and announce that a young boy named Jason is here and watch their reaction."

The sailor speaking to him stood. "You've got my curiosity piqued. I will go see myself." With that, he opened the door to the forward hold and left. He returned a few minutes later with an odd expression on his face. One of the sailors asked, "Well, what is it, Codd?"

Codd spoke with a little awe in his voice. "Well, when I said a young boy named Jason is here, they paused and then broke into so much wild cheering the soldiers had to push them back. The women then advised the soldiers to surrender if they wanted to live, because Jason the Juggernaut was going to get them. Boy, are you Jason the Juggernaut?"

"Of course." He smiled. "And since you, Codd, seem to be the bravest of sailors to face an angry group of women, would you escort me to see the Queen? I must verify she is here, first."

Codd nodded. "She has her own guarded quarters. Follow me."

Jason followed Codd to another hold where tarps, planks, ropes and barrels of tar and grease were stored for maintenance of the ship, then up a ladder through a trap door. This came to a hallway which ended in two doors; one door in the middle opened to the deck. A guard stood at each door.

Codd led the boy to the door on the left and explained to the guard, "The boy is here to attend the queen."

The guard looked at Jason, smiled, and muttered as he opened the door, "A boy with his toys could easily cheer her, and she could send him away if she doesn't want him...A little boy is here to see you, Your Highness."

Queen Overa, pacing the floor, turned to the guard angrily and spat, "I told you I was not to be disturbed by anyone, not even the Vizier."

Jason stepped in.

"Oh, Jason!"

The guard shut the door behind him.

"Jason, what are you doing here?"

"I jumped through a portal to rescue you."

"I am sorry you got involved, Jason." The queen looked around and sighed. "You see...I am running away."

Jason stood dumbstruck and confused.

Queen Overa continued, "I have made a deal with the demon Donjoni and his minions to release me, and although it cost all the money I have, it is now done, though not in the way I would have preferred. Now if you will excuse me, I have some business to attend to. Donjoni. Donjoni, where are you? I demand to see you at once!" Overa stood and repeated her call, stamping her foot to emphasize her urgency.

An oil lamp went out, and blue tinged smoke shot out the chimney, forming a miniature storm cloud mimicking the real storm that rocked the ship outside. The smoke became black and grew, coalescing into a hideous form; a black demon with orange eyes that blazed like molten metal appeared. Its over seven-foot stature forced it to duck in the low-ceilinged cabin. The room filled with an evil, dark aura. Donjoni hunched up against the ceiling, then squat walked over to the couch and lounged upon it as if he owned the place. "So, Overa, I perceive you are not happy with something?"

"That is right. I am not!" Overa said angrily. "I made a deal for only me to be taken away and paid well for it. Now, why have you taken the women and girls as well? The Vizier plans to make them into slaves for harems. Furthermore, they took the treasury of the kingdom."

"Ahh," Donjoni hissed. "I went to great effort to find someone to rescue you. I sent my minions far and wide to talk to heroes of all countries. Only one would do it but for a much higher price. That was the terms Vizier Keldokar demanded to make it worth his while to take you to safety. What do you care about a kingdom no longer yours? What do you care of women who turned a blind eye to your captivity? Now they are taken captive themselves. I would think that fair justice, fair revenge."

"I did not want revenge, just escape. Send them back."

"I cannot go back on my deal with Vizier Keldokar. You have chosen this path, and it chooses you. Freedom does not come without its price."

"Then I want to make a new deal with you, one that supersedes all previous agreements. What would it cost me?"

"Don't do it, Overa," interrupted Jason. "I will get them back."

The demon looked surprised. "The little boy speaks. You must be the Jason whom Akari spoke of. You should have accepted the offer to do this service for Akari. You could have saved Overa all this heartache, as well as the other women. And now back to you, Overa. I will send the women back at the cost of the thing dearest to you."

"I have nothing anymore, so demon, nothing is dear anymore. I accept your price."

Jason turned to interject as the demon said, "It is done. It has been a pleasure doing business with you, Overa." With that, the demon vanished in a clap of thunder.

Overa looked at Jason and said, "Oh Jason, I am sorry not to include you so you could go home too."

"It's okay," he said slowly, "That demon could not take me anywhere against my wishes, and I would not have let him."

Jason said nothing more as he walked to the couch and plopped down, while Overa stood in a self-sacrificing pose. He waited, as he knew the realization would soon sink in. In about a minute, she came over and sat beside him.

"Oh Jason, what have I done?" Overa cried. He just reached over and gave her a comforting hand. "What is it the demon took from me?" she wondered. "My freedom?"

"No," replied Jason, "because you were never really free to begin with."

"I will ask you what you mean later, but if not that, was it my soul?"

"I think not, for whether you realize it or not, there are things dearer to you than your own soul. Things only a mother or father could understand."

"Merinda and Kuari," she cried, squeezing Jason's leg and nearly crushing it.

"Merinda cannot be touched by the demon, for she belongs to the Creator now and is protected."

"Kuari?"

"I don't know—"

Suddenly, a thunderous knock sounded on the door.

"Jason, I think I am about to lose my freedom anyway."

"Not today, Overa."

"Why not?"

"Because the Creator and I are here for you now," Jason said as he hid behind the couch.

The door slammed open and in strode the imposing figure of Vizier Keldokar with two guards behind him. Vizier Keldokar stood dressed all in black with a broad belt and black turban around his head. "All the women have vanished." Accusingly, he pointed a finger at Overa, "What have you done?"

"I have sent them home," said Overa defiantly.

"Then you shall take their place. Turning to the guards, he said, "Strip her and we shall see if I will take her for myself, or send her to the slave market."

"No one touches her. Furthermore, drop your weapons," Jason rose menacingly from behind the couch with his compound bow at full draw.

"A little boy? Kill him," ordered the Vizier. The two guards charged while Jason shot the closest in the mouth, knocking him backward. The other guard jumped onto the couch with his foot hitting the top, pushing the couch back and over. Jason would have gotten caught by the couch against the wall if he hadn't leaped straight up, dropping the bow and landing on the back of the couch while at the same time trapping the man's swinging sword hand. Then he stepped inside and twisted the man's hand as he turned, trying to force the man to drop his sword. Although that did not work, the strike to the groin along the way did, and the result was still a dropped sword as the man reacted to protect himself.

The Vizier was not idle during this time, having begun an incantation. The queen had moved to the back of the room, wielding a silver candlestick as a club. The balance of the guard and Jason were less than perfect, considering the pitching and rolling of the boat, and they both fell. Jason recovered quicker, knowing he did not want to start a grappling match with someone so much bigger.

The Vizier cast his spell, and suddenly, Jason's arms felt like lead, like something was countering his every move. The guard viciously applied a choke-hold on Jason as Overa applied the other end of her candlestick to the back of the guard's head. He grunted and pitched over, unconscious.

Jason had wondered if he was immune to the forces of magic since he abstained from using it, but apparently not. Instead of trying to fight the forces, he willed his body to relax, to go with the flow rather than resist. Meanwhile, Vizier Keldokar began another spell. Overa rushed him with her candlestick, forcing him to break off and flee.

By now, Jason managed some form of movement, visualizing himself as a liquid and oozing the direction he wanted to go with virtually no effort. Overa came to him, concerned. Jason managed to smile and stand weakly but felt himself regaining control by the second. "If the magic affects even you, what chance do we have?" asked Overa.

"Overa, it seems the odds have been against me ever since I arrived here. If it wasn't for the Creator, I should have died many times. We will do our part and let the Creator do his."

About that time, they could hear men coming up to the trap door in the hallway. Jason, still sluggish, weaved drunkenly into the hallway. A guard had one-third of his body up from the hold.

Jason pulled his long dagger, slunk behind, and laid the edge of the blade along the man's neck and murmured, "I can kill each of you before you can make it up, and my God can easily sweep you into the cold sea with this storm if you try to come from the deck outside, so you and your men might as well wait to see who is the victor in this contest between your leader and I. Would you want to follow a man who can be beaten by a little boy?"

The guard nodded his understanding and carefully retreated down the ladder and shut the trap door. Jason had Overa stand on it, with orders to knock anyone on the head who dared to force it open. Just as a precaution, he barred the outside door to the deck. After a minute with no one else trying to enter, he tried the door to the Vizier's cabin.

It was locked. Jason had seen the chintzy lock on the other door, and with his dagger, he quickly lifted the bar and stepped inside. The swinging shadows gave the Vizier a weird, deranged look. The Vizier looked at him in shock. "How did you get past the guards so quickly?"

Jason pulled his bow full draw. "I am going to give you one chance to surrender."

"Surrender? Hah. I have made myself immune to your weapons. You will die slowly and painfully to my spells." The Vizier laughed.

"Wrong answer." Jason shut the door with one foot and shot one of the lamps and knocked the other two out with the tip of his bow, putting them in complete darkness in a matter of seconds. The Vizier laughed and made a light appear in his hand.

Jason drew and swung at it with his katana. The razor- sharp sword hit the mage's hand but did not cut him. The blow, however, did send the little ball of light flying and flickering out as the mage's hand hit the wall from the force of the blow. In the dark again, the Vizier began yet another spell.

Next, Jason cut into the mage's side, but when the blade hit the man's flesh, it was like hitting chain mail. Evidently, he was immune to swords as well. Jason sheathed his sword as the Vizier struck a vicious backhand to his face. It was weak for a man, but against a little boy, it sent him flying.

The mage followed Jason and sat on him, trying to choke him. Jason gripped one of the evil man's hands and used his other hand to push into the throat with his fingertips, pushing the wizard away. Then going against the finger joints of the hand he held, he hurled the sorcerer off him while the man's fingers made a popping noise at the violent motion.

"You little wretch!" he screamed. "You broke my fingers!"

"You must have forgotten to make yourself immune to me, Vizier," he retorted.

He then did a side kick to the warlock's shin and another punch to the face. The Vizier made it to the door and fumbled with his broken fingers at the latch. He opened the door and stepped out only to meet a smash in the face by Overa's candlestick. His immunity to weapons must have covered candlesticks too, because he brushed past her even though she struck him repeatedly. The Vizier struggled to unbar the door to the deck when Jason leaped into the hallway. "You don't want to go out there," Jason warned.

"Why not, you little imp?" he snapped impatiently.

"Because,"—Jason paused ominously—"my God is waiting for you out there!"

"Bah." The Vizier spat as he ran out on deck.

"Guards, guards, attend me!" the Vizier screamed. A guard pushed open an outside hatch on deck, looked out, and then shut it again quickly. Jason looked past the wizard to see the huge wave the guard saw, looming on the dark horizon behind the wizard.

He slammed and barred the door shut. "Hold onto that door handle, quick!" he cried to Overa. She grabbed it just as the wave hit the ship, heaved, and rolled the ship upside down all the way over to upright again. Regaining his feet after a few moments, Jason checked on Overa and saw she was okay. Opening the door, he went outside to check on the helmsman.

The helmsman, unconscious, had lashed himself to the boat but was tangled in the broken aft sail. Jason ran and cut the lines and started to drag the man down to the cabins. He heard a faint cry and saw the wizard struggling in the water.

He paused in shock when a large, tentacled creature broke the surface of the water near the vile little man, now frozen in horror as he saw the nightmare creature as well. It looked similar to a squid but half again larger than the ship. Yet it was wrong for a squid, because there seemed to be a hundred gray and brown tentacles, each ending in a clawed hand.

Just as the mouth cleared the water, he was surprised to see a gigantic fanged maw spewing water as it gave a huge roar, sounding like a hundred waterfalls at once. Cruel and comparatively beady eyes perched above the mouth and searched the water for its prey.

The Vizier gave another cry of terror and splashed noisily towards the ship. He made no more than five strokes when a clammy clawed hand suddenly grabbed him and pulled him toward the large gaping maw. The warlock struggled mightily as he was forced into the jaws, which snapped down with such force as to crush the mage in one blow. The maw opened again to gulp the now still form down.

The creature sank and disappeared beneath the waves. By now, two of the ship's crew had ventured out of the cabin and helped Jason pull the unconscious helmsman inside as quickly as they could. If such a large monster attacked the ship in this storm, they would not have a chance.

"What was that thing?" asked Jason of one of the men.

The man shook his head. "There are monsters that swim in the eddies of magic that defy all recognition. You said your god was out there waiting...

perhaps that is what your god looks like."

The other sailor was shaking. "Pray to your god that he doesn't eat us."

Jason replied, "That Leviathan is not my God, but I will pray for our deliverance."

He prayed for protection in their presence, and they waited.

The pounding ocean waves made it impossible to tell if the creature was attacking or if it was gone. After a while, it did not seem to make any difference if it was the monstrous storm or the terror of the deep tossing them about, but the ship remained undamaged.

After a while, as if having been appeased by a sacrifice, the sea calmed, and everyone rested. Jason found that though his former self was conditioned to the sea, his younger self was not and sea sickness set in severely, so much he wished to jump overboard to relieve the symptoms.

He went up top to steer, just to be in the fresh air. Although he had never sailed a ship of this size before, he had once converted his fishing boat to auxiliary sail and was familiar with the principles. The smallest sailboat to the largest sailing ship share the same principles. He particularly liked the lateen sailing rig and had used it once on an ice boat he had made.

When morning light came, land appeared in sight ahead. The helmsman, Skeg, and the navigator came on deck and took soundings to determine their location. The rest of the crew repaired the fore and aft sails while raising the first mainsail. The helmsman and navigator decided to maintain Jason's course to get a closer look at the land.

Jason went below deck to talk to Overa in her cabin.

"Where are you going to go now?" asked Jason.

"I must return to Chanderlon and see if Kuari is okay."

"And if she isn't?"

"Then I will call on the demon and see if he will trade me for her," Overa replied despondently.

"You know he won't."

"No, I don't know that. Why wouldn't he?"

"Because he delights in making people feel miserable."

"But what else can I do, Jason? I got her into this mess and it is up to me to get her out."

"Give your problems to Jesus the Creator," he responded as a matter-of-fact.

"Come on, Jason, can the Creator really straighten out a mess this big?"

"Of course he can. He will do it because he loves both you and Kuari."

"Jason, I have heard and seen how the Creator helped you and how both my husband and Merinda now follow him as well, but I am sorry, I cannot believe that a god or any spiritual creature can really care about us.

We are just too far gone."

"You may be right, but how can a god ever show he cares? Does he do it by giving you everything you ask for? As a queen, you can see how ultimately this is not good. In contrast, if he only gave us what we need, that would seem out of a sense of duty or obligation."

The queen answered, "He shows it by doing what I am about to do. I am going to give my life for my child, if need be."

"Right on!" answered Jason.

"What?"

"Right on. I mean that you are very right. That is exactly what my God did for us."

"You mean he gave his life for us?"

"Yes," Jason replied and continued to tell her about Jesus.

When he was through, she sat and mused while he went back to the sorcerer's cabin to try to find a place to lie down, on the verge of exhaustion. He found a bed and had just rested his head on the pillow.

At that moment, there was some excitement on deck and a sailor knocked on the door. "The helmsman wants you to come see this." He and Queen Overa went up on deck and looked to where the helmsman was pointing. Jason could see a small town on the coast with a castle in the distance and a large mountain behind and to the left of it.

"Why, it's Chanderlon!" Queen Overa exclaimed.

"Aye," concurred the navigator. "The boy was right on course through the whole night."

Jason bewilderingly shook his head. "I had no idea where I was going. I was so sea sick, I was just steering to keep the waves from rocking the boat so much."

"Where to, Captain?" Skeg said, looking at Jason with a big smile. It may have been a good-natured joke, but he wasn't going to let it pass.

He smiled back. "Take her right up the river, helmsman, to Chanderlon and a three-day shore leave for everyone!"

CHAPTER 46

A Leap into the Abyss

Shortly after the raid, Princess Merinda was holding her tearful sister as the men conferred around the planning table in the great hall. The king was too agitated to sit on the throne set up for him.

"Send out the knights," bellowed the king.

"But, sire, we have no way of telling where the kidnappers and thieves went!" exclaimed Sir Tadden.

"I don't care. Send them out to see what they can find."

"We should wait until daylight. In this storm, they will find nothing. We cannot even keep a lamp lit in this wind and rain."

"Then think, man, think. Did anyone see or report anything strange earlier today?"

"Why no, sire. Everything was as usual before the storm," reported the vexed knight.

The king paused in frustration when a small voice interrupted, "Father, I did. Well, at least Jason pointed out to Merinda and me a strange thing."

"Come here, child," said King Beldane, more gently. "Come beside me and tell everyone what you saw."

Princess Kuari stood beside him, wiping the tears from her face. "We rode our horses to the beach and saw a black ship sail in and anchor offshore. Jason was bothered it did not send anyone to shore. It just furled its sails and then all was still, with no more activity on deck."

One of the guards spoke up. "Yes, the attackers were dressed as foreigners, and a few of them wore no shoes."

"No shoes. What does that mean?" asked the perplexed monarch.

"It means, sire," interjected Sir Tadden, "that they were sailors. Leather shoes tend to fall apart at sea, so most sailors don't bother with them."

"Then get a boat and send a troop to check on them," commanded King Beldane.

"But," Sir Tadden started to protest, when suddenly a small explosion of white smoke puffed on the table before them all, momentarily blinding them. As the smoke rose, gasps could be heard throughout the room, both from on and off the table. Standing before them on the table were the missing women.

The king too jumped on the table. "Overa, Overa, where are you?"

As he was looking through the crowd of joyous women, two screams pierced the room. One was Princess Merinda, pointing at Kuari, who now screamed. Inky black smoke swirled around his daughter and in an instant hid her from sight.

One of his guards charged into the smoke, which now looked like a twirling tornado of filth, in an attempt to rescue the princess. The guard disappeared, then reappeared, flying across the room with great force. He landed painfully on a stack of benches used at meal time.

Everyone stood frozen with horror as Kuari's scream faded, as if coming from a deep hole. The black swirling smoke seemed to be sucked into a hole in the floor and as it disappeared, so did the last sounds of Princess Kuari.

"Quick!" shouted the king. "Search the whole castle from top to bottom. Find my daughter!"

Although guards and knights streamed from the room to organize a search party, few had hopes they would ever see the young princess alive again.

Around noon, a strange black ship sailed up the river to the docks of Chanderlon. The Monarch of Chanderlon was ready to receive the villainous ship with all the soldiers and knights remaining from the war. He was angry and ready to destroy everyone aboard when his wife, in a very unqueenly-like fashion, jumped off the ship's deck before it even reached the dock and ran to him.

"Tell me, Beldane, how is Kuari?" she asked breathlessly.

Seeing the concern of the woman he loved, he broke his stern countenance. "I... I don't know. She disappeared before our eyes in a cloud of black smoke. We searched the whole castle, but she is nowhere to be found. We hoped this might be another sorcerer's trick and that she was with you."

Jason joined them. "We have an idea where Princess Kuari is, but let's not talk of it here."

The king nodded and quickly led the entourage back to the castle. There, the royal family held a meeting with Jason, alone, in their chambers. Princess Merinda sat beside Jason on the couch as the king and queen paced.

The king spoke first, "Jason, it seems many evils have befallen us lately, and we have become dependent on the Creator and you for aid. We still live in a world of magic, despite ridding ourselves of priests and wizards. Without you, we are helpless."

Jason replied, "You were at the battle of the juggernauts, O King, and you know it is the Creator and not me who gives success. You have access to the Creator as I do, except for one thing. The poor relationship with your wife hinders the effectiveness of your prayers."

The king looked at Jason and then the queen severely, as though ready to argue, but instead, his countenance softened, "You are right, Jason."

King Beldane turned to Queen Overa and said, with emotion, "I am surprised to see you return of your own free will. I have never been the husband of your heart and have kept you locked up in fear of losing you. I know you will not believe this, but I have always loved you deeply, although now I see that it was a selfish love. I had hoped that over time you would see and somehow deem me worthy of your love, but now I see I was wrong.

"Overa, I now release you from me. You may live where and how you wish. But before you go, please know this: I have suffered as much as you, and when you depart to live your life of bliss, I will continue suffering for want of you." Upon saying this, the king removed his crown and knelt before Overa, head bowed.

Princess Merinda, next to Jason, grabbed and squeezed his hand as tears flowed from her eyes. Queen Overa leaned over to King Beldane, lifted his chin, and pulled him to standing. "When you took me from my simple life on a farm in Tycora, I suffered greatly, so I have only one thing to ask of you." King Beldane looked down, nodding. "Can I have a cow? Actually, not just one cow, but lots of cows?"

King Beldane threw back his head and laughed. "Of course, my love. You can have as many cows as you like. We can let Merinda run the kingdom, and I will help you milk them."

She smiled. "I like that. I think I am starting to like you, too!" She held his hand. "I have loathed you for such a long time. Please forgive me if I am not immediately the wife you want, but upon this promise, I am willing to try."

The king knelt again. "I will see to it you do not regret this decision."

After a moment, Queen Overa said, "Now, let's get our daughter back." They both turned to look at Jason expectantly.

"I will not lie to you," said Jason. "I do not know how to get your daughter back. I do not know how to travel the planes. Otherwise, I would have gone back to my home by now. But one thing I do know is that the gates of hell cannot remain closed against us. There are groups praying in earnest right now and be assured, the Creator has a plan."

Jason addressed Queen Overa specifically, "Think on this, Queen Overa. You were willing to offer yourself to a demon for your daughter's return, but are you willing to offer yourself to the Creator?" Then Jason left and went to the common garden to pray. He knelt at a stone bench and closed his eyes.

"Excuse me, little boy, I didn't mean to interrupt your praying." It was Akari.

Jason warded off a puff of smoke that accompanied his appearing and replied, "I suppose you are here to blame me for the queen's problems and Princess Kuari's disappearance because I didn't accept your offer and do that service for you?"

"Not at all," said Akari, "although it would have meant a bonus for me... But no, I am here to do a service for the Creator!"

"What do you mean?" Jason asked skeptically.

"I have been thinking about what you said about the freedom of choice and your bet with me. You proposed such an unthinkable thing of a demon serving the Creator, and I realized that just the fact that I could not do this really was a lack of freedom to do whatever I might wish. Your proposal was so radical. It would be rebellion and treason against the status quo—and then I think to myself, 'Hey, rebellion and treason are what demons do best. It is the stuff we live for!' This would be the rebellionest and the treasonest thing a demon has ever done. I would be the most hated demon in history—which, to a demon, is a good thing. The other demons would rally as one to tear me into atoms and torture each atom separately. Except that by doing such a deed the Creator would protect me. So then I would get to thumb my nose at all the other demons, another favorite demon pastime..."

"Okay, okay...I get it!" exclaimed Jason. "However, warped your reasoning, you have decided to do a service for the Creator?" "And at no charge too!" Akari rubbed his hands together gleefully.

"So what is it you are prepared to do?" asked Jason.

"I am going to help you get Princess Kuari back," the little demon announced grandly.

"Okay," said Jason, hardly daring to believe this was really happening, "I have some things to get and will be right back."

To Jason's sensibilities, doing anything with a demon was a sin, but the timing and declaration of the spirit to help the Creator seemed a matter of providence. Wanting to get back before the demon could change his mind, Jason rushed off, leaving the demon in the garden with his own personal visions of grandeur.

He picked up his weapons and backpack and ran back as quickly as possible. The little demon was still in the garden when he returned, standing on a flower pedestal bowing graciously to an invisible audience.

"Uh, Akari," he said, "doing service for the Creator is rewarding, but we try to do so with a little humility."

"Why, yes. Of course." Akari jumped from the pedestal, bowed his head, and gave Jason his most humble look.

"Well, I am ready. Let's be off," quipped Jason, wondering if he was betraying his trust in God by accepting the demon's help. Perhaps it was a lie or a trap, but what if the little demon's desire to do something for God was genuine? If so, then this was a rare opportunity and he could not deny anyone willing to serve the Lord.

Akari seemed to pull down a zipper to open a piece of fabric in space and stepped through. He followed and Akari zipped the hole back up.

"What joke is this, Akari? We haven't gone anywhere." Jason looked about.

"No joke at all. This is the netherworld that touches your plane. You will notice the vision is not as sharp and the breeze not as strong. You are now invisible on your plane, and with a little training, you could interact a little with the physical world from here. Gravity has little effect and you can pass through solid objects like a ghost. In fact, this is where many spirits of the deceased get stuck if no one comes for them. Even many demons and devils have chosen to live here for a short while.

"Now, I could have opened a portal straight into the Abyss, but we wouldn't make it in undetected and would be attacked. But going this route we can sneak into Donjoni's lair and back out again without him even knowing.

"If you look about the sky, actually beyond the sky, since distance is not such a big deal on this plane, either, you will see swirling light of various colors. Some are vortices of magical energies, while others are portals to various planes and dimensions. From here they open and close at random, making travel from this plane unreliable. If you look into the ground, you will see more swirls...see the one that looks like the afterglow of a nuclear explosion? That is one of the portals to Hell, and beyond that, the dark blue is the portal to the Abyss. Sometimes Pandemonium is that color too, but we will know for sure when we get there."

"Will we be going underground? How will I breathe?" asked Jason.

"Oh, we will be through long before you need to take another breath." Akari sunk into the ground, but Jason could still see him. Jason experimentally thrust his hand into the ground. There was a little resistance, kind of like cotton candy, then virtually none. He put his head in and followed Akari. It was true. He didn't seem to need to breathe.

He started off swimming but discovered he didn't need to, as he just moved wherever he thought. He didn't see as much as sense the boulders he went through, the bed rock, the veins of silver and gold, springs of water, and occasional rock-impregnated pools of oil.

He considered this the ideal way to explore. No wonder demons were sought after for their knowledge. When they went past the swirl of the portal to Hell a large monster came out, looking like a fish but with tentacles instead of fins and saber tooth fangs. It looked at them, then turned back into the swirling mists.

When they came to the portal for the Abyss, Akari checked it out first to make sure it was safe and not hiding some vile monster. Once inside, it resembled a long tunnel, similar to a space worm-hole in an old Sci-Fi movie. Outside the tunnel was a light gray substance, which the demon identified to Jason as the ethereal plane, a place where it would be easy to get lost were it not for these tunnels. Travel along the tunnel was very quick and opened in a swirling hole over a dark, barren red landscape.

Jason fell, immediately affected by its gravity. He rolled when he hit the ground, nearly breaking some arrows. Akari apologized for not warning him. The little demon also explained there were six hundred and sixty-six layers of the Abyss and that Donjoni, being a fairly minor demon, had a keep on the forty ninth level. Akari could teleport there, but to keep from being discovered they should enter the old fashioned way by traveling to the edge of the Abyss, a great hole that runs through all the layers, and jumping off to free fall until they reached the right layer.

"How far away is the edge of the Abyss?" asked Jason.

"My best guess, by looking at the terrain, about 350 miles," said Akari.

"Are we to walk through this desert the whole way?" asked Jason incredulously.

"Certainly, a little brisk walk is good for you," piped Akari.

"But that could take weeks, and then after we jump, how will we stop ourselves to land on the forty-ninth layer?"

"Well, I hadn't thought that far ahead," confessed Akari. "I figured we would sneak in, steal Princess Kuari from under Donjoni's nose and then sneak out, climb the forty-nine layers and then figure a way to jump to the portal and laugh about it over a root beer float or something—"

"About how long would you estimate this mode of rescue to take?" Jason interrupted.

"Ahhh, let's see... Three weeks to walk to the edge, one week of free fall, another month to Donjoni's palace. The rescue itself would be relatively quick—perhaps three days—then a month back to the edge, three years climbing the Abyss, then another three weeks coming back here, assuming the portal is still here... It would only take about three years and four months."

Jason sighed. "For an immortal like you, this may not seem like much time, but for a human in torment, every hour seems like a lifetime. I suggest we risk discovery and teleport in, snatch the princess, and teleport out," said Jason emphatically.

Akari shook his head sadly. "You know not the Abyss. It was made by the Creator as a place for demons and evil spirits to live and not continually pester the prime material planes. It was also built as a prison, so there are different characteristics of each layer. The lowest levels are completely locked, where no one goes in or out without the will of the Creator or by one with the set of keys.

"The upper levels are partially locked, restricting movement with a variety of strictures. At the forty-ninth level we could teleport in, but cannot teleport out for four days. Also, all teleportation is monitored by demons. Going in myself would arouse no suspicion at all, but with you—it would be such an unusual event it would attract an audience from all the kingdoms of the forty-ninth plane."

Jason shrugged. "Is there a place on that layer between areas that is not monitored?"

"No," said Akari, "demons are fanatical about spying on others, and even monitor areas of other demons, to see if there is any advantage to be taken of them. The only time we could teleport in undetected is if we did it right in the middle of a skirmish or war, and that would be more dangerous than teleporting directly to the presence of Donjoni himself."

Jason considered the implications and thought the best way was for Akari to rescue the princess by himself, teleport in, wait four days and then pop back with her. But he did not trust Akari to not change his mind, or to have the moral fortitude to perform such a task on his own.

"Then," Jason said, "we will take our chances and we will need help. Do you have any subordinate demons who could help us out?"

Akari thought hard. "I do have subordinates, but they are not stupid and would report us... But, wait. There are some who owe me and would be glad to get out from under the debt, although a favor of this magnitude would take some convincing—that is, assuming we survive teleporting in."

"Let's do it," said Jason.

"Okie dokie, I guess it doesn't really matter where we go, since they will find us, so we might as well go to the front gate of Donjoni's Palace. The view from there is really spectacular."

Akari grabbed Jason's hand, and he felt a rush of wind. Suddenly, they stood before the gate of a tremendous black granite structure. The palace beyond the gate, made from obsidian with huge domes, would put any palace built on his home world to shame. The palace was atop a jagged black mountain of volcanic rock. The sky, black as night with no stars, glowed dimly like twilight, but from no discernible source.

Below the mountain, he saw a breathtaking view of a vast black sea as smooth as glass, with a spider web of causeways, bridges, and isthmuses connecting a chain of islands of various sizes. In the distance, he could see dark, bird-like creatures flying, and nearby in the water he saw the body of a huge white worm break the surface and roll from sight.

"Beautiful, isn't it?" declared Akari, folding his arms with satisfaction.

"Yes, in a way...I could see why a demon would want to live in a place like this," said Jason.

At that moment, the iron gates creaked open and eight demons, resembling horned lizards the size of men, ran out and encircled them, followed by the tall, lanky Donjoni.

"What have we here, Akari? Why have you brought a human to our realm?" thundered the lord demon.

Akari stammered, "I... I am sure you recognize Jason, the little boy with Queen Overa? He has come of his own free will—"

"To rescue Princess Kuari," Donjoni finished for him, and then continued. "Akari, you should have known better than to bring a servant of the Creator here. Why, the boy practically glows with the Light. Of course, we can't keep him here for long, but to have such a delicious opportunity... We will crucify and torture him as long as we can. I have checked, and I see he has no magic on him to resist us or to harm us, so he is as helpless as any slave. Take the boy and prepare him for crucifixion and ready the flesh worms."

Worms again, thought Jason. Why do evil beings have such a fascination with flesh eating worms?

Akari had sort of side-stepped out of sight during Donjoni's dialogue, and Jason drew his two long daggers as a horned lizard- demon leaped toward him. Jason slashed quickly across the stomach and an ascending claw. The demon paused and looked at himself, but when he saw no damage, he smiled a toothy grin and slapped Jason to the ground.

Donjoni laughed and strode into the palace. Jason resheathed his knives and sat on his knees in an attempt to control his breathing, eyes closed.

Comparatively huge to this little boy, the rest of the hissing lizard demons rushed Jason all at once. Jason let out a kiai as he drew his katana, cutting in the same motion as he came up to one knee. His blade drew across three demons. They screamed in pain and surprise as Jason, in the next few moments, mowed down the rest. They writhed and dissolved into puddles of green ichor.

"How did you do that?" exclaimed Akari.

Jason spoke as he calmly cleaned the ichor off his sword. "The Japanese warrior believed his soul resided in his katana. After years of practicing Iaido, I suppose I have attained some of this ability, because I struck with my soul of light, which I am sure is doubly powerful in this realm of darkness. I suppose I could have done it without my sword at all, except a physical sword does help to focus it."

Akari moved toward the gate and said, "I now have hope we can accomplish our mission; you are more powerful than you appear."

"Even if I could not have done what I did, I have angels protecting me."

"There are angels here? I doubt that. As a demon I should be able to see them." Akari peered around.

"Yes," he replied, "as incredible as it seems, God sends angels to protect those who serve him, and even though we can't see them, we have faith they are here."

"I am serving God right now... Is there an angel protecting me, too?" asked Akari, a little dubiously.

"Undoubtedly, Akari,"—he laughed—"and I believe Princess Kuari has angels protecting her, too. I think very soon she will decide to follow the Creator without reservation."

Akari shrugged. He had occasional run-ins with angels, and they seemed little different from him, and for them to have an ability he did not know about was highly unlikely. In fact, at one time, eons ago, he had been an angel, and even then, he did not have the ability to hide from other spiritual beings. Perhaps Jason was misled by his archaic religion.

Akari led them into the main hall and took a side corridor leading past some apartments. He stopped at one that looked like it was decorated for Halloween, covered with streaks of blood with a shrunken head for a doorknob.

Akari addressed the doorknob, "Hi ya dork. Is Mincella in?"

The doorknob opened its beady black eyes and made a disgusted face as it looked down at Akari and replied, "Of course, she is not home, and she plans to not ever be here whenever you come to visit—do you get my drift? Your manners are atrocious, your diction is awful, you smell bad, and you are short."

The doorknob then shut its eyes tightly and tried to ignore Akari.

"Normally," said Akari, "I would torture you until you announced me to Mincella, for she would already know I am here, but I am in a hurry so I will be nice to you. Here is a bug I saved just for you."

Akari produced a big black beetle in his hands out of nowhere, as though he were a street magician, and fed it to the doorknob. The doorknob opened its eyes and chewed the bug with pleasure, then spat it out, because it couldn't swallow. Jason could hear a bell ring in the room and the door suddenly opened, exposing a luxurious apartment decorated in black and red.

The raven-haired woman framed in the doorway was fantastically beautiful in a wispy gown. Her cherry red lips contrasted with her milky white skin, and her sultry eyes reflected a hint of purple. Other than the two small horns protruding from her head and two large bat-like wings on her shoulders, her slim and graceful shape, barely concealed by her nearly see-through blue gown, would have put any fashion model to shame.

Placing a dainty hand over her brow, Mincella said, "Akari, I am not well today. Please call on me some other millennia..."

For once, Jason was glad his body was that of a little boy, which didn't have the torrent of hormones that ravaged older boys and men. Even at that, he couldn't help but stare.

Akari persisted, "I am not here to socialize, but to give you an opportunity to pay your debt from our bets on the Battle of the Juggernauts, by doing a small favor."

"Well, why didn't you say so?" Mincella dragged Akari inside. Noticing Jason, she said, "Little boy, didn't your mother ever teach you not to stand around with your mouth hanging open? It attracts flies, you know."

"Mincella," said Akari, "I would like you to meet Jason, the little boy you lost so much on."

"Ooooh, I wish I could skin you alive for what you cost me, young man," she spat, her claw-like nails making scratching motions toward Jason.

"Er, er, yes...But now, you not only can cure your debt with one small service, but we will let you in on a little secret so you can win big on the next event," squeaked Akari.

"In that case, come on in, Jason," purred Mincella, holding the door open for him.

"Thank you, ma...ma'am," he stammered.

"Oh, he is so polite. A rare thing for a human. Now, let's get down to business. What is it you need me to do?" Mincella said, as a matter-of-fact.

Jason looked at Akari and let him do the talking.

"We need you to teleport Jason and Princess Kuari out, which I can't do since we just now teleported in. The betting opportunity is that Jason is here to rescue Princess Kuari, and right now the odds running against him are a thousand to one down at the office."

"So tell me, dear Akari, what is it they do not know which will give me my edge?" asked Mincella demurely.

"One," said Akari excitedly, "is that Jason has the ability to destroy a demon without magic. Second is that there are a band of ninja angels sent from the Creator to help him, and lastly, if Jason can get the princess to you, you will teleport them out."

"Wait a minute. I haven't agreed to anything, yet. This will get me into huge trouble with Donjoni," said Mincella fervently. "Well, from what I hear, if anyone can handle the wrath of Donjoni, it is you. And if you have seen Princess Kuari, you know she is a looker. This is one way you can get rid of the competition and pad your account at the same time," said Akari sincerely.

"Hey, what was that about angels? I don't see any angels, ninja or not."

"I don't know, but Jason says they are here." Akari shrugged and looked at the boy pointedly.

Jason, too, shrugged. "I don't know how any of the spiritual rules work, but I am normally guarded by angels, and I can't imagine God sending me into the Abyss without some protection." Pulling his sword, he continued, "Perhaps my ability to use this was actually angels making the cuts for me, but anyway, I think it is enough for you to know that I am protected, which gives me an edge in this mission."

"And that goes ditto for me, too," said the little fiend, folding its arms smugly.

"Okay, okay, I'm in." Turning to Jason, Mincella said, "You, child, must get Princess Kuari to my room in the next two hours, or all bets are off. You understand?"

"Yes, ma'am."

"What a polite boy," Mincella remarked again as Jason and Akari left the room.

Walking down the hallway, Akari said, "Jason, I should warn you that Mincella is a succubus, so whatever you do, don't let her kiss you. She will drain the power and energy that is your life."

Jason changed topic and said, "I am impressed you actually bet on me at the Battle of the Juggernauts."

"Well, after you beat the super martial artist Maudid with the bees, I quit being stupid and started thinking that at least some things you said to me might be true. So now I am exhibiting a little faith of my own. Forget the odds if you have the Creator on your side."

CHAPTER 47

Ninja Angels

They entered a large room with many pools of various liquids, and a variety of demons of all shapes and sizes lounging in them while servants, some of them human, held towels and brought refreshments of foul-looking drinks and plates of live wiggly things. As Akari and Jason walked through, none gave them a second glance. Akari told him, "Since you are only human, try to avoid being splashed by some of the pools. Many demons have a fondness for acid baths that would eat your skin off."

They went down a stairwell into another long hallway with many rooms. Jason noticed a lack of guards and asked Akari about it. "The problem is that demons and their minions are too untrustworthy to be used as guard, so everything is guarded by strong magics that even affect demons. So do not think the lack of guards will make our task any easier. We will be able to walk right to Kuari, but getting her out will be hard." Suddenly, in the distance, a large bell began ringing. "Sounds like they discovered the demons who were to crucify you are missing, so now we are in lock down."

At that moment, two demons strode past them unhurriedly. "Doesn't seem like anyone is too concerned about the alarm," observed Jason.

"No, they are all headed to the betting offices. There they will get all the news, and the demons will lay their bets first before doing anything. The only ones we have to watch out for are Donjoni and his personal minions, of which I am one, so I know the drill. First, he will flash down to your most likely destination, Princess Kuari.

"Since you are not there yet, he will trust to his magical wards and then start a search with the lockdown. Second, he will lock the gates, and then search section by section, locking the areas behind him. The search will be slow, since Donjoni has few helping him, for all the bettors are loath to interfere. Not wanting to waste their ability to teleport, the search would be similar to one on your home world."

"How do the betting offices know about the rescue?"

"We made sure of that, by letting Mincella in on it. She will run down to the office and place her bet right away, and immediately the game is on. But this is one bet I will miss," said Akari woefully.

"Don't worry, Akari, the Creator will reward you."

"Oh, here we are. Princess Kuari is on the other side of this door." Akari opened the door, astonishing Jason that it wasn't even locked—a sure sign of a trap. "Akari, do you know all the traps in here?"

"No, the traps change frequently."

"In that case, would you mind holding the door open?" he asked as he stepped inside. The stench of an overflowing outhouse on a hot mid-July afternoon struck him. The room was oblong, with a pit running down the center about twelve feet wide. Black statues lined the edge, looking like ninjas in various poses, with a variety of weaponry.

At the bottom of the cavity was a trough cut in the floor, with an opening flush with the floor at both ends. Feces oozed in through one side and slowly exited out the other side. Princess Kuari, legs covered with filth, tried to help the flow of feces leaving the pit. If she did not, the feces would fill it, as evidence on the floor showed it had overflowed several times since Princess Kuari started shoveling. She was shoveling and pushing furiously, trying to keep the flow going. A sadistic mind designed this system.

Jason pulled out his rope, braced himself behind a statue, and lowered the rope. "Kuari, grab the rope."

Kuari, so lost in her misery, did not see or hear Jason at first, but when he called again, she ran to the rope. "Oh, Jason, I am so glad to see you! I have been praying to the Creator every minute, but did not really believe he would send you." Kuari climbed as lithe as a monkey and Jason helped her up to the floor.

"Jason, the statues are coming alive," cried Akari.

Jason looked to see Akari in a battle of his own, trying to keep the door from forcibly closing on him.

"Quick, Kuari, run out the door," he said and ran to the front of the first row of statues. They were indeed coming alive, head first. He did a flying kick to the chest of the first statue, sending it toppling like dominoes onto the others. As they struck, they crushed the others, destroying them. However, the ones on the other side of the room were fully animated and now coming like an army of dark shadows.

A gas as green as pea soup, and nearly as thick, fell from holes in the ceiling as he raced out the door, grabbing Akari on the way. The door slammed with an audible click of a lock, and greenish gas escaped from the edge of the door. As soon as the door shut, fine threads of spider webs started shooting from the walls and ceiling. Jason drew his katana and ran, pulling the princess, who in turn grabbed the little demon. Jason cut and slashed his way to the stairwell.

The room with the pools was now abandoned, its former occupants presumably down at the betting office gambling on Jason's chances at rescuing the princess.

Kuari called out, "Stop. I have to wash this filth off me."

"Kuari, we don't have time. Let's get you out of here first and then worry about that."

But Kuari insisted on washing, against Jason's wishes, while Akari, holding his nose, readily obliged her in finding a pool of water that wasn't acid. Despite his protests, Jason could only shake his head and stand guard. This brought to mind a country song he knew called "Waiting on a Woman." But even Jason had to admit she smelled awful.

Suddenly, three demons stormed the room from a side corridor. Kuari screamed, cutting her bath short. The hairy demons had small bird wings and stood over ten feet tall. They seemed to be half gorilla and half wild boar, with gorilla-like arms and the hind feet of a pig. They bellowed with pure ferocity. Jason felt a wave of fear as he charged to meet the spirits. He felt small and would have preferred to run away, but gave his standard growl, instead, which turned into a kiai yell.

Charging full speed, he ran right between the legs of the lead one, striking upward. The demon looked embarrassed as it fell. Jason kept running in a hook pattern, coming to the side of the demon on the right. He found himself in instant darkness. Nonplussed, he closed his eyes and struck, feeling his sword drive home, then left the sphere of darkness for the demon to die on its own.

Meanwhile, the third demon had cornered Akari and was about to smash him into the floor. Akari cried out, "Okay, Creator, your angel can do something now!" The huge fists stopped just inches from the little demon trying to cover its head, then suddenly the huge demon was flung back into a pool.

Puzzled, Akari looked at his hands and said, "Wow!"

The large gorilla-like demon was, for a moment, completely immersed. Enraged, the demon exploded out of the pool only to be met by a huge, flaming sword just inches from its face. The stunned demon froze in place, his eyes followed the sword up to its wielder, a twenty-foot-tall giant with enormous wings, its robe a dazzling white glow. The expression on the angel's face was anything but pleasant.

Dwarfed by the sudden apparition of good, the demon squealed in fear. As it fled, it changed into the form of a wolf and ran full speed down the halls, tail tucked between its legs. Akari meekly said, "Thanks, Angel." The angel nodded at him with a salute from the flaming sword and disappeared, fading out like a ghost.

"Come on," encouraged Jason to the stunned Akari as they ran from the room.

When they reached Mincella's door, the shrunken head hollered, "You can't come in."

Akari ignored it and grabbed the face, turning the knob as it tried to speak under his grip. Jason and Kuari followed Akari as the door opened. Before them, filling the entrance, was Donjoni. Mincella screamed from behind Donjoni, "Run, Akari."

Donjoni laughed. "I cheated and checked on who the first bettor was, guessing you had another ally. Now you might as well surrender. No one can get past me."

The doorknob said irritatingly, "Don't say I didn't try to warn you."

Akari looked up at Donjoni and smiled. "It is you who better surrender. You can't see my buddy here, but he is far bigger than you and has a flaming sword, too!"

Donjoni looked puzzled, "Usually you can't help but squeak in fear in my presence. Why are you tempting me to crush you, little one?"

"I told you, back off, you big bean pole. Not only do I have a huge angel on my left, Jason the Juggernaut is on my right and the Creator himself is hovering right over the top of you, ready to crush you if you make one false move, so step aside!" declared Akari, with a menacing glint in his eyes as he took a step forward.

"What? I see nothing except three little...Akari, what is happening to you?"

Indeed, Akari was changing before everyone's eyes. Donjoni stepped back, a little fearful as Akari grew to the height of Jason and sprouted white wings and wore a white gown. His horns vanished and his visage became that of a boy, albeit with eyes still glinting angrily.

"I serve the Creator now and am free of your rule, Donjoni. I am Jason's newest protector and companion. You cannot harm him or me!"

Donjoni stepped back, hands up as though to ward him off, covering a horrified expression. "Stay away from me, you little freak. I don't know what has happened to you, just don't touch me."

Akari looked past Donjoni to Mincella. "Since I am now free from this prison, we will not need your service, my love, but consider your debt paid. However, know it wasn't paid by me. It was paid by the Creator. Tell them, Mincella. Tell all the demons what you saw. It is true. We have free will and can change if we want to.

"Good-bye, Mincella. I hope you will follow me and someday learn to serve the Creator, too. You would make a beautiful angel." With that, Angel Akari smiled and grasped both Jason's and Kuari's hand. They felt a gentle breeze with a flash of light.

In a moment they found themselves standing in the common garden of the castle of Chanderlon, except that Akari was no longer anywhere to be seen. It was dark, but the fiery glow of the morning sun could be seen in the eastern skies. The castle was as still as a tomb.

"Let's go tell everyone the news," Jason suggested after a moment, but the excited girl was already dragging him along.

With a shriek of joy, Princess Kuari stunned the sleepy guards at the door with a hug each and ran through the main hall, whooping and hollering, "Everyone, wake up. I am back!"

She then ran to the royal quarters, hugged the guards there, and ran into the main apartment screaming, "Mother, Father, Merinda, I am home!"

Queen Overa was awake, kneeling at the open balcony, still dressed from a sleepless night of praying. When she heard Princess Kuari's voice, she gave a screech of joy herself and leaped up to embrace her. The king and Merinda soon emerged from their rooms and joined the joyful fray. Lords and ladies, as well as many children, crowded into the room, and Princess Kuari hugged them all. The king declared that day a celebration for the return of their daughter.

Feasting, music, and dancing began about noon. The party went into the royal gardens to play games and listen to Kuari's tales of the heroic deeds of Jason and how a little demon became a little angel. Jason, although he found it pleasant, found himself in a melancholy mood.

He felt a little jealous of Kuari, for whom God had moved heaven and earth to bring her home. Would not God do the same for him? He looked forward to a reunion such as this with his own family.

The castle opened its gate for the townsfolk, and soon there was dancing and rejoicing in the streets at the youngest princess' return. Gunther and Jason joined the knights in the courtyard to watch exhibition fighting, along with many others. After a few matches, the knights begged Jason for an exhibition.

Jason towed Gunther out as his partner in a demonstration of unarmed hand to hand fighting. First, Jason demonstrated breaking bricks and boards that happened to be the right size and then ran Gunther through his normal throwing routine from various attacks. Gunther was throwing Jason onto the hard stone pavement, for which Jason's skills were sufficient to prevent injury. Then Jason did an exhibition of his own throwing skills, appropriate to Gunther's ability to fall.

The crowd loved it, and the soldiers and knights were impressed. Afterward Codd, the sailor from the black ship, slapped Jason on the shoulder from behind. Though not generally a smart move to do on a martial artist, Jason felt no intent of danger.

"Captain Jason?" asked Codd. "Are you intending to sail with us as we head out in a few days?"

In truth, Jason had nearly forgotten about the ship. Kuari's disappearance had consumed his thoughts, and he had not yet considered future plans. He looked at Codd thoughtfully and replied, "Yes. The Creator has provided me with this opportunity, so perhaps it is what I am suppose to do. Spread the word that any of the original crew and soldiers who wish to sail with me are welcome."

"Very good, Captain. I think nearly all the crew will be there," Codd said as he disappeared into the crowd.

Gunther interjected, "I always knew you would leave sometime. Thank you for giving me another chance and spending so much time with me."

"You are very welcome and Gunther, you have been more than worth the effort. You are my good friend, and if I can I will be back to see you."

"Do you need me to go with you?" asked Gunther.

"Yes," said Jason, "but I also think the Creator needs you here to keep the light shining. So stay, for now."

"I feel that, too. Do you think the Creator speaks to me as he does to you?" asked Gunther.

Jason nodded, "Yes, most definitely, although most often the Creator speaks to me without words."

Two surprise visitors came the next day to Gunther's church service. Queen Overa and Princess Kuari. Both marched to the front of the assembly and publicly declared their decision to follow the Creator, and to denounce their sinful lives of before. The whole group went to the river, where Gunther baptized them. Jason watched joyfully, along with Princess Merinda and King Beldane. After the baptisms, Princess Merinda looked sad. Jason asked her about it.

Princess Merinda looked deeply at him as she spoke. "There is a ship at port claiming you are its captain, and it is leaving tomorrow. You will be on it, won't you?"

"Yes... I think my work here is done, at least for now. Perhaps the Creator will send me home or to another distant land on this world. If that is the case, you will hear from me frequently."

"Jason, you will always have a home here. I will miss you."

"Thank you. I will miss you, too. I promised to spend this afternoon with Nelda and Amanie, but I will see you tomorrow before I leave." At that, Princess Merinda hugged and kissed him and went to join her rejoicing family.

Jason went with the Killensdale's to the beach that afternoon. He talked a little with Lord and Lady Killensdale and then played in the water with

Amanie and Nelda. They talked long on many subjects and returned to the castle late that evening.

Early the next day, Princess Merinda accompanied Jason as he visited his ship while it loaded stores, preparing to leave. As they walked back to the castle Princess Merinda said, "Jason, you are the brother I never had. I am going to miss you very much."

"I am going to miss you, too. I almost wish you could accompany me like you did at first, ready to run off to a life of adventure, but I know you are needed here," he responded.

"Yes, Father wants me to study and join all meetings to learn how to run the kingdom."

"Is that what you want to do?" he asked.

"Yes," she replied. "I think I can do that and so much more."

"I am sure you will," he replied.

That afternoon the whole town showed up at the docks to see Jason off. Everyone from the castle came, from the lowest stable hand to the royal family.

He was surprised to see Yaveen, who made his way through the crowds of well wishers. "Jason, I am sorry I did not get to congratulate you in your victory with the juggernauts, but I was called away on urgent business."

"That's okay. I am glad to see you are all right."

"Yes, indeed. I have spoken with Princess Merinda and have heard how she will act as regent from time to time."

"She will need good people beside her. I know she will do well," replied Jason.

"Do not worry, young knight, for I will personally look after her in your absence."

"Thanks, I hope to talk to you more if I return." Jason moved away from the princess's sword instructor to others wishing to speak to him, many followers of the Creator. He was glad the princess would also have help from Gunther and the other Christians, for he was sure the gods would not leave her untested.

He visited with the royal family as the ship prepared to leave. They assured him that his room would always be prepared and ready for his return. Princess Kuari seemed particularly sad to see him go and hugged him hard.

She turned away so he couldn't see her cry. As he turned to the ship, both Amanie and Nelda intercepted him and hugged him hard as well. Both made him promise to return someday. Although he wasn't sure he could keep that promise, he made it anyway, for their sakes.

As he walked up the plank to the ship, he turned and summoned

Gunther. As Gunther stood before him, Jason said, "Send the light, Gunther, and remember to encourage truth seeking." Then Jason gave him his katana with its scabbard. "Sharpen your soul as though it were this blade."

"Thank you... Thank you!" Gunther croaked, full of emotion. Jason smiled. Gunther's voice was changing.

He then boarded as the ship pulled out. The crowd cheered and waved while he stood at the bow and enthusiastically waved back. Crowds lined both sides of the shore. After about a half mile, the castle guard lined the river shoreline.

When Jason and the ship came abreast of them, the sergeant called a salute. Jason saluted in return and held the salute the whole way. At the end of the line, the knights in full armor on their horses, with shields and lances, saluted as well. After he passed, the men banged their lances and shields together, and he could hear the men cheer.

Children ran along both shores shouting, "Jason the Juggernaut!" and stopped to salute him. He saluted them back. When the ship breached the mouth of the river to the open sea beyond, the people in the village wondered about the commotion at Chanderlon and gathered at the shore to wave. He waved back to them, as Skeg came to the bow with Jason.

"Well, captain, where to?"

Jason looked around and saw a bird flying out to sea. He blinked, for what he saw now was not a bird but a little angel— Akari? Jason blinked again, and again, it was a bird. "Follow that bird, helmsman. The Creator has charted my course, and he will reveal the destination in his own good time." Then Jason turned and entered his cabin as the ship sailed into the unknown.

CHAPTER 48
Deologue 8

The colossal black spider leaped off the wall of the cathedral, floating momentarily in space and then falling, legs splayed, down onto the small group of hapless lizard-like quasilings below. The small creatures screamed and tried to run, but got in each others' way.

Several were instantly squashed as the massive claws at the end of the legs landed on them. The horror then crouched over them, as the fore claws gathered the crying creatures into a pile. The mandibles scooped up three or four at a time to begin its grisly meal.

Just then, the giant Xan Rukkah walked into the room and paused, taking in the gory scene. "Axialla, it has been long since you have shown your true form."

One of the multiple eyes, comparable to the compound eyes of a normal spider, separated and floated free of its anchor to the dark head, trailing bloody-looking tentacles, hovering before the face of Xan Rukkah. Compared to Axialla's current form, he no longer looked giant.

"Go away," hissed the huge arachnid. "I am in a foul mood and wish to devour."

"Curb your appetite for a moment, my dear, for I bring both good and bad news about the Creator's champion," said the big god as his voice clapped like thunder.

"You mean champions," Axialla said, shaking a claw at him.

"No, there is only one. We learned this from the demons who have had some dealings with the child as of late. It seems the champion went into the Abyss to rescue a princess and the event has upset them greatly."

The floating eye returned to the spider. Axialla shrank back down to a woman, releasing her captives.

"But how can he be alive? How can he, a mere mortal, travel the planes? Is the boy a god, too?" she demanded.

"According to demons, he can regenerate to some degree, enough to have made fools of us. In traveling the planes he had help. Is he a god? I fear something far worse."

Floating up to the face of the giant, Axialla asked, "Is this the good news? What can be worse?"

"I... I fear the Creator is here, too. He is inside the boy," said the titan in a trembling voice.

"The Creator living inside a boy? Impossible. Mankind, even the children, are too corrupt for the pure and mighty Creator to possess them for long."

"I know not how, but it seems to be true. You and I have each lost a country to him, and now he is traveling by ship on to others. He must be stopped."

"I think it is time to fight this boy directly. What is his name? Jason?"

"Yes, they now call him Jason the Juggernaut. But what of our reputations if Jason defeats us?"

Axialla smiled, "And what of the reputation of the one who defeats him? He cannot defeat all of us. Tell the gods to use all means to stop him, for this is all-out war!"

The story continues in <u>Revenge of Skelleros</u>
Jason the Juggernaut, Book 2.

Jason the Juggernaut Quadrilogy

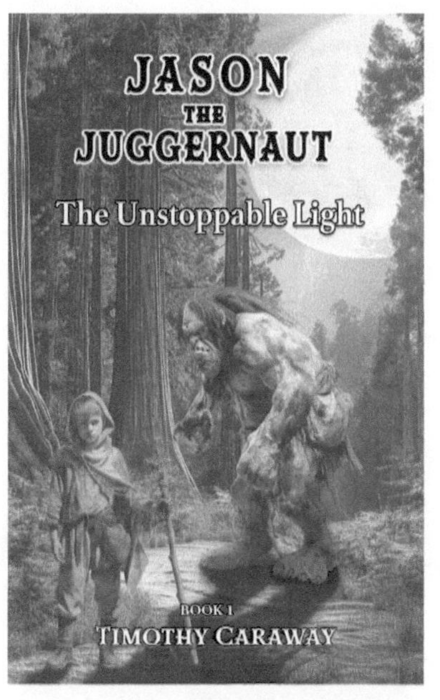

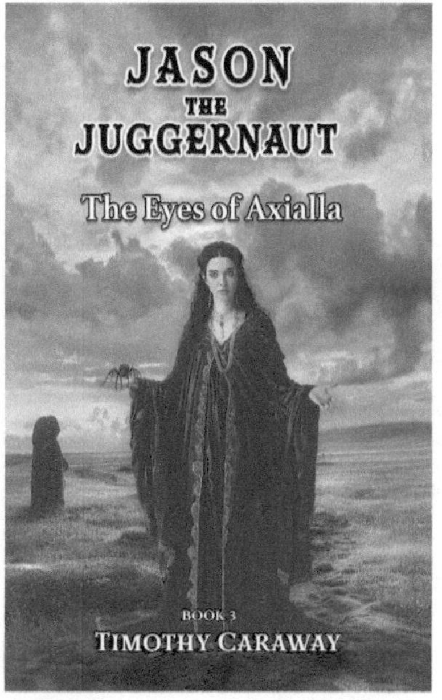